# The Scar of Aimsire

Tales of Aimsire - Book Two

A novel by: Scott Ladzinski

The Scar of Aimsire
Tales of Aimsire – Book Two
© 2025, Scott Ladzinski

This is a work of fiction. Names, places, characters, and incidents are the product of the author's imagination, and any resemblance to any actual persons, living or dead, organizations, events, or locales is entirely coincidental or used fictitiously.

## Sincere Thanks:

To all who purchased and read Book One so quickly after I published it, thank you! I can't even express how much your support has meant to me ☺

## Special Thanks To:

My beautiful wife, Sherri. Thank you, again, for all your love and support. I love you so very much and can't imagine trying to do this life without you!!

Ian for just being an all-around amazing young man. I love you, son!

Laurel (@laurelmladzinski on Instagram) and
Scott (@scotthaskinbooksandmusic on Instagram)
… I appreciate all the time you both took out of your busy schedules to help bring this second book to life. Thank you, thank you, thank you.

Ron Fortier for being the man who encouraged and convicted me to write the stories in my head. I deeply appreciate all the help you gave and continue to give me. As always, your guidance and mentorship have been invaluable! I hope my second book makes you as proud as the first one did.

For a map of Aimsire please visit:

www.aimsire.com

# Chapter 1 - Inductions

"Who am I? I'm a thick-headed twit."

Quickly covering her mouth to contain her laughter, Ceridwyn, Master Wizard of the Sun and one of the select advisors to High Consummate Lathai Thel'Radin as well as the Council of Elders of the Fara Commonwealth, still managed to spit out some of her tea. She caught her breath and wiped the front of her elegant robes with a towel.

"By the light, Aeolis, you certainly know how to turn on the charm."

"Begging your pardon, Mistress Ceridwyn, you're the one who asked me to tell you more about myself."

"Fair enough. I can't argue with that. Please allow me to rephrase. Tell me about your life growing up in the capital and how you decided to become a ranger."

The face of Fararalanthis' chief ranger lost the joy that was present during her laughter.

"There were happy moments, but my parents typically had somewhere to go, or some obligation that didn't involve me. Apparently, being born a Dawnwater requires that tradition and social engagements always supersede spontaneity or joyful expressions of family and love. Though I was interested, I didn't choose to be a ranger, it was expected of me.

"As soon as I was old enough, I was sent to ranger training without choice, as many males within the aristocracy are. I progressed through the fledgling orientation and was promoted to cadet in under a year. For decades, my father was very proud of me. Oddly, as I moved into specialist training, however, our relationship rapidly became strained.

"I know it's natural for families to go through this, but there was something different. He began looking at me with more suspicion than pride."

He went quiet as a look of sadness flashed across his face. Ceridwyn let him process his thoughts without interjecting. He looked her in the eyes before continuing.

"For as long as I can remember I have been driven by the need to be perfect. Thanks to that mentality, I thrived in the competition of ranger training. I was first up every morning, extra reps on the bow, more strength and endurance training than required, constantly pushing myself to be the best. Rapidly, the experience became more than simply following tradition. I genuinely found myself embracing the military lifestyle. In fact, I loved it and still do.

"The dark side of all this was that my arrogance grew right alongside my burgeoning ranger skills. I am sure that is what caused the rift between me and my father. When I heard he was killed defending the border near Forest Song Falls, something inside me never really settled down."

She reached across the table, placing her hand on top of his.

"My heart sings in sadness. I'm sorry, Aeolis. I did not know any of this and I certainly didn't intend to open old wounds."

"You have nothing to apologize for. I just wish our relationship hadn't soured before he died."

Ceridwyn squeezed his hand as she responded.

"Sadly, I have come to learn during my years of traveling that your story is no different than many I have heard. It seems to be a universal trait among royalty especially. There is a strange instinct bordering on obligation to procreate and produce an heir but as soon as the baby is born, they become a threat to power. It's a shame.

"The cycle is perpetuated when a child grows up like that. The idea of love and family gets lost in the selfishness of maintaining one's position. It's the primary reason I never wanted to be part of the aristocracy or academia. They both slowly devour themselves from within. Funny enough, life circumstances, or dare I say, maybe even God's will, took me down an unintended path and ultimately, I ended up entangled in both."

He listened and dared not move his hand out from under hers. The warmth of her skin was intoxicating.

"I envy you growing up in the forest during your early years. You were blessed to be away from it all."

"There certainly wasn't any politics or formal obligations. We were a family of weavers and seamsters. We had very little money, but plenty of love. Our family work was highly admired, not that it ever really mattered."

"What do you mean?"

"Those of 'higher station' would come asking us to design and construct beautiful garments for them. They would provide the softest silks and linens or pearls and gems to be woven in that sparkled like the stars. It became typical for them to agree to the price, but upon returning pay a tenth, or even less, demanding that we as their 'subjects' provide our service for the betterment of the commonwealth.

"Dare I ask? How is the commonwealth made better by forcing one's kin to work their fingers to the bone while dining, drinking, and lusting their own selves late into the night?"

Aeolis' eyes dropped as he felt a small measure of guilt push through him.

She continued, "My parents had no choice but to comply; we needed food. We are not farmers. Yes, of course, I can identify a strawberry or a tuber, but we never learned to work the land so we could thrive in its production. Our trade was making clothing, and our existence depended on the coin it brought in. In the end, my family survived despite our lack of dignity and even less to eat. Don't envy or over-romanticize my childhood, Aeolis. I am not this small because of genetics; malnutrition is the reason for my physical stature.

"I was one of the lucky ones, however. When I was one hundred and two my talent for magic was serendipitously discovered. I was whisked away in time to reverse some of the effects, but as you can see, not all of them."

There was no self-pity in her words. She leaned back, withdrawing her hand and picked up her cup of tea. She never broke eye contact with him.

Shamefully, Aeolis realized that he had never thought about what life was like for those outside the capital. He knew it very well could have been his parents who had done the sorts of things she had just spoken of.

"What if I was to say something to First Prince Jerrin? I could ask that those outside the capital be treated with more fairness."

"I am one of their chief advisors, Aeolis. Do you think I have not plucked the ears of the first prince and the High Consummate countless times about these sorts of things?"

Aeolis was about to speak when the barmaid approached.

"Can I get ya'two anything else?"

Ceridwyn smiled warmly as she responded, "I am fine, thank you. As usual, the beet soup was delicious."

The young girl turned to Aeolis. "You aw'right, too?"

"I am, thank you."

The young woman had just turned to leave when screams erupted outside. Aeolis and Ceridwyn stood in a flash as a loud explosion rocked the walls of the inn. Instinctually, Aeolis reached towards Ceridwyn to protect her.

She pushed around him and withdrew a lodestone from her robes, tucking it into the socket on her belt before dashing out the front door. He followed, going into the main street of the hamlet. Smoke was billowing into the air from the north side of town.

Aeolis queried, "Do you see anything?"

"It looks like the stable is on fire. Come, it's just around the corner."

As they made their way, she whispered magical words and the lodestone flared to life. Ceridwyn peeked around the inn but quickly withdrew. She spoke directly to Aeolis' mind to keep things quiet.

*"There are pieces of horse everywhere,"* she paused, *"...being eaten by an ogre and two trolls."*

Filling his lungs, Aeolis nocked an arrow and began to focus. He was about to draw and step around the corner when Ceridwyn's hand gently touched his forearm.

He slid back, *"What?"*

*"There is a signature. That explosion came from a wizard. I feel..."*

She went silent as they both felt static fill the air. Ceridwyn detected the ripples in Shakyna radiating outwards.

A fireball erupted from the tree line, smashing into the door of the jailhouse. Three blue skinned ogres charged from the shadows of the forest and crushed the stunned guard as he stumbled out of the burning building. They entered and the sound of a metal door being torn from the hinges immediately followed.

Ceridwyn and Aeolis watched the three ogres emerge with a reptilian dressed in scaled, black armor. The symbol of Nataxia was shamelessly displayed on his pauldrons.

4

Aeolis spoke to her mind, *"Looks like a prison break...my guess is these are survivors from the attack on Faralanthis."*

A second reptilian holding a gnarled staff and dressed in ornate robes stepped out of the trees and watched as the ogres and reptilian warrior returned. Several dozen humans were now armed and moving to defend their hamlet.

The reptilian wizard turned his slick eyes towards the group of men. His clawed hand came up and a fireball erupted from his palm, blasting one of the humans off his feet. The body burned to ash before it hit the ground. The rest screamed and charged.

"By the light. No, don't." Ceridwyn stepped out from behind the building and thrust out her hand. The ogre and two trolls eating the horse looked up just as her spell exploded in the middle of them, sending all three tumbling.

Instantly the reptilian wizard felt the pull through Shakyna. His eyes shifted and locked on Ceridwyn. His tongue flicked and caught her scent as a smile crossed his scaled face. Guttural clicks and hisses emerged from his mouth as he gave orders. The three ogres broke away and charged the oncoming group of defenders.

The ogres and humans smashed into one another; the barely trained townsfolk began to fall quickly. Aeolis stepped out and fired an arrow, hitting one of the ogres in the eye. The broadhead exited the back of his skull and the massive blue beast collapsed into his own footprints.

Ceridwyn grabbed Aeolis by the sleeve and yanked. The fireball that was aimed at his chest hissed by and singed his hair.

*"Aeolis, when the closest threat is dispatched, always kill the magic user next."*

Ceridwyn's lodestone blazed. She stepped around the corner and a solar flare exploded from her hand. The reptilian slipped nimbly to his right and the spell detonated in the trees behind him. Shattered, burning wood flew in all directions as the creature sneered at her. The reptilian warrior grunted orders to the ogre and two trolls near the stables. They had recovered from the explosion and charged the elves.

Aeolis slid his bow around onto his back and unsheathed his two elegant short swords. He spun and effortlessly cut down the first troll. He shifted his blades to attack again, but the swinging fist from the second troll caught him in the ribs. He tumbled into the dirt as the air evacuated his lungs.

Ceridwyn waved her hand and leapt into the air. The spell caused her to rise into the air and a second spell pulled Aeolis along with her. They landed gently and Aeolis got his feet under him again.

"Keep on the mage, I will handle these two..."

Using his natural speed, Aeolis charged and jumped with a twist, bringing the blades across. The troll swung at his face, but her hand separated from her arm as his blade met her wrist.

Howling, the troll stumbled forward. The awkward shift in her momentum caused her shoulder to impact Aeolis on the hip. They both hit the ground violently and slid in the dust. Seeing an opportunity, the ogre attacked. Aeolis rolled aside just as the creature's foot smashed down where his chest had been.

Stepping to gain an angle, Ceridwyn cast a burst of fire at the reptilian wizard. Just before the spell hit him, he brought up his clawed hand. The ball of fire stopped in mid-air. His yellow eyes glistened and he bared his teeth as the fire hovered before him. He thrust his hand forward. The spell grew in intensity and obediently flew right back at her.

Ceridwyn channeled Shakyna, pressing both hands forward and concentrated on the fireball. The spell stopped once again. She could feel the heat and the powerful push behind it. Wizards knew that reptilians were the kin of dragons. Their natural affinity for magic was well beyond anything an elf could learn in a lifetime.

*"Aeolis, I won't be able to keep this up for much longer..."*

Aeolis ducked as the ogre's massive fist whistled over his head. He countered by swinging up with his swords, catching the armor along the side of the beast's body. The metal sparked as he shifted to find an opening. The ogre was faster than anticipated and a second swing nearly caught Aeolis in the nose. He felt the breeze of the fist as he shifted back to avoid the blow.

*"Neither can I, but we can't leave these people to be slaughtered."*

The reptilian began exerting more power into his magic. Ceridwyn dug in her heels as she began to slowly slide backwards. The muscles in her cheeks ached as she clenched her teeth.

6

Flicking her eyes to catch Aeolis' location she spoke again to his mind, *"Duck down..."*

Aeolis immediately dropped as Ceridwyn channeled an exhausting amount of Shakyna through her body, shifting her hands towards the ogre. The spell exploded off the creature's chest and his smoldering body flew backwards.

Without hesitation Aeolis charged the two reptilians. The one in black armor sprinted and closed the gap with lightning speed. He jumped, swiping at the elf with his razor-sharp claws.

Twisting in the air, Aeolis dodged the strike and slid his swords up along the chest armor, etching two jagged lines in the metal scales. The reptilian hissed as Aeolis passed him and whipped his tail, catching the elf ranger in the face.

"Aeolis!"

Ceridwyn wrapped magic around Aeolis and yanked him back towards her just as the reptilian slashed at his throat. He landed beside her, clutching the flowing gash in his cheek.

She reached into her robes and removed a handful of reagents, throwing the spell components onto the ground around their feet before hissing words of magic. In a flash they vanished, immediately appearing at the gates of Gryphonledge.

+++

Jerrin looked up at the soft knock on his door.
"Enter."

Raspberry humbly stepped towards the elf prince's desk.
"Mr...er, First Prince Jerrin?"

"Yes, Raspberry, what do you need?"

"Well, sir, I mean, your princeliness, I just finished playing for your father, the High Consummate, I..."

Her eyes became slick with unshed tears. "...well sir, I don't think he's gonna get better. I played for him all morning. I prayed, I concentrated, the glow of grace was all around the room. It's just, he's still breathing with a strange, kinda, scratchy sound. Ms. Ceridwyn told me before she left that the light of his star is going out. I promise, sir, I am doing my best to heal him."

Leaning into his desk, Jerrin spoke matter-of-factly.

7

"Ceridwyn is right, soon the High Consummate will ascend to the constellations. That is inevitable. There can be no life without eventually passing to the next plain."

"I don't understand. Why did you ask for me to play for him then?"

"Myth'alas, my mother, and I want his passing to be as peaceful as possible. Your playing soothes him, as it does us all. You are honoring his soul by filling the room, and our home, with your music and Balaby's songs. That is all we are asking of you."

Raspberry remained quiet. It was clear by the look on her face that she understood what he said, but not necessarily what he meant. She remembered Mr. Lenly, the balladeer who had trained her, explaining that the songs God gives through Balaby, the tutelar who guides and mentors her, could bring more than just healing. Up until now, all she had really done was see people benefit when she played and sang. With a slight nod she looked Jerrin in the eyes.

"Yes sir, Prince Jerrin. I'll keep playing for him."

"Very good. Come back tomorrow morning, and again, my family thanks you for offering your gifts. Balladeers have become a rare thing. Having one as talented as yourself to offer his soul up in the twilight of his life is a tremendous comfort to us all."

Raspberry left the prince's office and made her way through the palace formed from castlewood trees. She stopped at Ceridwyn's home, grown from a tree right beside the one the elves had gifted her. She stared at the door and sadness filled her. It had only been days since she left with Aeolis, but she already missed Ceridwyn like it had been years. She was certain that her friend was off having a grand time traveling and knew her own place was here, assisting the Royal Family. She wiped away a small tear and walked next door to her home.

She stepped inside, placed her instrument on the chair, and looked up.

"Whoa!"

"Do not be frightened, little one. I will bring you no harm."

Raspberry instantly felt a sensation of peace. The elegant looking woman with soft, striped, green eyes, long black hair that shimmered like raven feathers, and delicate, porcelain white skin smiled. Somehow, Raspberry could instantly sense she was telling the truth and that there was no danger.

She scanned the woman's beautiful green dress and stopped at the highly detailed pink lotus embroidered on the left sleeve. It looked exactly like the one that used to hang on Mr. Lenly's healing room door.

"Who...who are you?"

"My name is Rajumin. I have traveled from the Vale of Ghosts to visit you."

"Me?"

"Yes, little one."

"Are you a ghost?"

Rajumin laughed as she responded. "No, sweet Raspberry. I assure you; I am quite alive."

"Okay. Well, how did you get in?"

"The door was unlocked."

"Umm, yeah, no, I mean, how did you get into Faralanthis? The guards are on extra high alert since the attack."

Rajumin smiled and looked out the window.

"Aimsire holds many secrets. There are passages and waypoints that allow those who know how to use them access to any place they desire regardless of any wall or army that has been put in place. The old ways have been lost for quite a long time, but life and light are returning. The people of this world are seeking truth, guidance, and wisdom once again. In a way, they are waking up to what once was.

"You see Raspberry, while the very creation of God's hands chose to look away, you, the created where never abandoned. God doesn't want thralls who follow mindlessly. When individuals ask to be left alone, they are left alone. It's a choice to follow and seek the light. Now that they are seeking once again, blessings are being poured out even more fervently."

She turned and looked at Raspberry. "Ameliara has told me about you, I had to meet you for myself."

"Ummm, Ameliara? The tutelar of healing?"

"Yes, Raspberry."

"You talked to Ameliara...Balaby's wife?"

"Yes, we spoke last night. When Lenly passed, that made you the last balladeer on Aimsire."

Raspberry fidgeted with her hands, not sure what to say next. Suddenly, she remembered what Ceridwyn would do in situations like this.

"Ms. Rajumin, would you like some tea? Honey mint tea is, umm, well...always nice for conversations like...this."

"Spoken like a true friend of Ceridwyn." Rajumin beamed.

"You know Ceridwyn too? Is there anyone you don't know?"

"I don't know you, but after what I've heard, I'd like to."

Slowly a smile crossed Raspberry's face. She investigated Rajumin's eyes and felt that incredible sense of peace once again.

"I'll go make us that tea."

+++

Kali stared out her bed chamber window, studying the burnt grass where she had blasted Rorie with a lightning spell. Her eyes traced the black lines burned into the grass. She reached into Shakyna, surrounding herself with the comfort of magic's catalyst.

She pressed her mind into the earth itself, feeling for the pulse of power, the deep heartbeat of energy that she felt come through her feet the day she fought Rorie alongside her cousin, Rayann. She knew the power was there spinning out of the core right beneath her feet...but felt nothing.

Contemplatively she meditated on the events, how the power had filled her, a deep and pure power she had never experienced before. It was far beyond anything she had been able to cast shredding Shakyna alone, and she wanted more.

"It's amazing, isn't it?"

The voice was not Rayann's. She whipped around and her hands came up as power and magic instantly flared to life. A wise looking young elf stared at her as Kali narrowed her eyes angrily.

"Who in the crevasse are you? How did you get in?"

The sharp featured woman in deep green robes trimmed in golden brown showed no sign of distress or fear. Her narrow, almond shaped, gold-colored eyes never twitched.

"Who do you *think* I am, Kali? Last time you heard my voice, you answered eagerly and without hesitation or anger."

10

Kali lowered her hands and gently shook her head in disbelief as she whispered, "No...you can't be."

"Yes."

Instantly Kali went to her knees. In her experience she knew better than to not kneel before a tutelar. Aviyana stepped forward, offering her hand and spoke as if she had read the young human's mind.

"Rise. The tutelary are not to be bowed to or worshiped. We are but the servants and messengers of God. Come and walk with me."

She stood as Aviyana reached out her hand. The instant their fingers touched they were transported to the meadow. Aviyana studied the scorched dirt and then looked at Kali.

"Most humans who would have attempted to channel that much power without knowing how would have cooked themselves in a most horrific manner and died."

"I am not most humans."

"Of course you aren't. Why else would I have come?"

Aviyana began to walk towards the cliffs that overlook the Sylph Sea and Kali hurried to catch up. As soon as they were side by side, Aviyana continued.

"Magically speaking, you are deeply talented, much more so than most. As such, I believe the restrictions of moon and sun magic will never be enough to satiate you. Besides just talent you have far too much ambition. In honesty, I am not even sure that what I am willing and able to offer you will be enough in the end."

Kali responded, "I have never felt as alive as I did when that power came up through my feet and out my hands. It was nothing like shredding Shakyna. The connection was direct, deep, immeasurable, almost...intimate. I want to learn more."

"That is because you finally cast magic as God intended, not under the perverted practices of the one cast out because of her rebellion. God has granted me permission to have this conversation with you, but my parents have petitioned to not bestow upon you what you seek. They say you committed an abominable treason to magic when you shredded Shakyna. They also believe you are unpredictable and it's too dangerous to offer you the gift of terra.

"I, however, appreciate your unpredictability. I believe it makes you capable of never being held to a single path but rather to know how and when to shift for the betterment of this world. With terra, you are connected directly to God's creation and therefore more deeply committed to preserving it.

"Aimsire has been dormant for too long. I was given permission to activate the ardor channels again so that God's life and light can flourish more abundantly amongst you. I seek those whom I can trust and have the strength to control the flows. In short, I am here to make the final decision about you.

"Very few magic users are centered and disciplined enough to wield this power, and we have lost so many wizards. You above all know this directly.

"You have walked the halls of she who rebelled; therefore, you understand treachery and the grief it brings to all. Conversely, you have now felt and are beginning to understand the ways of the light. Though I don't know the future, what I do know is that unless we commit ourselves without hesitation, this world may be spun off its axis and shaken apart. Shakyna is the binding force that holds it all in place. Because you mastered the shredding of it so well, ironically you understand it better than any wizard we have left."

Aviyana stopped when they reached the cliffs and turned to look at Kali.

"I granted you access that day so you could defeat your cousin. I needed to know if you had the strength to control terra without dying."

"So that was a test?"

"Of course it was a test. All wizards who follow God must be tested, that has always been the way. That is how we know you are committed to the light."

"What if it had killed me?"

"Then you would have died, and we would keep looking."

Kali's thin, charismatic, crooked smile crossed her face before she bowed her head humbly.

"If you feel I am suited and capable, Aviyana, I will follow your guidance and commit myself to the path of God's light."

Through her feet, Kali instantly felt the warmth of terra enter her body and course through her veins. She drew a deep breath and gasped as the power filled her. The slow, rhythmic pulse of the ardor channels tingled her toes.

Lifting her right hand, she stared at the blue glow emanating from her palm and the lightning that now snapped between the gaps of her fingers.

Suddenly, a sharp, unprecedented gust of hot wind blew in off the sea. It hit her face first and then flowed over her shoulders before coursing down her body. Kali's wizard robes changed in color to a dark, emerald green, trimmed in gold and brown.

Aviyana declared, "I charge you to walk this planet and protect its inhabitants from evil. Show them the light so that God may shine in their hearts and thoughts. Those of the moon are the shield. Those of the sun are the sword. But those who wield terra are the vindicators. They do what must be done, no matter the cost, even when it is the hardest thing to do. That is your path now. Even at your own expense if that is the need. Vigilance and sacrifice are your new calling."

"Thank you, Aviyana…" she paused.

"Say what else is on your mind, Kali."

She inhaled deeply and looked back at the spire of Faemley Manor.

"When Fifth and Piramay arrived, they were not here for any of us. They wanted the Staff of Terra."

Aviyana remained silent. Kali turned back to her.

"Why did they take it and flee?"

"For what exact purpose I do not know, however, they have been systematically reducing the northwestern coast to ash. Last night they razed Restwater Bay to the ground. Based on their pattern, Pearlport will likely be next."

"What can be done?"

"That is entirely up to you. The tutelary gift as God requires and guide those who receive, but as you told your cousin on this very spot, 'In the end you are only required to do two things in this life; you must make decisions, and at some point, you have to die.'

Kali felt a knot in her stomach as her own words came back to haunt her.

Aviyana continued, "The time will soon come when you are going to need to make some decisions. Will you throw yourself down on the rocks below to avoid that? Or, will *you* hide from the truth now that you know it?"

13

# Chapter 02 - Voices of Power

"Call the Commander!"

Aeolis and Ceridwyn appeared just outside the gates of Gryphonledge, unconscious in the center of the road. Six heavily armed steelguard ran to them.

"Get a healer! This one's injured!"

Hours later Ceridwyn's eyes fluttered open. The room was unfamiliar and smelled strange. She ached and turned her head, staring at Aeolis on the bed across from hers. His cheek had been tended to. The wound was dressed but there was still redness from the reptilian's poison. She clutched her ribs and sat up, breathing through the pain.

"You are going to be fine."

Turning her head towards the voice Ceridwyn whispered, "Archmaster Elgan."

"It is good to see you, Ceridwyn, though maybe not under these circumstances."

"Do you know…the citizens of Clay Water, are they…?"

"They are safe. We received a carrier pigeon from the platoon commander who had been sent to retrieve the reptilian. If it had not been for you and Aeolis doing what you did, the whole hamlet might have been wiped out before they arrived.

"Unfortunately, the reptilians escaped. We believe the mage was Nidhug. Based on the initial report, we know it was his brother, Rezren, who had been captured.

"We suspect that Nidhug knew the soldiers were coming to retrieve Rezren. When the platoon returned it was reported that the jailhouse was destroyed."

Ceridwyn stood and began to put her outer robe back on. She looked at Archmaster Elgan Qiyarius, the only elf left on the Circle of Six since Nimsul had been murdered. His skin was still smooth and youthful, but time away from the forest was clearly taking its toll. His green eyes were sunken under his unkempt, long, thin eyebrows. He still projected every measure of pride that would be expected from an academic, Fara Elf wizard, but the slight droop in the points of his ears was noticeable.

"Yes, I witnessed it. That blast of fire blew most of the front of the building to splinters. I tried to fight Nidhug; he was far too strong."

"Do not hold it against yourself. There was nothing more you could have done against a reptilian wizard. You did well and held them there long enough for the steelguard to arrive and save the rest. There have been many of these incursions into human lands since the thwarted invasion of our home. This incident was only one of dozens we have learned about. It makes sense they would come into human territory where they wouldn't be hunted by the rangers any longer.

"Rest yourself and report to the Circle of Six tomorrow at noon. We have had Lady Rose prepare rooms for you in the keep. Aeolis will be awake soon. Already he stirs."

"Yes, Archmaster Elgan. I will see you tomorrow."

+++

"I am glad to hear that the steelguard arrived. I just wish we could have done more."

"We both do, Aeolis, but at least we did what we could."

He turned and looked out the window across the vast city of Gryphonledge. Its gray buildings, all made of solid stone, reflected the strength of the human's central army command center which was housed here. This was the human capital and home of their king and queen. A heavy military presence demanded that everything be orderly and easily accessible in case a defense needed to be mounted. The streets were aligned in perfect order, and all roads led back to the massive keep in the middle.

Beyond the keep, to the north, stood the famous Wall of Tides. Seamlessly carved into the stone, it was the largest sculpture in the known world. Rising four hundred meters high and spanning five times as wide, it depicted a massive ocean wave jutting out and curling under itself, poised as if about to crash onto the city and engulf its inhabitants. The details were exquisite, showcasing bubbly foam, underwater plant life, and vivid depictions of fish, sharks, and whales caught in the surge.

The castle grounds were at the base, directly in the center. The shadow of the wall covered the back half of the compound where the gardens were, providing a pleasant and practically weather free experience for the king, queen, and their family.

Gryphonledge had originally been a joint dwarf and human mining town. Thousands of years ago, in collaboration and partnership, the two races worked together, harvesting the precious metals and stones formed by the magic energies running beneath the resource rich Iron Mountains. As the operation pushed deeper into the rock over the years, inventive and creative miners began to hew the stone into smooth, level streets and geometrically perfect buildings. A vast city carved from the rock itself without a seam or pinch of mortar.

Five hundred years ago, after a falling out between the races, the dwarves returned north, settling themselves once again amongst their kin in Quill's Gate. Hardly a dwarf had been seen on Aimsire ever since.

"Your meeting is tomorrow?"

Ceridwyn walked over and looked out the window, focusing on the Hexangular. It was an odd-looking building among the much more orderly that surrounded it. This was the building from which the Circle of Six governed the academia of wizardry. The building was mysterious and perpetually shrouded in a thin, sweet-smelling mist.

"Yes, tomorrow at noon."

"What are you going to tell them?"

She turned and looked at him. "The truth. The attack on Faralanthis. Nataxia's unexplainably sudden ability to open massive portals on Aimsire, Kali returning to Hailan Glen. All that has transpired."

Ceridwyn slipped her arm under Aeolis' and turned to look out the window again. She gently rested her head on his shoulder. His stomach went to butterflies, wondering why this sudden show of affection. Or was it? Perhaps it was simply comforting in the moment that he was the only piece of home she had right now. Either way, he was happy to let it linger.

She sighed, "I feel as if everything is about to change. Shakyna is stirring and the ground buzzes with strange energy. I can feel it like my own heartbeat. Something is happening to our world. Whether it is good or bad, I cannot determine."

The next morning, Aeolis arrived at Ceridwyn's chamber and knocked softly.

"Enter, please."

His breath caught in his throat as he stared at her. She had prepared herself for the meeting and was simply radiant. He did his best to quickly regain his composure.

"I asked for food to be brought up for you."

"That was very kind. I am not sure my stomach is settled enough to eat, however. What I would really like is…"

"…honey mint tea."

"Yes." A gentle smile crossed her face.

"Well, as luck would have it, I have some of that coming for you as well. It won't be honey from Rootvale, but I was told that the honey harvested in Goose Sky is richly delicious. It should all be here in a few moments."

"Thank you. That was very thoughtful."

Aeolis noticed the slight trembling in her fingers which was causing difficulty for her as she attempted to tie on her waist sash. She was normally a bulwark of confidence. This slight hint of vulnerability only made her more appealing and attractive to him.

"Would you like some help with that?"

Her cheeks went flush and she shook her head. "No thank you. I can manage."

He walked over and gently took the end of the sash from her hand.

"I have always heard and understand that you like doing things alone, but sometimes it's okay to accept help."

She reached up and gently touched the small piece of tartan cloth that was always pinned under her collar on the left side.

"It's not that I am refusing your help, Aeolis, I just…"

The sudden knock startled them. Ceridwyn cleared her throat and took the loose end of the sash from his hand, tucking it loosely so it would stay temporarily.

Aeolis walked over and opened the door. The scent of the honey mint tea instantly filled the room.

"Ahh, yes, thank you. Please set it over there."

The young woman who entered had the mark of a knight squire on her pauldron. Ceridwyn observed that she looked a little too old for one that typically held the rank.

The squire set the tray of food on the table near the window and spoke, "Before you depart Gryphonledge, Commander Lady Rose would like to request a meeting. She is very interested to hear about the attack on your capital city. She feels it might be related to the increased sightings of the Rage Queen's forces in our lands."

Ceridwyn inquired. "May I know your name?"

"I am Larissa, Commander Rose's squire."

Ceridwyn found it odd that the young lady only offered her first name. This was not customary for human knights as they often wanted their lineage known.

"The dawn of our friendship brings me joy, Larissa. Please tell your Lady Rose that I would be honored to meet with her after I conclude my affairs with the Circle of Six."

With a bow of her head, the squire left. Ceridwyn turned to Aeolis, her cheeks were no longer flushed.

"Again, I appreciate you thinking of having this brought to me. Tea will help settle my stomach."

+++

An hour and half later, the two elves left the keep and began making their way to the Hexangular. Ceridwyn spoke as they walked together.

"I really am fine to go alone. It is likely they won't want to hear your testimony until I have told them everything I came to inform them of. If you would like to see the city while I am in my meeting, I can call you on the winds when I know more."

"I have never been to Gryphonledge and fear I might get lost. As you are the only of us who knows this city, it's best that I wait for you and humble myself to being shown around."

She turned and looked at him. He offered her a playful wink and Ceridwyn smiled.

"Well, I must say, I have never been a gentleelf's escort. I just worry that you may get bored with waiting. I have no idea how long this is going to take."

"I will wait all day for you if need be."

18

As they approached the Hexangular, the sweet smell of spell regents and pungent components began to fill the air. Everything about the design of this structure was done to astonish and even create a small amount of fear. The mysterious nature of wizards was one of their most important powers. Knowing that they could inspire awe simply through their presence was something they had always leveraged. Ceridwyn stopped at the door and turned to Aeolis.

"You cannot enter, not until you are invited. I am sorry, that is just the way."

"I understand. It's not a problem; I will be under that tree when you return."

She turned and stared at the massive oak growing in a large patch of dirt surrounded by a solid stone planter.

"That oak there?"

"Yes. That oak, right there."

Ceridwyn's cheeks flushed ever so slightly as she turned and walked through the door.

The inside of the Hexangular was ornate and cold. Everything in this room spoke of superiority and power. It sickened her. She loved that she was gifted with magic, but the formal, elitist, and rigid academia that governed it was something she never subscribed to. She didn't care about rank or privilege; she devoted herself and learned magic so she could help those who couldn't help themselves.

"Thank you for coming."

Ceridwyn turned and immediately offered a respectful bow.

"Archmaster Reena."

Reena Elestandra was one of the friendliest and levelheaded members of the Circle of Six. Much like Ceridwyn, she never allowed the pride of wizardry to dominate her place within it. Her silvery gray hair was pulled back loosely, styled in a way that showed she had no plans to cast magic today. Though she was seventy-five, she still had a deep youthfulness in her face, which matched her joyful expression of welcome.

"I am sorry to hear what happened to you and Aeolis in Clay Water. I am also sorry to hear what happened in Faralanthis. Not only Archmaster Nimsul's death, but also how an army of such size managed to sneak in under our noses. It is something we are not taking lightly. We were happy to hear that the portals were closed before the entire invading army could arrive. I hope that whatever additional information you can report to us today will aid in providing deeper insight."

They began to walk and Ceridwyn spoke.

"Archmaster Reena, unfortunately I won't be able to offer much about the means of their arrival. What I can say is, there was some hope by the end of it all. Kali is the one who closed the portals. She has left the service of Nataxia and is now with Rayann Fionntán, in Hailan Glen."

Reena stopped. "Hamish and Ebonia's daughter?"

"The same."

Reena looked toward the chamber door and then back to Ceridwyn as she whispered, "Indeed that is good news." She paused. "I would advise you to keep this bit of information between us, for now."

Ceridwyn's face showed her confusion.

"But Archmaster, surely The Six will want to know."

Reena leaned in as she advised, "Some in The Six are deeply disturbed. The magic fields are in an upheaval. Motion and power are coming up through the terra like never before. Maise and Nicodemus are the most concerned. As terra wizards, they are more sensitive to the fluctuations than the rest of us. They fear that Nataxia has gained access to the ardor channels directly and may seek to use them against us."

"But the ardor channels have not been active or passable for many centuries. I don't see how…"

"Ceridwyn, I know, it doesn't make sense, but neither does this ambient magic her wizards are casting. Conclusions are being drawn before there is sufficient cause or evidence to do so. The hunting and murdering of so many wizards hasn't been helping and we have been unable to stop it. Our insights have been cloudy, almost as if they are being purposely thwarted.

"All this is why I am cautioning you to remain quiet in this one regard. Until we know more, we cannot allow wild theories to run amuck and I certainly don't want to introduce anything that might tarnish Hamish or Ebonia's memory. I promise, in due time, we will present this information. When all has settled enough to do so, we will call Kali to come testify before us. Hopefully sooner than later so we can start making a definitive plan."

"She won't come. She is not a wizard of the robes. The Circle of Six do not have authority over her."

"Don't worry about that. Her cousin is of the robes and before my husband left this life we were friends with her parents. We will cross that bridge when we come to it."

Looking at the door and then back to Reena, Ceridwyn gave a soft nod of affirmation before they walked into the council chamber.

The hexagon shaped room was intimidating, even to a seasoned wizard like Ceridwyn. Though she had been here countless times before she still felt a pull on her stomach as the nerves clenched her guts. Reena stepped forward and looked at the other four members.

"Master Wizard Ceridwyn Bolshoraes of the Sun."

In a flash, Reena was up in her chair, looking down at the center of the room where Ceridwyn now stood alone.

Ceridwyn turned her head and looked at the chair where Nimsul once sat. She felt a pull in her heart. Inhaling deeply to center herself she turned to look around the room.

"Archmasters, my heart sings to see you all again. I have come per your summons to offer my report."

"Before that, Master Ceridwyn, we have a different matter to discuss."

She turned and looked up at Archmaster Joziah, a moon wizard of great renown and power. He was a human in his late fifties, without a hint of gray in his black hair or a shard of humor in his body.

"As you instruct and desire, Archmaster."

Joziah stood and looked at the other four members before turning to look down at Ceridwyn again. He spoke without a hint of emotion in his voice.

"We, the Circle of Six, have looked into Shakyna. We have discerned the visions of the river, and it has been decided that you are to be elevated to the rank of Archmage, effective immediately. Your deeds and your power have grown in steadfast consistency to the benefit and service of Aimsire. Congratulations."

Ceridwyn's face showed her shock. She looked at Reena who simply nodded.

"My thanks to you, Archmasters, I…"

"I am not finished, Archmage Ceridwyn."

She turned and looked at Joziah again, bowing her head respectfully.

"We have also been discussing the vacancy in our chamber. The loss of Nimsul was a blow to us all. In addition to your new rank, we are also promoting you to be the sixth member of the Circle of Six. By the grace of God, long may the conclave of wizards survive upon and protect Aimsire."

She heard the words ringing in her ears. Again, she looked to Reena who was now displaying a soft smile. Ceridwyn turned back to Joziah and waited a moment. He offered no more words, so she softly cleared her throat to speak.

"Again, my thanks to you, Archmasters. I am honored that you would show this level of trust in me…however, I cannot accept your offer."

Nicodemus, a stern and ferocious looking terra wizard of incredible power leaned in.

"We do not make *offers* here, Archmage Ceridwyn. Your assignment to the Circle of Six is not only an honor but your duty as a wizard to accept when called."

"Archmaster Nicodemus, I understand that no wizard in the history of our world who has been offered a position on the Circle of Six has turned it down, that is, until now. I also know that there is no edict or law within the conclave that requires or binds me to accept, that is simply precedent and tradition."

Nicodemus furrowed his eyebrows as he sat back.

Reena looked at Ceridwyn and inquired.

"Archmaster, this is a prestigious honor. Why is it that you are not willing to accept?"

"Archmaster Reena, with all due respect, sitting in a place of authority has never, nor will ever be my place in this world. If it pleases you, I prefer to make my difference out there, where it matters most. My lack of truly ever understanding why God would allow so much suffering in this world notwithstanding, I chose to learn magic and even to be challenged or die by the Test of Ten Gates. My motivation has always been to assist and aid those who cannot or are powerless to help themselves. I didn't do it to become bound to a chair, making edicts and rules."

Reena leaned back and looked at Elgan, the sole elf in The Six. His face showed his disappointment but also reflected that he was not happy that Reena was right when she predicted to him that Ceridwyn would not accept.

He looked at Ceridwyn and spoke softly, "Archmage Ceridwyn, Shakyna has discerned and guided our decision. What would you have us do? Leave the Circle of Six in a vacancy?"

"No, Archmaster, I would advise you to keep looking, but first, that you would allow me to give you my report regarding Nataxia and her inevitable invasion of Aimsire, as I was summoned here to do."

+++

At the sound of footsteps, Rayann turned and smiled warmly to her cousin.

"Good morning, Kali. How did you sleep?"

"Fairly well, but I'm still adjusting."

She sat near the hearth and poured herself a much-needed cup of tea. Rayann sat next to her, wiping her hands on a towel.

"Adjustments take time, allow it. I have seen that you are getting more comfortable here, in fact, I saw you walking to the overlook by yourself yesterday. It filled my heart with joy seeing you move around the Glen and meditating to find your lineage."

"By myself? You mean you didn't see who was with me?"

Rayann laughed. "Kali, of course you were by yourself. I would have seen if someone was with you and besides, my attunement would have alerted me if anyone entered the glen unannounced."

Kali set her tea down and stood, offering her hand.

"There is something I must show you."

Leading her cousin upstairs, Kali walked over to the large, double doors of the dressing closet in her room. She pulled them open and stepped aside. Her robes hung on a mannequin, the black was gone, and they were now a splendid, deep, emerald green, trimmed in earthy brown. The heavy silk shimmered in the morning light as Kali spoke.

"I was not alone."

Rayann gasped as she walked over and looked at the garment. Her eyes traced the new embroidery on the left shoulder. Gold thread, dense and delicately stitched formed an arch with a solid dot below it. The symbol of Aviyana.

"Aviyana was with you? Is that what you are saying?"

"Yes. I pledged myself to her guidance at the overlook. What's more, the ardor channels have been activated once again."

Rayann paused for a moment as the pieces started coming together. She traced her finger over the golden thread as she responded.

"The Tower of Kells has been stirring. The center sits on a conjunction point and the cap stone has been humming. My grandparents used to talk about it, but I have never experienced it, until yesterday."

This time Kali smiled as she whispered, "I know."

Rayann's eyes went wide. "How?"

"I can hear voices coming from the tower. They have been calling me, and I have answered."

"They are beckoning you to unseal the door. It is our ancestors; you are to be the next Mistress of Kells!"

"No, they have been calling you and have asked me why you are not answering."

Rayann stepped back and felt a shiver run down her spine.

"You're right, I have been ignoring them. I don't know if I am strong enough."

Kali's eyebrows dipped. "That's fear talking."

"Of course, it's fear talking. To control the tower one must face the entirety of the Fionntán bloodline. One must prove they are worthy before the secrets are unveiled!"

"And why are you not worthy of such a thing?"

"I...I was born of two, not one. Yes, I can cast, but my true power was in The Bond, my connection with my brother. I couldn't even defeat him on my own. It ultimately took you and Myth to do that. I just don't see how I will be able to face the bloodline and show I am worthy or deserving of the honor."

"You are the last person I would have expected to hear that from. The whole time I was training all I heard about was how powerful you are. Fifth told me that I needed to be cautious when the time came to confront you, how your bloodline made you so formidable. Rorie said all the same, warning and cautioning me that facing you wasn't something to take lightly. Want to know something? It was all true. What's it going to take beyond your ancestors calling upon you to realize it for yourself?

"You arguably snatched the greatest assassin to ever live out from under the Rage Queen's grasp and turned him to the light. You opened my eyes and brought me back to my ancestral home. You showed a halfling that she has value in a world that told her she does not. By the light, you, a human, became a princess of the Fara. So, when are you going to finally step up and do something for yourself? This is your home; *you* are the one meant to be its matriarch, not me."

Rayann's head dipped. She inhaled through the tears and whispered, "So much has happened in the last year. I have a husband now, who, yes, also happens to be the Fara Elf Prince. I have our baby growing inside me. I am supposed to change the world, me, 'the one of different eyes.' Everyone whispers about how I am the one of prophecy. So…yes, I am scared. I am frightened to death of not ascending to a place where I meet everyone's expectations. Never in my dreams did I imagine I would ever leave this glen in the first place."

Kali's face softened. "Which is all the more reason you should take the highest place within it. Let's take a break so you can think. That breakfast you made smelled delicious. Let's go eat and continue this discussion on full stomachs."

+++

Appearing before the gate out of thin air, Piramay released three of her protective seals, charging herself with power, and swung the Staff of Fire. A blast of flame as hot as dragon breath engulfed the area. Twenty soldiers were instantly turned to ash and the soul well pulsed in Fifth's hand.

The bells immediately began to ring and the citizens of Pearlport scattered for safety. Nearly a thousand people instantly realized the stories of cities being razed to the ground south of them were true. The knights had been sending soldiers to defend

25

the remaining cities, but Piramay just proved how ineffective they were going to be.

The guard hastily began to close the gates, but a fireball the size of a boulder blew one of the stone towers to rubble. The right side of the gate collapsed and began to burn. Piramay advanced and Fifth was right behind her.

He swung the Staff of Winds. The flames rose and spread rapidly across the area as swirling winds whipped them into a blazing fury that no human could outrun.

Two knights on horseback came charging down the middle of the street, lowering their lances and thundering towards Piramay. Her laughter echoed off the buildings and she slammed the butt end of her staff onto the cobblestone. A wave of fire arched out before her, burning the legs off the horses. The knights hit the ground and slid to her feet. Fifth flicked his finger to turn them over onto their backs and wrapped them in binding magic.

Piramay sauntered over, looking down with a sweet smile.

"Poor, poor, knights. You cover yourselves in steel for protection and forget it's so much like an oven when heated."

She opened her hand and dropped a glowing ruby onto each knight's breastplate. Their armor began to glow bright orange and the sizzle of their padding and skin could barely be heard over their screams. She laughed and stepped over them, pressing into the town square. The small keep in the center of town was now shut. Those that managed to get behind the gate shivered as the smell of burning flesh and charred wood filled the air along with the choking ash. Fifth stepped up beside her and looked at the gate.

"One would think that being so close to Nethermen territory they would use stoutbark wood, not oak."

He pushed the Staff of Winds forward and a blast blew the gate off the hinges. Piramay thrust her hand forward as she released a fourth protective seal, increasing her power. She cast a succession of fireballs which tore through the troops advancing on them. The spell was so powerful it went through the soldiers and then into the portcullis that secured the keep. The entire front of the stone building began to collapse as the explosion rocked the foundation.

Fifth lifted the soul well and smiled. It pulsed with purple energy as the souls of the dying were sucked into it. Piramay stepped over and traced her finger across the gem. Sparks flicked off the surface where her fingernail made contact.

"So beautiful."

She turned casually as two more soldiers charged through the burning wood. Bringing her hand up the two instantly burst into flames and collapsed.

"So, Fifth, how many is that now?"

"We have successfully filled three soulwells, giving us the three thousand we need."

Piramay pouted. "What a pity, I was looking forward to visiting Northrim next."

She turned and stared at Fifth with a devilish grin. He handed the soul well to her and spoke, "There would be no harm in collecting a few more souls, in fact, having one more reserve of power could prove to be useful. There is one small matter we could address before erecting the towers."

Her eyes flashed and she turned, looking at the center spire of the keep as it creaked before collapsing into the flames. "Well then, to Northrim it is."

# Chapter 03 - Ascensions

Touching her fingertips to the charred dirt, a shiver ran down Rayann's spine. The lightning spell that burned these lines was so hot it had even melted the stones. She looked up at the window of her cousin's room. There was no question that despite how young she was, she was exceptionally powerful.

Turning back, Rayann's eyes followed the path of burnt grass where the lightning had etched a scar into the meadow but closed them when she reached the place where Myth'alas had cut her brother down. Even after all he had done, she couldn't bring herself to look at the place where Rorie had perished. While she knew the actions he had provoked against them could have only ended the way they did, she still found it incredibly painful to know her twin was dead. Admit it or not, there was deep emptiness inside her now. First her parents, then Rorie...she wondered if the void inside her, caused by their deaths, could ever be filled.

Reaching to her belly, Rayann inhaled the fresh, salty air. Yes, of course it could. She had Myth'alas now, and this little miracle growing inside her. They were not the family she was born into, it was even better, they were the family she chose. She knew in time she would move on. Her grief would fade, and she would release the anticipation she once had of walking through this life with her brother.

Suddenly, the silver capstone that topped the Tower of Kells pulsed. The energy filled Rayann and she turned to look at the manor. The beautiful, monolithic stones defied all logic, and yet, they made perfect sense. Her head was full of beautiful memories, but simultaneously, every tragedy in her life. The voices called out to her once again. Rayann's throat went dry with fear as she responded.

"Yes, I hear you."

Entering her ancestral home, Rayann moved through the central halls towards the massive, magically sealed doors that provided access to the Tower of Kells. Her hands began to tremble as she rounded the last corner. The voices of the deceased Fionntán surrounded her, muffled as if she was hearing them while under water. She reached the end of the unlit hall and the darkness lifted. To her surprise, the sealed doors were open.

Rayann paused and stared beyond the threshold. There was nothing but a magical, infinite void. It was as if the opening was sucking all the light in and devouring it. She closed her eyes and concentrated, drawing power from the moon and surrounding herself with Shakyna. Pressing her mind into the magical, golden river, she calmed her breathing. The catalyst of magic and life reached back. Its energy surrounded her on command as the hollow walls of juxtaposed granite reverberated. She opened her eyes and bravely stepped forward.

Instantly, Rayann was standing in a twisted, freshly burned forest. She recognized her surroundings; she was north of Faemley Manor. Everything was coated in greasy black ash and the smell of charred wood filled her nostrils. The tree line was ahead, barely visible through the smoke rising from the smoldering ground. She shivered, but moved forward, staring at the sliver of light between two gnarled trees.

As she exited the tree line, Rayann stared at Faemley Manor. Most of the structure was in ruin. Her eyes traced the blackened stone and shattered shimmer glass. The entire meadow was charred and held no life, except for the place where Kali's spell had blasted Rorie; there it was bright, emerald green, and full of life.

Where Myth had cut Rorie down, tall wildflowers sprung up in dazzling colors, swaying gently in the salty Sylph Sea breezes. She approached and reached out, touching some of the pink milkweed blossoms.

"You never should have broken with me, sister."

Whipping around, Rayann's hands flared to life with bright blue light. She stared into the face of her brother. His eyes were swirling gray with dazzling white light flaring beneath the pupils. His beard was longer than she had ever seen him wear it and long burn marks stretched across his pitch-black robes where Kali's spell had twisted itself around him.

"You have no power here, Rorie!"

"Oh, sweet sister, in fact I do. So long as you live, you will never have that which made you whole. Me."

Without even lifting a finger, a blast wave of energy pulsed off his body. Rayann was thrown and landed on her back in the unburned grass.

"Ironic, that our cousin weakened me, your husband finished me, and now, forever, you get to fear me."

"I do not fear you."

"I know you as well as I know my own mind. We shared knowledge, emotions, life, even our mother's womb. You are lying to me and to yourself."

He was right, she was terrified. Rayann lifted her hands and screamed as a blast of gravity erupted from her palms. The energy which could have moved ten men simply passed by, swirling the ash behind him into the air.

Reaching up, a tendril of dark energy from his hand clasped her around the chest and brought Rayann to her feet. He lowered his chin and began to close his fingers. As he did the energy constricted her ribcage and she felt the air in her lungs begin to be slowly squeezed out.

"So, what now, brother?" She coughed. "You intend to kill me? Here? In this ash world you now live in?"

"I am not going to kill you. It will be far more satisfactory to just torture you a bit and then let you live a long, unhealthy life. The ash all around you shall flow through your veins. It will grind away at your heart with every thump. Each time you feel the scrape of it, you will remember me. Your dead brother, killed by your selfish actions."

The strength of his spell intensified and Rayann could feel the ash beginning to rub against her skin. Her womb throbbed as the life within it tried to resist what it was feeling. Myth's face flashed in her mind, Kali's words rang in her ears…she pushed back and Rorie screamed as a pulse of bright blue energy traveled back at him through the connection and blasted him off his feet.

She positioned herself into a combat stance and thrust her hands forward before he could get back up. A sphere of blue energy surrounded him. He stood and flicked the energy shield.

"How many times have I witnessed this spell? How many times has it surrounded me as a means to protect? How many times have I watched you collapse it and crush your enemies?"

"Too many times."

"Correct! Too many times."

"You are not strong enough to counter this spell, Rorie. Not even in this place."

30

"Your words linger too long, sister. Even now, you can't bring yourself to harm me. Go on then, do it."

Rayann's eyes flashed. "I never intended you harm. Severing our bond, absorbing your magic, none of that was intentional. I loved you. I still love you!"

"Which is why I continue to grind away at you. Tik-tok, sister. The gnomish clock is counting down. Do you have what is required to kill me? Perhaps it would help if I dared you to do it like when we were children, when you felt that you needed to prove yourself to mum and pa?"

Angrily she gritted her teeth and drew in Shakyna. He smiled as she completed her spell. The bubble collapsed. She exhaled sharply; he stared back, there was no trace of harm to him.

"Oh, sister…"

Rorie thrust his hands forward and his magic bore down on her. Spheres of inky black smoke that looked like skulls rapidly streaked towards her. Arcs of turquoise energy erupted from Rayann's hands, deflecting them. The diverted shadow skulls blasted craters in the ashy ground. As he intensified the power and speed of his attack, some of the magic swerved around her and began to burst holes in what remained of the outer walls of Faemley Manor. Dazzling arrays of color sparked through the air with each impact.

The intensity of his barrage was beginning to take its toll. Her eyes teared up with exhaustion. Through the light and shadow erupting between them, she would catch glimpses of his face; he was not drained in the least. She pressed her heels into the patch of green grass and drew all the energy she could, deflecting one last burst of his assault before her magic left her.

The spell hit her in the center of her chest. Any energy she had left was drained by its effects. She lay on the ground, panting and reeling in pain. The ash floating through the air began to cling to her sweaty skin.

Rorie knelt beside her. She tried to stand and get away from him, but he placed his index finger on her breastbone and effortlessly pressed her back down. She had nothing left. He stared at her and drew a heart on her cheek in the wet ash.

"The hatred that sprang from your heart was something I never thought you were capable of, Rorie. Somehow, despite our bond, you were able to always hide that side of yourself from me."

"I hid nothing from you. There was no hatred in me until you stole our gift."

"Yes, there was, I can see that now. I can see that you are the reason that Kells was locked. The ancestors knew. Mama and Papa knew. It's why they never attempted to unlock it. If they did, you would have had access to the greatest archive of magic on Aimsire. They denied themselves so as to also deny you. I was too naïve to see it, even though I was the only one who had direct access to your mind."

"And what makes you think you are worthy of Kells, sister?"

"I am worthy because, though I never wanted to leave, I did. I now see that there is hope for this world. The dormancy of this glen, and this tower, is unacceptable. It is an affront against God who wants us to spread light and love. If I am ever granted access, I will ensure that the power which flows through Kells be used to bring joy and life to the world once again."

Rorie stood and looked down at her. His face suddenly morphed as his robes became pristine white. The ash left the air, and the glen exploded into a splendid array of vibrant color.

Rayann gasped as energy filled her body and fresh air filled her lungs. She looked up and a man with the kindest face she had ever seen reached down to help her to her feet. He was Rorie's height, and his thick, snow-white hair reached all the way to his waist. His dark skin was flawless and smooth.

"Grandpapa?"

"You have done well, granddaughter. We had to know your brother's mind was fully separated from yours. It would be too dangerous to permit one who would use the power and knowledge for ill to enter Kells."

"Thank you, Grandpapa. I can feel all that is within. If I may ask, how do I start?"

Rayann's Grandmama appeared behind Rayann and spoke. "Stay your path; make all this new knowledge a part of your journey. Though you are bonded to the elf prince, you are still a Fionntán. Never forget that. Love your husband. Love your child and any that may follow. Allow their love to fill your heart and give you purpose."

Her Grandpapa spoke. "Do all your Grandmama says, but also know your power and resolve comes from your bloodline as well. Be wise, and bold. Trust those around you but also be cautious and brave."

Tears filled Rayann's eyes as she nodded. "I promise both of you, I will."

"Welcome home, Matriarch of the Glen, Mistress of Kells."

The landscape swirled and evaporated. Rayann felt the cold stones against her cheek and opened her eyes. She was lying on the floor just inside the threshold of the Tower of Kells.

"Rayann?"

She lifted her head and turned towards Kali who was kneeling in the hallway, just outside the door.

"You made it back; that's a good sign."

"How long was I gone?"

"Four hours."

"What?!"

"I followed you when I saw you pass towards the tower hallway and watched as you were sucked into the void. I could barely see you for the first hour, but slowly the darkness lifted, and finally light flared."

Rayann groaned as she sat up, her body was stiff from lying on the stones.

"I had to face him again. But it wasn't actually him. It was a test to prove I am worthy."

"Clearly you passed; I heard the voice just before you woke. 'Welcome home, Matriarch of the Glen, Mistress of Kells.' Not to say, 'I told you so,' but I did tell you that you were the one our ancestors were calling out to."

"Yes…you were right. The ancestors granted me the Tower of Kells and all it holds."

Kali shifted her gaze. "May I have permission to enter?"

"Of course, cousin."

As both women stood, Kali stepped through the double doors. The round room stretched out before them. Comfortable seating and tables formed a circle in the middle. Painted portraits of the Fionntán lineage were hung all around the room. Glittering light filled the place, but there were no torches or windows.

Kali spoke in awe. "It is absolutely beautiful."

"Yes, it is. This is the Room of Welcoming, a place of comfort and intended for debate, conversation, and learning."

Kali turned and looked at Rayann, cocking her eyebrow. "How do you know this?"

Laughing, Rayann responded. "Suddenly, I am filled with all sorts of new insight. As soon as Grandmama said her words my head was flooded with more knowledge than I think I have learned in my lifetime. I suddenly know every detail about this tower, and this manor. I know where every book is, why the walls hum with energy, and what we need to do to start unlocking it."

"We?"

"Of course! We are the last Fionntán. It is up to us to unlock the secrets of Kells and use that knowledge to spread life and love. Together, we will change the world."

+++

Raspberry quietly entered the chamber of the High Consummate and sat beside his bed. Her heart hurt as she watched his slow, labored breathing. She desperately wanted to make him better, despite what everyone was saying. Last night she had meditated on her mentors' words. She remembered Lenly's kind eyes and the way he spoke to her. She desperately wished she could talk to him now. She looked at her shimmering blue shirt, the one he had Mirelle make for her. With a small nod of confidence to herself, she knew what she needed to do.

"Good morning, Mr. High Consummate, sir. It's me, Raspberry. I wrote a new song for you last night. I came this morning to play it for you. I've been spending so much time with you, but we've never had a real conversation. I wish I could ask you to tell me your stories, I'm sure they would have been wonderful. Before I sing this for you, I just wanted you to know, I wish we had gotten that chance."

She stared at his sunken, motionless face. After a moment she brought her lute to her chest and strummed. Instantly the golden glow of graceful light filled the room;

*"Lo' in the twilight, the dove settles in,*
*He coos and fluffs into roost.*
*Pausing in silence where the moon and sun banter,*
*And nighttime is now introduced.*

*Did he accomplish all that he yearned for,*
*Could he have stridden for more?*
*His eyes start to tingle as sleeps taking over,*
*The constellations he soon will explore.*

*Peace to the mountains, peace to the prairies,*
*peace to the brooks, and the trees.*
*In the still of the darkness he watches the water,*
*Content in all that he sees.*

*Carry on my two sons, carry on my dear wife,*
*I promise your lives shall endure.*
*Onward and yon ward, into the heavens,*
*My spirit shall now be made pure."*

Raspberry felt a strong hand gently squeeze her shoulder. She gasped and turned in surprise, staring into the strong-featured face of Myth'alas.

"Mr...er, Prince Myth'alas! I'm sorry, I was just playing..."

"I know, little one. You have no reason to apologize."

"What do you mean?"

Myth'alas gave a nodding gesture with his chin and Raspberry turned to look at the High Consummate. He was surrounded in a gentle, golden glow, and he was no longer breathing. She started to cry and Myth'alas knelt in front of her, placing his hands on her shoulders.

"Do not cry, for this was the purpose. He needed to pass in peace. You made that possible. Jerrin and I agreed on it. It's probably the first thing we have agreed on since I was born."

He winked and she could not help but chuckle. He stood and looked at his father.

35

"I will let Jerrin know so you don't have to. It's my duty, not yours."

He walked to the door but turned to look at her again before he left.

"Raspberry?"

"Yes, Mr. Myth?"

"That was the most beautiful song I have ever heard. Rayann was right about you. Your heart is as pure as she professes. You truly have an amazing gift."

Her cheeks went as red as her hair and her instinct was to explain herself. Suddenly, she remembered Ceridwyn's words and looked up at the prince, smiling confidently.

"Thank you, sir."

"I will go speak to my brother. Do not feel that you need to linger at my father's side. Of course, you may if you wish, but if you would like to go get some rest, please feel free to do so."

Myth'alas departed. Raspberry slung her lute over her shoulder and looked at the High Consummate. She tilted her head slightly and joy filled her heart. For the first time since she had been coming to play for him, there was a smile on his face. He finally looked at peace.

+++

"So that is it then?"

Jerrin leaned on his elbows and looked across his desk at Myth'alas.

Furrowing his brows, Myth'alas spoke plainly.

"That's all you have to say?"

"What else is to be said? We knew this was coming."

"All the same, I will go inform our mother. The situation calls for slightly more empathy than you are clearly capable of summoning."

Jerrin stood and leaned on his knuckles.

"Is that so? Where were you the last hundred years, brother? All of a sudden, you're the reliable shoulder to cry on during our families' darkest hours?"

Any other being who had said such a thing would have been immediately invited to settle a comment like that with steel

36

on the dueling ground. Myth'alas chose to swallow his pride and stared silently at his brother.

Finally, he spoke. "I will go inform our mother."

"Myth'alas."

"Yes, Jerrin?"

"I am not finished speaking with you."

"All the same, my guess is mother has already felt the shutter of her life mate's death. She needs to be comforted."

"I agree, but we need to discuss the ascension."

"What of it?"

"Now that father has passed, I will become High Consummate and you will be elevated to first prince."

"I understand how ascensions work. Again, what of it?"

"I have not been overly fond of your residing in Hailen Glen as opposed to here in our castle where you belong. Though I don't understand why you would desire to live in human territory, I have tolerated it."

"Tolerated it?"

"You have a role within the commonwealth to think about. The elven nation needs you now more than ever. I insist that you return here and live with your own kin."

"No."

Jerrin walked around the desk and stared up into the eyes of his brother.

"That was a direct order from your High Consummate."

"To the crevasse with your orders, *High Consummate*. I have been away from my bride for over a week tending to this commonwealth. You said these late nights were to be temporary. I have a wife, and a home, and soon, I will have a child. I refuse to allow my family to linger for my return as I sway to your every bidding and commandment."

Jerrin took a step back and stared at Myth'alas who was now crossing his arms over his broad chest defiantly. He exhaled his frustration.

"I should have figured."

"That's right, you should have. This is how those who find love move through life. They have families, and I will not have my child raised here to be judged by those who can't see beyond their own noses. No child of mine is going to learn the prejudice and snobbery of 'our' kin."

"Careful what you say."

"Or what? You'll attempt to excuse and justify the fact that the Fara still own their own kin as slaves? That we claim dominion and kill any elf that opposes our rule? That we haven't left our forests for centuries to help spread God's light which was our charge as the first created on Aimsire?"

Jerrin inhaled in anger and walked back behind his desk, sitting roughly in his chair.

"If you weren't my brother…"

"…we would already be on the dueling grounds 'discussing' your comment about where I have been the last hundred years. I assure you, brother, it's a conversation you wouldn't have enjoyed."

Turning on his heel Myth'alas left. Jerrin stared at the door, contemplating his brothers' words.

+++

On the cliffs high above the city of Northrim, Fifth stared through a gap in the rocks. Piramay approached and glanced over his shoulder as she spoke.

"Looks like they are well aware of us. That's going to make this all the more fun."

Fifth estimated. "There must be two hundred knights, plus the soldiers. Unfortunate for them and highly profitable for us."

"They are digging in and attempting to form a defensive trench perimeter around the main gate. Do they think we will be arriving on horses? These fools are so predictable it's pathetic."

He mocked. "Look how fervently they are digging. At least no one can say they lack ambition. I propose we wait until after sunset. We have hit every other town in the daylight; they won't be anticipating a night attack. Over there, in the harbor, see that merchant ship with the blue sails? That's where we should start."

Piramay snickered. "What are they loading? It looks like…kegs of gunpowder. How wonderful. I have a special little trick that will truly set this attack off with a bang."

They stepped back away from the cliff's edge and sat in the cool shadows.

"Piramay, I should tell you what I plan for us to do with the harvested souls from this attack. As you know we have all the energy we need to accomplish our mission. To truly strike fear into the citizenry of Aimsire and establish ourselves as the absolute power of magic and authority, we must also strike down the pillars that are already established."

Piramay's vicious grin crossed her face. "You mean to destroy the Hexangular and those who rule from within it."

"Correct. How did you know?"

"What else is there? The elves are more pomp than authority anymore. The humans have their military might, but they are no real threat. The Nethermen may venture south once we have set our banner, but they are non-magic users. Easily controlled.

"The only true potential threat is the Circle of Six and the few remaining wizards they can assemble. If we strike down the leadership of their academia and then begin to weaken their power by harvesting the energies of magic, they will be powerless. I am all for it. As you said before we started this whole campaign, 'the risk will be worth the reward.'"

"Yes, it will be, little phoenix, yes it will be."

"So, once we have a fourth soul well of energy, what's your proposal for eliminating our rivals?"

"No strategy will be needed. With as much power as we have now, we'll just walk right in their front door."

# Chapter 04 – Path of Constellations

Ceridwyn read the parchment and looked up.

"The star of our High Consummate has extinguished."

In unison, she and Aeolis spoke as they bowed their heads respectfully, "May the memory of his light never cease to sing in our hearts."

With a sigh, Ceridwyn tucked the note into her robes and looked out the window across the rooftops of Gryphonledge.

"The Rite of the Eclipse is in two days. Myth'alas has asked me to return immediately to assist."

"And what of me?"

"Aeolis, you are the Chief Ranger, of course he wants you there." Ceridwyn turned with a coy smile.

"Did he say that specifically?"

"No...but he did mention if you show signs of being possessed by any more demons, he will run you through."

The brief second of shock was immediately replaced by his laughter. He lunged at her, squeezing her tightly in a flirtatious hug, pretending to subdue her. She squealed and feigned defeat, but then quickly cleared her throat and stepped back as she placed her hand over his heart.

"Aeolis, I'm sorry. I should not have..."

"Should not have what? There is something between us, I feel it. I know you are a wizard, and I am a ranger, and yes, that presents potential difficulties. But still, I just need to say..."

"Aeolis..."

"Begging your forgiveness, I must say this. You saved my life, for that I am grateful enough. That said, have you really not felt it as well?"

"Aeolis, you are a fine elf. Though you were a pompous snob prior to your...event, I have seen the change in you. I want to believe it's real, I mean, I know it is, however, I just–" Ceridwyn turned and looked out the window again. Her eyes immediately became slick with unshed tears as she reached up under her collar, placing her finger on the piece of tartan cloth pinned beneath.

He gently reached, placing his hand on her shoulder and turned her so he could look into her eyes. She was crying.

"What? What is it about me that you don't approve of?"

40

"It's not you, Aeolis."

She removed his hand from her shoulder and took a moment to settle her emotions. After she gathered her thoughts, she looked into his eyes.

"When I was a young mage, just months after completing the Test of Ten Gates, I was sent on a mission by the Circle of Six. As you likely remember, centuries ago, wizards and knights were often paired together in cooperation for the benefit of Aimsire. I was assigned to a mission with a knight of the hammer. He was a very kind human named Sir Thomas Galbraith."

She cleared her throat as her cheeks went flush before continuing.

"We were sent north into Knockingwood to investigate a disturbance. A small village called Asdinshire had been sending carrier pigeons informing the Hexangular about strange noises and purple, flashing lights up in the cliffs. It had been going on for weeks, but when a couple of their townsfolk went missing, they asked us to investigate.

"I have always had a knack for uncovering things, and Sir Thomas was reputed to be quite a sleuth himself. We ventured out. I, the bright-eyed fledgling wizard, and he, the experienced knight. From Gryphonledge we traveled north, getting to know one another as we traveled along the salted roads. I was young and inexperienced in more ways than just wizardry, but I recognized that he was captivated by me.

"I admit, I found him quite charming at first, but very quickly, I found him to be…handsome as well. It was his character more than anything that enamored me. He was always so polite and genuinely empathetic to any along the way that needed our assistance.

"'It's the simple things that bring the most pleasure,' he used to say anytime we stopped to lend a hand. Being of more humble origins than most Fara Elves, I always managed to find satisfaction in the smaller things life offered. I think it was that, and his disregard for all the pomp and circumstance I had seen in most knights that ultimately attracted me to him.

"Over a month of travel later we were just a day's ride from Asdinshire. It was getting dark, so we decided to set camp. As usual, he offered to take the first watch so I could rest. Two hours after sunset I heard his war cry and sprang up from my blankets. Two, decaying, zombie-like humans were approaching us. I can still remember their glowing, purple eyes. Before he could draw his sword, I incinerated both with a single spell, and the night went quiet. Of course, neither of us could sleep after that and we hurried to town at the first light of dawn.

"We made our way to the village; the fear in the air was palpable. After meeting their magistrate, we were given a cottage to stay in and set up our headquarters for the investigation. Oddly, upon our arrival, there were no more disturbances in the hills.

"At night, when we were done with our busy day, we would have dinner with the townsfolk at The Chuckling Goat. It seemed like little more than a typical human tavern and inn at the time, but now it's a place that will forever remain in my heart. It was there I got a chance to really observe and understand humans.

"We elves like to think they are brutish and power hungry, stripping the lands for their own benefit while hastily warring with any who stand in their way. Yes, of course, there are some who are like that, but I discovered when it comes to humans, the norm is their hearts are often filled with more good than evil, and their intentions tend to follow in the same manner.

"Weeks turned to months as we interviewed everyone within kilometers who had any information or witnessed the disturbances. We made daily treks into the hills searching for any signs of necromancy. We were certain that's what it was, especially given our own encounter with those undead humans. The hardest part was we both consistently felt the evil in the air. Not a day in the woods was absent of the feeling we were being observed. Every time we thought we might be getting close to something; we would hit another dead end."

Ceridwyn reached up and unpinned the piece of tartan from under her collar and brought it out, staring at it lovingly.

"What did flourish during those many months was my relationship with Sir Thomas. We had stopped sleeping in separate beds after four weeks, and though I am embarrassed to admit to you now, things blossomed faster than I ever thought I would involve myself with another."

She began to blush as she gently stroked a finger along the fine wool.

"We were six months into the investigation and the day of our breakthrough finally arrived. The night before, there had been horrific squealing and flashes of purple on the north ridge. We went up at first light and found dozens of slaughtered elk. The blood had been completely drained from their bodies. It was sickening. I cast 'reveal magic' to find that there were indications of dark sorcery everywhere. Thomas found a minute trail, I confirmed the path with a 'reveal' spell, and we hiked several thousand meters into the cliffs. We thought we had finally made a discovery. A well-hidden cave was before us. In our zeal, after so much time and work, it never occurred to us that it was all a set-up.

"We entered the cave and immediately made our way for thirty minutes through a twisting pattern of tunnels. The evil we could feel was the only thing thicker than the atrocious smell in that cavern. We pressed on. Finally, we entered a large, dome shaped room. Purple and green light glowed from enchanted skulls all around the perimeter. Thomas drew his blade and I felt the pull of magic a split second later. I never had a chance to counter or warn him.

"A whirlwind of power scooped us up and flung us to the center of the room. Slimy black roots sprung from the floor and bound us to stone tables. I felt a painful, dark hex enter my body that clutched at my tongue and wouldn't allow me to speak. I was helpless. No magic. Thomas was a meter away, bound tightly. He had managed to turn his head towards me just before the roots pinned him down and covered his mouth. His eyes said it all, he wanted to apologize for not seeing the trap sooner.

"A dark figure emerged from the shadows and made his way towards us. He stared at me with his mirrored eyes. Later, I would come to learn that this man, if you can call him that, is Fifth. He spoke to me first and his voice was sinister and gravely. 'Ceridwyn, I hear you have completed the Ten Gates. What a delight to finally meet you face-to-face.' He then turned to Thomas, 'And, Sir Thomas Galbraith. Honorable and gallant Knight of the Hammer. I must say, I have only come to know you in the last few months, however, I am quite impressed.'"

Ceridwyn's voice began to quiver softly.

"Fifth turned to me and placed his hand above my navel. 'So, little Fara, this is when things get interesting. I have been watching you both,' he turned to Thomas. 'There are secrets in this womb, tucked away, even from her lover.'

"As Fifth turned back to look at me, I sent a missive to Thomas' mind, even though I had never done so between us up until then… *'It is true Thomas, I am pregnant, but I wanted to wait until we were done with the investigation to tell you. I didn't want your mind to be clouded. We were so close to calling in the guard to take over…I am so sorry!'*

"Instantly, Thomas' mouth began to move as he attempted to speak, but Fifth flicked his fingers and the slimy vines tightened. I could hear his jaw dislocate as his eyes welled up with tears from the pain. 'Tsk, tsk, Sir Thomas. I am the only one permitted to speak. You see, you two have set back my experiments and research. Just as my time has been penalized, so too there must be a penalty paid by you as well. I will give you the choice, sir knight, since you are the superior in rank it falls on you to decide. That is the price of leadership. Will it be the life of your unborn child? Or yours? I assure you; I will only kill one of you.'

"Fifth's face curled into a devilish smile. He watched me as I twisted and attempted to send Thomas another message on the winds. The agony from his attack on my mind hit me like a mountain falling into the sea. I buckled under the strain of the bindings as my body convulsed from the pain. Thomas looked at Fifth with pleading eyes and the pain instantly stopped. Fifth nodded, 'Very well, sir knight. It is decided. You are the one whom I shall kill.'

"Fifth waved his hand. A shadow leech slithered from the darkness and crawled on top of Thomas. It clutched at him with those appalling tentacles, became translucent, and forced its way through his chest."

Aeolis felt a cold sweat on his forehead and reached, gently taking her hand.

"That is how you knew what it was that had possessed me."

"Yes, Aeolis. What happened to you was the second time I had seen such a thing."

She wiped away her tears with her sleeve and clutched the tartan cloth tightly.

"What happened next is etched into my mind deeper than anything else I have ever experienced in this life. Within seconds, the shadow fiend had taken root. A thin, white line appeared around my Thomas' pupils. The bindings that held him down released and he stood. Fifth looked at Thomas and spoke, 'Good, the creature has taken hold of your will. As I promised, I will only kill you. The shadow fiend, however…,'

"There was no hesitation. Controlling Thomas' body, the shadow fiend drew the dagger from his scabbard and pierced me, right into the womb. I felt one small kick, and it was over. The pain of the wound was a moon cast shadow to the agony I felt in my heart. A mere second later, a guttural scream escaped Thomas' throat and he began to melt away. His skin, blood, and bones dissolved as if he had been dipped in acid, right before my eyes. I turned my eyes and looked at Fifth with hatred and he spoke flatly, 'Little dear, this is the way of punishment. One dies, and the other is left to suffer the lesson so they may tell the tale.'

"I woke up in our bed at the cottage. To this day I can't tell you how I arrived, but I remembered everything else that had happened. I also felt that the child, murdered in my womb, was gone. I am certain Fifth had somehow removed it. I wrapped myself in Thomas' tartan cloak and didn't leave the cottage for weeks. It is only because of the kindness of the townsfolk, bringing me food and water to sustain me, that I survived.

"Two months later, after I had recovered physically, I cast what I intended to be my final spell. I transported myself to Rootvale and moved back into my family's home. I vowed to never use magic again and returned to work as a seamstress. For years I stayed in seclusion.

"Finally, one day, Nimsul came to visit. He offered no pressure; he didn't even ask me once to join him back in Faralanthis. He simply came to talk. I refused. He continued to show up twice a week and we would sit by the brook that ran beside my parent's home for hours on end drinking honey mint tea in silence. It took a year, but finally, I told him the whole story.

"After I was done, he said, 'Ceridwyn, you don't have to practice magic ever again, but God has given you a talent, and I don't believe you will be whole unless you follow the path that was placed before you. Additionally, though I dare not speak on behalf of him, I don't believe that's what Thomas would want your life to become either. If you ever feel you are ready, speak to me on the winds.'

"He stopped coming to visit me after that. Two months later my mother brought me a new set of robes. She had been constructing them for me every night in secret after I had gone to bed. As she looked me in the eyes she simply said, 'My beautiful daughter, though I love having you in our home, your place is not here.' She handed me the robes and I cried immediately. In my heart, I knew she was right. I saw that the level of injustice and evil that had been done to me could not be left to linger on this planet.

"After I settled back in Faralanthis, I made a promise to myself that I would never love again. I did not want to offer any advantage of that type or to increase an enemies' leverage over me as I had with Thomas. My personal vow upon returning to the robes was if I did fall in love again, I would quit magic. That brings us to this moment. Here I am. Wearing these robes. Deeply in love with the chief ranger of the Fara. Honestly, Aeolis, now that I am at the crossroad of my own words, I don't want to give up either my robes, or you."

Aeolis felt his heart twist in his chest as she concluded the most painful story he had ever heard. How she had managed to survive such a thing and then stand up again to move on with her life, he simply could not understand. To know she had suffered so intensely made him yearn to reach out, draw her into his arms, and hold her tightly, but he knew now was not the time to do that. Aeolis was not able to speak for many moments. He simply sat with her, but finally he found the right words.

"Ceridwyn, I have found the promises we make to ourselves are the hardest ones to uphold. Simultaneously, they tend to be the least rational. I have spent my life trying to prove something to someone. To my father, that I was worthy to carry on his legacy. To my mother, that I was the son and child she always wanted me to be. To Jerrin, that I could lead the rangers. To the elves of Faralanthis, that I could be the line of defense and protect us from outsiders. Ultimately, I failed in every aspect. I allowed that same darkness that took Thomas into my body. Yes, I know you said it was something I could not have been prepared for, but even still, I can't help but wonder.

46

"What I do know is I would be dead if not for you. You were the only one who dared to even investigate what was happening to me. It was you who stood up to my bullying and defiance of your presence. It was you who stared into my eyes, recognized what was going on, and withdrew the darkness from within me. You did more than save my life that day, you saved my soul, and my heart. That day I realized how truly empty my life was. You brought the light back into my heart, and from the light, I am learning how to love."

He leaned forward and brushed a tear off her cheek.

"I cannot control my emotions, I never could. My heart is screaming at me to not let you go. To see you look at me with such love but also such sadness, however, is something I can't endure. Beyond that, it's certainly not fair to you. I understand your vow, and I respect it. If it will make it easier for you, I will leave you alone. Knowing that an elfess like you, even despite my brutish behavior and the fact that I attempted to kill you, could still see something good in me, that it might have led to something more? That can be enough to give me great hope that I can be a better elf. I admit, it will be hard, but I can let it be enough."

Ceridwyn smiled sadly. She recognized they both found it easy to unburden their thoughts with one another. She slid beside him and placed a soft kiss on his cheek before slipping her arm under his and rested her head on his shoulder.

Exhaling softly, she whispered, "Please don't leave me alone…but please have patience. I just need time to think all this through. If it puts your heart at ease, know that I care for and dare I even say, love you deeply."

"If it takes an eternity, I will wait for you."

+++

Larissa knocked gently on Lady Rose's door. She was a hard-headed, strong-willed young woman full of potential, the exact kind of person Lady Rose desired in a squire.

"Enter."

She walked in and stepped up to the desk. Her deep green eyes focused on her commander. She waited patiently as Lady Rose finished applying her seal to a parchment.

"Yes, Larissa. What can I do for you?"

Larissa bowed her head. Not a single strand of her tightly pulled back, raven hair with red highlights fell out of place.

"Lady Rose, Ceridwyn summoned and offered me this note to deliver to you."

Rose took the note and broke the seal;

*"Commander Rose,*

> *Life and light to you. It is with a songless heart that I must inform you, our High Consummate has passed to the constellations and I have been summoned back to Faralanthis. Prince Myth'alas has requested my assistance in the arrangements for the Rite of the Eclipse so his father may ascend, and his brother, Jerrin, may take the role of High Consummate. I deeply apologize and mean no offense in not meeting with you as I told your young squire that I would. I give you my word, when next I am able, I will return, and we can have our audience with one another.*

*Until our hearts are near,*
*Ceridwyn Bolshoraes, Archmage of the Sun"*

"Unfortunate."

"What is unfortunate, Commander?"

"The High Consummate of the Fara has died. Ceridwyn must return to see to arrangements."

"He's dead? When? How?"

Lady Rose raised an eyebrow and looked at her young squire curiously.

"Why the sudden interest, Larissa?"

Clearing her throat, Larissa regained her composure.

"It's nothing, just unfortunate, as you said."

Lady Rose noted the change in demeanor but put it out of her thoughts, for now.

"Yes, it is. Please see that they are escorted safely to the border."

"Commander, they've departed, by means of magic."

"Of course they have."

Rayann and Myth'alas looked out across the great elven city of Faralanthis from the balcony of the throne room. She turned and went up on her tiptoes so she could kiss Myth'alas. He smiled, ran a finger along her forehead, and tucked a stray curl of hair behind her ear.

"I love you, wife."

"I love you too, Myth."

"Jerrin asked me to move back here. I told him no."

"It's no surprise. You two are of completely different minds. I admit, I have been wondering about what to do in that regard. Now that Kells is unsealed, I don't know what the right answer is. I could live here; we could raise our child here. Kali could stay at the manor; she'd be more than fine on her own. The ingress works both ways. I could move between here and there just as easily as you have been."

"Rayann so much has changed here, but so much remains the same. Half-breeds are accepted in the human territories, but not in Shimmerwood. Our child would always be looked down upon. Because I am first prince, nobody would dare to do so openly, but the Fara are much too prejudiced and set in their stubborn superiority."

"I just want you to be happy. If all of this starts to put unnecessary strain or anxiety on you, that would be the worst."

He placed his hands on her cheeks and leaned down, kissing her deeply.

"You and our child are my only priority. I will do my duties to the utmost of my ability and I will need to spend a lot of time here but starting tonight and for every night until our last, I will sleep with you, in our bed, in Hailen Glen."

Rayann felt her cheeks go warm and hugged him tightly, pressing herself into his broad, muscular chest.

"Alright you two, that's enough of that."

Myth'alas and Rayann turned to see Ceridwyn walking onto the balcony with a warm smile, Aeolis followed right behind her. Rayann walked over and was about to bow her head in respect but, before she could, Ceridwyn embraced her in a welcoming hug. Rayann gladly accepted.

"Welcome home, Ceridwyn. I heard the news. Congratulations on your promotion."

"Don't remind me; academia and hierarchy are so stagnant and meaningless."

Myth'alas stepped up to Aeolis and placed his hand over his heart. Aeolis mirrored the welcoming before he spoke.

"May the memory of your father's light always sing within our hearts, Prince Myth'alas."

"Thank you, Aeolis. How are you feeling?"

"I am completely back to full strength, thanks in no small part, to Ceridwyn."

"That is good news. Tomorrow morning, I would like to see you at first light. We need to formalize your rank as Chief Ranger under my command now that I am First Prince."

"Of course, my Prince."

"MS. CERIDWYN!!!"

Raspberry came sprinting onto the balcony and smashed her little body into Ceridwyn's. Ceridwyn laughed as she hugged her friend.

"I missed you so, so, much! I have bunches of wonderful things to tell you!"

"My heart sings now that we are near once again, Raspberry. I look forward to hearing your story after the Rite of the Eclipse."

Raspberry stepped over and gave Rayann a warm hug.

"It is good to see you too, Ms. Rayann."

"And it is always a pleasure to see that big, bright, beautiful smile of yours, Berry."

Looking around, Raspberry suddenly remembered.

"Oh dear! I'm supposed to play at the ceremony! I need to go! See you all soon!"

As she sprinted away Myth'alas remarked. "You were right about her Rayann, the dirge she sang to assist in my father's passing was the saddest, and yet, most beautiful song I have ever heard."

"I will never forget that first night I met her in Brighton, it was the joy I heard in her music that truly changed my opinion of the world."

Ceridwyn stepped up beside Rayann. "Agreed. I am not sure Aimsire has ever had a Balladeer as gifted as that little one."

+++

Raspberry finished her closing song. The assembled within the Hall of Stars bowed their heads and spoke in unison.

"May the light of his star always sing within our hearts."

Ceridwyn stepped forward.

"On behalf of the royal family, thank you for seeing High Consummate Lathai Thel'Radin to the constellations. We conclude."

The assembly of Faralanthis' nobility made their way out of the hall. Jerrin stepped over to Raspberry.

"I appreciate your playing for my father again, my family thanks you."

"Sure, High Consummate. It was my pleasure to help."

Ceridwyn smiled proudly at Raspberry from behind Jerrin's shoulder. As he turned to leave, she walked up to her friend.

"That was truly beautiful, Raspberry."

"Thanks, Ms. Ceridwyn."

"Come, let us all have some tea."

Myth'alas, Rayann, Aeolis, Raspberry, and Ceridwyn left and sat in the royal gardens. After the tea arrived, Ceridwyn lifted a cup to her nose and inhaled.

"It's the simple things that bring the most pleasure."

Ceridwyn turned to Rayann. "How are things in the Glen?"

"Well, I unsealed the Tower of Kells."

"You did what? That's...well that's wonderful news!"

"Yes. Just prior to that Aviyana appeared to Kali. She has pledged herself to terran magic. The manor began to buzz with power just after and that is what motivated me to unseal the door. I can't get her out of the library. She's been specifically focused on the ardor channels. Aviyana told her that they have been activated once again."

Raspberry suddenly perked up. "Oh! The ardor channels! I know what those are! Ms. Rajumin told me all about them."

Shocked, the entire group turned. Ceridwyn reached and touched the top of Raspberry's hand.

51

"Did you say, Rajumin?"

"Oh, yes Ms. Ceridwyn, she's very nice. We had a long conversation in my house while we drank honey mint tea. I remembered how to make it from the way you taught me to. It was a perfect conversation for tea and cakes."

Ceridwyn pressed Raspberry. "During this conversation, she told you about the ardor channels?"

"Yeah! I asked every question that came to my mind! She told me that there are many mysteries on Aimsire, and one of them is the ardor channels. She said that if a person knows how to use them, they can go anywhere on the planet in an instant. It's pretty incredible. She also said they are what bind the planet. Shakyna surrounds everything and helps to sustain all life, and ardor holds it all together. That's how God designed it.

"Ardor is very powerful, and the terra wizards can use it for their magic. It makes them the most powerful wizards because the source is right under their feet, whereas the power of sun and moon wizards has to travel all the way from the constellations."

Ceridwyn turned and looked at Aeolis and Myth'alas. A hopeful smile crossed her face. Suddenly Raspberry blurted out again, "Oh, yeah! She also said she knows you, Ms. Ceridwyn. We didn't talk much about that, but she did mention it."

"Yes, I have had the privilege to speak with her in person. Did she tell you anything else?"

Raspberry tapped her chin.

"Well, she said something about life and light returning. She also said that people are starting to seek for truth again. OH, and that God's eyes are turning back to the citizens of Aimsire! She also mentioned something about the core being rushed."

Ceridwyn's eyes went wide. "Rushed? Do you mean, roused?"

"Huh? Oh, yeah! Roused!"

Ceridwyn smiled as many of questions in her mind had just been answered by this information.

Aeolis set his cup down.

"I wonder if this is in part to what is happening along the west coast?"

Myth'alas immediately inquired, "What do you mean?"

"While we were in Gryphonledge, the human armies were on high alert. Apparently, there are armies razing all the towns and villages along the west coast."

Ceridwyn corrected him. "Aeolis, the reports did not say armies, they specifically said, 'two magic users.'"

"Of course, but that had to be a loss in communication or exaggeration. I mean two individuals? I admit, I don't know as much about wizarding magic as you do, however, even two that moved beyond Archmage and reached the level of Eldedorach would not have the power to burn cities to the ground, that level of magic would tax them to death."

They all turned as Myth'alas spoke, "It is not impossible. You said the cities were being razed, that means fire."

"Yes, Prince, fire and wind," Aeolis confirmed.

"It's Piramay and Fifth." Myth'alas exhaled slowly as his eyes filled with concern.

"What?" Ceridwyn nearly dropped her tea.

Myth'alas continued. "Fire and wind. Think about it. There is no magic user as attuned to wielding fire as Piramay. She is not a magic user of Aimsire's traditional wizardry learnings. Whatever her source of power is, that's a secret she has never revealed. What I do know is that she utilizes a complex system of magical seals to keep from overheating herself while casting.

"As she releases seals, her power increases, as does the risk of literally boiling her body to death. I assure you she has spent a long time learning to tiptoe on the edge of power and safety. I have watched her burn small villages to ash in minutes. We know Fifth has the Staff of Winds; he revealed it during his fight with Kali at Hailan Glen. Nothing pushes fire faster than strong winds."

Ceridwyn's face went pale as she set her cup of tea down on the table.

# Chapter 05 – Four Thousand Souls

As the sun set, Piramay released three, glowing, marble sized orbs from her hand. The objects streaked through the air along an arced trajectory and landed so precisely on the merchant ship it was as if she placed them by hand on the deck. Instantly they burned through the wood and into the hold, igniting the gunpowder. The merchant vessel exploded in a massive mushroom cloud; the only thing louder than the screaming was Piramay's maniacal laughter.

She and Fifth moved along the shoreline and entered the city near the docks. Fifth was right, the Northern Command who had been preparing to defend Northrim were never expecting an attack like this.

Pillars of flame erupted from Piramay's hands with so much force it stripped the street of its cobblestones. As they peeled up off the ground, the stones glowed white hot and smashed into the wooden structures, setting them ablaze. Using the Staff of Winds, Fifth propelled the fire and blazing hot stones into the surrounding buildings.

Gathering some of the fire towards her, Piramay swirled the flames like molten liquid, filling it with her magic to intensify the heat. Fifth created tornados with his staff to carry the magically enhanced flames into the air. Two dozen spirals of flame twisted upwards and detonated a hundred meters above the city, raining fire down onto the rooftops. It had only been half a minute and already the entire harbor district was ablaze.

Fifth sneered. "And here they come…"

Piramay turned and flicked her hand. The ashen Staff of Fire appeared and she used the tip to draw an arc in front of her. A barrier of flames rose up between them and the soldiers.

"Route them! Find a way 'round!"

Commander Liam Stenberg of the Order of the Shield barked orders to his soldiers of the steelguard. He was a handsome man, honorable, tall, blonde, blue-eyed, and the first-born son of the family. The Stenbergs were one of Aimsire's oldest lineages of knights and were highly respected among the people. None of that mattered now. The four dozen soldiers that were with him obeyed and broke into two separate groups, trying to find their way around the flaming wall.

"There."

Piramay looked through the flames, pointing at the group that had split to the right.

Fifth followed the path of her finger and pointed the Staff of Winds. A violent gust pushed the inferno around the soldiers and their screams came and went quickly. He turned as Piramay was conjuring a large ball of fire, caught it in the winds of the staff, and slung it like a mortar shot where the other soldiers had advanced. It exploded on the roof of a half-burned building, sending sharp, burning shrapnel in all directions. The soldiers fell instantly.

Seeing his rally of troops annihilated so quickly, Liam turned his horse and retreated to the central, defensive perimeter.

"Awww. He doesn't want to play anymore."

"Patience Little Phoenix, there is nowhere for him to run."

Lifting the soul well, the gem pulsed with energy as the lifeforce of the dead were drawn into it.

"Come, they are clearly huddling into the walls through the center of town that we saw from the ridge. Their gathering together will make this easy."

+++

"What happened? Where are your steelguard?"

Lady Kellan ran out from behind the makeshift wall, grabbing the reins of her brother's horse as his shocked face turned back towards the carnage.

"Four dozen; dead in seconds..."

"Liam!"

Turning back to his sister, he snapped. "What are you doing out here?! Get behind the wall, Kellan!"

"Liam, this wall is a funnel. They will rain down fire again and we will die in mass! We must spread out. This isn't a phalanx line battle. We need to move and surround them!"

"You are not the commander of this sector, I am! Now get back behind the wall!"

Lady Kellan stared at him with her sharp, blue eyes, and turned angrily, moving back into the defensive perimeter. She may have been barely twenty and only a Knight of the Burnished, the lowest rank of the knighthood, but she could identify a bad situation when she saw one. This assemblage that the high command had put in place was fine for an army closing in through the streets. The moment she saw fire come from above, however, she knew it would be nothing less than a slaughter.

Her soldiers approached. "What did he say?"

"Nothing worth repeating." She looked around briefly and then spoke again. "Come with me."

The seven members of the steelguard under her command immediately obeyed. She had been granted her ladyship into the order of the knighthood six months ago but had already proven herself fighting the Nethermen. These troops trusted her implicitly. They moved to the north and then circled through the defensive obstructions, coming to an opening in the defensive perimeter. A senior knight in the Order of the Lance stopped her.

"Where are you going, Lady Kellan? Why are you not with your brother?"

"We...um, we are scouting. Our detachment is moving around and using the cover of darkness to see if we can provide a flanking maneuver."

"Good. Smart of Sir Liam to suggest that. Be careful. May God and Dionadair guide you."

"Thank you, sir."

They passed through and her sergeant shot her a mischievous glance for lying to a commander. Kellan narrowed her eyes as she whispered, "Don't say a word."

After making their way to the fishing shacks on the coast, Lady Kellan led her small contingency along the line of grounded boats. A second wave of fiery tornadoes went into the air and they watched in horror as concentrated fire rained down into the city once again, immediately followed by the screams of the dying.

"That looks like it was right above the central command area, your Ladyship! How can we fight against such a thing? Lady Kellan, what are we to do?"

"Our duty. Come on."

Lady Kellan led her troops along the edge of the northern shoreline districts, listening and watching for the enemy. An explosion caused all of them to turn and one of her men came up beside her.

"We can still escape, my Lady, on one of the boats…we don't have to…"

"Our job is to protect this city, at all costs. Do you all still trust me?"

"Yes ma'am, of course."

"Then no more talking of retreat and remember your training. I promise I will not intentionally lead us to slaughter."

As they rounded a corner in the shoreline market and began to cautiously advance back towards the heart of the city, more explosions reverberated through the air. Kellan paused. Her throat was dry and the fires all around them were pulsating unbearable heat. She was sweating through the thick linen padding she wore against her skin and her plate armor felt especially heavy. Calming herself, she turned to look back at her soldiers. They were terrified, she could see it in their eyes, but they were still loyal and staying with her.

"Okay, let's…"

A blast of wind knocked them to the ground. They tumbled and clattered for several meters before stopping. Immediately, Kellan tried to stand, but slimy vines erupted from the ground and held her and her soldiers tightly. They were trapped like rats in a cage. Additional vines sprang up and covered their mouths to keep them from speaking. She shifted her eyes and watched as a pale, silver eyed, black robed man approached.

Piramay sauntered up behind Fifth and stared at Lady Kellan, and then her soldiers.

"Well, well, well…what have we here?"

"Apparently they were trying to take a bite out of us in a flanking maneuver, Little Phoenix."

"We can't allow that now, can we?"

Fifth brought his hand up as Piramay was about to incinerate them. He lifted the soul well; its pulse had gone quiet.

"The well is full. Their death will not fuel our efforts."

"Perhaps not, but it would still be fun to watch them cook in their armor."

"Nevertheless, their death would be inconsequential. Let's leave them to tell the tale of how their city fell in mere minutes. It will spread fear about us, and fear is a powerful weapon."

Piramay knelt and looked into Kellan's eyes.

"What pretty blonde hair. This one has strength; it's bursting from her hateful stare. I like her."

Piramay kissed her index finger and pressed it against Kellan's forehead. Kellan narrowed her eyes and Piramay sneered in return.

"Goodbye, little pretty."

"That's enough for now, my Phoenix. We have a mission."

"Indeed, we do." She stood and turned to look at Fifth. "Onward then?"

In a blinding flash of purple light, they were gone. The vines instantly released, and all eight gasped for air as their mouths were uncovered. Looking around, Kellan saw nothing but horror. Every building she could see was on fire. The heat was far too intense for them to advance any further.

"Steelguard, back to the coast. We can't get back through this and should try to cool ourselves. When the fires burn themselves out…we will search for survivors."

+++

Piramay and Fifth appeared on the ridge overlooking Gryphonledge. Two guards posted on the rim immediately began to draw their weapons, but Fifth lifted his hand and crushed them with a spell. The two wizards casually stepped over the bodies and approached the edge looking down at the mysterious Hexangular.

"Look, Little Phoenix, there is light coming from the council chamber windows, they must be in a late session. How perfect."

"Shall we introduce ourselves?"

Fifth lifted his hand and instantly they were transported into the council chamber. The five current members of the Circle of Six felt the pull of dark magic as the two swirled into view and instantly went into action. Joziah began casting protective barriers over his comrades, while Reena and Elgan conjured fire in unison.

58

Lightning and burning stones began to rain down on Fifth and Piramay from Maisie and Nicodemus.

A blast of wind swirled from the center of the room, followed by a bright purple flash of light from the soul well in Fifth's hand. Their spells were instantly banished, and all five wizards of the council were flung into the walls behind them. Dark energy pinned them, bound their hands tightly, and swelled their tongues so they could not speak.

Piramay sauntered up the stairs to the large, upper ring and began to pace around the circle, looking into the eyes of each Archmaster with an enchanting smile as she passed.

"Archwizards of the Circle of Six. As you know, my name is Fifth, and this is my esteemed partner, Piramay."

Piramay offered a formal curtsy. "A pleasure to finally make your acquaintances, I'm sure."

Fifth continued. His voice echoed ominously off the walls. "Following our efforts, as I know you have been, I am certain you have come to understand that we are the new power on Aimsire. The old ways of your God are gone. Magic as you know it is dead. As a result, those who govern the practice of its mysteries and power must be made an example of. That is the price of leadership."

Fifth placed their fourth soul well on the floor. He looked around the room quietly, making sure to establish eye contact with each of the five council members. He waved his hand and the device began to hum and vibrate.

"Come, Little Phoenix, we won't want to be around for what comes next."

In a brilliant flash of purple light, they were gone. The Circle of Six watched in horror as the device began to bounce around and flash intensely.

+++

Commander Lady Rose Fairwind sat in her chambers. Her short, chestnut brown hair peppered with a hint of gray was pulled back neatly. Her bright, youthful, hazel eyes moved slowly as she read the evening reports. Known for her consistent fairness and empathy to those under her command, but also for her uncompromising expectation that her orders be followed when given, Lady Rose was known amongst the knights and the steelguard as "The Velvet Hammer." It had been three years since she was given command of the central army at the age of forty-five. During that time she had more than proven herself to be a highly competent leader.

A bright flash illuminated the city. She looked up from her desk as the explosion on the other side of Gryphonledge lifted into the sky like a scroll unrolling into the heaven's. She stared in horror as the purple flames and sickly green smoke were suddenly accompanied by a thunderous roar that shook the keep. Seconds later, massive chunks of the Hexangular's stone walls began raining down into the city.

"Larissa! Rally the steelguard!"

Grabbing her war hammer, she ran to the hallway and dashed down the stairs onto the front observation platform of the keep. She screamed to Sir Ordin Wolfrider, one of her Knights of the Lance, and this evening's watch commander who was stationed on the street below.

"Go to the castle! See that the High Guard have secured the Royal Family. After that, return to me immediately!"

With a sharp salute, Sir Ordin was on his horse and thundering towards the castle.

Larissa returned, panting as she reported, "Commander, I lit the beacon to alert the guard as you ordered. I stayed to watch and confirm from the tower deck. The troops are taking their defensive positions and lighting their signals. I also saw the knights assembling to their stations."

"Well done, Larissa." Lady Rose turned to look at the plume of smoke.

"What did those bloody wizards do this time?"

Lady Rose and Larissa watched as the green smoke rapidly spread through the air over the city. As the smoke thinned they could see that the top five floors of the Hexangular were gone. A jagged, hollow shell was all that remained.

Larissa swallowed hard. "It was not the Circle of Six, Commander Rose."

"How do you know that?"

"There's... malevolence in the air."

Lady Rose turned to look at her squire.

"I don't know how you always seem to be able to sense these sorts of things. If you have sensitivity and magical abilities, we might need to think about transferring you into the knightchanters."

"With all respect, Commander, I would prefer to remain under your leadership."

Rose let it go for now; this wasn't the time for such a conversation. She hurried down the large stone steps to the courtyard and turned to a young squire.

"Young lady, assist Larissa, we need my horse and hers as fast as possible."

"Yes, ma'am!"

Minutes later Larissa led the two horses out of the stable. They mounted and rode for the gate. As they made their way, the ominous cloud continued to thin and spread over the city. The moon's silver light was filtered through the green smoke creating an unnerving atmosphere. The wounded were being tended, but from what Rose could see, they were mostly injuries from retreating. Nothing too serious. She offered a silent thanks to God that this happened at night when the streets were mostly clear.

Halfway to the gate, the clack of hooves echoed through the streets and Rose looked up as Sir Trystan approached on his horse, Glaive.

"Commander Rose, I have the wicket gate sealed and I sent two dozen soldiers to the Hexangular to investigate and report. Our spotters on top of the wall are glassing the hillsides. There is no sign of anything."

"Well done, Sir Trystan. Larissa, go find the soldiers Sir Trystan sent. Assist them and report back to me if you uncover anything."

"Aye, ma'am."

Larissa was off like a shot and Rose turned back to Trystan.

"Any idea what it was?"

"No, but the fire was purple and the lingering smoke is green. Who ever heard of such things?"

"Wizards."

Trystan's lip twisted in agreement.

"Good work here, Trystan. I need to go send word about what happened. When Larissa returns, please have her meet me in my quarters. If you see or hear anything, and I mean, *anything*, you send a runner immediately."

"Yes ma'am, I will. If I may ask, Commander, who are you going to send word to?"

Rose turned and looked at the smoking shell of the Hexangular.

"Ceridwyn, the elf wizard who was visiting two days ago. She was the last to address them. I heard she was one of their top advisors and apparently, they wanted her to join the Circle of Six. It makes sense to let her know…besides, she's the only wizard I know the location of."

+++

It was midnight. Piramay and Fifth appeared at the crossroads north of The Shawl. The small guard station that housed a dozen soldiers where the three roads met was quiet and still. Without a word, Piramay's hand came up and a fire ignited just outside the door to draw them out. The twelve soldiers on watch came running from within and Fifth casually lifted his hand, casting a cloud kill spell.

They twitched and died on the road almost instantly. The two wizards entered the building and Fifth unrolled his map on one of the tables. He pointed.

"These spots mark the tower locations. We need to place one soul well at each. I assume you still have the one I gave you?"

"Of course."

Piramay removed the elegant device and placed it on the map. Fifth removed the other two from his robes and for a moment, they stared at each other in silence.

"This is it, Little Phoenix. Today you will die but then rise again from the ashes. The spell is going to take us to our limits. Only with the power of the three staves to shield us do we even have a chance. Because they will bear the brunt of the burden, they will be destroyed in the process. Once the spell is complete and the towers rise from the earth, our bodies will go dormant to recover. We shall rest for four and a half months by my calculations."

"You never mentioned this, Fifth. That is a long time to be vulnerable. Even with the Circle of Six gone, there are wizards remaining in this world who will certainly try to find a weakness in the towers and destroy us."

"Yes, however, the spell will also fracture the sky. The sun and moon wizards will be weakened, as will their power. We will be drawing Lúth directly from the constellations. Combined with ardor being drawn through the towers, a temporary, protective barrier will be in place that nothing on Aimsire will be able to compromise. Unfortunately, we will not be able to keep it in place indefinitely. Until all three towers are in harmony the process will not be complete but once it is, the barrier will cease to exist."

"Are you still considering...her, as mistress of the third tower?"

"Piramay, we have discussed this. Kali is power-hungry. She will be lured in like a moth to the flame. When she joins us, she will bind Shakyna to the towers and complete the process. You saw her raw talent in the Glen. She summoned the power of terra without ever being taught. You and I, we are not wizards of this world. We need someone that can bind Shakyna and ardor so the towers can be sealed to the core. She is the only choice."

"I have warned you, Fifth. She is not capable of loyalty."

"Not to people, but she is to power. The allegiance of three with the same desire is what solidifies that loyalty. An individual cannot control the balance, but three can. Kali will understand this, and she will comply. Remember, I am the one who trained her. I have been into the deepest recesses of her mind. I know her better than anyone else. Even better than she knows herself."

Piramay was caught in a struggle. She wanted this power but would need to compromise to achieve it. Though she did not trust the snit, she could not disagree. Kali just might be capable of loyalty to herself and therefore remain stable. That was, if she even joined them in the first place.

"You are certain she can be compelled to join us?"

"Leave that to me. For now, focus on this evening."

Though Piramay had always found Fifth's brand of magic to be vile and disgusting, he always had an effective insight into the way of things. That was why she trusted him. With a gentle nod, she agreed to move forward.

"Good." Fifth scooped up the two soul wells. "Know that I trust you above all others, Piramay. I assure you; I have thought this through. Soon, we will be more powerful than the tutelary themselves. Once we defeat them, we will even be able to challenge God."

"I trust you as well, Fifth. If not, I would have informed Nataxia of your schemes and delightfully roasted you on her marble floor."

Fifth laughed, knowing she spoke the truth. They walked out of the guard station and onto the crossroad.

"Just over the rise, a thousand meters, you will find a chunk of obsidian. I buried it there decades ago and it marks the center of your new home. Place your soul well on it in the etched grooves. I will place the other wells and meet you back here."

Forty minutes later, Fifth watched Piramay as she appeared over the rise, walking back towards the crossroads. Approaching him, she noted that the Staff of Winds and the Staff of Terra were standing straight up in shimmerstone mounts aligned with the soul wells. A third, the one she was walking towards, sat empty.

Piramay stopped and flicked her hand. The ashen colored Staff of Fire appeared, and she knowingly dropped it into place. Silently, Fifth walked into the middle of the staves. Piramay moved to a marked spot across from him and took her place. Just before they began, Piramay twisted her hands and the ten seals that helped contain her power appeared and hovered before her.

Moving her hands up, she twisted the seals like clockwork and removed all ten barriers to the power within herself. Her eyes began to glow, and she stared at Fifth with purpose.

Simultaneously, they closed their eyes and began to chant. Piramay had made the memorization of this incantation a part of her daily rituals for the last month. She was not a typical magic user. Her abilities were not of traditional origin, but she understood all the dangers of wielding energy this powerful.

As their hands moved in sync, the three staves began to glow. A triangular wall of light connected at the corners by each staff surrounded them. Piramay's auburn hair swirled as their bodies became the conduits to focus the energies. Thin arcs of light shot from the tip of each staff, circling through the sky like tracers, connecting them to the soul wells.

Instantly, the three wells opened like flowers blooming, and the shrieking screams of the dead echoed across the open fields. Lines of light pulsed under the ground as the ardor channels absorbed the power of the souls, sent it to the staves, and then the arcs of light sent it back to the soul wells.

Piramay felt as if her body was going to be shredded and her spine screamed as if she was on a torturer's rack. She bit her lip until it bled and pressed her feet to the ground, pushing her hands forward.

*"Yes, Little Phoenix, yes…stay with me, stay with me…"*

Suddenly, each soul well emitted purple beams of light to a focal point high above. Dark clouds full of the faces of the dead began to swirl like a cyclone, spinning violently as the screams were carried through the dark air. The epicenter of this triangulation began to blaze brighter and brighter until it flared, and a massive crack appeared in the sky. Peaceful, golden light streamed through, bathing the entire area with shimmering twinkles that danced and darted around.

Piramay screamed and opened her eyes as she focused her concentration, staring at Fifth. He was as calm as he ever was, focused on her face, his hands pressed out, palms towards her. As the energy continued to build between them, even in her unshakeable confidence, she began to wonder if her body could take much more.

He whispered. *"Stay with me…"*

She exhaled a final scream of courage and pressed the power flowing through her blood to its limit. The vortex from above concentrated and settled in around them. Lúth mixed with the ardor below and then exploded outwards beyond the soul wells. The colliding energy mixed with shadow and fire burned every living thing in a two-kilometer radius as it passed over.

A deep rumble from the core caused all of Aimsire to shudder for a mere second. The effect was so rapid most who felt it passed it off as imagination. Those sensitive to magic, however, felt knots and sickness in their stomachs.

The soul wells rattled and then sunk into the dirt. Three massive holes opened in the earth and spires, twisting and writhing like living creatures emerged from the ground, growing hundreds of meters into the sky. The tops pulsed and sent shockwaves of electrified energy back and forth to one another and then to the hole in the sky. The moon and sun dimmed slightly as the magical energy was sucked from them and the distortion of pure magic radiated from the entire area like a plague slowly spreading across the land.

One final explosion from each of the three towers blew clouds into the sky. The staves shattered as Fifth and Piramay collapsed onto the road. The last souls fizzled from existence as the invisible, protective barrier materialized into place. Fifth lifted his burned cheek from the dirt and gazed upon his partner. She was barely breathing. The magic had shredded all the clothing from her body. Her skin was peeled into curls, scorched black, and all her hair had been burned away. Despite that, she was alive.

"Sleep mighty Phoenix. We shall be...united...*soon.*"

Lifting a shaky hand, he touched the tip of her finger and whispered the final word of the spell.

"Reschackv..."

They disappeared, wrapped in their towers. Now, they could rest.

+++

The alarm bells across Gryphonledge instantly erupted again as the night sky to the southwest exploded in thunderous light, fire, and shadow. Larissa had just returned to Lady Rose from the Hexangular ruins with her report and went to her knees, clutching her stomach.

"Larissa!"

Rose lifted her squire effortlessly and carried her to her own bedchamber as she screamed.

"Summon the healers!"

She laid Larissa in her bed and turned to look out the window. The horror of the lights and the sounds of explosions over the horizon caused her mouth to go dry.

"By the tutelary...what now?"

# Chapter 06 – Ashes to Ashes

"I am growing impatient with all the failures and incompetence that surround me! Why have the traitors not been brought before me and laid at my feet?"

Nidhug and Lorcan bowed their heads as Nataxia paced around them like a cat about to devour her prey.

"Mistress, Fifth's magic is not traceable, you above all should know this…" The back of Nataxia's hand cracked against Nidhug's cheek. His head recoiled from the impact, but he remained passive as he brought his eyes back to hers.

"I apologize, Mistress." His tongue flicked and his slit pupils narrowed as he looked at her.

"What about you? Anything to add?" Exhaling angrily, she looked at Lorcan.

"Only that there is more news that we have not yet shared."

"What?! Why won't you speak?"

Nidhug responded. "Mistress, Northrim has been added to the list of coastal cities that have been razed to the ground. We hesitated to inform you as this could mean being struck again."

Nataxia narrowed her eyes on him. Her voice devolved to a low growl. "If it were not for your past loyalties, I would kill you both here and now. I have been waiting far too long for the traitors to be laid at my feet, and in that time, they have marauded up the coast, destroying, but *not in my name*."

"Yes, Mistress, as I have explained, I cannot trace their magic. We have attempted to intercept their pattern, but they strike too randomly. Even Northrim was not the last of their latest moves, there is more."

"What, *more*?"

"Last night the ardor channels pulsed violently across the world, I could also feel the core of Aimsire stirring. As a result, I have lost my ability to travel upon the ardor. I was, however, able to trace the lines to the anomaly. I located them. The sensation was faint but I could sense the results of their spells."

"What are you trying to tell me?"

"I believe Fifth and Piramay have found Lúth. The traitors have created an anomaly. Though it was difficult to see the vision through the twisting magic, it appears they have…grown three towers from the dirt itself and are now protected by the raw energy. It pours from a crack in the sky, pulsing like a heartbeat, faint, blanketing the land in golden light."

Hearing that Fifth, the creature she had created like a mother, who's purpose and mission was always to find the raw source of magic and return it to her, had again betrayed her, caused Nataxia to go into a rage. The news struck her more deeply than any treason or setback she had ever known.

Maintaining her poise, she stepped over to one of her massive Netherman guards, grabbed the hilt of his sword, and withdrew it. Without hesitation she ran him through. His armored body clattered to the floor and she watched as the life bled out of him. She flung the fouled blade against her throne. It bounced back, clattering and splattering thick blood as the reverberating steel clanged down the stairs, stopping at Lorcan's feet.

"Pick it up."

Lorcan looked at her in shock. "I SAID PICK IT UP!"

Bending down, the massive Netherman brought the blade up and stared at the Rage Queen. She walked over and touched the tainted blood on the black steel. It began to hum and a smokey aura wisped around it.

"This is yours now. Replace your blade with this one. The magic within will make you twice as strong."

She turned to Nidhug.

"As for you, take my army, they are assembled here and north of the Dungeon Sea upon Aimsire. I put you in charge of them all. Use my portals and go to the lands of the Icy Marauders where our last gateways exist. They have assembled their armada and will transport the armies to Northrim so we may begin to march south. Destroy everything as you pass. Leave not an individual, nor even their cattle or livestock alive.

"When you arrive at these towers, figure out how they did this. We will defeat them, and when we do, I will make you the Archmaster of Lúth. Fifth and Piramay have deceived me for the last time, but I have *your* loyalty, and I will reward you once you have brought back what is rightfully mine. I need not remind you, only I have the ability to control this power!"

"Yes, Mistress."

+++

*"Rayann, can you hear me?"*
*"Yes, Ceridwyn. Did you feel it last night as well?"*
*"I did. May I use the ingress to visit you?"*
*"Of course."*

Ceridwyn watched the magic kindle and the portal sparked to life. She stepped into the gateway Rayann had created between Hailan Glen and Faralanthis. She walked into the living room and both Kali and Rayann were there to meet her. The look on Ceridwyn's face was solemn and serious. Rayann's empathic abilities could feel the concern and confusion in her. It was all the more reason that Rayann approached and hugged her in a welcoming embrace. As they stepped back from one another, Ceridwyn handed Rayann a small piece of parchment.

"I received this from Commander Lady Rose Fairwind. It arrived just before dawn via passenger pigeon."

Kali stepped forward and read the note with Rayann. It only took seconds before they looked back at her.

There was a slight trepidation in Rayann's voice as she spoke. "The Circle of Six? Gone? And…towers? This doesn't make any sense."

Kali interjected. "What do you intend to do?"

Ceridwyn looked at Kali. "I intend to go and meet with Commander Rose, investigate the destruction of the Hexangular, and see these…towers for myself. But I do not wish to go alone."

"I will join you." Kali's response came without hesitation.

Rayann watched her cousin disappear up the stairs to gather her traveling items. Once she was alone with Ceridwyn she whispered, "What do you think it is?"

"I have no idea. Never have I even heard of such a thing. With the exception of her name and title, nothing Lady Rose wrote in that note makes sense to me."

"I am worried about Kali. Right after the tremor we awoke and found one another. She took me to the library in the Tower of Kells, speaking nonstop. She kept going on about the ardor and Shakyna, flipping through books faster than possible to read them. She said she felt it all unraveling, as if being consumed like fuel in a fire."

"Will she be alright to make this journey and face what we are about to see?" The feelings Rayann felt coming from Ceridwyn were as serious as the look on her face.

"Yes. She's not unstable and she is far more sensitive to such things than you and I. I just don't want anything to happen that will cause her–" She paused and swallowed hard, "I don't know, I'd rather not say it."

Ceridwyn took Rayann's hand. "If she was visited by Aviyana, we can hold fast to the confidence with which she was gifted terran magic. Aviyana is not known for granting access in haste. Yes, some have fallen, but we must trust the decisions of the tutelary, after all, they get their instructions from God directly."

Rayann agreed. "I will go pack. Will you be transporting us all there?"

"No, I will take us on the ardor channels."

Ceridwyn and Rayann turned to look at Kali, who was already back. She was in her travel cloak and the pungent smell of fresh spell components was wafting from her robes.

"Are you sure you know how to use them?"

Ceridwyn wasn't meaning to be condescending, but she knew that Kali had been a terran wizard for only a short time.

"I am sure. The books within the Tower of Kells taught me everything I needed to know, and I have already traveled on the ardor channels to test my knowledge. I assure you; I can get us to Gryphonledge."

"You already…"

Ceridwyn interrupted. "Rayann, please go pack, we need to depart soon. While you are gathering your things I will speak to Lady Rose on the winds and let her know we will be arriving shortly. I do not know if she will understand where the voice is coming from, but I will do my best to communicate with her."

Rayann understood and went upstairs without protest.

Ceridwyn turned to Kali.

"Will you excuse me as I call out on the winds?"

After she saw Kali's nod of agreement, she bowed her head and closed her eyes. After a short moment of silence, she looked back up with a smile before she spoke.

70

"I trust you and I believe you are capable of getting us there across the ardor channels. Before we depart, is there anything else you can tell me?"

"The sickness we felt was Shakyna being shredded, similar to the effects when ambient magic is cast around wizards. This wasn't ambient magic however, it was something else, something much more sinister. Obviously the feelings didn't linger permanently but other than that, I can't say. After reaching into the ardor I can tell you that the aftershocks traveled across the world, following the energy lines. Additionally, the moon and sun have dimmed. You are not working with as much source power as you are used to."

"Yes, I know, I felt it. Has Rayann said anything?"

"She is aware. My advice for both of you would be to rely on lodestones more than you typically do. Naturally it is going to take longer to charge them, but at least you will have them as a back-up."

"I had thought of that as well. Are you not feeling any difference?"

"I am."

Kali didn't expand on her answer. She decided for now to keep it to herself that she was in fact feeling an increase in terran energies. Whatever was happening was causing the core to emit power more vigorously. It had been intense enough to cause her concern. Wielding terran magic was dangerous enough as it was, however, if weakening the moon and sun wizards was part of some unknown strategy, perhaps killing those of the terra by overloading their bodies was the other.

Rayann returned and spoke with conviction.

"I am ready."

Rayann turned to her cousin as she asked her question. "Are you sure about traveling along the ardor?"

"Yes, I can do it. I can also say, it isn't nearly as jarring as traveling by teleportation."

Kali led them outside. Rayann sealed the door and approached, offering a slight nod that all was in order.

Ceridwyn spoke. "Kali, one last thing. I would advise that we arrive with space between us and the main gate. I am sure the soldiers and knights are on high alert. After all that has transpired in the last two days, three wizards appearing from thin air will be quite jarring if they didn't receive the message and aren't expecting us."

Without another word, Kali reached her hands out. The moment Ceridwyn and Rayann's hands were on top of hers, all three were sucked like lightning into the ground. An instant later they stood half a kilometer outside the massive main gate of Gryphonledge. The alarms did not sound and four individuals on horseback rode towards them. It was obvious by their non-aggressive approach they had received the message.

"Well, Ceridwyn, looks like that worked." Kali flashed her charismatic, crooked smile. "Good idea to send that message."

The three wizards started walking and as the two groups came together, the four riders dismounted. Lady Rose brought her hand to her heart in the traditional greeting of the elves, attempting to make Ceridwyn feel welcome. Ceridwyn gently brought her hand over her heart and then turned it forward, opening her palm to Rose in response.

"Ceridwyn, thank you for answering my summons and for letting me know you were coming with companions. I don't know how you whispered in my mind like that, but you are right, we are on high alert. Having awareness of the unusual method of your arrival is appreciated."

"My heart sings now that we are able to meet, even under these unfortunate circumstances."

Lady Rose made introductions. "This is my squire, Larissa McCulley."

Larissa bowed her head respectfully and brought her hand up over her heart in a perfect elvish greeting. Ceridwyn immediately recognized something familiar about her but kept it to herself. She returned the welcoming gesture.

The other two knights began to remove their helmets.

"This is Sir Ordin Wolfrider, one of my top generals and chief advisors, and this is..."

As he removed his helmet, Rayann could not help but blurt out happily, "Sir Trystan."

There was a look of shock on Rose's face as she turned to her Captain of the City Guard and lifted an eyebrow.

"You two know one another?"

"Yes, my Lady, I met Rayann Fionntán and her brother when I was serving in Brighton. Tell me, Rayann, how is Rorie?"

Rayann cleared her throat uncomfortably.

"Rorie and I…, let's just say our lives took different paths."

"That is unfortunate. May I ask who this is?"

Rayann could feel Trystan's attraction to Kali immediately.

"This is my cousin, Kali Fionntán Wizard of the Terra."

Trystan bowed his head warmly.

Lady Rose shot a glance at Sir Trystan.

"Well, now that we have the introductions out of the way, may I suggest you settle in and we meet in my headquarters in an hour? Ceridwyn, I assume you will want to stick around as we investigate and discuss what is happening. I have requested rooms be prepared for you and your companions in the keep just in case. I do not want this to come across as overly presumptive, so let me add you are obviously under no obligation to stay."

"Thank you, Lady Rose, I believe we will stay at least a short while."

"Will you be needing anything else?"

"Yes, actually," Rayann replied. "May my room have a bed for two? With your permission, I would like to have my husband join me here. To accommodate that, I will need to create an ingress for him to travel back and forth to Faralanthis. I assure you it will not compromise your security."

Lady Rose understood immediately. Rayann was obviously human, but she was married to an elf, which wasn't common.

"Faralanthis? Yes, that will be fine. We will find a private place where you can create your ingress. The city is in a state of panic, I don't want to introduce anything 'magical' in public. In fact, I should warn you that your welcome is likely not to be a warm one. I am going to assign soldiers to escort you, at least around the city. I want to assure you that it is not for a lack of trust on my part. I am doing this purely for appearance's sake and so that the citizens of Gryphonledge will feel more at ease."

Kali's face showed her displeasure. Rayann sensed her cousin's irksome feelings and reached out to calm her.

"That is understandable, Lady Rose." Ceridwyn bowed her head respectfully.

"Then I shall see you all in one hour. Larissa, please escort Ceridwyn until I assign a knight to accompany her. Sir Ordin, please stay with Rayann, and Sir Trystan, please escort Kali."

The three immediately saluted and in unison responded. "Yes, ma'am."

Lady Rose effortlessly mounted her horse and rode back to the main gate. Sir Ordin looked at all of them with a warm smile and gestured with his hand as he grabbed the reins of his horse.

"Shall we?"

+++

Lady Kellan Stenberg sat on the dock and stared at what was left of the cargo vessel still smoldering in the waters of Northrim Harbor. She couldn't bring herself to look at the city behind her. One of her soldiers approached and sat.

"Ma'am, is there anything I can do to help you?"

She turned and looked into the face of Erika Tiliz, a sergeant of the steelguard, and Kellan's best soldier. Her sunbleached hair, dark mocha skin, and narrow, hawkish eyes, permanently squinted from growing up where the sun never ceases to shine, were exactly commensurate for a person who came from the Plains of Azshemi.

"No, thank you. We need to go at least search."

"I will inform the troopers."

Erika stood and wanted to say more but couldn't find the words. Deep down she already knew there were no survivors and this was likely the reason Lady Kellan had been hesitating to take the patrol in.

After a few moments Kellan approached. Her soldiers were ready. They had found some fish drying on racks and were eating it for breakfast. Erika walked up to her commander.

"Ma'am, would you like some?"

"No, I am not sure I could keep it down."

"Ma'am, all the same, you are going to need your strength, no matter what we find."

Kellan had learned not to argue with Erika even though she outranked her. She was one of the best sergeants in Northrim. Erika had a strong will and a big heart and Kellan was more than aware that Liam had assigned Erika to watch after her. She took the dried fish and ate it as she briefed her troopers.

"We already know what we're going to find, but our duties require us to go. My orders for this mission are simple. Search for survivors and try to not to breathe in too much ash."

Solemnly, they walked through the streets between the blackened shells of the buildings, jumping at any sound they heard. It was a long forty-five minutes as they made their way slowly to the central command in the town center.

"I have never seen anything like this, my Lady."

Erika spoke into a piece of fabric covering her mouth. In shock, she scanned the blackened suits of armor and melted steel weapons laying all around them. The only thing left of the people was ankle deep ash. Lady Kellan began to walk where the tents had been set up for the high commanders and Erika grabbed her by the arm with a vice-like grip.

"OW! Erika!"

"No, my Lady. Don't go over there."

"What? Why?"

"You two!"

Two privates of the steelguard came at Erika's command.

"Take our Lady over there, give her water."

The two soldiers began to escort her, but she pulled away.

"Erika, what is it?"

"Please go with them, Commander Kellan. Trust me."

Confused, Kellan stepped away with the soldiers. Erika turned and walked over to some rubble and knelt. She moved the scorched rock and brushed the ash off the pommel of an elegant sword. The crest of Stenberg came into view.

Exhaling sadly, Erika brought her hand to her heart, closed her eyes and whispered.

"May the tutelary guide you to the constellations. Go with God, find your happy field and peace, Sir Liam."

Erika solemnly returned to her commander and handed her the sword.

"I am sorry, your Ladyship."

"Oh no. No." Kellan took the sword, and her hands immediately started to shake and tears welled up in her eyes. The soldiers remained quiet.

A moment later, a delicate, feminine voice broke the silence.

"May Liam's soul find rest."

All of them spun and brandished their weapons. Two figures, a male and a female, dressed in elegant battle garments stood staring at them.

"Who are you?! Identify yourself by order of the King!"

The adrenaline had brought the authority back to Lady Kellan's voice.

Stepping forward, the male of the two spoke. He was tall, strong, and confident. His medium hued skin had undertones of blue in it, and his long, silvery hair shimmered as he moved. Deep blue eyes with a trace of silver around the pupil stared at Kellan.

"My name is Nolore of the Silentclaw, and this is my cousin, Rajumin of the Silentclaw. Fear not, we come in peace and mean you no harm."

Lady Kellan and her soldiers lowered their weapons, going to their knees in reverence. Kellan spoke softly, "Is it true? You are the Silentclaw?"

Rajumin stepped forward. Her skin was porcelain white unlike her cousin's, and her hair was long, shiny, and raven black. Her eyes were the kindest Kellan had ever seen, and their striped, deep green also had a thin line of silver around the pupil.

"Soldiers of Aimsire, please return to your feet and do not kneel before us. We are but messengers and servants of God. We are not to be worshiped."

Kellan and her steelguard stood. She looked at Nolore and Rajumin for a moment before finally finding the courage to speak.

"I am Lady Kellan Stenberg, this is my Sergeant Erika Tiliz, and these are my soldiers of the steelguard. How can we assist you?"

"There have been increasing traces of dark magic and even darker energies. What happened yesterday, however, caused God to issue commands to the tutelary as well as send us, the Silentclaw back into the world in order to assist Aimsire once again."

Nolore looked around, tracing the burnt buildings with a melancholy gaze.

Lady Kellan nodded. "We knew they had been burning the coastal cities. It was only a matter of time before they hit us. We thought we were ready. I don't know who they were–"

Nolore turned to look at Lady Kellan as he interrupted her.

"We do, and it is not the burning of the cities that prompted our return, but instead what we just returned from seeing."

"Begging a pardon, Nolore, but if not the razed cities, then what? Thousands of innocents have died at their hands. In a little over a month they have razed no less than ten villages and cities to the ground. Surely the tutelary have noticed."

"*God* has noticed," Rajumin interjected. "We, as well as the tutelary, are not to intervene at every step of Aimsire's citizenry or their actions. *Our* purpose is to provide guidance and help when there is no other choice. Since the Dawn Light, God has given you the freedom of will to make your own choices. God listens and will answer prayer but has also provided you what you need to handle your lives in this grand creation you have been gifted with. Intelligence, strength, wisdom, discernment, leadership, mercy, rational thought, empathy; all of these and more are among the gifts you have been given. Most seem to have forgotten that. Last night, however, this world was compromised in a manner that does require our help."

"I don't understand." There was anger in Kellan's voice.

Nolore explained. "You have no means to understand, at least not yet, for what happened occurred far from here. We have come to transport you there, to the epicenter so you may know."

"Why me? Why us?"

"Because *you* survived, and the high command of the central guard needs to know what you know."

Erika asked. "Where do you intend to take us?"

"To the Vale of Ghosts and then to Gryphonledge."

+++

Entering his brother's workspace, Myth'alas approached as Jerrin looked up.

"What can I do for you, First Prince?"

"Did you feel the tremor last night?"

"I did. The mystics are working on it."

77

"No need." Myth'alas threw a parchment in front of Jerrin. "This arrived from my wife a short time ago."

Jerrin's brow furrowed as he picked up the parchment and read Rayann's words.

"This makes no sense."

"We agree, it doesn't, but that's what she said. I have come to let you know that I am leaving within the hour to join her in Gryphonledge."

"How many times do I have to tell you that your duties are here, among your kin?"

"Our entire world is at stake. It is Fifth and Piramay, do you not understand?"

"What I understand is that I am the High Consummate of the Commonwealth of Elves, and you are the First Prince. Our duty as brothers in the Royal Family is to see to the safety and well-being of our kin. That...Sinner King of theirs can handle whatever is happening in his own kingdom."

"What makes you think they are going to stop because we have archers on the border? If they burned coastal cities to the ground, how can you be so blind to think they won't do the same to our forests? You like to hold it against me that for a time I served Nataxia, but I know her, and if she is somehow behind this it is about complete and total domination of this world. Nataxia is at war with God. She cannot strike directly, but she can strike us, the children. That has been her plan all along."

Jerrin leaned back. "Very well, you have my permission."

"I didn't come seeking your permission; I came to tell you I was going."

"When are you going to come to respect that I am your High Consummate?"

"When you come to respect that I don't walk in your shadow any longer. Yes, you are my High Consummate, but you have taken it upon yourself to treat me like a fae wild my entire life. The same kin you shamefully continue to allow to be enslaved and treated like street scum. I am your brother, but I also have so much more to lose now, and I won't let it go without a fight."

Myth'alas snatched the parchment off Jerrin's desk and left. Rounding the halls of the castle he went into his room. Kali was waiting for him to transport them back to Gryphonledge.

"How did he take it?" She arched a knowing eyebrow as she observed the anger on his face.

"As I expected he would. I am packed, we can just go."

Without another word, Kali reached her hand forward. He reached back, pressing his palm to hers and they disappeared into the ardor channels.

+++

Rayann laid her head on Myth's bare chest. It had been a long day. Endless hours of meetings with Lady Rose and her high commanders had taken its toll. She was mentally exhausted and physically spent. As she listened to her husband's heartbeat, she began to cry.

"What is it, beloved? Why are you weeping?"

"Myth, my dearest love, our baby will be here before we know it. What is happening to our world? What kind of a place are we bringing an innocent child into?"

Myth sat up, gently bringing her up with him. He watched as the firelight danced over her snow-white curls and lavender eyes. He reached up and tucked a stray tendril behind her ear.

"By God's grace we will fight with everything we have. We will not let evil win."

"Beautiful words, Myth, but how? You saw the same sketches as I. You listened with me to the reports the soldiers with their magnifying lenses kept sending all day. Now they want us to go tomorrow morning and see for ourselves. Of course, I want to go. I have always been told that I am the one who is going to change the world. That through my actions the new era of enlightenment would be introduced. I just never imagined something like...*this*."

Myth leaned in and kissed her before staring into her eyes.

"If you are to fulfill that prophecy, it begins by walking the right path. You told me your cousin told you that on the cliffs. You believed her and I believe her. Yes, we are walking into an unknown; this is completely unprecedented in the history of our world. These are the sorts of events, however, that create great turning points. If you were truly created to be the one who brings Aimsire into a new age, then it needs to happen by the defeat of a great threat. That's the only way people will open their eyes to see and their ears and listen. Unfortunately, it always seems a tragedy is required before people start to pay attention."

"Deep down I know all this, husband. I just don't want anything to happen to our child."

"I promise, Rayann, by all the strength in me and all the prayer I can offer, I will never allow that to happen."

# Chapter 07 – Amongst the Ruined

Ceridwyn smiled as she finished reading the note that had arrived in the middle of the night. Aeolis and Raspberry would be arriving just after dawn to join them. High Consummate Jerrin had assigned Chief Ranger Aeolis to the envoy in Gryphonledge to assist the first prince and help assess the situation.

Raspberry was under no such orders, but according to the message insisted that she come along for 'friendship reasons'.

"Ceridwyn, are you alright? I don't believe I have ever seen you smile like that. In fact, you're blushing."

She looked at Rayann as she tucked the note away.

"It is a long road we walk in this life, full of turns and mysteries."

"What's that supposed to mean?"

"Nothing…for now." She looked at Rayann sideways with a coy smile.

Myth'alas entered the room and saw the two women whispering and giggling.

"I am not sure what you two are up to, but when a male enters a room and two females act like that, it usually means mischief." He winked at his wife.

"My beloved, it is nothing like that." Going up on her tiptoes, Rayann kissed his cheek.

"Prince Myth'alas, I received a note this morning. The High Consummate is sending Aeolis and Raspberry to join us. There was also personal news for you, but I think it will be best to have Aeolis explain."

"Fair enough. When will they be arriving? There are torches lit in the courtyard and squires preparing the horses. I am sure the commander has already ordered our mounts be saddled and prepared."

Rayann answered, "Kali left not long ago to bring them back; she should be here any minute."

A few moments later, Kali appeared with Aeolis, Raspberry, and a young elf in ranger armor. He was around one hundred years old. His adolescent body was gangly, thin, and still developing its muscle, but Myth'alas could immediately see that he held himself well and was sure footed.

81

As they approached, the young elf looked at Myth'alas with awe as his hazel eyes scanned every detail of the prince in a heartbeat. Bowing his head respectfully and placing his hand over his heart, he handed the prince a wax-sealed parchment.

"My First Prince, High Consummate Jerrin has commanded. I am to give you this, and my service."

Looking at Aeolis in confusion, Myth'alas took the parchment and read;

*"First Prince,*

> *Greetings in the name of the light. Because we are not seeing eye-to-eye as of late, I have been pondering your obligations to the Commonwealth on my own. I would have preferred to have this conversation in person, but you stormed out and left me no choice but a letter. The young elf before you is Olwa Pilininge. I have assigned him to you as your new adherent.*

> *Part of your duty as First Prince is the training and mentoring of the future generations in our royalty. Olwa has proven himself and as you know his family has a long tradition of dedication to the Commonwealth and the Royal Family. His father, Ky'ly, has requested this assignment personally. After some thought, I felt it was a good match.*

> *Watch him as if he was your own heir. Teach him, mold him, and protect him.*

*Until our hearts are near,*
*Jerrin, High Consummate of the Elven Commonwealth*

Myth'alas looked sternly at Olwa. Instantly the young elf's face crumbled under the pressure of the prince's gaze, and he lowered his eyes.

"Olwa."

The young elf looked up.

"First lesson. When confronting a frightening situation, never break eye-contact. Keep your focus. Agreed?"

With a nod, Olwa communicated his compliance.

Myth'alas tucked the note in his leather armor and turned to the group.

"Shall we go see these towers?"

Ceridwyn interrupted. "Prince Myth'alas, allow me to go first, follow in a moment. I should be the one to let them know we need more horses."

As Ceridwyn entered the courtyard she saw that Myth'alas had been right. A contingency of knights and steelguard were waiting, sixty strong and in full armor. Horses had been prepared for them. Lady Rose approached offering a greeting.

"Good morrow, Ceridwyn. Are the others on their way?"

"They will be along shortly. I came to inform you that three more from Faralanthis have just arrived. We will need horses and hopefully accommodations for them as well."

Lady Rose looked at the archmage with annoyance and then shifted her gaze to the rooms where the guests were housed.

Ceridwyn recognized her error in not informing the commander sooner. Though Lady Rose had no formal authority over her, she understood they were in human territory, in her city, and everyone was on edge. She bowed her head respectfully.

"Commander Rose, I came before the others to offer my apology. I made a mistake. It will not happen again."

As she straightened back up, Ceridwyn continued.

"Without excuses, I just found out myself. A pigeon arrived in the middle of the night and the message was delivered to me this morning. It was from High Consummate Jerrin, he had directives for us. The others that arrived a few moments ago are Aeolis Dawnwater, the Chief Ranger of the Fara Commonwealth, Raspberry Fiddlebow, a halfling and Balladeer of Balaby, and Prince Myth'alas' Adherent, Olwa Pilininge."

"Prince Myth'alas?"

They turned and looked at Larissa. Ceridwyn nodded to confirm what she had just said.

"Myth'alas is *here*?"

"Yes, Larissa, he is Rayann's husband."

Commander Rose immediately recognized the sudden change in her squire's behavior again and her odd new interest in the elves. She turned to her sternly.

"Larissa, tonight I want to see you in my tent. Privately."

Larissa bowed her head in compliance. Rose shifted her attention to a group of squires.

"I need two more horses and a pony for the halfling, double-time."

The squires were off without hesitation. She turned her attention back to Ceridwyn just as the group came up behind her. Every soldier and knight were in awe at the size of Myth'alas. He was as large as Sir Ordin and his presence was undeniable. Immediately, Prince Myth'alas bowed his head respectfully to Commander Rose.

"Thank you for your permission to enter the city."

"Of course. Ceridwyn has informed us of the others. I also have her assurance that there will be no more unannounced arrivals. As much as I appreciate having you and these wizards join us, this is still my city to protect, and I need to be made aware from now on of the comings and goings of your companions."

"It was an oversight. You are right, it is your city, and we will comply. On behalf of us all, I apologize."

Lady Rose extended a hand and Myth'alas clasped her forearm firmly.

"Apology accepted."

The squires returned with the horses and pony shortly after all introductions were made. Lady Rose addressed the group.

"We have several hours of riding. Let's move out."

Passing through the main gate, the soldiers formed perfect columns and moved down the road. Half the knights moved ahead and the other half took position in the rear. Raspberry came up alongside Ceridwyn.

"Is everything alright Ms. Ceridwyn? You look sad, and it seems like everyone is on edge." She glanced towards the front of the entourage. "Ms. Rose looks angry."

"Lady Rose has much on her mind, Raspberry. She oversees protecting every life in the region. Her behavior is understandable and forgivable given the circumstances."

"I heard about these…tower thingies. Something inside me said I need to come and see them with you. What are they?"

Ceridwyn turned to Raspberry. "I do not know, little one. We are all going to find that out together."

She looked up at the tear in the sky, writhing and glowing ominously in the distance.

+++

The closer the column advanced, the more fixated Kali, Rayann, and Ceridwyn became on the fracture in the sky. The sensations of magic were oddly muted and the terrain with its twisting valleys and gorges did not allow for a view of the towers at any point during the journey. After riding for six hours, the group came to the bottom of a large rise. Hundreds of soldiers were present and military tents stretched to the top. Lady Rose halted the column and approached the three wizards.

"When we reach the top, we will be looking down into the Dale of Still Mead. From there, you will see what we are up against."

Several steelguard split off as the group made their way up the hill. By the time they reached the top, it was only Sir Ordin, Sir Trystan, Larissa, and Lady Rose accompanying the group. The moment the towers came into view, Ceridwyn gasped and brought her hand up over her mouth. Rayann went pale and felt her throat go dry with fear. Only Kali seemed to maintain her composure.

"Wow'za! Those are some really scary lookin' towers. Look at all the lava flowing from the fiery one and swirling around the bases of all three! How are they not burning up?"

Raspberry's eyes were wide with inquisitiveness.

Rayann came to her senses at the comment and felt little more than curiosity from Raspberry. She reached out with her empathic abilities so she could assess the rest of the group and felt almost nothing from Kali.

"Kali?"

"Yes, cousin?" Kali turned.

"What are you feeling?"

"Can you not tell?"

"No, I can't, and you are the calmest of us all right now. Please, tell me."

"Myth'alas' suspicion was correct. It was Piramay and Fifth who did this."

Ceridwyn swung her horse around. "How do you know that for sure?"

"For sure? Is any more evidence needed? Look at them. That tower on the left, black, abstruse and slick, purple flashes of light around the capstone. The one that looks like crystalized fire, magma pouring from its walls, filling the valley with a molten lake. It had to be them. They came to Hailan Glen with Rorie but not to fight us. Once they had what they wanted, they escaped."

"The Staff of Winds?" Myth'alas inquired.

"Yes. As you all know, the moment Fifth locked it with the Staff of Terra and stripped it from my hands, they fled. They did not come for you, or me, or Rayann; they came for the staff. Piramay had the Staff of Fire; all three are artifacts from the tutelars of magic. Somehow, they needed them to help do…this. Artifacts hold incredible power within them, my guess is the towers are what's left of those staves."

Suddenly, Sir Trystan made his observation known. "There are three towers. Who occupies the third and why does it seem dormant compared to the others?"

Kali turned and looked at him.

"That, Sir Trystan, is the greatest mystery."

An hour later, the group was down at the bottom of the rise in the command tent gathered around a large map on the table. Sir Ordin pointed.

"Right here, on the western side where the two roads once came to a fork, there is a gap in the magma. I sent Sir Gregory this morning. He has been scouting that area with his troopers all day. He will be back tomorrow at dawn to give us his report. Once we know what he and his platoon found, we can make an informed decision.

"My hope has been to line this ridge with trebuchets and bombard the Gray Tower since it is closest. If we can collapse one, perhaps it will weaken the other two. This is, of course, all speculation based on the very little we know."

"That's a bold move considering these are wizard towers." Kali cautioned.

"What do you mean?" Sir Ordin inquired.

"I mean that these were not built, they were grown. That's what the reports said. You don't simply knock down buildings infused with magic by throwing stones at them."

"No building or wall on Aimsire can withstand a bombardment forever, especially from *our* trebuchets."

Kali narrowed her eyes. "Just because they are on Aimsire does not mean they are *of* Aimsire."

Sir Ordin stood to his full height and looked down at Kali. He was not accustomed to being talked back to. Just as his chest began to puff out aggressively, static filled the tent and Kali's eyes glowed faintly. Rayann reached, grabbing Kali by the shoulder to calm her.

Realizing the tension was building, Lady Rose stood and shot Sir Ordin a look so firm it immediately caused him to stand down. She then addressed her soldiers.

"It has been a very long day and we all need rest. I believe we should adjourn and retire for the evening."

Rose turned to the wizards. "I want to thank you for your patience and your assessments. You were asked to come and be part of this process on purpose. We need those who can speak to the curiosities as opposed to what can only be seen."

She looked at Sir Ordin briefly. He knew exactly what her statement meant and she looked back at their guests as she continued.

"I have had spacious, comfortable tents prepared for you. I would appreciate it if you would stay in the encampment tonight and return here at first light so we can hear Sir Gregory's report together."

"We can do that, Commander Rose." Myth'alas spoke for the group.

Rose nodded in thanks. There was a growing respect for him in her expression as she extended her arm. After their farewells, the group made their way to a row of tents that lined the road. Each was under watch by two members of the steelguard.

Bidding others a good evening, Aeolis and Olwa took the first tent. Raspberry ran to the second and peeked inside.

"WOW, pillows, and a feather mattress! I've never camped like this before!" She turned and looked at Ceridwyn. "There's even two beds! We should share this one!"

As Raspberry disappeared into the tent, Ceridwyn turned to Rayann.

"What a gift to have that kind of joy even in such dire circumstances."

"Since the first moment I saw her, joy is all I have ever felt flowing from her heart."

"That's good. I fear we are going to need as much joy as we can get. I will see you in the morning."

Ceridwyn stepped in and hugged Rayann tightly. Rayann had been noticing that Ceridwyn was being much more affectionate towards her lately. Their interactions were rapidly becoming far less formal even though Ceridwyn had been promoted to the level of Archmage. They were increasingly becoming friends as opposed to wizards of rank.

"Hey, Ms. Ceridwyn, ya' comin'?" Raspberry's head poked out of the tent flaps.

Ceridwyn stepped back and winked at Rayann as they both giggled at Raspberry's enthusiasm.

Kali was standing off to the side in silence and Myth'alas approached her.

"Would you join us in our tent for tea before bed? I would like to discuss some things with you before tomorrow morning's meeting."

"Of course. I too was hoping we could talk."

Rayann, Myth'alas and Kali entered one of the two remaining tents. Just as the soldiers closed the flaps behind them, Kali lifted her hand to keep Rayann and Myth'alas from speaking. She reached into her robes and removed some spell components, sprinkling them on the floor near the entrance. Whispering words of magic, the reagents flared to life and a dim light burst forth climbing the walls of the tent until it came back together at the top.

"A cone of silence, so our conversation remains private."

Myth'alas grinned in satisfaction.

"I will make us some tea." Rayann turned to the small, coal, tent stove, and swung the kettle over the burner.

"Thank you, beloved." Myth'alas and Kali sat before he continued. "You left a lot out when you were speaking to the human commanders about how you knew who was responsible."

"As did you." Kali grinned wryly.

Myth'alas huffed in agreement but then became serious.
"How do you think they did it?"

"As of yet their using the staves is all I have pieced together. From there, I truly don't know. What I can tell you is in all my years of learning from that merciless, inhumane, sadist, there is no limit to his ambition. Fifth is incredibly intelligent and finding Lúth has always been his primary directive. Nataxia tasked him to find it so that she could use its power to enter Aimsire once again and sow chaos before destroying the tutelary and ultimately challenging God once again."

"Do you think that is what's pouring through the fracture in the sky? Do you think she will come through that gateway?"

"I believe it is Lúth, but no, she will not be coming. Fifth is ambitious. I don't believe he has any intention of turning over that kind of power to the Rage Queen."

"Why not?" Rayann set the cups of tea down as she asked her question.

Kali answered her. "At minimum, the very fact that she had him seeking Lúth means she is too weak to enter Aimsire without it. Fifth knows that if he can control that power, he can control her. My guess is this is just the beginning. I have a notion that he might even be planning to overthrow her and attempt to become a tutelar himself, or worse.

"Given his interest in death and all the conversations he had with me about unlocking power from the souls of the deceased, what better position to be in than to control every one that has passed through this life and entered the Crevasse?

"When I destroyed Bonstar Steeple, I was using a device he invented called a soul pearl. The reports of villages and townships being destroyed up the coast finally make some sense. Somehow, he must have been capturing the souls of the dead. Maybe as a means to garner enough power to grow those things. I don't know. It's all theory."

Though Rayann had never had a single interaction with the necromancer, she shuddered at the thought. She asked a question.

"Why three towers? If it was Fifth and Piramay, Trystan made a good point, who is occupying the third?"

"My guess is nobody." Kali's face remained blank as she answered. "Like all things on Aimsire, there needs to be balance.

Even whatever this is. A third tower suggests that these two efficacies cannot exist without a fulcrum to harmonize them. The bursts of energy that are flashing between them are also occurring towards the Gray Tower. Though they are not nearly as vibrant. It is possible that its existence is to provide the hinge point between the two. The power flowing from the sky fracture was more concentrated over the Gray Tower. Perhaps it acts as a distribution point, or…some sort of energy storage like a giant lodestone. I really don't know; again, it's just theories."

"Kali."

"Yes, Myth'alas?"

"How much time do we have?"

"I don't know. It could be days; it could be months. No matter how much energy they channeled through whatever means they did, God's natural laws apply. Their bodies had to act as the conduits. That is the way of magic on Aimsire, no matter what the source of power. As you know, wizards' bodies get taxed physically as they channel. That is the check and balance put on magic users so none become too powerful.

"I can't begin to fathom how much power it took to grow those abominations. It's hard to speculate or take a guess as to how much recovery time is needed without all the information."

"So, we are up against a gnomish clock and we don't know how much time we have. Worse, we don't know what they are planning to do once they awaken."

Myth'alas scratched his chin as he leaned back in his chair.

Kali added. "We know enough about them that whatever they are planning won't be for any benefit but their own. If they were capable of doing what they did up the northwestern coast without unlimited power, one can only imagine what they will do once they have truly unlocked it."

Instinctually, Rayann placed her hand over her womb. She looked down at the growing bump in her belly which she just noticed was now starting to show through her heavily pleated wizard robes.

+++

Commander Rose leaned in. It was late and they all needed sleep, but she wanted some answers from her squire first.

"Larissa, I am not going to command you to tell me, because you know that is not how I want things to be between us. However, in the order of things, I am your commander and you are my squire. I need you to come clean with me. What is going on?"

She swallowed hard and stared at her feet. Inhaling deeply, she knew the time for any and all deception with her commander had just come to an end. As she looked up she ran her hand along the left side of her head, tucking the hair back behind her ear.

A ring on her middle finger glowed brightly. Right before Lady Rose's eyes, Larissa's ear changed. It wasn't sharp and pointed like an elf, but it had a lift to it, and a blunted, round point appeared at the top.

Blinking her eyes as if she was seeing things from lack of sleep, Rose shifted her gaze before locking eyes with her Squire.

"You're half-elven."

With a sad nod Larissa confirmed and then blurted, "Aye, Commander Rose. Beyond that, I am Myth'alas' half-sister."

Very few things caught Rose off guard, but this news certainly did. She leaned back in her chair and folded her hands under her chin.

"Well, if anything, all my questions as to your unexplainable dexterity and endurance during training sessions have finally been answered."

Larissa laughed sadly and then leaned over her commander's desk.

"Please don't tell him. I am the bastard child of his father's love affair with my mother. Yes, I am a half-breed. We are not welcome in elven territories. He would never accept me."

Rose smirked as she responded, "Larissa, for the first time in our many years together I can't believe I am about to say this, but you aren't paying attention."

"What?"

"You are so focused on Myth'alas that you have completely lost sight of his wife. She is human."

"Yes, I know...I just..."

"Larissa, additionally, she's pregnant. I have a feeling that Prince Myth'alas is going to be okay with you being a half-breed."

"She's…pregnant?"

"Her robes hid it well until she sat down with us for supper. Four or five months along if I'm not mistaken."

"Fine, Commander, but the Fara Elves, they don't live in the same world as us. They are pompous and prejudiced, highly judgmental and vicious towards outsiders."

"Larissa, you are generalizing. You spent the day with us, and Myth'alas. Did you get any of that from his behavior?"

Clearing her throat, Larissa whispered, "No."

"Exactly. Now heed my advice. You need to tell him. I don't mean that as in he *needs* to know, put plainly, his finding out is inevitable. What I am saying is you need to be the one who gives him this news."

Larissa was about to interrupt but Rose's hand shot up.

"I am not finished. In just this one day of spending time with him I can tell you, if Prince Myth'alas is anything, he is intuitive. Not to mention I had a little investigation of my own done. Ceridwyn can do something where she looks into, what did they call it, 'The Silver Waters', and mysteries are revealed to her.

"Rayann is an empath, that should be clear to any of us who spent time with her. She can feel emotion and if she really wants to, read your mind. Kali, well, there wasn't much on her. But you heard and saw the way she reacted to Sir Ordin when he tried to intimidate her. She's clearly fearless, highly intelligent, and can put pieces of a puzzle together quickly. Normal people don't stand up to Sir Ordin.

"If you don't say something to him soon, one of them is going to figure it out and inform him. You need to ask yourself; how do you want him to find out? Through one of his trusted sources, or personally, from you, his sister. If I were you, I would think hard about that."

Larissa shed a tear and nodded. Rose smiled and reached across the desk grabbing her squire's hand.

"Nothing needs to be decided at this very instant. Sleep on it. I will see you at dawn."

+++

Lady Kellan turned to Erika. "Have you ever seen such an amazing place?"

"Never in my days could I have even imagined, much less expected, a place like this could even exist, my Lady."

Looking out from the observation balcony, the two women took in the Vale of Ghosts. It was less a vale, and more a thriving city, crystalline and beautiful. The structures were massive, with doorways that seemed to extend into the heavens, and the Silentclaw who occupied it walked around with purpose and conviction.

"Are you ready to depart?"

Nolore had a large bag slung over his shoulder as he approached. Rajumin was right behind him.

"Yes, I mean, I would love to stay, but I understand we have probably been here long enough. We need to get back. To leave such a beautiful place, however..."

Nolore smiled. "Well, Lady Kellan, perhaps I will bring you back some time, and reveal all the mysteries of this place."

"What my cousin means is flirt with you and ultimately fall in love with you."

Nolore spun and shot his cousin a look. Rajumin raised her hands in mock surrender.

"Prove me wrong."

Shaking his head, Nolore spoke to Lady Kellan.

"Please excuse my cousin, what she lacks in social graces, she more than makes up for in her service to God under the guidance of Ameliara."

"And what my cousin lacks in straight-forwardness, I make up for him with mine."

She winked as Nolore went flush with embarrassment. She turned to Kellan and Erika.

"And with that, we shall be off."

Lady Kellan gathered her soldiers. Without needing to be told they arranged themselves in a circle with Rajumin and Nolore. In a flash, they were gone.

+++

Bold'Rock had smelled the smoke from miles away. As he and Pela'Rock arrived at the top of the easternmost ridge he looked down into Northrim.

"There is nothing left, my Pela. The whole city is burned black. There must be a thousand ships in the harbor, all with Nataxia's symbol on their sails."

Pela crawled up beside him and gasped.

"Did they do this, father?"

"No. Look."

Pela'Rock followed the path of where he was pointing. Only a handful of the ships were anchored near the shores and being unloaded while the rest remained in the harbor. The water lines suggested they were still laden with cargo. Supplies lined the shore but much larger areas had been cleared to stockpile more.

He continued. "They are just arriving; most are still on the boats waiting to dock."

"Then who?"

"Who wields fire? Who left during the battle of Hailan Glen?" He turned and looked at her.

"But...why?"

"I do not know, daughter, but I know it is not safe for us to linger here."

They cautiously made their way south, traveling as quick as possible and used the mountains as cover to avoid the human patrols until they arrived outside Riverhorn. Traveling by way of these mountains meant they were trespassing through the territory of the Shatter Stone Clan. Being of the Ice Rock Clan, they would have been killed on sight if spotted.

As a Netherman, Bold'Rock had incredible endurance and required little sleep. After what had happened at Hailan Glen, he had made a special harness for carrying Pela'Rock on his back. She was small and light and could sleep in it so they could travel for longer periods of time. They had also been practicing with it, designing new attack techniques where she rode on his back and sprung up at the last second, keeping her safer as they approached their enemies.

Looking down into the valley from the forest's edge, Bold'Rock spoke.

"I need you to do something."

"Of course, father, anything."

"I need you to write a note and send it to the elf prince, Myth'alas using one of the human's pigeons."

"What? Father, no!"

"Listen to me, Pela. We can trust him; he allowed us to live. There is honor in him. I do not know the shapes for writing the common language, but you do. Write down what I say and send a pigeon to him in Faralanthis."

Pela'Rock did not agree with his request, but she was obedient when given instructions by her father. She produced a stick of soft silver and some parchment, then sat.

"Daughter, write these words…"

# Chapter 08 – Discordancy

Sir Ordin puffed his pipe as he waited with Sir Gregory, a man so strong he looked like he had been carved from granite. His ebony skin was a stark contrast to his silver armor. A sturdy, square jaw, deep, dark eyes, stern brow, and only half an ear on the left side of his head left no question that he was one of the toughest warriors in the knighthood.

"How close did you get?"

"Within a kilometer or so, but the terrain is rough where the earth was churned up. It was getting too dark to see effectively so I brought us back."

"Well, I look forward to hearing the full report as soon as Lady Rose arrives."

"What in the crevasse!?"

Sir Gregory unsheathed his weapon and his captains and lieutenants did the same as Prince Myth'alas approached with his companions. Myth'alas stopped twenty paces away and stared at the man. He casually brought his hand up to the hilt of Blue Moon but did not withdraw the magical blade from its scabbard.

The air around the three wizards began to buzz dangerously. Aeolis adjusted his stance, and Olwa shifted in beside the prince, also grabbing his sword.

Raspberry looked around curiously and declared, "Hey, what's going on? I thought we were all friends!"

"Sir Ordin, that's him. The Crimson Wind. He is a servant of Nataxia!"

Sir Ordin dropped his pipe and grabbed the hilt of his sword but did not withdraw it.

"Is that true, Prince Myth'alas?"

"It is true that I was once an agent of the Rage Queen, yes. Though I do not recognize this man, it is entirely possible that I made movements against him or others associated with him."

"He has no place here, Sir Ordin, not among us!"

Rayann took a deep breath and reached out to feel Sir Gregory's emotions. There was genuine fear and anger in his heart towards her husband. Releasing her draw of power, she brought her hands up as a show of peace and amicably stepped forward.

"Gentleman, please. Let's all stay calm. Prince Myth'alas is not your enemy. He is reformed and walks in the light. The Ceremony of Coruscation proved his heart is no longer of the darkness."

Sir Gregory's hand tightened so his leather glove creaked gently. He kept his sword steady, pointed at Myth'alas.

"The ceremony of what? No tricks from you are going to change my mind, wizard. Years ago, he cut down four of my knightchanters in a matter of seconds while we were on operations in Knockingwood!"

"Yes, I remember that day. In battle your men fell to my blade, but we are no longer adversaries, I assure you."

"Assure me? I assure you that I am about to uphold my vow to avenge them."

"Halt!"

Sir Gregory was just beginning to charge as Lady Rose's voice boomed out. "What is the meaning of this!?"

Sir Gregory turned and addressed their commander.

"That is the Crimson Wind, Commander. The wizard killer. He is the one I wrote about in my reports. He is an agent of Nataxia, the Rage Queen."

Lady Rose calmly shifted her eyes and looked at Myth'alas. "Are you?"

"The answer is, 'not any longer.' It is true that for a time, I served the Rage Queen, but it is also true that I now walk in the light. By the love of this woman," he gestured to Rayann. "And by the grace of God, I was brought back from darkness. It is a very long story, Commander Rose, one I would be happy to tell you sometime when tensions are not so elevated. Right now, I propose instead that we focus on what's over that hill, listen to Sir Gregory's report, and decide what to do next."

"And how do we know you aren't a double agent?"

Myth'alas looked at Sir Ordin. It was a fair question.

"First, Sir Ordin, I would not be in the company of these wizards if I still served the Rage Queen. Second, I would not have been restored to my place among the Royal Family of the Fara, and third…" He unsheathed his dagger and drew the blade across his palm. Holding his hand up so all could see the blood trickling down as he spoke.

"By my blood, I make this oath of steel. On my honor and my life, I bind my promise to you, Sir Ordin. Therefore, by these words, I walk in the light, under God's guidance, and I will fight by your side. I pledge to purge the world of this evil we face. Either by victory or my death."

Lady Rose watched Myth'alas and when he was done speaking, she addressed Sir Ordin.

"I don't know how he knows the words of the blood oath of the knights, but you can't deny that he has just said them. By his honor and his blood, his life is now bound to you in truth, Sir Ordin." She looked back at Myth'alas intently as she continued speaking to him. "Should he break his vow, may God strengthen your arm and Dionadair guide your blade to strike him down."

Sir Ordin nodded and released the grip of his sword. He turned to Sir Gregory and spoke an order, "Stand down."

Sir Gregory and his men obeyed, but Rayann could still feel contempt in his heart. She knew it would take time, but had confidence that Myth'alas would prove himself honorable and reformed to these knights.

Moments later they were all inside the command tent, listening to Sir Gregory.

"Along this ridge there are flat spots. Though the ground has been churned up I believe we can set up our trebuchets. Here, where the salted road once existed, I want to send a small squad along that ridgeline to confirm that the ground is solid enough to bear the weight of our siege machines."

Lady Rose inquired. "You were not able to determine that while you were there?"

"No, ma'am. As I told Sir Ordin earlier, we were only able to get within a kilometer or so before darkness set in. We glassed the area thoroughly with our aggrandizers, but the ground may be undercut through here. I believe it is solid; however, the low light and late day shadows didn't allow us to confirm. I have a squad ready to go in deeper and investigate."

"These are good findings, Sir Gregory. Well done." Lady Rose looked up at him approvingly.

"Thank you, Commander. With your permission I would like to get the squad moving. It is roughly an hour's ride to the high point; from there I can observe, and it will allow for a full day's light so they can conduct their mission."

"Permission granted; however, I will be going with you." She turned to the wizards. "And I would like to request that you three come along as well."

Ceridwyn nodded. "I will go."

"As will I." Kali chimed in.

Myth'alas stepped forward. "Not to speak for the group, but I feel that all of us should go. We didn't come here to sit around in camp. Aeolis, Olwa, and I have gifted sight. We can see further and sharper than even your aggrandizer lenses. Raspberry here, well, she is very clever and I'm certain will even sing a blessing over the troops before they depart."

Lady Rose glanced at Sir Ordin who gave the slightest nod of agreement and then concurred with Myth'alas.

"Very well. Everyone grab your gear and get something to eat. We'll meet back here in thirty minutes. Larissa, gather some squires, have them get horses prepared while you get ready."

"Aye, Ma'am."

+++

By mid-morning, the group was settled in on the southern highpoint overlooking the churned landscape. The Black Tower was before them and Ceridwyn shuddered knowing who was inside. Sensing her unease, Rayann approached and whispered, "I am with you, friend."

Ceridwyn simply reached and grabbed Rayann's hand, squeezing softly.

Raspberry played a song. There were no lyrics, but it captivated them. She focused on the six scouts. Golden light swirled around them and they breathed easily as strength and courage filled them. She concluded and Sir Gregory stepped forward to proclaim the directive for their mission.

"Move down to where the road was destroyed, hook into the embankment, and scout that area thoroughly. Primary objective is to make sure that the ground is solid enough to hold our trebuchets. Once you are in a safe location, glass those towers and search for anything. Weak points, makeup, mortar joints, type of stone… anything that will give us an advantage. Understood?"

"Aye, sir!" The six soldiers spoke in unison.

As they departed, Aeolis spoke to Myth'alas' mind. *"It would have been better for them to shed the steel armor so they can move more quietly and quickly."*

*"This is not our army, Aeolis. We need to allow them to run things their own way."*

As everyone on the rise watched the six soldiers making their way, Kali stared at the towers. From this vantage point, the Gray Tower was even more fascinating. Being closer allowed her to see that the tower was not as dormant as she first assumed. Delicate lines of turquoise fire curled up from the base, swirling and combining with thin wisps of shadow. The golden light of Lúth that poured in from above met the flames halfway down, forming a faint ring that swirled delicately. She was mesmerized, it was the most beautiful harmony of magic she had ever seen.

Kali's eyes lingered for a long time on the confluence where the magic's met but shifted her gaze as the six scouts approached the broken landscape.

"Sir Trystan, may I borrow your aggrandizer?"

"Yes, of course."

Trystan handed over the elegant magnifying device of Gnomish design.

"If you twist that little nob there…"

"Yes, Sir Trystan, I know how they work."

Clearing his throat nervously, he stepped back. Kali brought the focusing lens to her eye and watched as the scouts got closer to where the road was destroyed. All the observers were silent. This was the closest any had been to the towers since their creation. The tension in the air was palpable.

Lowering the aggrandizer, Kali watched. The scout's steps were slowing but they were still moving forward. She shifted her gaze to the Gray Tower. The ring in the center was beginning to swirl more aggressively.

She looked back at the six and whispered, "Wait…"

The swirling ring of converged magic flashed and sent a shockwave up the tower walls. As fast as lightning the energy spread across an invisible dome that covered all three towers and traveled down until it impacted the ground. The six scouts were instantly vaporized. They turned to black dust and their armor clattered to the ground into the piles which were all that remained of their bodies.

Larissa gasped and clutched her stomach. Ceridwyn and Rayann did as well. The sickness from the distorted magic flashing over them. Kali was unaffected. Lady Rose stared in horror and Sir Gregory ran to his horse, mounted, and thundered towards where his troopers had fallen.

Commander Rose screamed, "Halt! That's an order!"

Sir Gregory ignored her and rode the distance between them and his scouts at a full gallop.

Lady Rose looked at Sir Ordin before turning to Kali.

"What in the crevasse was that?!"

Kali stared at her in silence.

"Answer me!"

"You do not command me, Lady Rose. This situation is not as simple as you and your knights have been trying to make it out to be. I have been attempting to warn you. These towers are not natural nor of Aimsire, they are born of magic stolen from God. Clearly there are defenses in place, but as I am not one of those who conjured this magic and brought it into our world, I have as few answers as you do."

She returned her gaze to the Gray Tower. The magic had calmed. She looked at the walls through the aggrandizer lens and watched the fire that surrounded the base. The magma was boiling in calm, steady patterns. Through the aggrandizer she watched as dozens of black orbs floated to the surface. They began to swirl and moved to the center of the three towers, drifting in a measured pattern. Kali turned to Lady Rose.

"Something has awoken."

"What?"

Kali handed her the aggrandizer and pointed.

"Look for yourself, there, in the center."

"Those floating orbs? What are they?"

"I don't know, but they just surfaced. Things just got even more complicated."

+++

Hours later, they were back at the Command Tent. Sir Gregory pounded his fist on the table and looked across at the wizards.

"All this damned sorcery and bewitchment you people bring! Nothing but trouble! All my life! Why God allows magic is beyond reason!"

Lady Rose spoke. "I believe it is time for you to step outside, Sir Gregory. Sir Ordin, take him for a walk."

Ordin ushered Gregory out of the tent and Lady Rose turned her attention to the three wizards.

"I am sorry."

Ceridwyn interjected. "There is nothing to apologize for, Lady Rose. He has every right to be upset at the loss of his soldiers."

Rose nodded to her in thanks for her understanding.

Rayann could feel the tension in the tent increasing even after the two knights left. She smiled at Raspberry whose eyes were glassy with confusion. The little halfling smiled back but it was obvious she was overwhelmed with emotion.

Rayann spoke to her mind. *"Berry, I know you are upset, however, will you play for us please? Something soothing that will bring hope and comfort."*

Raspberry gave a slight, almost unnoticeable nod and brought the lute to her chest. With precision and practiced accuracy, she strummed. Rayann glanced around as everyone occupying the tent instantly felt the warmth of Balaby's song and she could feel the emotions calming. The little halfling's eyes were closed as she played. Rayann whispered to her mind again.

*"Thank you. Please keep playing for us, as we sort all of this out."*

Rayann broke the silence. "How long will Sir Gregory and Sir Ordin be gone?"

"Until Sir Gregory calms down."

"That won't do. Given what happened that could take weeks. If we could get him back, the music will soothe him."

Rose looked at Larissa. "Please retrieve them."

With a sharp nod, Larissa was off. A few minutes later, Sir Gregory and Sir Ordin returned. Myth'alas nodded at Sir Gregory with a look of understanding. Both had lost soldiers in battle.

Ceridwyn stepped up to the map on the table and cleared her throat.

"It's safe to assume that whatever those things Kali identified floating in the magma are, it's likely to make any response more difficult."

"Whatever they are, they are alive." Kali informed them.

She walked up to the table and continued, "Just before we left, they started to open like water lilies. I don't know what they will become, but they are not passive."

Exhaling slowly, Commander Rose looked at her two trusted knights and then back to Kali.

"Well, I am not risking any more lives until I know more."

Kali agreed. "That is understandable, Lady Rose. I will go by myself tomorrow morning and investigate further. I will get as close as I can and try to figure out what they are. Now that I have felt its magic signature, I will be able to sense where the barrier is and can avoid contact with it."

"With all respect, Commander, allow me to accompany her." Sir Trystan interjected.

Rose looked up at Trystan. There was hesitation in her eyes and she remained silent a moment as she considered his request.

"Permission granted, but on one condition. You listen to whatever Kali says. This is her mission and she is in charge. If she says stop, you stop. If she says move, you move. We are dealing with the mysteries of her world, not ours."

Sir Trystan looked at Kali.

"Aye, Commander. I will."

"Then let's all get some dinner and rest up. To say this has been a long day is an understatement. You two can leave at first light tomorrow."

+++

The next day, just before dawn, Kali stood at the top of the hill overlooking the Dale of Still Mead. She could hear the soldiers awakening down in the encampment behind her, hundreds strong.

More had arrived late last night. It was becoming clear that the position of the knights and steelguard were that they would need to engage this enemy in force. Deep down, she felt the inevitability of that.

Closing her eyes, she prayed to God for strength and asked for Aviyana to guide her. She felt nothing, only the words, 'that, Kali, is entirely up to you' echoing in her mind. Opening her eyes, she stared at the towers and followed the lines of energy to the fracture in the sky, high above. The magic pulsed and she felt a rattle in her heart, as if a dragon had awoken, caged within her, shaking the bars to get out.

"Good morning, Kali. Are you ready?" Sir Trystan greeted her warmly.

"Well, I am the one who has been standing here waiting. Seems like the answer is obvious."

His cheeks went flush.

"Yes, I'm sorry. I stopped at the chow tent and packed us a wrapped lunch in case our mission went a little…"

Without a word she reached and touched his hand; they disappeared in a flash and appeared a short distance uphill from where the scouting party had been killed the day before. Trystan blinked as he looked around in surprise, speechless as to what just happened.

Kali flashed her charismatic, crooked smile when she saw that her actions had bewildered him. She turned and walked confidently towards the edge of the warding. The Gray Tower called to her. She watched as the swirl of magic began to build again.

Hesitantly Trystan followed, keeping his eyes fixed on the empty suits of armor. When she was ten meters from the deceased soldiers she stopped and turned to him.

"Do you see the junction on the Gray Tower? Where the magic comes up from the base and the golden light comes down? The energies meet right in the middle. It's very faint, but if you focus it will reveal itself."

"Yes, I see it."

"Keep focused on it and take a step with me."

They stepped forward, and the swirl built ever so slightly. "Did you see that?"

"Yes!"

"Now look at the center of the magma, where it turns like an eddy. As I said last night, they aren't orbs anymore."

Trystan saw movement, like something swimming beneath the surface and whispered, "I have never seen anything like this."

"They are elementals. Rayann and I went back to the Tower of Kells last night and did some research. The black pods we saw floating yesterday were their birth. They are growing, like children. What's more curious is why they were created. These towers were not put here to grow elementals."

Trystan furrowed his brow as she continued.

"The next thing to show you requires your trust. Do you trust me, Sir Trystan?"

He beheld her blue eyes. They were like exquisite crystals. Fragile and delicate, as if they would shatter if he dared to stare at them for too long.

"Yes, of course I trust you."

Kali whispered soft words of magic and gently kissed him on the forehead. He felt a warm jolt. It spread across his face and the veils were lifted from his sight. The landscape was a dazzling display of dancing lights, flowing like a river across the entire area.

"I have given you sight into the fields of magic. The golden light you see that flows like a river is the catalyst for our spells. We call it Shakyna for it is the very essence of God flowing upon our world. It brings life and light to all Aimsire. The blue glow you see emanating from the ground is the effusions from the ardor channels below the surface. They are like a web, even perhaps, a fisherman's net that surrounds our world, binding it all together. God set it in place during the Dawn Light. Now look at the towers."

Trystan complied. There were twisting ribbons of energy flowing between the tops of the black and fiery towers. Dark pulses shot from the Gray Tower towards the other two, fading halfway in rhythmic patterns, as if trying to connect, but unable.

"I see it, but what does it mean?"

"It means I was wrong. The tower is not a lodestone. It requires and seeks a master. The continuity between the three is incomplete. Three towers and only two masters suggest there's a potential fragility we can exploit, but it won't be easy."

She waved her hand and the magical sight left Trystan's eyes. His face showed his disappointment, but also his infatuation with her.

"You are simply amazing."

"No, Sir Trystan. I am just a wizard."

"A beautiful wizard."

She ignored it, turning back to the towers as she spoke.

"Perhaps things are not as grave as I had first predicted."

He watched her as he focused on the cool moisture in the middle of his forehead where she had kissed her spell onto him.

+++

"Elementals? What are elementals?" Ordin had never heard the term.

Rayann placed a large book on the table and opened it so Ordin, Gregory, and Rose could see the illustrations from *The Slemon's Archive of Aimsire's Creatures*.

"They are beings grown by a mixture of elements and magic. Very complex, extremely difficult to create, and there are no less than four dozen of them floating in the lake of magma. Based on the research Kali and I have been doing, they are in their infancy, but still extremely dangerous. It is likely we will see them emerge from the fire and walking the area under the warding within two weeks."

"Do they mean to attack us?"

Kali spoke up. "That's certainly possible, but our sense is they are for protection, not an assault."

"How can you be so sure?" Gregory's voice was laced with obvious distrust.

"I can't be sure, Sir Gregory. Like you, we are piecing together what we discover and trying to figure out the rest along the way. If the research my cousin and I have been doing and the knowledge it brings are so offensive to your ears, we can start keeping it to ourselves."

"Sir Gregory, mind your tone."

Lady Rose glanced at him and communicated every ounce of her authority. She turned back to Kali.

106

"Your counsel is more than welcome here. Is there anything else?"

"There is, but not about the elementals. There is a broken band of energy, a weak link if you will, between the Gray Tower and the other two. I was wrong about the Gray Tower possibly being a lodestone. The three towers are in fact a trinity. The power of that trinity, however, is as of now, incomplete."

"What does that mean?" Ordin leaned in curiously.

Sir Trystan interrupted. "It means, sir, that the whole is greater than the sum of the parts. Two towers have masters, one does not. This project of theirs is incomplete." He cleared his throat. "I only know this because Kali was gracious enough to share her theory with me while we were still on mission. Without a master, the third tower is likely weaker."

Kali looked at Sir Trystan. She could sense there was wisdom in him and he had been truly listening to her. Looking back at the three senior knights she continued her report.

"From what I discerned during my last visit to the warding; it is a complex series of layered spells. It's possible that if we attempt to negate the power and breach it, our magic will simply be absorbed. If the worst was to occur, it could strengthen the shield. There is also a chance, theoretically, that we can create an aperture."

Kali walked around and stood beside the knights. She placed her finger on the map at a spot adjacent to the Gray Tower.

"Based on my visions into the fields of magic there appears to be a slight fluctuation, a weak spot if you will. Right here. If we can create the door, your soldiers can move in."

"Excellent. Then let's start planning the assault."

"It's not that simple, Sir Gregory. Magic this intricate has never been seen on Aimsire, at least not in any of the knowledge we have been able to uncover. There is still work to be done to see if getting through is even possible.

"Beyond that, I am still not convinced that your trebuchets will be more than pebbles bouncing against steel. Additionally, if you end up needing to fend off these creatures, they are born of magic and fire. Your weapons will not be effective and you will have to get right up on them to strike."

Sir Gregory huffed. "That is what we do, Kali. We are knights and strike up close, facing our enemies at arm's length."

"Elementals wield magic as well as brawn, Sir Gregory. You will be fighting both their incredible strength as well as their fire. There are frost spells we can apply to some of your weapons and armor. They will only last a short time, but it could be helpful. Again, I can't promise you anything, this is all untested theory."

Hearing Kali's thoughts, Myth'alas scratched his chin and looked at his wife. He placed his voice directly into her mind, *"I need to speak with you and Kali when she is finished, in private."*

+++

Sir Trystan stood on the road with Kali outside the command tent. The hours of scouting and then meetings all day left him exhausted, but he smiled all the same.

"We dance well together, you and I."

"What does that mean?" She cocked her head to the side.

"I mean, we work well together. What we did today. It gave the commanders a lot to think about, we should be proud."

"All we did was force new questions; nothing was answered."

"One thing was." His voice was slick and sly.

Kali was less than impressed with his tone.

"And what was that, Sir Trystan?"

He moved in a little closer.

"I know you're the most amazing woman I've ever met."

Kali had never experienced a man attempting to flatter her like this, but she recognized it. She stared at him in silence. It was obvious that he was about to lean in again, so she stepped back.

"I'm not what you think I am. There are many who came before me. I am only standing on their shoulders."

"You are too humble."

"Oh, Sir Trystan, I am not. I just know I have a lot more to accomplish before being the most amazing anything, anywhere."

Kali walked away and left him on the road.

Before the meeting adjourned, Rayann had asked Kali via mindspeak to meet with her and Myth in their tent afterwards. Kali entered and could immediately feel the need for privacy. Without being asked she cast her spell again to seal out prying ears.

"No need to ask what this is about. Let's get to it."

Myth'alas helped his wife sit and then offered Kali a chair before he spoke.

"We need more than frost spells on steel. That isn't going to do it."

"I know. I had to offer them something."

"I have something."

"What is it, beloved?" Rayann inquired.

He turned to his wife and laughed. "You are both going to think I'm mad, but here goes. Bold'Rock's daughter is a frost sorceress. The cold she conjured when I fought them was incredible. Her pull on the magic field was undeniably powerful, even I could sense it."

Rayann shook her head in disbelief, but Kali spoke first.

"Brilliant idea, Myth'alas."

"Have you two lost your heads? He is a Netherman. Beyond that little issue, we know nothing about either of them. These are Knights of Aimsire, they would never allow it."

Myth'alas knelt and grabbed Rayann's hands.

"I know. That said, it might be crazy enough to work."

"Who even knows where they are, or if they will answer if we summon them?"

He handed her a small parchment.

"I received this after breakfast; it was routed from Faralanthis to Gryphonledge and a runner brought it here. In this note they confirmed all that happened along the west coast and have requested solace in Hailan Glen."

Rayann read the parchment and looked up at him.

"Oh, my beloved Myth, this is a long shot at best."

"What else do we have?"

Kali took the note. After reading it she added. "The girl does have talent. Even engaged in battle against Piramay and Fifth I was feeling her pull all the way across the glen." She turned to her cousin. "Long shot or not, frost kills fire."

"I don't know. It's one thing to bring them; it's another to convince the knights."

Myth'alas smiled. "Let me worry about that."

Rayann heard her husband's words. After a moment she spoke in alignment with him.

"I trust you, both of you."

Myth'alas turned to Kali.

"How tired are you?"

"Not tired enough to quit. Just tell me where we're going."

She reached out her hand.

+++

Nolore, Rajumin, Lady Kellan, and her squad appeared outside Gryphonledge. From the walls, the guard sounded the alarm and the steelguard were dispatched. The defensive force approached but lowered their weapons when they identified Lady Kellan as a Knight of Aimsire. The captain approached and addressed her.

"My Lady. May I request your identification, please?"

"Lady Kellan Stenberg of the Northern Command. This is Sergeant Erika Tiliz, and these are my troopers."

"And them?"

"Nolore and Rajumin, of the Silentclaw."

"Silentclaw?"

The captain turned to his sergeant. "Alert the guard, send a carrier pigeon to Commander Rose, have rooms prepared."

"Aye, sir!"

The sergeant was off like a shot and the captain dismounted as did the handful of soldiers that were with him. They all went to a knee. Nolore stepped forward.

"Stand, good soldiers of Aimsire. We are but messengers and servants of God. We are not to be knelt to."

The captain and his soldiers returned to their feet. His eyes filled with tears.

"This is a glorious day; we have been petitioning and praying to God for it. Now victory is assured."

"No victory as of yet, good man. There is still plenty of fight and a long road ahead."

# Chapter 09 – Politics and Pride

The first day of winter arrived. A sharp chill lingered in the air and news of the arrival of the two Silentclaw had spread quickly. Despite the cold, Gryphonledge was bustling with new hope, and life.

"Thank God for your arrival and Dionadair for his guidance."

Lady Rose was in awe. She stared at the two Silentclaw and for the first time in a very long time, felt a seed of faith sprout in her heart.

"We are but servants and messengers. We will do what we can." Rajumin smiled.

Turning to Kellan, Lady Rose spoke sympathetically.

"I am sorry for your loss, Lady Kellan. I met your brother Sir Liam many years ago. He spoke highly of you. He was a good man and an honorable knight."

"He may still be alive." Kellan whispered.

Rose nodded out of instinct more than agreement as she glanced at Nolore. The report Kellan, Erika, and their troopers offered, corroborated by the Silentclaw, left no question that this squad were the only survivors. It was natural to hang on to hope, so Rose stayed silent on that matter.

She continued with the conversation. "Well, for now we shall fold you into our ranks until I can reach Commander Steelpike. First, I want you and your squad to take a few days off. You have been through a lot and need rest."

Rose turned to Larissa. "Be sure that Lady Kellan, Erika, and their troops have what they need. House them in the diplomat quarters near the castle for now so they can have some privacy."

"Aye, ma'am, I will."

Larissa escorted them out and as the door closed Rose turned to Nolore and Rajumin.

"What other news can you share? We've received hardly a word from the northern command as the attacks were moving up the coast. The few carrier pigeons which did arrive often bared messages that made little sense but always insisted the situation was under control. Clearly that wasn't the case."

Nolore responded. "Nearly every town or hamlet of size on the western coast has been razed. All your keeps along the mountain ranges are intact, however, with the harbors destroyed they are short of supplies. Many of the soldiers that were stationed along the coast are dead. Worse, Nataxia has landed an army in the ruins of Northrim. They have nowhere to march but south."

"Of course. We will begin to prepare with haste." Rose squeezed the words out between her teeth.

"Commander." Rose turned to Rajumin. "The tragedy of those murdered is not insignificant, but we must focus on the three towers. You can fight the army if they make it this far south, however, those towers are the real threat right now and why we have arrived to assist you. They can destroy everything on Aimsire if we don't figure out how to topple them."

"So, you don't know how to destroy them?"

"No, but we will help you and the wizards figure it out."

Rose inhaled deeply and rubbed the headache behind her temples as she spoke again.

"The Circle of Six were killed just before the creation of the towers. The only wizards in the city are the three that arrived when I requested Ceridwyn come to discuss a completely different matter, a discussion we never got to have. The Central Command has no remaining knightchanters, and Ceridwyn has informed us that there are very few if any remaining wizards in the world."

Nolore spoke. "I have heard the two that came with her are members of the Fionntán family, can you tell me where they are?"

"Of course. I can have them summoned for you."

"No, please. I would prefer to meet with them in private."

"As you wish. Along the eastern wall of the keep we have many great chambers. I have them housed there. You may go at your discretion."

"Thank you, commander." Nolore bowed his head respectfully, a gesture Lady Rose did not take for granted.

+++

An hour later, Nolore and Rajumin approached and stood before Prince Myth'alas and Rayann's door. The guards were astonished as they stared at the two Silentclaw.

Rajumin raised an eyebrow after the long silence and smiled at the two men.

"Could you please announce us?"

The soldiers came out of their trance.

"Yes…yes of course, goddess."

"I am not a goddess. We serve God and are but servants and messengers."

As they entered, Myth'alas and Rayann stood waiting. Myth'alas brought his hand over his heart and opened it in greeting. Rayann bowed her head respectfully.

"Greetings and peace to you. I am Nolore, and this is my cousin, Rajumin. We have traveled from the Vale of Ghosts by directive of God and under the guidance of Ameliara and Dionadair to assist you."

Myth's normally stoic face softened with gladness. Rayann felt her husband's heart fill with joy before she spoke.

"Thank you for coming. How can we help?"

Nolore replied. "We will need a full debrief of what you know, but first, can you please summon Kali."

Compliantly, Rayann closed her eyes and summoned her cousin via mindspeak.

"I just requested Kali join us, she is on her way. She's housed just next door, so…"

The door opened and Kali walked in. Rajumin inhaled softly, immediately walking over and embracing her like a long-lost sibling. Kali's eyes went wide and she reluctantly returned the hug, staring at Rayann with a look of shock.

"It is so good to see you, Kali. After what happened to your parents, we thought the worst. When word reached us that you were alive and on Aimsire, my heart was overrun with joy."

Kali gently pushed away as she responded, "Thank you, but who are you?"

With a slight flush, she answered, "You may call me Rajumin. I met you when you were but four weeks old. Your parents, Ebonia and Hamish brought you to the Vale of Ghosts when they came to request the Silentclaw return to Aimsire. God had not deemed it yet. After they departed, we received word that their ship had gone down during a storm in The Tempest. Thinking you had suffered the same fate…ahh, your little face has always lingered in my memory."

"That's not what happened. It wasn't a storm."

Nodding her head in affirmation, Rajumin spoke warmly. "And thank God for it."

"Thank God? We were attacked and my parents were murdered. I was kidnapped, taken to the constellations and had my mind clouded and manipulated. This was done to forge me into a weapon to sow chaos under the banner of Nataxia. Why thank God for that?"

Nolore interjected. "Because you are alive and here now. Brought to be in just the right place, at just the right time. Your journey has prepared you and formed you into what you need to be for God's purpose."

Kali turned and looked at him. "How very poetic, but there are many questions that romance and prose do not answer. Being in the right place at the right time doesn't mean anything without the information to make beneficial decisions. Nor does it explain why God would allow such a thing to happen in the first place."

"God's eyes never left you and will ultimately use all things for good. You can rest assured of that. In the meantime–" Nolore reached into the bag he was carrying and handed Kali a stack of books. "Perhaps this gift will get you started in answering some of your questions."

Kali's eyes went wide. For a wizard, there was no greater gift than knowledge. Though she did not know the nature or content of the books he was handing her, she knew that coming from a Silentclaw meant they were significant.

He spoke again as he pointed to the book on top. "This one will probably interest you the most."

She read the cover out loud. "'*The Treatise of Lúth*'. Indeed, this will prove valuable."

"The presence of Lúth is why God and the tutelar commanded us to return. It is not meant for mortals."

"Thank you for this gift." Kali stared at the book like a hungry child who hadn't eaten for days.

"The Tower of Kells would be an appropriate place to house those when you are finished."

"Of course. I will see to it."

Nolore turned to Rayann.

"Speaking of The Tower. We felt the shift in ardor and Shakyna. There is a new Mistress of Kells."

Her cheeks went flush and she nodded.

"Yes, it is true. My ancestors have granted me The Tower."

"Well, the Mistress of Kells cannot be expected to fully find her place without this."

Nolore brought his palms together, then turned them parallel to the floor. A thin line of lavender light appeared and moved towards Rayann as he separated his hands. Nolore finished the spell and a smooth, finely polished, stoutbark wood staff hovered before her. The tip looked like a miniature version of the spire atop the Tower of Kells.

"This is the Staff of Kells. It draws its magic directly from the tower itself. No matter where you are on Aimsire, with this staff you can call upon Kells and wield the power within."

Rayann remembered her father talking about the Staff of Kells, but he spoke as if it no longer existed. She stared, seeing the place worn smooth into the wood where countless generations of her family had grasped it. She was frozen in awe.

"Take it, Rayann. You are the Mistress of Kells. The staff is yours now."

She looked up at Rajumin with moist eyes and slowly reached out, grasping it. The power flowed through her and she cried tears of joy.

+++

Lorcan and Nidhug stood on top of the scorched walls of Northrim keep. Nidhug bared his teeth and pulled his cloak tightly over his neck as the snow fell.

"Cursed cold. We should have been here months ago."

The massive Netherman secretly snickered at the reptilian's attempts to warm himself. He spoke as they looked out across the burned city.

"Months ago, our queen bid us to attack the elves. There was no power to reopen the portals once the one who could shred Shakyna so efficiently fled."

"Don't remind me."

Nidhug turned and walked along the battlement. His dew claws tapped the stones with each step. He stared at the army outside the main gate, spread out like a plague which would soon be released upon the land.

"My brethren will be here in a week. Be sure the army is prepared to move out the moment they arrive."

"Why does it take so long?"

Nidhug turned and looked up at Lorcan.

"Their chains have lingered since the end of the rebellion. The ardor flows have provided new power to free them, but it will take time."

Lorcan huffed in frustration. "Soldiers who sit in the cold become restless, fat, and weak. They need battle and the smell of blood to stay hungry and strong."

Without a word, Nidhug turned and walked to the main chamber of the keep. Lorcan followed and they approached a large map. Rezren looked up and his tongue flicked as he caught the grimy scent of the Netherman. His scaled, black armor shimmered in the firelight and his orange eyes shifted back to the map. Snarling under his breath, he pointed a long claw, tracing the edge of the mountain range.

"The humans built wide, military roads. With our speed we can move down the range with ease and resupply at each of the human cities. The two traitors eliminated half of the northern army. The rest will fall easily."

"What of the Nethermen?"

Rezren looked at Nidhug. "Easily purchased, or killed, makes no difference."

Lorcan added to the conversation. "If we can entice them to join our ranks with the others it would give us an advantage. Humans fear us, that is why they have built so many fortresses along the mountain range. Nethermen despise the humans for it. They might welcome an opportunity to fight."

Both reptilians looked at the normally quiet creature.

"What do you propose, Lorcan?"

"The Shatter Stone Clan are the most aggressive and live along this border. They will likely engage us if we simply march by. If I go and speak with their chief, I can negotiate his loyalty."

"How do you know they won't kill you on sight?"

"Though I no longer live among them the Shatter Stone are my clan, I am one of them."

He lifted the large human shield that now acted as the spaulder on his left shoulder, revealing a scar that had clearly been branded into his skin.

"If I request a parley, by our traditions they will allow me to speak."

Nidhug stared at him for a moment. His tongue flicked and his eyes narrowed.

"You have seven days before the assemblage arrives. I suggest you get going."

+++

"All of a sudden and without permission you are using my diplomat quarters to house soldiers?"

The squat Sinner King paced around Commander Rose's office as he spoke. He turned and looked at her with dark, beady eyes. His plump, fat cheeks squeezed out of his neck collar, and the over-ruffled, floral, heavy fabrics reeked of perfume and richly scented powder.

"Sire, they are the only survivors of the attack on Northrim. I offered the quieter quarters so they could enjoy some comfort. They need proper rest and recovery before I bring them back into our ranks."

"What of *my* family? What about *our* quiet and comfort? Did none of this occur to you? Hmm? Those chambers are to be the buffer of the city noise so we can relax in our gardens. How are we to enjoy our breakfast if we hear the merchant carts rolling by, or…soldiers gambling, drinking, and making whatever merriment they may in the name of 'rest' and 'recovery'?

"We cannot rule unless we have proper rest and quiet so our minds can remain still and purged of distraction, Commander Rose. I shouldn't need to explain this to you, again."

"Have they been disruptive, my king?"

"No, but they could become so. They are soldiers after all."

Internally, Rose was screaming at this man and wanted to throttle him, but as commander she maintained her calm.

"You are right, your highness."

"Yes, of course I'm right. You will have them removed, immediately."

"Sire, since you are here, I should inform you that I have been giving the matter of your family a great deal of thought. The war council met this morning. With circumstances as they are, we feel it would be best for you to begin your journey to your castle in Pearlpoint Harbor for the winter right away instead of waiting until the end of the month. The cold is setting in and if that isn't enough, we will likely be facing a battle with whomever created those towers soon. For the safety of your family and yourself, I would advise that you depart tomorrow morning."

The Sinner King looked out the window.

"Well, yes…it would be quieter and warmer there. I do despise the snow. Are you sure you won't need my input on the coming battle?"

"I assure you, your majesty, we will find a way to manage."

"Yes. Perhaps." He glanced sideways at her in a very condescending manner. "As you know, I am a master of military strategy. Perhaps I will send pigeons to offer my advice as ideas come to me. You will need direction, after all."

"Your correspondence and advisement are always welcome. Send them directly to me and I will see that they are brought before the council."

The king lingered several moments, staring out the window and tapping his chin as if he was thinking. Rose didn't have time for this, but she let him walk through his overly dramatic routine. She already knew how it was going to end. Finally, he smacked his lips and nodded his head.

"Yes, for the sake of my family's safety, we will go. I shall advise you from the castle at Pearlpoint. These are not times to put important leadership in jeopardy. Afterall, what would you do without me?"

"Exactly. Of course, we don't want your safety compromised, sire."

"Good! Then I decree that we shall leave at first light tomorrow morning! Order to have all arrangements made. I am late for my next appointment."

"As you declare it shall be done. I will order preparations."

The Sinner King exited and Larissa stepped from her place beside the wall, smirking at her Commander. She covered her nose to block the lingering perfumes. Rose simply rolled her eyes and sat down, rubbing her temples.

Larissa spoke gently. "Would you like some tea, or food, Lady Rose?"

"No, thank you. At least we can now claim martial authority and move forward with all the planning. Not having to deal with his distractions will allow us to better focus and move more quickly as necessary."

"At least you ordered preparations for his departure two days ago. Wouldn't want him late for his wig powdering or whipped cream puffed pastry now would we?"

Rose huffed before leaning back in her chair. She inhaled deeply before speaking again.

"How are you doing? Have you spoken to Prince Myth'alas as we discussed?"

"Not yet. There has not been a good time."

"Well, I agree, things have been nothing short of chaos the last few days. I know this is going to sound crazy, but even in all this there are traditions to be observed. As I met with the War Council this morning, High Moon was mentioned. As you know, it's in three days."

Larissa crinkled her brow knowingly.

"You mean to still have the festival?"

Rose smiled. "Yes, Larissa. I know it may seem foolish, but as of now things are calm. Relatively speaking I mean. When those towers awaken we will more than have our hands full. With the Silentclaw arriving and the need for a long breath before the winter sets in, we have decided to have the Feast of High Moon. We will also be honoring our fallen steelguard and knights up north. Being a social gathering, maybe it will afford you the opportunity to speak with your brother."

"Commander, for what it's worth, I think it's a good idea. Thank you for helping me find an opportunity to speak with him."

"Larissa, do me a favor?"

"Of course, commander, anything."

"Don't be so nervous about the conversation as to neglect telling him yourself as we discussed. Not as your commander, but as your friend, promise me."

Larissa swallowed hard as she paused before giving a single nod with her response.

"I promise."

+++

After her evening meeting with Lady Rose, Ceridwyn went to the ruins of the Hexangular. Her steelguard chaperons stayed close but also allowed her some space. All the work she was doing with the knights had kept her from coming to do a proper investigation. It mattered little. There wasn't much left and the lingering magic signatures were the same as those around the towers. There was no mystery as to who was responsible.

Moving around the rubble she paid her respects and offered prayers. Finally, she decided to take the long route through the merchant district back to the keep.

As she made her way and looked through the windows, she immediately recognized the elegant, fancy dress she had seen in Fogburgh. Looking up, her heart filled with warmth as she read the sign above the door, 'The Curiosity Shoppe'.

She turned to her escorts.

"I will need a few moments. If you don't mind, please wait outside."

"Of course, Mistress Ceridwyn. We will be right here if you need us."

Upon entering, the familiar little brass bell rang and the smell of dyes and cloth hit her nose.

"Mirelle?"

A melodic response came from the back room.

"One moment."

Ceridwyn could not help but smile as she waited. Soon enough she heard the whirling of a stitching machine stop and seconds later Mirelle walked through the door and into the front room. Her eyes went wide as she saw Ceridwyn standing there and she spoke with delight in her voice.

"Ceridwyn! How good to see you! I'd heard wizards arrived after what happened. I'm so glad it's you."

She walked over and Ceridwyn brought her hand to her heart and then opened it in greeting.

"My heart sings to see you again. I had no idea you left Fogburgh. What prompted that?"

"After Lenly passed, I felt it was time for a change. I mean, I grew up there, it was all I ever knew. As much as I loved that little fishing village, I always wanted to live in the capital. It's been very good for business as well. I don't have to travel near as often and there's many more customers who seek fine clothing here."

"That is understandable. I see you still have that fine dress in the window."

"Yes, the Baroness who ordered it never returned. It's been so many years. It was to be for a turning-of-age party. I've no idea why they never came to pick it up and I'm sure the little one I created it for has well outgrown it. A shame really, it would've looked dazzling on her."

"Well, I am not sure if you heard, but Commander Rose has decided to proceed with the Feast of High Moon and I find myself without a proper dress."

Mirelle could not help but smile. She walked over and took the dress from its hook in the window and handed it to Ceridwyn.

"I'm sure this is about your size, please have it. I'm happy to make hasty adjustments should you require them."

"Oh no, that's not what I...please, let me compensate you at least."

"Ceridwyn, I insist. This gown was paid for in advance. Besides, a celebration is exactly what I created it for. Believe me, it'd bring me great joy to see such a fine garment lovingly worn rather than just hanging sadly in my window."

Ceridwyn's cheeks went warm and she took the dress.

"Thank you, I will cherish it. Perhaps, since you don't want payment for this dress, I could hire you to make another?"

"Of course, I'd be happy to."

"Wonderful. This other garment is not for me, however, and would need to be completed before the festival. I know that is a quick turn-around so I would be happy to assist in any way I can but would like it to be of your design. We can work together, if you don't mind. I will be your assistant."

"I'd be delighted to work with you."

"Splendid. So, here's what I am after. The dress needs to be small and should have a certain, eclectic feel to it. Oh, and it needs to be made with blue fabric."

Mirelle smiled, knowing exactly who it was for.

"I still have her measurements. I'd be honored to do this for our little Ladybug."

## Chapter 10 – High Moon

After multiple trips to the north over the next few days to find Bold'Rock and Pela'Rock, Kali and Myth'alas located them. Kali stood near the entrance of the cave, scanning the valley far below. Now that Riverhorn was the northernmost populated human city with a keep, the knights and steelguard were making heavy modifications to the defensive perimeter.

The wooden walls in the town center were being reinforced. In addition, hastily constructed watchtowers and emplacements now dotted the landscape. While she watched them work, scurrying like ants across the landscape, Kali listened to the conversation between Myth'alas and Bold'Rock.

"We will grant you solace in Hailan Glen. I do this with the asking of a favor."

"Of course, we will compensate you."

"Compensation is not what I mean. Normally a mercenary would be paid in coin, what I am asking is that you would fight for us in exchange. A massive battle looms, we will need all the soldiers we can get, and more specifically, we need your daughter's sorcery."

"My Pela's cold is required?"

Curiously, Bold'Rock turned to look at her. She shrugged softly and he turned his gaze back.

"I don't understand this bargain, Warrior Prince."

"As you know, the two wizards, Piramay and Fifth, fled during the battle in Hailan Glen."

"Yes, most dishonorable."

"Perhaps, if you look only at the surface. They did not come to fight; they came to steal an extremely powerful weapon, the Staff of Winds. Once they acquired what they sought, there was no reason to continue fighting."

Bold'Rock scratched his thick, black beard.

"Understandable, though they did pledge to fight for the queen. Of course, so did we until we saw that it was wrong."

"Yes, and I appreciate that you changed your mind. Fifth and Piramay on the other hand had an ulterior motive. After they acquired the staff, we believe it was combined with two others. It gave them the power to create three towers. A triangulation of raw energy which we are certain is being harvested for evil purposes. We fear they intend to use this magic against all the living creatures of Aimsire."

"I still don't understand why this means you need my daughter's cold magic."

"As a protective measure, they have grown fire elementals. My thought was that with your staff and her sorcery, it would give us an advantage in the battle."

Bold'Rock turned and looked at Pela.

"We have never seen a fire elemental or fought one, daughter. Do you feel confident in going to battle against them knowing so little?"

"We have fought others who wield fire, father, and I was able to freeze them. I don't know why it would be any different."

Bold'Rock looked at her a moment, studying her eyes. He could always see if she was feeling fear by looking into her eyes. He rarely saw it.

Turning back to Myth'alas he asked, "How safe is your glen?"

"Safer than any place on Aimsire. Nobody will be able to reach you. You will feel more secure than the elves in Shimmerwood."

"I agree to your terms."

"I am glad to hear it."

Myth'alas stuck out his hand and Bold'Rock clasped his forearm in traditional warrior fashion.

"So, the biggest trick is going to be convincing the knights to allow you two to join us."

Bold'Rock quirked his head as he spoke, "You have not spoken to them about this bargain?"

"No. Worry not, if I can't convince them of this arrangement you and your daughter are still welcome to stay in Hailen Glen for as long as you like, with no further obligations."

"That is not the way of the world, Warrior Prince. There must always be an exchange."

"That you pledged your willingness to fight with us will be enough. When the time comes, I feel confident that I can convince the knights."

Raspberry looked up from her pages of music as someone knocked on the door.

"Come on in."

Ceridwyn entered the room and smiled.

"How are you my little friend? I have hardly seen you for the last few days."

"Yeah, sorry Ms. Ceridwyn I'm sad and haven't felt too social. I've been writing and praying instead. I still don't know why my song didn't protect those soldiers."

Ceridwyn sat next to Raspberry before responding.

"You can't stop every bad thing from happening or help every time. That's not how life works. Believe me, I know myself from personal experience. What matters is you tried."

"I know Ms. Ceridwyn, it's just confusing. Sometimes when I sing and play, everything works out great. Other times, well…you saw what happened to those poor soldiers."

"I did," Ceridwyn reached over and took Raspberry's hand. "I also understand."

Raspberry leaned in and rested her head on Ceridwyn's shoulder, sitting quietly for a few minutes. Finally, Ceridwyn broke the silence.

"You know the festival is tonight, yes? Rayann told me you don't plan to attend."

"Yeah, I think I'm just gonna stay in my room."

"Not to be overly assumptive, but that doesn't sound like you. I have never known you not to attend a party or play for people at any chance you get. Based on what I have seen in preparations, this is going to be a grand affair. I'd hate for you to miss it."

"Ms. Ceridwyn, it's…well, what I mean is, I do kinda wanna go. I just don't feel like being all festive and stuff right now. Also, I'm a bit afraid the soldiers might not want me there. It's hard to explain."

"Berry, believe me, I understand how you feel. If you don't mind my asking, do you celebrate the Festival of High Moon in Weefolk Wood?"

"Ha! Yeah we do! Halflings will look for any excuse to throw a great party!"

Ceridwyn laughed at Raspberry's enthusiasm.

"So, I have noticed. May I ask then, do you understand why the Festival of High Moon is celebrated?"

"Sorta. I mean, it's the first festival of winter. Giving thanks for the harvest and coming together to celebrate all the hard work that was done to get everything ready for the cold season."

"Yes, all of that is true, but there is also a deeper purpose and reason. Did you know that the Festival of High Moon is the only celebration that all Aimsire celebrates in almost identical ways?"

"No. That's pretty interesting!"

"I agree. The festival was originally held to commemorate the Dawn Light, when God created all the beauty and splendor of Aimsire. For humans and elves in particular, it also came as a date to mark the partnership and peaceful exchange between us. This festival is about God's light and all the life, optimism, peace, and joy it can bring. It helps us to remember that we should continue to pursue these things.

"It's always held on the first full moon of winter because it signifies that even when things are about to become the darkest, God's light still brings us hope. To be perfectly honest, given what we are surely about to face, I think it's the best holiday that we could be celebrating right now. For what it's worth, I hope you will reconsider attending."

Raspberry's eyes glassed over and she nodded.

"I'll go. I heard that people get all fancied up for this though. I don't really have pieces of clothing like that. Maybe you can help me dress up my balladeer shirt, or perhaps we can go through my stuff and find something appropriate together?"

"It just so happens that I can help."

"Thanks. If anything, just getting to spend a little time with you will be nice."

"Yes, I apologize that I have not been available. The knights have been asking a lot of us all."

"They haven't asked much of me, especially after what happened."

"I realize that, but I assure you it has nothing to do with what transpired at the towers. You have significant talents, they just haven't seen it yet."

"And humans don't really like wee-folk."

"I can see how your journey in this life would give you those feelings, however, I don't think that's entirely true. They just don't know you quite yet. My guess is before all of this is over, their eyes are going to be opened and they will see just how special you are."

Raspberry smiled and her cheeks went flush.

"You really think so, Ms. Ceridwyn? I just wanna help."

"I know you do. I promise if you give it time, they will want you to help too."

They hugged one another tightly and held their embrace of friendship for a while. Raspberry enjoyed the comfort of it. Finally, Ceridwyn said, "Now, about what you should wear this evening..."

She turned and gestured with her hand. Magically, the door popped open. Raspberry turned to look as Mirelle walked into the room. She was already dressed for the festival and Raspberry squealed.

"Ms. Mirelle!"

She bolted across the room and smashed her little body into her friend, hugging her tightly. Mirelle laughed as she stroked the halflings' bright red hair.

"It's good to see you again, Ladybug."

"My goodness! Why are you here? I mean, I love that you're here! It's just...this is a really long way from Fogburgh!"

"I moved here a few months ago. The Curiosity Shoppe is now on Maker's Row, just off the Market Square."

"Wow! Can I come visit you like I used to?"

"Of course. I would have invited you had I known you were about! You are always welcome in my shop and my home. You know that."

"I know, I mean, I remember you always saying that I just like to make sure."

Mirelle smiled and brushed the wrinkles out of Raspberry's sleeves as she continued.

"Three days ago, Ceridwyn and I talked about how someone was going to need a special dress for tonight."

Raspberry turned to Ceridwyn with a smirk.

"You knew I didn't have clothing for a festival…"

Ceridwyn smiled as she responded.

"Indeed I did. I also discovered, quite by accident, that Mirelle had moved here. I could think of no one better to come up with something wonderful for you."

Mirelle left the room and returned in seconds with the most exquisite blue dress that Raspberry had ever seen. It was pleated and stitched in such a way that even the movements of being carried made it come alive. Darker blue within the folds exaggerated the shadows and large ruffles were set in perfect alignment with one another. Ribbons in every color fell like living rainbows along the shoulders. Beads and ornate shellwork were stitched across the bodice like scaled armor. Mirelle knelt and presented the garment to Raspberry.

"This, Ladybug, is a garment worthy of Aimsire's most unique individual, who, I might add, happens to also be its finest Balladeer. It's one of a kind and inspired by the lost lore of the merfolk, I remember you always loved those stories. Ceridwyn and I spent the last three days working on it together."

Raspberry ran her fingers along the fine silk and stopped when she touched the embroidery along the center of the chest. The golden thread shimmered and formed the symbol of Balaby right above where her heart would be once she put it on.

"Wow. It's the most beautifulest dress I've ever seen. Thank you, *both* of you! I can't wait to put it on!"

"Well, we have two hours. Let's get you ready."

+++

Tonight, Gryphonledge was not a city on the brink of war with a strange, foreign invader. Instead, it was a place of joy, happiness, and plenty. Apart from the wall guard and roving patrols, Lady Rose had authorized the entire city to take the night off and celebrate. The streets were alive with the sound of minstrels and merriment. Even the steelguard who were still on duty wore crowns of specially grown snowdrop flowers, or sprigs of late autumn blooms on their armor.

The Hall of Gems and Merriment within the castle had been opened now that the Sinner King was traveling to Pearlpoint. He had clearly been so focused on himself he had forgotten there might even be a festival, which settled with Rose just fine. Eventually he would receive word but she would deal with that when she needed to.

The entire castle compound was alive with laughter. The delicious smell of roasted meats and mead filled the air. Lady Rose was speaking with Sir Ordin and Sir Gregory when the appearance of Prince Myth'alas and his entire collective of companions caught her eye. She turned to her subordinates.

"Come, let us welcome our guests."

As she approached Prince Myth'alas, he greeted her first in the manner of the elves and then extended his hand in the greeting of warriors.

"Thank you for coming, Prince Myth'alas. You and your compatriots are more than welcome to eat, drink, and explore the castle grounds without restriction."

"My thanks to you, Lady Rose."

He turned and Rayann stepped forward, followed by Olwa, Aeolis, Ceridwyn, Kali, and finally Raspberry. The little halfling was practically floating in her fine dress. She looked around the hall in amazement and spoke as she shook her head.

"I have never seen such a marvelous room. It goes up so high. Wowza! There are even paintings on the ceiling!"

Rose nodded. "Yes, the king doesn't miss a detail when it comes to decorating his home."

"Or the chance to spend the people's coin."

Rose elbowed Sir Gregory playfully and gave him a smirk. "Not tonight, Sir."

He chuckled and raised his cup in compliance before taking a hefty swig of mead.

Lady Rose turned back to Raspberry.

"I must say, that is a beautiful dress and quite appropriate for you. It's as if it was tailored just for your sake."

"It was! Ms. Mirelle and Ms. Ceridwyn made it for me. Ms. Mirelle made Ms. Ceridwyn's too!"

Rose observed Ceridwyn's dress.

"Also, an elegant garment."

Ceridwyn agreed. "As a tailor myself, I believe Mirelle is one of the finest clothing makers I have ever met."

Rose raised an eyebrow at her compliment. Knowing that coming not just from a wizard but also an elf, meant it was not misplaced.

"Well, I would like to meet her if possible. I don't normally dress fancy like this, however, protocol and politics sometimes require it."

"She's right here and just so happens to live on Maker's Row."

Ceridwyn gestured and Mirelle stepped forward bowing her head respectfully.

"Good evening, it is a pleasure to meet you."

"It is nice to meet you too, Mirelle. Please enjoy the castle grounds and let Larissa here know if you need anything."

She took a quick look around at their faces and smiled as she continued, "Well then, let's relax and enjoy the festival."

+++

Joy and cheer filled the air. Even Commander Rose was finally persuaded to have a small chalice of the fine mead that Sir Ordin and Sir Gregory had been deeply indulging in.

Kali had managed to slip away and was standing alone on one of the small castle balconies overlooking the city. She was leaning on the rail, tracing the silhouette of the jagged ridgeline, lit from behind by the moon. Beyond that ridgeline was the Dale of Still Mead. Even from here she could feel the Gray Tower. Its pulse radiated through the ardor channels. The dragon in her heart stirred.

"Beautiful, isn't it."

She immediately recognized his voice and exhaled softly, responding without turning her head.

"Yes, Sir Trystan. The night sky is crystal clear which makes the full moon all the more beautiful."

"You don't find the city beautiful?"

130

He stepped up beside her and placed a silver chalice of mead on the ledge.

"No, Sir Trystan, I do not. I find it cold and practical, just like any center of military operations should be."

"I'm surprised you think that. Gryphonledge is bustling with exciting and attractive features. Did you know that the entire city is carved from a single piece of rock without a seam or the use of mortar? There is a clock tower in the town square designed by gnomes which reaches fifty meters into the air and the springs never need winding. We have skybridges that span the big river flowing from the wall that offers incredible views. We even have fountains and gardens watered from nothing more than the artesian springs that come up out of the ground. Perhaps tomorrow…"

"No, Sir Trystan."

She came off her elbows, stood up straight, and turned to face him.

"Kali, I was only…"

"I know what you are trying to do."

He sighed. "Well, would you at least share a chalice of mead with me?"

She looked down at the ornate, silver cup before shaking her head.

"I am sorry, no. I do not allow my mind to be clouded."

Trystan turned and looked out across the city as he set his cup down in exasperation.

"Why do you always call me, 'Sir'?"

"That is your title, is it not?"

"Formally, yes, but not among friends."

"I didn't realize that we had become familiar enough with one another to be friends."

"Well then, let me say I hope we will become so."

She could see his desire for her illuminate in his eyes.

"I know you do, but it is not realistic, and frankly, not appropriate. We are on the verge of war; nobody may come out of this alive."

"That's exactly why we should live in the moment, grasp what is here, now. We need to live and love."

She laughed. "Pretty poetry with no practicality, Sir Trystan. I would rather learn all I can and increase my chances of

131

survival than hunt and peek for stolen kisses in the moonlight. Couples don't fall in love in one evening. At most, they foolishly indulge in those moments you are speaking of in order to satisfy a passing trickle of desire."

She could sense his frustration as he turned and looked out across the city once again. After a moment, he broke the silence.

"Kali, I want to tell you that for me this wasn't about a fleeting moment. I think you are the most amazing woman I've ever met, dare I say, the most amazing woman on all Aimsire. I sincerely hoped we could get to know each other a little more."

"I know, Sir Trystan. I have heard you every time you say it. Thank you for bringing me some mead, it was a kind gesture."

She left and Trystan stared out over the city once again. Never had his charms been rejected so whole-heartedly. It confused him at first, but the more he lingered on the conversation, he only began to desire her more.

+++

Larissa watched Rayann stand to go and refresh her plate. She leaned in and whispered, "With your permission, Commander?"

Rose turned and noticed Myth'alas was alone. She offered a quick wink, communicating her approval.

Larissa approached her brother and offered a traditional elven greeting. He stood and returned the gesture before speaking.

"May the moon shine brightly upon you this evening, Larissa. This is a fine affair. I must admit I have not attended a Festival of High Moon in over one hundred years. It is refreshing to see and feel all the hope in the room."

"Yes. It is always the most beautiful festival of the year. All the candles and torches combined with the late autumn flowers hanging so delicately before the winter sets in. It reminds us that spring and the warm sun will return again soon."

"The elves celebrate in a similar manner, only the lighting is different. We have no torches or candles. Our clerics and vine binders fill the forest air with energy, causing the fae lights to glow more vibrantly as they dance over the city. It's like the stars are hovering right before your eyes."

"It sounds beautiful. I would love to see it someday."

"Perhaps, next year. When all this is behind us, we can have you and some of your comrades to Faralanthis and…"

"I'm your sister."

Prince Myth'alas' eyebrows went up and his head shifted slightly to the side as he watched her cheeks go as red as roses with shame and embarrassment. Sheepishly, she lowered her gaze.

"I…what I mean is. I'm your half-sister. Our father met my mother in Clay Water one hundred and twenty-five years ago. I have little details about what went on between them, I mean, besides the obvious, or how long it lasted, but…"

"Larissa."

"Yes?"

"I know." He smiled lovingly.

"You– you know? How?"

Myth'alas reached down and took her hand. He lifted it up so the Ring of Concealment on her finger was between them. He then lifted his other hand and showed her his own ring.

"The ring you wear was our father's. The one I wear was my mother's. They had them crafted a very long time ago so they could travel through the human territories in disguise. I knew fathers had been 'lost' some time ago, but I spotted it immediately when we first met.

"I asked Rayann for a little assistance and she informed me of what she discovered. I know it might have been an intrusion without your permission, but I needed to know.

"Your mother gave it to you seventy-two years ago just before she passed, and that likely means our father gave it to her as a gesture when he broke things off. I was satisfied with the revelation and didn't say anything out of respect for your secret."

Larissa stared at him a moment.

"You aren't angry with me?"

"There's nothing between us over such a thing. What is there for me to be angry about?"

"I don't…I don't know. Maybe, that our father had indiscretions with humans? Perhaps you didn't know about that. Or…, or that you didn't know about me. Perhaps because your sister is a half-breed. I…"

Myth'alas lovingly interrupted. "Larissa, I'm not angry with you."

She looked into his stoic face a moment before she smiled with relief. Her eyes welled up and she whispered, "Well, it's good to finally meet you, brother."

"And you as well, little sister."

He stepped forward and gave her a warm, genuine, brotherly hug.

# Chapter 11 – Into Silence

The 4:00am tower bell tolled.

Kali hadn't slept a wink after leaving the festival.

She turned her head and looked out the window. Though it had dimmed since the appearance of the towers, the full moon was bright, casting silver light across the floor. Her mind was going a thousand places at once. Every event of the last few weeks swept through her thoughts in circulating waves with no conclusion.

The inevitable confrontation with Fifth and Piramay was approaching. She could feel it in her bones. Mostly, she felt the Gray Tower pulling at her. The distant call, charming her to fall deep into its sway.

Swinging her feet off the bed, she stood and walked to the wash basin, splashing the cool water on her face before staring into the mirror. Her heart stirred again as the dragon rattled the cage. She felt a frigid, eerie shiver run up her spine as the smell of sulfur filled the room. She watched her reflection as her pupils began to glow and the translucent, shadowy form of a dragon's face slowly surrounded her own.

A gravelly voice laced with power and sultry danger whispered, "*You are not destined for mediocrity, girl. Your potential for greatness is stifled by your unwillingness to embrace the darkness that you keep locked up within you.*"

"Our destiny is what we make it. It's our choices that determine who we are."

The dragon wisped, flickering like the smoke coming off a dying candle.

"*Of course you may say what you wish, but we know you are only hiding from yourself. How long can you do so, child? If you deny who you are, eventually the valve breaks, and your true nature will burst forth on its own.*"

"I am not who I was raised to be. I was clouded and manipulated."

"*The Rage Queen can only encourage an angry heart; she cannot create one. To say so is an insult to God. Speak your self-denial all you wish, but you were born to be exactly what you are.*"

"No. That is *not* who I am."

The dragon laughed.

*"The light may fade, but an eclipse can only last so long. Afterwards, then we shall see..."*

The shadowy face faded as Kali's eyes returned to their crystal blue. She furrowed her brow and reached for her midsection as her stomach tightened.

"God, give me your strength. Aviyana, grant me your guidance."

+++

Commander Rose heard the plunk of the message slot and got up. She went out into the sitting room of her quarters and gathered the morning reports from the basket under the chute. She sighed as she looked at the small scroll with her unbroken wax seal on it. The carrier pigeon had clearly not been guided to the roost of the Northern Command and had returned with the parchment still attached. She was beginning to fear the worst.

"Commander?"

She looked up at the door where the voice had come from and smiled knowing her squire waited and listened to know if she was awake before knocking or speaking.

"You may enter, Larissa."

She walked in and looked at her commander's eyes in concern, noting the exhaustion.

"Couldn't sleep again?"

"I slept, just a bit restless."

Larissa walked to the hearth and swung the tea kettle off the coals. She poured two cups and sat at the table, setting one in front of her commander.

"Is that the scroll you had me send last week?"

"Yes, it came back, again."

"That's twice now. Do you think..."

"I don't want to think about that, Larissa. Nolore said an army had landed in Northrim after it was razed to the ground by those magic users. I am certain that Commander Steelpike is moving to counter the threat. My fear is he's not aware that the coastal cities and Northrim are separate issues. He needs to know but equally important is that I need to know if I should start sending troops north to protect the central territory border. I'm getting daily requests from all our harbors and cities asking for reinforcements and I have no *bloody information* to make plans or decisions upon."

"You've got that little crease in your forehead, which means you are forming a plan anyway. What is it?"

Rose chuckled; her squire knew her all too well.

"Ceridwyn and Kali are able to move around with magic. Rayann clearly has her own method, building those portal devices. I am weighing if we should ask them to send a scouting party all the way north and bring back some information. At minimum that would let us know what's going on."

"They seem eager to assist. There's no harm in asking. If you want my thoughts, I'm sure they will do it."

"Please send runners to them with a request to meet me at noon. Send one to Lady Kellan and summon her as well."

"Of course, Commander Rose."

+++

At precisely noon, the guards outside Commander Rose's office announced the arrival of the wizards. Rose and Larissa stood as they entered along with Olwa, Aeolis, Myth'alas, Lady Kellan, Nolore, and Rajumin. Rose was surprised to see the Silentclaw and bowed her head respectfully.

"Nolore. Rajumin. I did not expect you."

"We were visiting the wizards when the summons arrived. If you don't mind, we would like to listen in. Any information you have discovered about the towers is useful to us."

Rose replied to Nolore. "I have not summoned them regarding the towers; however, you are welcome to stay. It was you who gave us the original information I would like to discuss."

"What information? About Northrim?"

"Yes. I have not been able to reach the Northern Command. You had told us that Nataxia landed an army after those two magic users destroyed the city. I don't know what is going on up there, and I need information in order to deploy my resources where they will be the most effective."

Kali spoke. "Myth'alas and I told you that Riverhorn is the northernmost inhabitable city and when we were there it was being

137

reinforced. The steelguard are building emplacements and fortifying the walls. Obviously, there are still defenders doing what they can."

"Yes, I know that, however, Commander Steelpike is not responding, nor getting my scrolls. It is unusual and has me deeply concerned."

Rajumin stepped forward. "Commander, you need to focus on the towers; that is the real threat."

"I appreciate that, Rajumin, however I am responsible for the defense of the people all the way to the central commands northern border."

"By focusing your efforts on the towers, that is exactly what you would be doing."

"Yes, but I must protect them from any and all invaders. I appreciate your words. I have three towers to the southeast and may have an active army marching on us from the north. These are *both* priorities within my sworn duty."

Rajumin glanced at Nolore but said nothing else.

Rayann could feel the tension rising within Rose. There was no anger or fear, but there was certainly a great deal of confusion and lack of focus. She spoke softly to keep things calm.

"Commander? What have you summoned us here to discuss?"

Rose cleared her throat and picked up the message scroll.

"I have had Larissa send this twice to Last Wall, the command headquarters for the Northern Army. It has returned, undelivered both times. I don't know if that means the Northern Command has advanced to mount a defense, or if the Nethermen have taken advantage and attacked or laid siege to the castle. There has been nothing but silence since the arrival of the Silentclaw and Lady Kellan. I need to send scouts and establish contact with the steelguard and knights in Riverhorn."

Sensing where this was going, Ceridwyn spoke up.

"That would take months. I assume that by asking us here to discuss it your intent is to request we transport them there?"

"That was my hope."

"Traveling by magic is not a delicate or easy affair. It becomes increasingly taxing on the wizard when they transport more than just themselves."

"Admittedly, I know little about how you do what you do. I am asking because I am out of ideas."

Ceridwyn turned to her fellow wizards.

"What do you two think?"

"One of us would obviously have to go to bring everyone back." Rayann's glance shifted from Kali and then back to Ceridwyn. "Being a sun wizard, you are the obvious choice."

Ceridwyn turned to Kali. "What about the ardor channels? Could you use those?"

"Circumstantially, yes, but I need to stay and focus on my work trying to find a way through the tower warding. A reconnaissance patrol would likely take many days, even weeks. That would put me behind on my work to figure out the intricacies of the warding."

With a nod of agreement, Ceridwyn turned and spoke to Commander Rose.

"We will figure something out."

"Thank you."

"How many do you wish to send and when?"

"In the next day or two if that's possible. As for who should go, Lady Kellan is part of the Northern Command, she's the obvious choice. I suggest we send her and her squad so they can give their report."

"Eight is too many."

"Again, exactly why I need your input. I don't know about these sorts of things."

Aeolis inquired. "Lady Kellan, are your soldiers trained for reconnaissance?"

"No, they are sword and pike."

"If I may suggest, then. Elven rangers are the fastest and quietest on Aimsire. Should any scouting or reconnaissance be needed while we are there to gather more information, I could be of assistance. If I go with Lady Kellan instead of her soldiers, it would be less taxing on Ceridwyn. It would also allow me to act as envoy to the Northern Guard so they know that the elves are doing what they can to stand behind them."

"I will go too."

They all turned to Olwa and his face showed his resolve.

"Though I am not commissioned yet, I am in the training to become a ranger. I could help with this mission."

Lady Kellan asked Ceridwyn. "How many can you comfortably transport?"

"Four is reasonable."

"Could you do five?"

"Yes, but that would be the maximum."

"Then, Commander Rose, I would also request that Sergeant Erika Tiliz accompany us. She has been stationed in Northrim for ten years and her reputation precedes her. The additional information about the attack she could provide would also be valuable."

"Approved. See it done."

Lady Rose appealed to Nolore and Rajumin.

"I know you disapprove, so first I want to apologize for not heeding your advice. It simply comes down to this, I must know what is happening in the north."

Rajumin spoke. "Commander, you are a leader, and you must follow your heart. But know that Nolore and I cannot be involved. Our directive is to work on finding a solution to destroy the towers and seal the crack in the sky."

"Thank you, Rajumin. Yes, I understand, and we do appreciate your continued work here, regarding the three towers."

"We have a lot to prepare," Ceridwyn declared. "Rayann, Kali, could you two assist me with mixing components and preparing the spells?"

"Of course, Ceridwyn, I am happy to help."

"As am I."

Suddenly, Rayann could sense the deep stirring of emotions within her cousin.

+++

Erika pressed her question. "We're going back north?"

"Yes. Commander Rose has directed us to connect with the Northern Steelguard in Riverhorn and return any and all information we can provide."

"But…a scouting mission? How do we even know that there are still soldiers in Riverhorn?"

140

"One of the mages, Kali, and the elf prince have already been up there to negotiate with an ally. Apparently, he also has a companion whom they wanted to recruit for the inevitable assault on the towers. They could see the steelguard from the ridges above as they worked to reinforce the defensive perimeter."

"My Lady?"

"Yes?"

"Nothing about this sounds remotely sane. We are not scouts. Why send elven rangers? I'm sorry, I just feel like I need to know more about what this all means,"

"Are you questioning Commander Rose's orders?"

"Of course not, I…"

"Good, because I am the one who requested you go with me, so if you were, you would also be questioning mine."

Kellan turned away to check her equipment.

Erika could hear the quivers in her ladyship's voice.

"My Lady, you know I am with you. Until the end and always. I would never question your orders."

Kellan's shoulders dropped and Erika could hear her sniffle. She walked around so she was facing her knight commander again. There was moisture in her eyes.

"I'm sorry, Erika. I was also hoping…"

"I know, but I think you already know that we aren't going to find him."

"He could still be alive…"

"Kellan."

She looked up at her sergeant who just addressed her as a friend instead of a subordinate.

"I know what you are feeling. I lost two brothers just before I joined the steelguard. Also, I was first sergeant under your brother for five years before you came along. I made a vow to him that I would serve you as loyally."

"And protect me."

Erika laughed. "Yes, Liam asked that I watch over you. I never really saw it as protection, however. You are a capable warrior. I am more of an…experienced guide."

"I know, and I am sorry I snapped at you. I just miss him."

"We both do. Let us honor his memory by doing our duty. Per the commander's orders we will go in the spirit of maintaining peace and protection for those whom we have vowed to defend."

Kellan stared at her a moment before nodding in agreement.

Erika walked over to the corner of the room and picked up the sword that had belonged to Liam. She walked back and handed it to her knight commander.

"Fight in his memory. Avenge him with every measure of your strength."

She hesitated but reached and took her brother's sword.

"I will."

"And I will be right beside you, Lady Kellan."

+++

The laboratory level in the Tower of Kells was spacious and easily accommodated Kali, Ceridwyn, and Rayann. The three worked together, mixing the components Ceridwyn would need to transport the group to the north. They were also mixing enough for her to cast spells while she was there if need be, and what she would require to get them all back safely.

Rayann inquired. "Ceridwyn, are you sure about this? This is a lot, even for you. Five people with all their equipment?"

"Quite sure. If I pace myself, I'll be able to manage. We offered our assistance to Commander Rose when we arrived, and though you're the empath here, even I could feel her struggling."

"There is no fear in her, it's remarkable. She has a steadfastness that is almost inhuman. It's as if she was born with strength and will instead of having developed and learned it over the course of her life."

"What in the crevasse is that supposed to mean?"

Ceridwyn and Rayann turned to look at Kali in shock. Ceridwyn was furrowing her brow at the tone in which Kali spoke, and Rayann suddenly realized that her cousin had been blocking her emotions so they could not be felt.

"Kali? Are you feeling alright?"

Kali looked at her cousin and relaxed her expression.

"I'm...fine."

She set down the herbs she was working on and walked out of the room. Rayann whispered to Ceridwyn.

"She's blocking me."

"Obviously something is wrong. Perhaps she blocks you so that instead she can talk to you. Go, I will be fine with my friend here, the old mortar and pestle."

With a wink, Ceridwyn shooed Rayann out and went back to work.

Rayann walked into the manor and up to her cousin's room. Kali was staring out the window at the meadow where she had first channeled terran magic. The instant Rayann walked in, Kali asked without turning to face her.

"Have you ever felt split? As if you know who you are but there was something else in you fighting it? As if, you were forcing yourself to be who you are instead of just being?"

"I have. When I left Rorie and everything transpired the way it did, I was in agony. When Myth was recovering from his infection and I managed to get a little time to myself in between tending to him, I would sit and think about every single decision I had ever made that led to that point.

"I had no idea where Rorie was. I had no idea that he held such contempt against me. I received no pigeons or scrolls, I'm still not sure why. In all of that I also knew if I left Myth he would likely die. I couldn't travel and leave him. Finally, I thought Rorie was dead because of me. I went through an entire spectrum of emotions and feelings. It was as if everything I thought I was simply was no more."

"I figured that was what you were going to say."

"Kali, what's wrong?"

"The Gray Tower is calling to me. It's been speaking to me in the form of a dragon. I am capable of controlling it, that might be why I'm being courted to bind myself and become its mistress."

"What?" Rayann went pale and instinctually took a step back. "What do you intend to do?"

"What do you mean?"

"What do I mean? The single most malevolent event that has ever happened to Aimsire is calling you to join in? Do you intend to do so?"

"Of course not. I have vowed to fight and destroy the towers. I am working on how we can breach the warding and knock that tower down. Do you doubt me?"

"No, but you just asked if *I* feel split. You implied you are fighting yourself to be who you are. Is this all because..."

"I was once in the service of the Rage Queen?"

"Yes. I mean no. It's complicated to say."

Kali shifted the topic. "Rayann, at any time since our reunion when you have felt my emotions, did you ever sense any malintent within me?"

"It's not that simple. I wouldn't just poke around like I'm in a library. I have sensed anger, and frustration on occasion, but not at a level I would say is more elevated than I have sensed from anyone else or have even experienced myself at times."

"Your eyes tell me that you're speaking the truth."

"I am. I realize your life was utter turbulence the entire time you were growing up. You have shared what it was like being raised in that environment. However, I can't bring myself to believe that Aviyana would have taken you as a wielder of terra if she felt you were evil."

"I never said 'evil'."

Rayann exhaled in frustration. "Fine."

Kali continued, "When Aviyana spoke with me, she said she liked that I was unpredictable and had walked in the darkness."

"That doesn't make sense. She must have meant that as a metaphor."

"There were no metaphors. I was chosen because I know both sides and can maintain a level head when necessary without coming to rash decisions or knee jerk reactions."

"Can't you see it though? Yes, Kali, you have walked in the darkness and now darkness stands in the form of three towers. The occupants of which are bent on the destruction of all we know and love. You are standing in the light by working to end this evil.

"I have listened to you talk to the knights. I have watched you analyze and decipher the information we are getting. You have been levelheaded and systematically figuring out how we are going to knock those blasted things over. I won't give up on you, so don't give up on yourself."

Kali sighed. "I'm not giving up, cousin. But you need to know, it's more comfortable for me to walk in the darkness than in the light. All the insights and revelations of what and why those towers exist are coming to me more easily every day. Ultimately, I'm just trying to solve the greatest mystery these towers have presented so far."

Rayann looked at her with quizzical concern.

"And what mystery would that be?"

"How do I fit in?"

+++

"My Prince. My heart sings to see you."

Olwa bowed his head and placed his hand over his heart, then opened his palm, extending it towards Myth'alas in greeting.

"I wanted to talk to you about this mission. As my adherent, in the future I would like to discuss these sorts of things with you before you volunteer."

"I'm sorry. You are right, I broke protocol and should not have spoken without your approval or permission."

"Olwa, you don't need my permission to speak. If I am to mentor and guide you, we need to talk about missions or training you wish to pursue. In this case especially because I won't be going along."

"Yes, my Prince. Whatever punishment you feel is necessary, I will…"

"Olwa, look at me."

The young ranger looked up and stared into Myth'alas' patient face.

"Do you believe I came to talk to you because you are to be scolded and punished?"

"Yes."

"Well, then let me start by saying that is not why I am here. In the few training sessions we have had, you have shown you are more than capable and smart in your decision making. With this war coming, and with you as my ward, we need to discuss your assignments before you take them on. That's all. You are free to follow whatever path you wish. Additionally, I'm not going to force you to do everything exactly the way I do."

Olwa seemed perplexed that he wasn't being spoken to more sternly. Myth'alas patted him on the shoulder.

"Aeolis is a fantastic ranger. It will be good for you to be under his guidance for this outing. Make sure you listen to him and follow his instructions. Trust him, for he is trustworthy.

"Above all, remember your training and think before you act. This mission is not without risk. After the meeting with Commander Rose, I spoke to Ceridwyn about joining the group, but she was resolute that five was the most she could safely transport. If it wasn't that I knew Aeolis will be a great teacher and guide in my stead, we would be having a different conversation."

"Yes, my Prince. Again, I am sorry. In the moment I recognized there was an opportunity for me to be involved, so I seized it before it passed."

Myth'alas smiled at his adherent.

"I wholeheartedly respect that you saw an opportunity and seized it. May God watch over you."

+++

Lady Kellan had just finished her dinner and gone to her room. She drew her brother's sword from the scabbard and stared at it. The ornate, swirled, forge-welded steel was exquisite, and finely crafted. Runes were etched into the fuller near the cross-guard, and the soft leather of the grip felt good in her hand. This was her family's sword. The blade had been in the Stenberg lineage for so long there was no written record of its origin. Traditionally, it had been handed down to the first of each generation who achieved their knighthood. The sword had been given to Liam; it was never supposed to be hers.

She could still remember attending the ceremony. Her father stood proudly and handed the blade to his son saying, "May this weapon, Falling Sky, aid you in bringing peace and justice to all of Aimsire."

She checked the edge; it was razor sharp. Bringing the blade up so she could stare at it in the lamp light, she whispered, "I will bring you honor as I take up your blade against our enemies, brother. I will not let you down."

There was movement outside her window and she stood. She looked out and found herself staring into the face of Nolore. Instantly, she heard his voice in her head.

*"May I come in?"*

Not knowing how to speak back to his mind, she spoke aloud. "Yes, of course."

She began to step towards the door but suddenly he was in the room, standing behind her. Startled, she swung around, the blade still in her hand. Nolore caught it by the edge as it came up between them. Her eyes went wide as she looked at his hand firmly grasping the steel without even a trace of injury.

"How...?"

"Please sit."

With a smile, he released his grip and gestured.

She sat and he picked up Falling Sky's scabbard before sitting down across from her.

"To what do I owe the honor of this visit, Nolore?" Her voice was shaky.

"I came to offer you a more personal farewell before you depart tomorrow. As you heard, Rajumin and I are forbidden to be involved. However I need to tell you, it's not a safe place you are traveling to. Stay on high alert the entire time you are there."

"Thank you. I admit, this is not the sort of mission I am normally part of, but with Erika and the elves at my side, I am confident we will be successful."

"The Rage Queen's entire army is up there. They will attack on sight and won't offer quarter or mercy should they overtake you. They are not here for prisoners. I wanted to tell Rose personally at the meeting, but as you know, I am forbidden by the High Borne to get involved, even if it's just information."

Swallowing hard, she stared into Nolore's eyes.

"Then we will be as cautious as possible. Thank you for telling me. Will you get in trouble for that?"

"Possibly."

She could see there was more he wished to say, but he remained silent. After a moment, he handed the scabbard to her.

"That is a fine sword. It has served your family and Aimsire well over the course of its life. I am delighted to see it is in the right hands once again."

She felt sadness overtake her, but she kept a brave face.

He spoke again. "May this weapon, Falling Sky, aid you in bringing justice to all of Aimsire."

+++

Ceridwyn was up early and gathered all the scrolls and spell reagents she and her friends had prepared. She placed them in her travel pack and began the short journey to the keep.

As she walked, Aeolis stepped up beside her from the shadows, attempting to startle her.

"Hello there."

She didn't flinch. A flirtatious smile crossed her face which she dared not turn to show him, yet.

"Were you breathing out of your mouth, Chief Ranger Aeolis? I heard you in the shadows before I even left my room. It sounded like a boar grunting and trying to find a mud pit."

"What? Impossible!"

"Aeolis, perhaps it slipped your mind that as an elf I possess sharp ears as well?"

She turned her head, revealing her smile. Happiness sparkled in her eyes and he noted the increasing blush in her cheeks. He gently took her hand as they walked together in silence. His stomach filled with butterflies and his heart stirred as he dug deep to find new courage as their fingers intertwined.

A mission within the mission entered his mind, one that would require more vulnerability towards another than he had ever thought was possible. He resolved himself to take the chance and just as they arrived at the portcullis he released her hand and gently touched her shoulder.

"Ceri."

"Yes?" Her voice was anticipative as she turned to him.

"I just want you to know that no matter what we find out there, protecting *you* is my top priority. Please do not take that the wrong way. You know I am in love with you. When all this is over, my only prayer is to share as many sunsets as possible with you by my side."

It was the most forward he had ever been with her and it didn't go unnoticed. She paused a moment before responding.

"My sweet Aeolis, my heart sings joyfully whenever you are near. That my life should be graced with someone new whom I can cherish and even love is more than I could have ever dared pray for. I understand that you want to protect me, but who among us knows how many our days will be?

"We are fighting for a better world and that fight is dangerous. To perish for a cause as important as this, that could be considered an honorable death. So, we will go, together, and if we die, we die together. But if we live…"

She paused and sighed heavily before pressing her gaze deeper into his eyes and bringing her face closer to his.

"I want to live, with *you*. Knowing there is a glimmer as faint as the smallest star in the sky shines that we might find a path through this? To breathe in the dream of spending the rest of our natural lives together watching sunsets by one another's sides? But mostly by your words to me this morning, my sweet Aeolis, I am filled with more hope than I have felt in a very long time.

"Understand that I still have my doubts regarding God's providence because of my experiences. I admit, I'm scared. However, perhaps I can trust again. I lost so much while believing I was under divine protection, but lately, I can't help but feel a pull in my heart that God is, indeed, watching over us through all of this."

She placed a gentle kiss on his cheek.

"I accept your vow of protection because I know you mean it, and I know you will honor it."

"I will, you have my word."

She stepped close and slipped her arms around him, hugging him tenderly for a moment in the crisp, morning air.

"Who knows what we are going to find up there? We must be cautious and pray we aren't about to step into a hornet's nest. If the Rage Queen's forces are there when we arrive, they will not take kindly to us. Even worse, if they have magic users with them, there is a chance they will sense our arrival immediately and gain the advantage."

"I agree. We will be cautious and we will keep our heads."

+++

The large council chamber of the keep had been cleared. Aeolis and Ceridwyn walked in, the last to arrive. Commander Rose offered a nod in greeting as the two elves entered and turned to the assembled.

"Thank you, again, to all of you. I know that three of you are under no obligation to obey my commands. Your willingness to undergo this mission as volunteers has been duly noted. I appreciate that you are putting yourselves in danger not only for the safety of the citizens of Aimsire, but also for me.

"As for you two," She turned and looked at Lady Kellan and Sergeant Erika before continuing, "Though you are obeying orders it does not in any way take precedence over your willingness to help me gather information. Please know that your wholeheartedly embracing this mission so I may make better decisions has also been written in my report. I cannot express my gratitude enough."

Aeolis bowed his head respectfully. "We understand your need for information. If this is what we can offer to help you focus, then we are happy to do so."

Ceridwyn observed that the ring of reagents had already been prepared. She looked up as Rayann's voice filled her head.

*"You're blushing again, my friend."*

*"Hush. My cheeks are merely pink from the cold."*

*"Then why is your heart racing like a rabbit dashing to avoid a pursuer?"*

Rayann winked as Ceridwyn glared at her playfully.

*"You can tell me all about your tardiness this morning when you return."*

*"Do you think we will return, Rayann?"*

*"You must. Who else is going to help me teach my child about the simple things?"*

*"Then by the light, dear friend and princess, I vow to tell you everything when we return."*

Ceridwyn felt sad, but a sudden confidence filled her thanks to her friend's words. She turned to the assembled.

"As you can see, Rayann and Kali have prepared a ring of reagents to transport us north. Though they are not sun wizards, I have written the spell on these scrolls and taught them the incantation. I assure you they are capable of getting us there safely. By having them send us, I will spend no energy.

"Once we are there and have completed our mission, I will recreate what you are seeing here in order to get us back safely. Hopefully, under peaceful circumstances. Any questions?

The group showed their understanding. Ceridwyn addressed Erika and Kellan directly.

"Have either of you traveled like this before?" Both soldiers shook their heads and Ceridwyn continued, "Well, it's going to be a bit jarring. This is a long distance we are traveling. What would normally take months is about to happen in seconds. Erika, your leather armor will insulate you from the effects, but Kellan, it's going to be worse for you with all that steel you're wearing. The metal is going to act as a conduit."

"Should I take it off?" There was concern in her voice.

"That's up to you, but we don't know what we are transporting into. We may arrive and need to act instantly."

Erika spoke. "I suggest leaving it on, if you are unable to raise your sword arm, I will protect you, my Lady."

Ceridwyn gestured to the circle.

"Please place your packs on the ground beside you. Kneel and have your weapons directly in front of you where you can grab them immediately if necessary."

The group followed Ceridwyn's instructions.

Kali turned to Commander Rose, Larissa, Myth'alas, and the two guards who would be watching the door.

"We need you to exit the room. Rayann and I require full focus and concentration. Do not allow anyone in. One mistake and we will send them off to who knows where, or worse, kill them. Commander Rose, you will need to leave this room in its current state. The magic trace by which we send them will imprint on Ceridwyn and allow her to follow the path back. This ensures they will arrive right here."

"Understood. I will station guards to make sure nothing is disturbed. I will also assign a runner to come get me the instant they are back."

Commander Rose addressed the party as they took their positions.

"May God protect you and Dionadair guide you. I will be praying for your safe return."

As the door closed Kali returned to the circle and looked across at Rayann. She then looked at Ceridwyn who nodded that the group was ready.

Kali and Rayann lifted their hands. The scrolls Ceridwyn had written and infused with sun magic hovered before their faces and both began to speak the ancient words of magic in unison.

To Kellan and Erika, their sounds resembled the hissing of snakes. The words they uttered were strange, foreign, and beyond any reasonable comprehension.

Together, the wizard's hands moved in mirrored, rhythmic patterns and their voices began to elevate in volume.

Kellan could feel the air around them beginning to vibrate as Shakyna swirled at the wizard's commands. She looked down at the crisscrossed swords on the floor in front of her. Liam's blade ready to be grasped by her dominant left hand, her own blade prepared for her right. Closing her eyes, she thought about Nolore's words.

Everything blurred together. Her thoughts, the smell of burning herbs whipping around the room, the strange words uttered by the wizards. She began to feel dizzy.

A sudden, vibrant flash of light which Kellan perceived through her closed eyelids caused her to squint. Air whistled all around her as if she was caught inside a blacksmith's bellows. She dared not look to confirm. Her ears rang louder and louder for several seconds until suddenly, there was only silence and cold.

She was laying on her stomach and barely felt the snow against her cheek before the world went dark.

# Chapter 12 – Shivers in the North

Kali fell to her knees as the spell sent the party north. She felt lightheaded and focused on slowing her breathing. Her clammy palms pressed against the cold stone floor as the pungent odor of the burnt, crackling reagents filled her nostrils. With exhaustion woven into her words she spoke to Rayann.

"How on Aimsire is Ceridwyn going to channel that much magic and bring them back by herself?"

Hearing no answer, she looked up. Rayann was curled into a ball, clutching her stomach.

Kali immediately got to her feet and ran around the circle. She grabbed her unconscious cousin and yelled, "Myth'alas, come, quick!"

He went for the door. One of the guards managed to grab him, doing his best to follow Commander Rose's orders that none were to enter. The soldier was knocked flat with a single, sharp jab to the chin.

The latch shattered as Myth'alas kicked the door open. In an instant, he was at his wife's side.

"What happened?"

"I don't know. We finished the spell; it was far more taxing than I could have ever imagined. I looked up after catching my breath and this is how she was."

With no effort, Myth'alas scooped up his pregnant wife and carried her to their quarters. Kali was right behind him. Rose and Larissa followed but stopped when the door was closed before they could enter the room. Larissa's eyes went wide with surprise as she turned to her commander.

"It's fine. Please stay here and report back to me after you know how she is. I will be in my quarters."

Rose turned and quickly made her way back to the meeting chamber. Several guards had come at the sound of the commotion and were at the door. Two were helping the guard Myth'alas had struck get back to his feet. She looked at him with sympathy as she removed a linen cloth from her pocket and dabbed at the blood on his face.

"Thank you for following my orders. Unfortunately, I couldn't anticipate they would get in the way of a husband who was focused on protecting his wife. Go get yourself checked out and then take the remainder of the day off to rest. Report directly to me in the morning and let me know your condition."

She turned to the sergeant.

"Please have a smitty brought and get that lock repaired. The rest of you stay here until you are relieved. Nobody enters this room until the party returns, not even me. I want nothing in there disturbed."

She made her way up the spiral stairs to her quarters and locked the door behind her. Now that she knew she was alone, Commander Rose exhaled the tension and fear she was feeling. She looked at herself in the mirror and began to cry for the first time in a long time. Had she just made a huge mistake?

+++

Ceridwyn inhaled the fresh, cool, northern air before opening her eyes and glancing around. Aeolis and Olwa were inside the tree line of a small clearing. Erika, Lady Kellan and herself were outside the trees in the open. They were kneeling in approximately half a meter of snow.

The party had landed much further spread out than their formation when they left. She felt concern knowing this was a bad sign in terms of where the spell had brought them. She observed Erika who had moved from her position and was now kneeling beside a groggy Lady Kellan. The young knight's face was green with nausea.

She turned and caught Aeolis' eyes. He offered a silent gesture that he and Olwa were well. She smiled lovingly and gave a signal that she was moving to speak with their human companions.

"She'll be okay, just takes a bit for the effects to wear off." Kellan's words came out slurred and slow.

"Tha' was'h lot worsh than I though' it wa' gonna be."

"I am sorry. It can take hundreds of years to get used to it."

Erika quipped. "Well, unfortunately we don't have that kind of time."

Ceridwyn spoke sympathetically.

"Lady Kellan, I knew that coming such a great distance might be…"

Kellan bent over and heaved the contents of her stomach into the snow. Ceridwyn handed her a small vile.

"Here, drink this; it will settle your stomach."

Without questioning the wizard, she drank the contents. Her lips twisted at the taste, but the color immediately began returning to her face.

"Are you okay, my Ladyship?"

"Yes, Erika. Thank you." She turned and looked at Ceridwyn, handing her the empty vile. "And thank you…for whatever this was."

Ceridwyn placed her hand on the young knight's shoulder.

"We will move out as soon as your stomach is settled, but please, take your time."

She made her way to Aeolis. Erika was fascinated that she couldn't hear Ceridwyn's footsteps on the crunchy snow. It was like she was floating.

They spoke barely above whispers as soon as they were side by side.

"How is Lady Kellan?"

"Queasy, but she'll be fine. I gave her some tonic."

"Good."

She glanced around the treetops. "The air is eerily calm."

"I sense it too. When would you like to move out?"

"As soon as Lady Kellan is ready. Aeolis, something went wrong. We are not where we intended to be. I only have enough reagents to create one circle and don't want to do anything until we know for sure where we are and if our arrival was detected."

He nodded in understanding. The humans had gathered their gear and began making their way over. Ceridwyn turned as their companions arrived.

"Do you recognize where we are?"

Erika answered. "That spine of rock is Shatter Stone Ridge. It runs for hundreds of kilometers from north to south. Unfortunately, we are on the eastern side. We should be much further west than we are."

Hearing her response, Kellan became more aware of their surroundings.

"Wait, this is Mistwood Forest. We are closer to Northrim than we are to Riverhorn." She turned to Ceridwyn. "How did we land so far northeast of our destination?"

"A simple miscalculation? Perhaps the spell was chanted incorrectly? The dimming of the sun and moon altering the pathways? The distance we traveled? The amount of metal we brought? There are far too many variables at play, it's hard to say for sure.

"We all knew this was a risky venture from the outset and we transported blindly. I have never been here and therefore had no frame of reference as to where we should touch down. I did my best to craft the spell and follow the path described to me. At least we are all in one piece."

Kellan pulled out her compass and map to acquire more accurate bearings.

"Based on my map, we are almost due east of Pearlport Keep. We should head northwest, towards the western side of Northrim Bay. The trade routes between Northrim and Pearlpoint closely follow the coastline. Once we are on the main road, we can go west over Pearlpoint Pass."

"I don't think it's a good idea to take the main road. It would be better for us to stick to the cover of the forests."

Kellan responded. "I don't disagree, but there are farms along the road. We might be able to acquire horses so we don't spend all our energy tromping through the snow. It would also do us well to warn the residents to get south if the armies haven't advanced this far yet. I am a Knight of Aimsire, they will trust me.

"Additionally, Shatter Stone is formidable and can only be safely crossed in a few places. Pearlpoint Pass is the best option given our location. We know those mages attacked Pearlpoint Keep, but maybe we can search for food and resupply. At minimum it gets us over the pass and onto the western side of the ridge where we need to be."

The elves agreed and they moved out. After a few hours of slow walking, the party approached the road. Aeolis gave a gesture for them to stop as he and Olwa scouted ahead. After a brief recon of the area, the two rangers returned.

"The road is undisturbed. No army has been through here."

"That's good," Kellan concurred. "At least we know they are still north of us. If we cross the Shatter Stone and make a hard push, we could probably be to Pearl Point in two days, well, if we can acquire some horses."

"And if we can't?"

"Given this snow, four to five days at best."

"My Lady, though it is the wrong direction we intend to travel, Raven Summit is just a few kilometers northeast of here. It's the last village before the pass and as you know a trade hub. There is a family I know who own a large farm on this side of town. They are friendly and it is a large place. I am sure they would have horses we could purchase."

"Perfect. Let's head there, get warm, and hopefully get mounts."

The salted base of the main road made the snow less deep. The group got onto the pathway and began heading towards the farm. Aeolis was in front, several hundred meters ahead of them, scouting as they advanced. He spoke on the winds to Olwa and Ceridwyn every few minutes to give them updates.

As they continued, Ceridwyn glanced at Lady Kellan. All she knew of the young knight's past was that she was once stationed here and that her brother had died during the razing of Northrim Keep. Hurrying her pace, she came up alongside her.

Kellan turned to look at Ceridwyn. She was fighting back fear and sorrow, it was obvious. With a soft, sympathetic smile, Ceridwyn reached and squeezed her on the forearm, silently communicating that she understood.

Aeolis spotted a large farmhouse on top of a high, snowy hill and stopped. The hillsides all around the property were terraced and clearly used for growing crops. This place looked just like what Erika had described. He called for all to advance.

He whispered to Erika. "Is that the place?"

"Yes, but there's no smoke coming from the chimney, that's never a good sign."

Aeolis agreed. "I suggest we get into the trees and make our way under the cover of the forest. It will be slower, but until we know if the house is inhabited, we shouldn't take any chances."

The thinned out trees along the road didn't offer much concealment. The rangers led the group deeper into the timber until

Aeolis was comfortable with the better cover they now had. He took point. Erika took second position, followed by Ceridwyn, Lady Kellan, and Olwa covering the rear. They spread themselves out in a wedged line and began to make their way.

Suddenly, all three elves stopped and squatted low, gesturing for their human companions to do the same. Ceridwyn saw the armored figures through the trees right after Aeolis had and she spoke directly to the two humans' minds.

*"Four scouts walking towards us. They are approximately twelve hundred meters away."*

Erika nodded that she understood and turned towards Kellan who returned the gesture. The two humans took defensive positions, watching in the direction Ceridwyn was looking.

Olwa moved along the far side of the group and got even with Aeolis. The two rangers looked at one another to confirm location and then slid into the shadows of the trees. They covered the widest gap between their companions and the patrol creating a kill zone should it be required.

Olwa spoke to Aeolis on the winds. *"They are moving again, meandering more than patrolling."*

*"They aren't paying much attention to their surroundings either. Clearly, they don't expect to find anything."*

The group of four men stopped. One of them leaned his war hammer against a tree and blew into his hands before opening his trousers to urinate an image into the snow. Their laughter carried across the landscape.

Olwa spoke to Aeolis' mind once again. *"I don't know the rankings of the Rage Queen's armies, but the one who put his weapon down has five stripes on his left pauldron. The one to his right has two; the other's each have one. Easy to assume who's in charge."*

Aeolis focused on the man. He was large, gruff, and his jovial laughter didn't match the scars and jagged tattooing on his face. Clearly, he knew how to make war. The four men began to move again, zigzagging quietly as they spread out.

It seemed like hours as the squad kept approaching. They were only two hundred meters away from Aeolis and Olwa now. Suddenly, the soldiers looked to their left and stood at attention. A heavily armored reptilian approached, moving through the snow with ease. She towered over the largest of them and a large sword was strapped to her back. She approached the scouts with purpose. The man in charge saluted. She spoke harshly without returning the gesture and pointed back towards the farmhouse.

Ceridwyn watched as the reptilian reprimanded them. She felt a flickering gust of wind behind her and looked down. A crisp leaf passed by her, tumbling gently across the snow. Her stomach knotted up as she shifted her gaze cautiously towards the patrol. It only took seconds before the reptilian's tongue flicked and her head snapped in their direction as she growled.

"Elf!"

Drawing her weapon, she hissed orders at the four humans. They spread out quickly and began to walk, this time, with dangerous purpose. Ceridwyn sank low, hoping the white cloak she was wearing would provide enough camouflage against the snow. She reached into her robes, removed a lodestone and tucked it into her belt socket. Next, she removed a handful of spell reagents to have them at the ready.

Aeolis spoke to Ceridwyn on the winds.

*"They are coming straight for you. We are going to have to shoot them."*

*"Patience, Aeolis."*

This was not the first time she had been in a precarious situation and refused to panic. She glanced at Olwa, he was perched on a branch, his bow up and ready.

Erika anxiously remained tucked behind a large boulder; she couldn't see anything from her position except Ceridwyn.

The reptilian's tongue flicked systematically, searching in earnest for a second dose of scent.

Erika watched Ceridwyn. She knew that wizards were powerful, but with her armor and spear, so was she. Ceridwyn glanced at her and Erika gave a slow, purposeful nod. Ceridwyn was about to send her a missive, but Erika stepped out from behind the rocks and whistled.

All four men and the reptilian charged. The two on the edges fell simultaneously as Olwa and Aeolis fired in unison. The reptilian halted and followed the trajectory of Olwa's arrow. She immediately identified his silhouette in the trees and charged the young ranger. Her shrill roar split the air and the sound of horns far off in the distance began to ring out in response.

Olwa fired another arrow. The reptilian easily dodged and came towards him with blinding speed. Leaving her feet she swung the massive two-handed sword. Olwa sidestepped the blow that would have severed his leg, moving towards the trunk of the tree. The branch where he had been standing broke free, cut clean. Olwa shadowskipped with graceful precision to another branch in a nearby tree. He was higher up now and trying to find an advantage.

The reptilian landed in the snow and spun. Olwa's next arrow hit the creature's chest armor dead center and shattered, harmlessly falling to splinters. The serrated broadhead barely made a scratch in the hard alloy. The reptilian leapt into the air, cocking her sword back like a gnomish spring. Using her left foot, she accelerated her momentum by pushing off a thick branch and closed the distance between her and her opponent.

Olwa spun, unsheathed his sword, and deflected the blow. Never had he felt an impact with such power and he barely maintained his balance. The reptilian clawed the trunk of the tree as her blow glanced off Olwa's sword. She swung her body all the way around the trunk and landed nimbly on the branch, facing him. Her clawed feet gripped, etching jagged lines into the bark.

Aeolis spoke on the winds to the entire group.

*"Whoever else is with them, they have all been alerted!"*

Ceridwyn looked at Aeolis. He was drawing another arrow after sending his missive. The feathers brushed his cheek and he fired. A lone soldier, several hundred meters away, had just crested a nearby hill. He fell into the snow as Aeolis' arrow streaked out of the sky and hit him directly in the neck.

Aeolis turned as he heard steel hit steel. Erika was fighting the two men; her double-bladed spear whirled, simultaneously deflecting blows while striking at her opponents. Lady Kellan was running to assist. He spoke to Ceridwyn.

*"Start making that circle. We need to get out of here."*

Erika moved with the formidable precision and accuracy that her years of training had provided. She had killed one of the men and Kellan arrived just as Erika cut the patrol sergeant down. The young knight's face showed her anger as she grabbed Erika by the arm and shook her.

160

"Don't you ever do that again!"

"What would you have me do, my Lady? Let them walk right on top of Ceridwyn? They were heading straight for her. She was a sitting duck."

"She had it under control. You put yourself at unnecessary risk."

"They are dead, Lady Kellan, I'm alive. You are my commander, but don't talk to me like…"

Three blasts of a war horn split the air. They looked towards the top of the distant hill; a dozen men and two reptilians had crested and were making their way towards them.

Kellan let go of Erika. "You are my Sergeant. I need you. Don't risk yourself like that. We fight together, and we use our heads."

Erika was angry, but she let it go. Together they turned and ran towards Ceridwyn.

Erika asserted. "We will hold them off. You need to get us out of here."

"I need time. Do what you can to keep them at bay."

"Fall back and prepare your magic. We can handle this lot."

Lady Kellan and Erika turned, running as fast as they could straight up the middle of the clearing towards the oncoming threat.

Olwa backed up as the reptilian inched closer.

"Pretty little pup, aren't you? Not even a scratch on that fancy armor."

The reptilian's tongue flicked as Olwa defiantly narrowed his eyes.

Her massive sword came at him again; he dropped his blade and jumped backwards drawing his bowstring and fired. He landed gently on his back, the impact cushioned by the deep snow. The arrow caught the reptilian in the soft underside of her chin. The beast slumped forward, bounced off a branch, and her lifeless body tumbled to the ground beside him.

Olwa exhaled gruffly as he heard Aeolis' missive about the enemy being alerted. The large group was getting closer. Two of those advancing were already on the ground thanks to Aeolis' arrows and Olwa added a third with a quick shot before recovering his sword and shadowskipping to a new position.

Now that the attention was off her, Ceridwyn bounded across the snow like a deer fleeing predators. She needed to put a little more distance between herself and the melee so she could work. She heard the horns again and the rallying cries of soldiers echoed across the valley. She heard steel ricochet off steel as her companions covered her retreat.

She thought to herself. *"Just what we needed, a whole army of bored soldiers who suddenly have something to kill."*

Suddenly an arrow passed through one of the spell bags hanging from her waist. It never hit flesh but the sound of fabric tearing and the instant sparkle of spell powder illuminating the air caused her to miss a step. She hit the snow with a heavy thud and slid to a stop. She looked up to her right; five soldiers were coming from a small gap in the trees. One was reloading his bow while the other four charged, their eyes reflecting their thirst for blood.

She threw the handful of reagents she was still holding towards them and hissed. Shakyna swirled and the snow around her twisted like a dust devil. The four soldiers hit the ground, instantly succumbing to her sleep spell. The archer watched his companions fall and became enraged. Ceridwyn had just revealed that she was a wizard.

The man hastily let his arrow fly. It was an errant shot that she didn't even need to avoid. She got to her feet and began to sprint again, taking cover behind an enormous, fallen oak that was nearly twice as tall as she was standing at full height. Another arrow whizzed over the log. She spoke on the winds to her companions.

*"There are soldiers back here too. I have an archer who is firing at me, once I have him handled I will...by the light, frost troll coming up on us from the rear!"*

Aeolis turned and saw the massive creature smash through the trees. He didn't have a clear shot and was about to move towards Ceridwyn and clear his angle when he heard a loud clash of metal. One reptilian was slumping over, dead. The other had just swung its tail and knocked Kellan back with a blow to her chest. Erika was closing, but the beast was going to deliver the death blow before she would arrive. Aeolis drew and fired. The arrow penetrated right behind the eye, and the reptilian collapsed under his own weight.

Aeolis yelled to the group.

"We must fall back towards Ceridwyn and protect her!"

Olwa fired and struck a soldier in the center of his chest just as more began advancing from the valley. He did as Aeolis commanded and began retreating.

Ceridwyn could hear the human approaching and the frost troll was heading straight for her, unencumbered by the snow. Her ears twitched as she listened. The archer was advancing cautiously. She watched the troll, he raised his massive club over his head, taking aim to deliver the blow. Just as he started to swing, Ceridwyn drew power from the lodestone, lifted her hand and hissed words of magic.

A blazing light shot from her palm and blinded him. He howled as he swung. She dashed between the troll's legs and the club hammered the fallen oak, right where she had been. The log shattered and split, opening a gap. The concussion from the impact knocked the archer back. She spun and cast another spell, increasing her strength as a beam of light wrapped around the man's chest.

Using the power provided by her magic she yanked as if pulling a rope and threw him into the troll. The blind, enraged creature, unaware of who or what just hit him, grabbed the soldier, and tore him in half.

Ceridwyn gathered Shakyna and pulled energy from the lodestone. She thrust her hands and smashed the troll in the back with an inertia spell that knocked him forward into the snow. His head bounced off the log and he was out cold.

*"Make your way back towards the troll, I am forming the circle. It's only unconscious, so be on alert."*

The group was systematically withdrawing. Along the perimeter, Aeolis and Olwa would move to the rear side, fire their arrows long enough for Kellan and Erika to move back, and then repeat the cycle. The soldiers in Nataxia's army continued to appear from seemingly nowhere.

Knight and sergeant fought as one, side-by-side. Their arms screamed at them as they pushed their muscles to the limit, cutting down anything that got within range. Arrows whizzed through the air, as the elves on their perimeter continued to pick off the advancing enemy.

Suddenly Aeolis came up alongside them. His bow was on his back, and he was holding his swords. Erika saw that his quiver was empty.

It was only a few seconds until Olwa was with them as well. His sword and dagger held proper in his hands, the four of them continued to fight and retreat as fast as they could.

Ceridwyn had the reagents spread on the ground. She withdrew the scroll from her belt and began to unroll it. The snap of a branch caught her attention and she looked up. A boleadoras was tumbling end-over-end through the air, heading straight towards her. She gasped and leaned back to dodge. The leather cord hit her just above the wrist and the two lead balls wrapped tightly. The heavy ends smashed into her forearms just below the elbows, instantly bruising her to the bone. She wailed in pain and dropped the scroll.

It was a futile struggle to untangle herself, the leather held tight, binding her arms. The soldier withdrew his sword and charged, confident that he had trapped her. Unable to wave her hands and cast a more powerful spell, she removed a vial filled with healing serum from her chest sash and flung it towards him. She hissed the words of a simple cantrip, instantly boiling the potion within.

The vial exploded as the pressure built, sending shards of glass and molten, viscous liquid into his face. He screamed and dropped his blade clutching his shredded eyes. The sword slid in the snow, stopping near her feet. She went to her knees and used the edge of the blade to cut herself free.

Ignoring the incapacitated soldier, Ceridwyn picked up her scroll. With a quick glance she saw that her companions were getting closer.

*"I am going to start the spell. Keep fighting and hold them off until I tell you to enter the circle."*

The scroll she had prepared in Hailen Glen obediently hovered before her face and she stared at the powerful words. Her strength was utterly consumed and her arms throbbed, but she began to speak the ancient words. As her body became the conduit, Shakyna swirled as she drew on the power of the sun. The burn of so much energy passing through her was excruciating, however, she was their only hope to escape. Deep down, she knew this could kill her, but better for one to die, then all.

Far to the north more soldiers continued to appear, advancing like angry dogs in the now trodden snow. The four had managed to thin out those around them enough that they could turn and start running.

Kellan yelled. "Keep going, I can cover the rear. Get to Ceridwyn."

Erika, Aeolis, and Olwa ran towards the unconscious troll. Aeolis picked up the quiver of arrows dropped by the dead archer, handed half to Olwa, and the two climbed on top of the fallen oak. They began to systematically pick off the faster soldiers that were closing in. Erika ferociously cut down the helpless blind soldier and then turned, staring through the gap in the oak log. Slowed by her heavy armor and exhaustion, Kellan was still well behind them. She began to go to her, but Aeolis screamed.

"No, we will cover her. Get to the circle, protect Ceri."

Erika felt hesitation, but knew he was right. They could keep Kellan covered from a distance. She turned and saw a soldier advancing on Ceridwyn from the tree line. Her spear became a blur as she engaged her enemy. His head was on the ground within seconds. She looked back at the two rangers. They were on the ground now that Kellan was closer, continuing to fire through the gap. Their arrows whizzed past the young knight, some missing by mere centimeters before striking her pursuers.

Ceridwyn's exhausted voice entered their minds.

*"Everyone...get in the circle..."*

Erika looked at the wizard as she stepped over the reagents. Her eyes were blazing like fire and the spell components began to burn themselves into the snow. Aeolis and Olwa entered next, firing their last arrows. Kellan sheathed her family sword and began to sprint as fast as she could. She was nearly there.

Ceridwyn heard Kellan's heavy footsteps and glanced, speaking to her mind.

*"Six more seconds...keep running..."*

The timing was perfect. She shifted her gaze back to the scroll. The letterforms dissolved with every utterance, manifesting the power locked within them. Knowing Kellan was going to make it, she assimilated the remaining power of the sun she had drawn into the spell. She could feel her spine compressing under the pressure.

The clang and crunch of the heavy mace caving in the side Kellan's plate armor echoed in Ceridwyn's ears. She turned wide eyed just as the spell successfully consummated.

Kellan stumbled and hit the ground. Blood instantly splattered her lips as her armor tore into her side and her lungs were pierced. The light flared and the smell of burnt reagents filled the air. Kellan slid in the snow. Her outstretched fingers stopped just outside the edge of the smoldering, smokey ring.

Her companions were gone. The physical pain of her injury and the fear of her circumstance slammed her simultaneously.

The soldier who flung his mace in a desperate attempt to stop her arrived first and violently flipped her onto her back. She gasped involuntarily and her eyes went wide as the mangled, jagged armor ripped deeper into her shattered ribs. He lifted her by the front of her breastplate, revealing the blood-soaked snow beneath her.

"Looks like we get ourselves a little blonde prize in the end, lads!"

He drew his dagger and looked into Kellan's eyes as a detestable smile crossed his face. Slowly he brought the blade up and placed the cold steel against her neck.

Suddenly, the sky went dark and the snow swirled all around them. Kellan heard wind as violent as a storm coming off the northern seas. The man's head lifted from his body, tumbling through the air. A massive impact caused the ground to shudder like the tremors of an earthquake. Dazzling shimmers glistened above her. Her vision was getting blurry, but she reached for the beautiful flashes of pearlescent light. Warmth radiated back, just beyond her fingertips.

Fire engulfed the area. The screams of dying, burning men and the hiss of melting snow temporarily pulled Kellan out of her daze. Every breath she took hurt worse than the last. The roar like a forge came again. More screams and hissing snow as steam and the smell of burnt flesh filled the air. She lifted her chin and saw the glistening scales along the underside of the dragon's neck flex and ripple as the flames erupted from the glands within its maw.

166

It took mere seconds to eradicate the danger all around her. The dragon stepped aside so he was no longer standing in protection over her. His face came close and the warmth of his breath caressed her cheeks.

"Hang on, Kellan."

Gently wrapping his front claws around her, Nolore vaulted into the air, lifting Kellan with him. The massive thump of his wings caused the trees beneath them to shutter so violently that all the snow was removed from their branches. The two of them lifted into the sky.

Nidhug observed all from the farmhouse on the hilltop. His eyes traced the flight path of the ascending dragon, watching Nolore's silver, glistening scales until they were out of sight. He turned to Rezren.

"So, the Silentclaw reveal their true selves once again. I must return and report to the Rage Queen. She will be interested to hear this information from me personally."

# Chapter 13 – Languishing Souls

Erika dove and reached for Kellan; her body did not land in the snow but instead on the cold stones of the chamber floor.

"My Lady!"

She screamed in anger and stood, rounding on Ceridwyn with her fists clenched.

"Take us back! Now!"

Ceridwyn's eyes rolled up into her head and she collapsed. Erika reached for her but Aeolis grabbed her arm and spun her around so they were face-to-face.

"How? How do we go back, Erika? Look at her!"

He knelt and cupped Ceridwyn's cheek in his hand. She was cold, sweaty, and pale. Her labored wheezing was disturbing to his ears as he spoke with insistence.

"Olwa, go inform Prince Myth'alas."

The door opened and the four guards entered. The corporal immediately turned to the runner.

"Summon Commander Rose."

Olwa brushed by them in haste and the runner disappeared up the stairs.

Aeolis picked up Ceridwyn and stood, looking at one of the guards. His face was filled with stone cold determination to take care of her.

"Take me to the infirmary."

The soldier immediately complied and led the way.

Erika investigated the circle where Kellan would have been. Two drops of her blood were all that had been brought back. The sound of the war hammer impacting her knight commander still rang in her ears. She fell to her knees and beat her fists on the stone, crying out in anguish.

+++

Nolore felt Kellan's warm blood dripping down his claws. He spoke to her mind, *"Hang on, Kellan. Don't give up on me."*

In a brilliant flash, he was instantly high above the Vale of Ghosts. He dipped his wing, and made a wide arc, beckoning the dragons below as he rapidly approached the ground.

"Summon Rajumin!"

He landed and took his humanoid form. Not knowing why Nolore brought a human to their vale once again, many of the Silentclaw did the same to hide their true selves.

After unbuckling Kellan's armor, he gently removed the breastplate before tossing it aside. Kellan weakly looked up at him. He could see she was fighting death.

"Stay with me, Kellan. Help is coming."

She attempted to speak, but nothing more than a soft gurgle escaped her blue lips. Her head turned lazily to the side as the light of life left her eyes. Her hand fell limp to the ground, and Nolore exhaled heavily in anguish.

A moment later, Rajumin arrived. Nolore could feel her presence behind him as he whispered, "It's too late. She's gone."

"Yes, Nol, she has left this life." Rajumin knelt beside him. "It will only be by God's grace that she returns to us. I will proclaim petitions on her behalf."

Rajumin looked at the gash exposing Kellan's ribs, it was massive. How she managed to hang on with such an injury was a testimony to her strength and will to live.

Nolore stared at Kellan's blood speckled cheeks and gritty forehead. Sadness and anger began to well up inside him. His cousin felt his pain. She placed her hands on the knight's breastbone above the heart and closed her eyes.

"God above all gods, since the Dawn Light, you have charged those of us that follow the guidance of your servant Ameliara to walk as the embodiment of your divine, healing light. You have instructed us to go into the world, to heal, cure, and ease the load of all your children. I ask if this be within your mercy and will, may this Lady Knight walk further in her life. If the light of life you put within her was snuffed out earlier than your will desires, I beseech you. Please restore her broken body and return her soul before it is consigned to the Crevasse."

Nol clutched Kellan's left hand and watched her face as Rajumin prayed. There was a flash under Rajumin's palm and a soft, restorative glow of green light emerged. The glow was steady at first but then began to pulse like a heartbeat before wrapping itself around the young human.

Kellan's fingers twitched and he watched the gaping wound in her side close itself up, replaced with new flesh and without a scar. His eyes went wide as she reached up. Her right hand grasped for his tunic and her fingers closed around the soft silk.

Softly and steadily, she began to breathe again.

+++

Trystan hastily entered the infirmary. He saw Aeolis huddled over Ceridwyn. Her breathing was labored, and her skin lily white.

Commander Rose entered a few seconds after. She glanced around the room and spoke.

"Where are Erika and Kellan?"

"Lady Kellan is dead."

Rose turned and looked at Erika who had answered the question as she entered the room.

"What?!"

"She's dead, thanks to that wizard there." Her words were filled with malice and she pointed aggressively.

Aeolis stood angrily and glared at Erika. His hands balled into fists.

"What did you just say?"

"We fought for Ceridwyn, Lady Kellan hardest of us all. You assured us that if we protected her, she would bring us back. We did all that was asked of us under the lie of protection."

"How dare you. We promised no such thing. You are a seasoned soldier, there is no assurance in combat, you know this. Given the size of the force that came down upon us, it's a miracle any of us made it back."

Rose stepped between them.

"Erika, go get yourself checked by the surgeons and then get some rest. Report to me tomorrow morning."

Erika glared at Aeolis over Commander Rose's shoulder before she exited the room. Prince Myth'alas passed her in the doorway and watched her go before turning to Commander Rose.

"Olwa informed me. I am sorry, Commander."

Rose exhaled softly and turned to Aeolis.

"What happened, exactly?"

"We arrived northeast of our intended location and on the wrong side of the Shatter Stone Ridge in Mistwood Forest. Collectively, we agreed to move north and attempt to acquire mounts. Once secured, we planned to cross Pearlpoint Pass and travel to Riverhorn. When we reached the main road that moves along the coast, we noted that the snow was undisturbed and there were no signs that any sizable group had moved through the area. We concluded that meant the army had not made it that far south. Erika knew of a farm northeast of our location just outside of Raven Summit."

"Yes, I know that trade hub."

"As we approached the farm we made contact with Nataxia's army. I assumed it was a forward scouting unit of some type at first, but then the whole Crevasse broke loose."

Rose turned to Larissa. "Make three copies of all you just heard and send our three fastest carrier pigeons to Riverhorn. They may or may not make it, but I need to at least try and warn them."

"Aye, Commander."

Rose looked at Ceridwyn. The elf always had a fragility about her, but lying there, still and unconscious, she looked like she would shatter if touched. She shifted her glance to Aeolis.

"Please keep me informed of her condition."

Lady Rose turned and left the room.

After she left, Myth'alas inquired.

"Is there anything else?"

"Kellan was mere steps from the circle when she was struck by a two-handed war hammer. It knocked her to the ground and I assure you my Prince, no soldier was close enough to swing it. It was clearly hurled at her. She was instantly bleeding heavily but alive when we transported. All I can say for certain is her fate was sealed. If the injury didn't kill her, and it certainly would have, the soldiers that were advancing likely finished her."

Myth'alas stayed silent, and Aeolis continued.

"My Prince, I must add, there were reptilians with them. We killed three, but, if they had those…"

"Then they are all there. Nataxia has been working for ages to release them. Nidhug and Rezren were the only two that she was able to rescue and escape with during the banishment."

Aeolis nodded in agreement before he spoke again.

"If I may ask, is Rayann in the keep? Can you summon her? I would like to request that she reach into Ceridwyn's mind. I need to know what she is thinking, if she's still…with us."

"Rayann is not available. I'm sorry."

"I see. She is back at the Glen?"

"No, Aeolis, she is in labor."

+++

"He is beautiful."

Kali smiled at her second cousin, pressing her lips gently against his forehead.

Rayann looked down at the swaddled child lying peacefully on her chest and brushed some of his thick auburn hair away from his face.

"He has his father's bright green eyes. You'll see when he wakes."

"What did you name him?"

"Braeren. It means 'inspired' in the elven language."

"Inspired. That's a beautiful sentiment. I am so glad that everything with him was okay. I was scared when I saw you lying on the floor."

"The midwife said he is perfectly healthy and just…how did she put it? 'Jolted out of me.' There were no signs of trauma or injury, and even though he arrived a little earlier than nature intended, he has all his little fingers and toes."

Kali lovingly stroked his hair and smiled. "That is certainly good to hear."

"Cousin, has there been any news about Ceridwyn?"

"She is still in the infirmary; the healers have no answers. Raspberry went and played for her last night, but she did not stir. Aeolis still hasn't left her side and refuses food or drink."

"I see."

Myth'alas entered and immediately walked over to his wife, kissing her gently on the forehead and then did the same to his son.

"How are you feeling today, my beloved?"

172

"Happy it's over. I just wish I could go visit Ceridwyn. It is sad that such a tragedy had to occur at the same time this little miracle was brought into our lives."

Myth'alas exhaled softly. "Well, the worst of it may not be over. I need to go to Faralanthis and give word to my brother of what is happening, including that a new prince has been born."

Kali inquired. "How is he going to take it?"

Knowing her question had nothing to do with the updates about the approaching army, Myth responded.

"Well, he knows that Rayann was pregnant, but given his deep-rooted ways, I am certain he won't celebrate or be overcome with joy."

"Would you like me to go with you?"

"I appreciate the gesture. Getting me there and back on the ardor channels in secret has been well enough, but I am certain you would not be welcome to have an audience with the High Consummate. I will use the ingress. Olwa will be accompanying me for the journey, but I will need to speak with Jerrin alone. While I am there I will appeal to the practical side of him and see if he will contribute rangers or any assemblage of troops to assist us. I may be the Prince General, but he still has little trust in me and refuses to allow me final say for deployments. Especially outside Shimmerwood."

Kali offered. "Have you spoken to Commander Rose? If not, I can go do that for you."

"Yes, she is still bereaved over what happened to Lady Kellan. I have asked Raspberry to go play for her and see if it will bring some comfort. My sister also tells me she has been taking starshade elixir for at least a week to ease her mind."

"Starshade? Very risky if she keeps doing that too long."

"Apparently it's the only way she can sleep. I do not envy her. Clearly, the anxiety and pressure of fulfilling her duties are becoming overwhelming. She is more than capable but given all that has happened so rapidly it's quite understandable."

Kali nodded in agreement. "I will increase my efforts to find a way through the warding. I can start living at the forward encampment on the outer rim of Still Mead. I will ask her if I can use her command tent. It is spacious and has all the maps. Perhaps that is a way for me to bring her some comfort, or at least, take some of the strain off her."

Kali turned as Braeren cooed and his eyelids flittered open. "You are right, cousin; he has his father's eyes."

+++

The next morning, Larissa approached the guards outside Lady Rose's quarters. She smiled and bowed her head in greeting.

"Good morning."

She knocked. "Commander?"

There was no response.

Pushing the door open, she entered and looked around. Maps and unopened correspondence lay on the large table near the hearth. The fire was going and the room was warm, but did not reflect the normal orderly condition she typically found it in.

Entering the bedchamber she frowned as she looked at the empty vial on the nightstand beside the bed. She set the platter of food down and walked over to her commander. Reaching gently, she shook Lady Rose.

"A new day has dawned, m'lady. Unfortunately, you are being summoned to join the land of the living once again."

Rose groaned and worked to turn herself over. Her head pounded and she grimaced through the pain. Blinking several times to bring things into focus, she saw her squire standing over her, smiling.

"I swear, sometimes when I see that perpetually cheerful smile, I want to have you hanged, Larissa."

"Indeed you could do so at your pleasure, Commander, but who then would have the courage to wake you when the rising sun dared not?"

Rose managed a chuckle before dragging her sore body up into a sitting position. Larissa picked up the empty vile and showed it to Rose.

"This is making things worse, my Lady. You really need to stop taking it."

She could hear the concern in her squire's voice and nodded as she took a long drink of water without speaking.

Larissa placed the vile on the platter.

"Kali is outside. She wishes to speak with you. If you like, I can tell her to come back when you have had a chance to bathe and dress."

"No, it's fine. Welcome her in and offer her tea. I will be out shortly."

Ten minutes later, Rose emerged from her bed chamber. She was still in her night clothes but was now wrapped in a thick cloak.

"Good morning, Kali. What can I do for you?"

Kali approached Lady Rose, noting the dark circles under her eyes.

"Stick out your tongue."

"My tongue? Why?"

"Please, just do it."

With enough trust to mask her apprehension, Rose complied. Kali looked in her mouth.

"Another week or so and your throat will be too swollen to breathe. I would strongly advise you stop consuming starshade. It tends to do more harm than good in the end."

Rose glanced sideways at Larissa. She was the only one who knew and had clearly told Myth'alas, or maybe just Kali. She exhaled and let it go. She knew that her squire was only being concerned for her health.

"Very well, Kali...and you too, Larissa. I will stop. I certainly don't want to cease breathing. Was that the only reason you came visiting this morning?"

"No. I would like to request permission to use your tent at Still Mead as my personal command center. It is large, there is a bed, and an iron stove to keep it warm. You haven't been staying there and it would give me a chance to focus and concentrate on finding a way through the warding. Moving back and forth between there and the Glen has been fine enough, but I think staying at the forward base might help morale and demonstrate to the soldiers that I am committed to the cause."

"Just the soldiers?"

Kali smiled wryly as she immediately picked up on the implication.

"Aren't you too, a soldier?"

Rose huffed. "Indeed I am. Permission granted. As you said, I haven't been using it. I will write up an order within the hour and you are welcome to stay there as long as you need to."

"Hopefully it won't be for too long. I am making progress."

"That is good to hear. Is there anything you can share?"

"Only that I know the warding wraps the entire area like a sphere. Using the ardor channels isn't possible. I'm still trying to decipher the complexity of the magic. God's natural laws are still in play, I just need to unwrap the riddle. There is an answer and I will find it."

"Thank you, please send a pigeon or, of course, you are always welcome to come tell me in person if you discover anything else."

Kali bowed her head and left. Larissa brought a cup of hot tea and set it on the table.

"Would you like help going through this pile?"

"No. But thank you."

"Oh, and Prince Myth'alas thought it would be beneficial to have Raspberry come and play for you this evening. She will be here at sunset. Her songs are quite soothing, as you know. Perhaps you will find it a pleasant alternative to waking up with splitting headaches after ingesting that gunk."

Rose smiled at the joke, but it faded fast.

"It's not songs I need, Larissa. It's hope."

+++

Ceridwyn had finally awoken and was moved to her quarters in the great rooms next to the keep. Aeolis did his best to tend to her, but she was still deeply grieved. She barely spoke and when she did, it was short, simple answers.

He brought her a cup of honey mint tea and set it on the night table. She whispered softly, "Thank you." But offered no other words.

"Is there anything else I can get you?"

"No, thank you."

"Ceri, it wasn't your fault."

"Two seconds, Aeolis. If I had been two seconds quicker."

"There is no way to verify if that would have produced a different outcome. That weapon came out of nowhere; none of us saw it coming. Olwa and I were watching diligently. If either of us had seen him we could have intervened. It was simply the chaos of battle. Nothing is guaranteed."

"Kellan is dead. That is guaranteed." She turned and looked at him with swollen, red eyes.

There was a soft knock on the door. Aeolis opened it and welcomed Rayann in. She entered with Braeren in her arms and sat beside her friend. Though there was still sadness on her face, Ceridwyn couldn't help but smile.

"My heart sings a new song. He is so beautiful, Rayann. Congratulations."

"His name is Braeren, for his birth is the result of his father's journey. An elf who was once lost, then found, and ultimately forgiven by God's grace and love for us all."

Ceridwyn looked at Rayann but before she could speak, Rayann continued, "Dear friend, we are all grieved by the loss of Lady Kellan. She was a bright and wonderful young woman. Her heart was pure. Though we didn't have a great deal of time to get to know her; that much was certain."

"I can still see her face, Rayann. I can still hear the awful sound of that mace wrenching the metal she wore. I can still see the fear and anguish in her eyes as she hit the snow and slid towards us, knowing she wasn't going to make it."

Without asking, Rayann reached into Ceridwyn and found the memories of the battle locked in her mind. She observed, like she had been there and witnessed them herself. Tears immediately filled her eyes, and she gasped with grief at what she saw.

"Yes, my friend. I can see it now too and it is a horrific sight. Together we share that perspective now. Please allow me to grieve with you so you don't need to do it alone."

Ceridwyn didn't answer and instead reached out her hands.

"May I hold him?"

"Of course."

Ceridwyn cradled him against her bosom and inhaled his baby scent deeply before she whispered, "It is good to meet you, little Prince Braeren."

At precisely sunset, Raspberry was at Lady Rose's private quarters. Expecting her, the guards opened the door, allowing her access. She walked in and smiled when Lady Rose greeted her.

"Good evening, Raspberry. Thank you for coming. Can I offer you any tea, or cakes? Larissa brought some for us to share just a few moments ago."

"Aww, no thanks, Ms. Rose. I've discovered that I can't really eat and sing at the same time; makes an awful mess."

Rose chuckled. "Quite understandable. Well perhaps you can have some after or take a portion when you leave then?"

"Sure, that would be great! I do love cakes."

Raspberry offered her contagious, bright smile once again as she sat down across from Lady Rose and continued speaking.

"Prince Myth'alas tells me that you can't sleep. I wrote a new song for you; I think it could help. I don't know. Sometimes my songs work, and other times, they don't. I'm sure willing to try if you are, though."

"I am. Raspberry, before that, if you don't mind, I would like to ask how you decided to become a Balladeer?"

"Hmm, nobody's ever really asked me that, I guess because all my friends already know. Well, I'm the oldest kid in my family and was raised in a home full of musicians. My mother was a singer. My father, well, he couldn't sing so great, but he sure could play instruments, any instrument!

"My brothers and sisters all played and sang or danced. Growing up, our house was always just…full of music. After the soldiers came and told us we couldn't live on our farm anymore we moved south, deeper into Weefolk Wood and…"

"Wait."

Raspberry stared at her.

"The soldiers? Soldiers told you that you couldn't live on your farm?"

"Yes, Ms. Rose."

"Knights and steelguard of the Northern Command?"

"Yeah. I had just come of age when it happened. We lived in Hobnob, right where the three rivers come together. There were about four hundred or so of us weefolk there. The steelguard were expanding a wall and building some kind of keep or something, to make a defense place. They said they had no choice but to put it right where our village is. Then they told us we had to leave, so we did. I helped my family move all our stuff and then decided, since we were already on the move, maybe I would just keep moving, and see the world."

"I had no idea that the Northern Guard were displacing people. There are no directives for such a thing. I am sorry that happened to you. Did they not compensate you for your land?"

"Nope, not a copper. It's okay though, you just have to get used to stuff like that when you're one of the weefolk, Ms. Rose."

Rose observed Raspberry's face. There wasn't a hint of sadness, so she queried further.

"Are you not sad about it?"

"No. Well, I was, but we set up a new village along a beautiful stretch of the river where the ground looked good for farming and my family says they are happy there. I send a pigeon every now and then to check in on them."

"Yes, well, as I said, I am very sorry that the steelguard did that to you."

"Aww, it's okay."

"No, Raspberry, it's not. That goes against everything the knighthood stands for."

"All the knights are human, Ms. Rose. Anyone who isn't human isn't as important as them."

"Do you really believe that?"

"No, but that's how they've always treated us. You're all bigger and much stronger, plus you have all those weapons. We couldn't fight you even if we wanted to. At least they gave us a chance to pack up and move instead of just beating us up before throwing us out. Sometimes that happens instead."

Rose exhaled angrily and made a mental note to discuss this story with the Northern Commander if she ever managed to get ahold of him. She'd see to it that at minimum some form of compensation be offered to those displaced. She lifted her chin and spoke again.

"Well, about your becoming a Balladeer..."

"OH, yeah! So, in my travels as a minstrel, I eventually met Ms. Rayann and Mr. Rorie. We traveled together a bit and then we had a fight with some goblins. Mr. Rorie got hurt and we took him to Fogburgh. Ms. Rayann had to go because of the summons, so I stayed with him at Mr. Lenly's Healing Room. Mr. Lenly loved the way I played and told me my gifts were deeper than just some sort of family talent. He said, 'God has given you a special gift, a way to play that could also make things happen'.

"As he started teaching me, turns out he was right. Not surprising really, he was right almost all the time, except when it came to putting cinnamon on green beans, BLECH! Anyway, the more I learned and memorized and prayed, stuff did start happening when I would make music. It's not easy, mind you, and I still can't make it happen every time, but usually good stuff occurs if I really concentrate. People get happier, or feel courage, and a few times, they've even gotten better if they were sick. I like when that happens best."

"That is wonderful, Raspberry. I am glad you have found a calling. You clearly enjoy making music, the times I have heard you play, I admit, it is quite captivating. I too once had a calling. I fear I've let it slip though. Somehow, I just can't bring myself to pray or feel like it matters anymore."

"That's sad. Did something happen to you?"

"In a manner of speaking. Nothing that I can really put my finger on. Just a sort of, slow drifting away I suppose. Like a ship that once had direction of sturdy conviction, but then the winds died and the sails fell."

"Hmm. Well, I could play the song I wrote for you. Maybe that will help put wind back in those sails. Want me to?"

"That would be lovely."

Raspberry unclasped the latches which held her instrument in its case and removed the lute. She looked at Lady Rose with a confident nod before playing a brand-new song of rest, hope, and peace.

Half an hour later, Raspberry emerged from the room with a few of the cakes neatly wrapped in a linen napkin. She looked at the two guards who were staring at her. There was an awkward moment of silence before she finally spoke.

"Ummm, good evening?"

One of the guards knelt.

"That song was amazing. Did our Commander enjoy it?"

"I think so. She fell asleep, so that's good."

"You think it's good she fell asleep during your song?"

"Sure! That was the whole idea."

She confidently handed a cake to each of the soldiers and smiled brightly.

"One for each of you. They smell like lemon. Lemons aren't especially easy to get in the winter yah' know. That makes these cakes pretty darn special."

She spun on her heel and skipped through the hall before disappearing down the stairs, making her way back to her room.

# Chapter 14 – Shades of Gray

Prince Myth'alas waited patiently as his brother scratched his signature on several parchments without even acknowledging his presence. Finally, the '*tink*' of the quill hitting the bottom of the inkpot rang out and the High Consummate looked up.

"What can I do for you, brother?"

"You have a new nephew. His name is Braeren."

"Do I? Braeren? Interesting choice for a name."

Myth'alas stayed patient as he continued.

"Would you like to meet him?"

"I assume eventually I will have to, but I am quite busy at the moment. Someone must run the commonwealth while someone else is off attending to the troubles of humans."

"What in the crevasse is wrong with you?"

Angrily, Jerrin pounded his hand on the desk.

"You know exactly what is wrong. You have no respect, no ambition, no loyalty to the commonwealth. You defy me at every opportunity and in the meantime, I am forced to linger in the duties that should be ascribed to you, Faralanthis' First Prince."

Myth'alas nodded and then motioned towards the door.

"I need to come with me."

"What?"

"Please, brother, just come with me."

Jerrin exhaled angrily, came around his desk and followed Myth'alas to the portal chamber.

"This is ridiculous, First Prince. Where are we off to?"

Myth'alas spoke calmly. "Still Mead."

"Why do I need to go to human territory?"

"It's better if I just show you. Please, brother."

Jerrin angrily activated his Ring of Concealment and his facial features became more human.

"Let's get this nonsense over with."

Myth'alas held up the port key and spoke the words that Rayann had taught him. He stepped through and his brother followed. Instantly they were standing in Gryphonledge Keep. Myth'alas escorted Jerrin to the gate beyond the courtyard. He spoke words to a much larger portal and it flared to life. Rayann, Kali, and Ceridwyn had constructed this one weeks ago to assist the soldiers traveling to Still Mead. Though some feared to use it, others found that traveling instantly was much more satisfactory than hours of walking, especially when they were moving supplies.

The brothers appeared at the corresponding portal, behind the forward camp in Still Mead. Without a word, Myth'alas began the long walk to the top of the hill. Jerrin stared at the fracture in the sky, unable to find reasoning for its existence. The assembly of soldiers and knights who made up the military camp paid them little attention as they passed.

Finally, the elven brothers crested the hill and stood atop the massive cauldron that overlooked the formerly lush Valley of Still Mead.

Jerrin whispered. "By the constellations."

"Yes, Jerrin. Look at it. This is what I have been trying to explain to you. You continually refuse to listen to me so I knew it was time for you to see for yourself. This is not a human problem. This is an Aimsire problem. Those towers are not here to glorify God nor for the welfare of our world. In fact, it's quite the opposite.

"The two wizards who created these abominations are former servants of Nataxia herself. We know they are working for their own means now. What's worse, Nataxia's troops are advancing from the north. Reports claim it's her entire army and they have reptilians with them."

Jerrin turned and looked at his brother.

"I had no idea."

"Of course not, I've only told you a dozen times. You are too stuck in your own head to see the wider horizon line before you. You always have been."

"Don't presume to talk to me like that. I am still your High Consummate."

"It's time you let the formal titles go, big brother. How long will you reign?" Myth'alas pointed at the towers and continued, "This is not going away, nor will it end unless we end it. Put aside your acrimony towards me. Put away your disdain for humans and their 'Sinner King'. Lay down your contempt and sour thoughts about all of it. This threat is real and must be dealt with."

Jerrin looked at the towers again.

"So, what would you ask of me?"

"Allow me to deploy the rangers and our soldiers. Let me bring them into the ranks of this army, under my personal command. We need to fight alongside the knights and their steelguard."

"I will consider your words and speak with the Council of Elders, but I make no promises."

+++

Olwa entered his parents' lavish home. They lived in a cluster of castlewood trees within the ornate and highly desirable Blooming District just outside the main gates of the palace. It was an area known for its beauty, exclusive gardens, wealthy inhabitants, and massive dwellings.

"Mother? Father?"

"My master, Olwa. Branch's heart sings and her love is happiest to have her eyes on you again."

He smiled and leaned in, giving Branch a warm hug. She had sold herself into lifelong service of the Pilininge family over one hundred years ago for three vials of medicine to save her mother from illness.

Branch was a Fae Elf, from the southern forests known as The Tangles. Being the wildest of the elves, the Fara considered them uncivilized and inferior in every way. The irony being, that it was the Fae who were in fact, the purest and most attuned to the ways of the forests above any other race of elves on Aimsire.

Branch's bright eyes, banded and sharp like the color of blue spruce needles, shimmered in the fae lights as she looked up at Olwa's face. She had raised him, not his own mother. She was the one who tended to him, cared for him, and she still loved him fiercely.

Reaching gently, Olwa took her hand. Her dark, olive skin was a deep contrast to his pale, pinkish hue. Colorful threads of natural twine were woven in her hair and at the end of several dozen locks she had shells, polished stones, and glass beads woven into the naturally striped brown and green strands.

"I have told you there is no need for such formality between us, Branch. I am not your master, nor will I ever be when I am head of this house."

184

"All you wish to say master, Branch listens."

She smiled timidly and turned her eyes to look at the floor, releasing his hand as she heard footsteps approaching.

"Good evening, my son."

Olwa shifted his gaze and smiled respectfully.

"Good evening, mother. The house is lovely, as always."

He was lying through his teeth. He hated this place and everything it represented. He longed to be back in Gryphonledge among the soldiers and new friends he had made. The gray, hard stones of the keep and stink of the human city were more inviting than the ornate silks, rugs, artwork, and decadent adornments in his parents' cold home.

"Well, of course it is, my son." She turned to her house elf. "Branch, what is wrong with you? Why do you linger in your duties? Offer Olwa some refreshment or at least take his tunic."

"Branch is so very sorry, mistress. Branch is was just happy to see master Olwa and has forgottsen hers'self."

Ky'ly entered the room.

"Whist. Off with you."

Branch tucked her head and disappeared into the house.

"Welcome home. To what do we owe this visit? Why are you not with the prince?"

"Prince Myth'alas is currently taking a meeting with our High Consummate. We agreed it would be good for me to stop in and say hello to you both. Our duties have caused a lapse and I realized it had been some time since I have done so."

Ky'ly tilted his head and stared at Olwa's face.

"How did you get that bruise behind your ear?"

"I was on a scouting mission. We had an…altercation, and I was forced to kill my adversary."

"I see. Well, clearly the prince still has some work to do in teaching you to defend yourself. Come, let us sit and catch up."

"Regrettably, father, I need to be off very soon. The Prince only gave me a few moments and then we need to return to Gryphonledge."

"I see. Very well. It was good to see you again."

Ky'ly left the room. Olwa exhaled his anxiety slowly as he watched his father walk away.

"Must you leave in such haste, son? We haven't seen you for a moon's cycle. I am sure Rainwen, your beloved, would be delighted to see you as well. Are you sure you don't have time? Maybe even just for supper?"

"I apologize, mother. I need to gather a couple small items from my room and should get back to Prince Myth'alas. I don't want to keep him waiting."

+++

Kali sat in the command tent, deep in thought, hunched over the map table. Dozens of pages of parchment were spread around, notes and observations she had been making about the towers and the warding.

It had only been twenty-four hours since she took residency, but the time was already paying off. Being consistently closer to the warding was helping her discover the answers she had been hoping to find.

She was studying the map when she heard the burning wood inside the pot belly stove crackle loudly. She turned and watched as the flue closed on its own, causing the smoke to build up in the combustion chamber. She stood and narrowed her eyes, suddenly feeling the cage that held the dragon in her heart rattle.

The smoke from the wood seeped through the seams at the top of the stove, and the dragon's head began to form above the blistering hot iron. The acrid smell of burnt wood filled the tent as the dragon's eyes flared to life like smoldering embers.

*"You atrophy, child. I can see the lack of true challenge beginning to take its toll. Will you allow it to wither your power and consume you completely?"*

"Who are you?"

The dragon laughed.

*"I am you, Kali, and you are me. I am the core of who and what we are. The voice that tickles your ears when you go astray. I only get louder the more you deny me an audience."*

Kali stepped forward and looked the dragon in the eyes.

"All are multi-faceted, but none are bound to an absolute fate. Last time you trespassed in my presence, you made it sound as if I have no choice."

*"Oh, child. You always have a choice, but as you know, all choices bear consequences."*

"And what consequence do I face if I deny your words, fight these urges, and ultimately find a way to destroy this threat instead of embracing it?"

*"I am no fortune teller. What I know is that it will always linger in your mind. The power that could have been yours. The pulse and the flow of energy beyond your wildest imaginations. Access to the most potent magic ever known on Aimsire which you could have wielded on command."*

"But at what expense?"

*"Ahh, Yes, there is always forfeiture for great endeavors."*

"I will not extinguish this world or kill those upon for my own gain as Fifth and Piramay are so willing to do. If I have learned anything, there is no balance in that."

*"Balance in this world is like the tides and the winds. It is interchanging and constantly fluctuating. You do not control the direction in which the wind sends the clouds, or the schedule of the seasons. Only God can do that.*

*"You do nothing to contribute to them, and yet, they exist. Their place is secure. They were there before you were born and will be long after you are gone. Balance is nothing more than the natural tipping and resetting of the scales, not induced by the actions of one person living their short life.*

*"The arrogance of those who claim that they matter in the natural dance of anything are swimming upriver during the spring run-off. Kicking feverishly, exhausting themselves all while being swept downstream. They live in delusion that they are doing something noble, contributing to a greater cause that will never be resolved. Creating balance in this world has never been yours to give or take."*

Kali quietly stared at the dragon. Her eyes narrowed as the smoky face wisped.

Catching her expression, the dragon continued.

*"However, there is an opportunity. We could be that fulcrum of balance you desperately desire to be. We are strong and know the way of wielding power. We can hold that tower. The gray gem is planted in the terra, a direct connection to the core of this world. The very core from which you draw your power. You can*

187

*align the towers. You can never be the balance for the world, but we can be the balance there.*"

"No."

Kali swirled her hands and gathered Shakyna. The dragon's face diffused as blue light manifested itself within the center of its head and broke the shadow to pieces. Kali was panting and the laughter of the dragon echoed in her ears.

Bursting from the tent, Kali felt hot and uncomfortable. She ascended the long hill and began to walk the ridgeline that surrounded the cauldron. Hearing horse hooves behind her, she stepped aside so the rider could pass, but the sound stopped.

She turned and stared at Sir Trystan seated atop his mount.

"Well, fancy meeting you here." His voice was chipper.

"Yes, a strange coincidence, Sir Trystan, especially after I asked permission to use Lady Rose's command tent and handed her order to you personally. Surely you aren't so misinformed that you didn't read the edict for yourself?"

"Hop on. Glaive is strong enough for both of us. The cauldron gets rough up ahead. I can get you across safely."

"Can you?"

As fast as he could blink, she was three hundred meters away, beyond the rocky portion of the path and back on the softer, grassy road, walking by herself once again.

"You little minx." He whispered to himself with a smile.

He tapped Glaive on the haunch and crossed the distance between them, siding up with Kali quickly.

"That was a fancy trick. Funny too."

"I am glad I could amuse, Sir Trystan. Now if you please, I desire to be alone."

Trystan nudged Glaive and turned the great war horse sideways, blocking her path.

"It's not safe out here, Kali. I can't in good conscience allow you to wander this close to the towers without an escort."

She flipped her hood back and glowered at him.

"Do you find me so incapable that I can't protect myself from the squirrels and rabbits that roam these hills, Sir Trystan?"

He was mesmerized. Every time she got angry with him, she was that much more beautiful. He imagined what it would be like to press his lips against hers. To feel the warmth of her skin and exchange breath.

"Kali, please understand. I know you are capable, however, I oversee the city guard. I am tasked with the protection of Gryphonledge's citizens and guests, alike."

"Then go protect your city! Do it as best you can against those." She pointed at the towers. "This is not a game. The magic from those abominations will roll over Gryphonledge in less than a heartbeat. Fifth and Piramay burned every coastal city in the northern territories to ash before they erected these towers. How much more powerful do you think they are now?"

He turned and looked at the towers; she could see his face change as reality hit him.

"That's right. You finally understand. If we don't find a way to stop them, these two will eradicate anything that gets in their way."

Trystan turned back to her. "What do we do then?"

Kali laughed sarcastically. "That is the great mystery that I have been trying to solve, Sir Trystan."

She stepped around Glaive and began to walk away. He slid off the saddle, and reached, grabbing her by the shoulder, turning her to face him. He did so, partly to continue conversing with her, but also in the hope that he could set up a kiss.

"And we are all grateful for it, Kali. That is why Lady Rose brought you here. That is why I am glad you are here."

She winced. Though he hadn't meant it, the rough tug on her shoulder had hurt. The dragon in Kali's heart stirred as she looked him in the eyes and suddenly, her face softened.

He saw it and felt hope. Had he finally managed to find a chink in her armor? She was going to allow this.

Kali stepped up to him and pressed her hand against the center of his breastplate. He inhaled deeply in anticipation as she began to go up on her tiptoes, approaching his face.

The area on his breastplate where her hand was touching suddenly became as hot as if it had just been pulled from a blacksmith's fire. He howled in pain and Glaive stomped the ground in protest. Trystan looked down; the imprint of her hand was melted into the steel.

He looked into her eyes, his expression a combination of fear, and shock. Her finger, still glowing from her spell, came up and she pointed into his face. Her voice was dangerously low and serious.

"Don't you ever grab me like that again."

Trystan put his hands up and nodded regretfully.

"I…I'm sorry, Kali. I was only trying to…"

There was a flash of light and she was several hundred meters away, walking along the cauldron again, alone.

+++

Myth'alas came to his adherent's room in the keep and knocked. Olwa bid him entrance. As the prince entered, he stood and formally greeted his mentor.

"My Prince, I was not expecting you. How may I serve?"

Walking over to the table Myth'alas looked at the drawing. It was an incredibly detailed rendering of the three towers.

"This is very impressive. I didn't know you had artisan talents."

"Few do, my Prince. I don't tend to talk about it much."

Nodding his head in understanding, Myth'alas continued.

"I need to discuss Bold'Rock and Pela'Rock with Commander Rose. My meeting is in fifteen minutes. I was hoping you would join me?"

"Of course. I will gather my things."

"You have been a little quiet since we returned. Is everything alright?"

"No. My mother and father, I…I just don't want to be in their home any longer. I am not of age yet and tradition still binds me to them. I am just thankful that I have this assignment so I don't need to keep pretending that I believe or agree with everything they stand for."

Having known Olwa's parents for many hundreds of years Myth'alas knew exactly what Olwa was getting to. He didn't wish to add fuel to the fire but knew he needed to say something.

"As your tutor and mentor, I would advise you to be patient and not do anything rash. Not that I am the greatest example. From my lessons learned by the mistakes I made, however, know that

190

it's here…," Myth'alas tapped him in the center of the chest, "where you will find the answers you are looking for. They might not always be the easiest answers, or the simplest road, and yes, there are times when those answers will even be wrong.

"Life's lessons come in many shapes and forms. Asking questions to confirm your discernment is never a bad thing and modeling your life to resemble someone you admire is always a great approach to finding happiness. Lastly, and most importantly, I would advise you to pray for guidance. God answers in whispers, so you need to listen carefully. Make sure your ears are always open so you can hear that small, still voice. I say that, wishing I had done so myself."

"My Prince, I've spent my whole life trying to be what my parents want me to be. I don't have the strength to confront them."

"And that's okay, for now. As you said, you have not yet come of age, but you are getting close. If you are still happy with the arrangement I can see to it that you remain my adherent. I'll be honest, I did not want one, but Jerrin forced you on me. At first, I thought you would only be a burden, but now I am glad I didn't protest. You are a fine young elf and I am happy that you are by my side. Yet another lesson that I needed to learn."

Olwa smiled and brought his hand to his heart.

"Thank you, my Prince. I am honored by your words."

"I am honored by you and your presence in my life, Olwa. Aeolis reported to me how you behaved and performed when you were up north. To say I am proud of you is an understatement. I know we have only had a few training sessions so far; all the chaos of this situation has made it difficult to really focus on teaching you combat skills. Starting tomorrow, at dawn, however, I will no longer practice alone. You will start joining me."

"I would be honored."

"Good. Now, let's go talk to Commander Rose and her subordinates. They aren't going to like what I have to say, but it's important for them to hear my proposal. Oh, and bring that drawing of yours."

Ten minutes later, Myth'alas and Olwa stepped into Commander Rose's War Council Chamber. Sir Ordin, Sir Gregory, Larissa, and Erika looked up as they entered. Immediately, Erika's face showed her displeasure and she returned her gaze to the maps. The others were more gracious and offered gestures of welcome.

Rose stepped to Myth'alas and clasped his hand in greeting.

"Good morning, Prince. What would you have us all speak with you about?"

Myth'alas gestured to Olwa who unrolled his illustration of the towers and placed it on the map table.

"I know there is disagreement on the greater threat. In my mind, both the advancing army and the towers are of equal importance, so it becomes a matter of priority and diligence to eradicate one, then focus on the other. I've made it no secret that I feel we should focus on the towers first.

"If Nataxia's army makes its way through The Bind before we have handled the towers, we will be split between the two. Given the limited resources we are working with, that would be the end of it."

"You are the Prince General of the elves," Sir Gregory interjected. "How about you bring some of your resources to join the fight?"

Patiently, Myth'alas responded. "I know it seems like it should be that easy. Yes, I am Prince General Myth'alas of the Faralanthis Armies, however, as you are aware, I had a falling out, for a time, with my family. Though my brother has restored me to the position of Prince General, for now it remains just a title. There is a lingering lack of trust, and he still insists that he give final approval of all deployments.

"I even showed him the towers personally to instill a sense of reality and urgency. I believe he is finally listening, but I can't do anything underhanded. We just need to be patient and allow him time to make a decision."

"Well, isn't that a wonderful story? We get to keep dying until the king of the elves makes up his mind."

Myth'alas glanced at Erika as she offered her sharp words. Her bitterness was understandable, so he let the comment go. Instead of answering, he pointed to the illustration of the towers.

"This is the closer threat. Kali assures me she is making progress and hopes to understand the compilation of the warding's makeup soon. I saw that the construction of trebuchets along the

192

crucible ridge was progressing quickly. Once a breach is formed, we can put that part of the plan into action."

"No offense meant here, prince, but what is your point?" Myth'alas looked to Sir Ordin.

"My point is that we need troops on the ground to protect the machines. They will be vulnerable during their part of the operation so we need more troops to protect them."

"To echo Sir Ordin's words, what is the point? We know all this."

Myth'alas turned to Sir Gregory.

"I have at my disposal two individuals whom I believe can help us."

Erika laughed. "Two? You offer two? That is what you came to say?"

"Not just two people, two very capable and powerful individuals. Bold'Rock and Pela'Rock of the north."

Erika stepped forward, fuming. She knew by the makeup of their names that Myth'alas was suggesting Nethermen join them.

"The Crevasse will become ablaze and all the souls within disentombed from the ice before I fight beside Nethermen. The very fact that you would even suggest this is deplorable."

"Erika is right," Sir Ordin agreed. "The Nethermen are our enemies. They have wreaked havoc in the north for as long as there has been a north. They have no compassion and less honor. We could not trust them to stand at our sides and fight; they might turn on us at any moment."

"What if I told you that only one was a Netherman, and the other was a human? What if I told you that he refers to her as 'daughter' and her to him as 'father'? He is an outcast, sent away from the Ice Rock Clan and sells his services to survive."

"So not only a Netherman, but a mercenary as well? This just keeps getting better and better."

Becoming impatient with her interruptions, Commander Rose turned and gave Erika a hard look. She receded back to the maps, pretending to study them, but kept her ears locked on the conversation.

Sir Gregory queried. "How do you know we can trust them?"

"I have already given them payment. A place to live in exchange for their services in the upcoming battle. They are residing in Hailen Glen even as we speak. She is not only a human, but an incredibly gifted ice sorceress. I know from having personally engaged them in battle. I was victorious, but few times in all my days have I been challenged so fiercely.

"They fight in tandem; he also has magic. A staff with a crystal in the center that sends forth cold and ice. I know little about them as a pair, but what I can tell you is there is a true bond between them. Most of all, they are running from the Rage Queen as well, meaning, they have every reason to fight alongside us."

Sir Ordin scratched his beard before looking at Gregory and then Commander Rose.

Rose studied his face for a moment and then addressed Myth'alas.

"Is there anything else you want to add?"

"Only that I understand this is your army. These are your lands and I will abide by any decision you make. I will respect your authority so long as we are within your walls and in human territory, no matter what decision you make in this regard.

"That being said, Nethermen take their oaths seriously, even until death. It is their tradition to keep their word, at all costs. Bold'Rock broke his word when he fled the service of the Rage Queen. He did so not due to a lack of honor, but because his eyes were opened to the truth. I believe that when he gave me his word in exchange for a safe haven to raise his daughter, he truly saw the light and will fulfill it."

He then regarded Sir Ordin. "I pledged my life to you, Sir, by the blood oath of steel. Commander Rose and Sir Gregory stood as witnesses. On that same oath, I give you my word that these two will fight with us, and for us, without complicating the plans. They will be under my command so as to not confuse any of the authority that your commanders have over your soldiers. Lastly, I vow that I will kill them personally if they betray us."

"We will discuss it." Rose concluded. "I will send word when we have made a decision."

"Thank you."

Myth'alas and Olwa left the room. Rose turned to speak with her subordinates as the door closed behind them.

"I can't believe you defied an order from the First Borne. His directives came directly from God. By the stars, what were you thinking?"

Nolore turned and looked at Rajumin, his face showing his conviction.

"They were sent on a mission doomed to fail from the outset. I could not let her die."

"Just her?"

Nolore's face dropped and he whispered, "Yes."

The frustration on Rajumin's face was clear.

"You know you could lose your flight over this, or worse."

"I know."

She walked over to him and lifted his chin with her finger so they were staring eye-to-eye.

"This fascination you have with humans has always been your weakness, but it might have gotten you in real trouble this time. Just promise me it won't go any further. You know what horrific penalties we face when our kind tries to mate with…"

She went silent as Kellan walked into the room. The young knight had been given access to a place to bathe and clean herself. Rajumin had also supplied her with fresh clothing to wear. Upon entering the room, she immediately sensed the tension between the Silentclaw cousins.

Clearing her throat softly, she spoke, "Am I interrupting?"

"No more than my cousin already has, Lady Kellan."

Rajumin smiled warmly, approaching the young knight.

"It is good to see you looking refreshed. The expression on your face alone says you are more relaxed."

"What happened?"

"All I can say for now is clearly you still have a purpose. God always offers grace, but restoring the dead back to life is not something that occurs regularly."

Kellan's voice quivered. "I don't understand. I was dead? So much is unclear and my thoughts are gray. I even have this strange feeling, like I was…flying? I don't know, it's all so foggy. I even hallucinated that I was rescued by a dragon."

Rajumin glanced at Nolore and then back to Lady Kellan.

"Though you were severely injured, your memories are not as unclear as you believe them to be."

"What? No. Dragons have not been seen on Aimsire for so long that their existence is more legend than believed fact. It couldn't have been."

Rajumin simply smiled and extended her hand.

"Walk with us."

As they navigated through the massive dwelling, Kellan looked at Nolore.

"Are you alright?"

"I am fine, just thinking."

The three of them walked out onto a large balcony and Rajumin whispered, "I need your trust."

Kellan nodded more instinctually than in truly understanding. Rajumin leaned forward, placing a kiss on her forehead. There was an immediate sensation of warmth that covered her face and a flare of light like staring into the sun erupted before her.

Kellan shielded her eyes and blinked to clear the flares. Suddenly, she gasped as she looked out across the Vale of Ghosts. Dozens upon dozens of dragons in various colors were flying over the massive valley while some were on the ground, relaxing in the sun. Others were perched on rooftops and the battlements, keeping diligent watch.

In the distance, a castle made from what looked to be a single, massive chunk of shimmerstone, glistened as the sun bounced off the walls in a thousand directions. The buildings were more like glorified landing places and dragons came and went.

"I…oh my…"

Rajumin smiled. "Yes. It is often overwhelming to those who have never seen it. The domicile we are standing in is yours to use until we determine what needs to be done next."

"What do you mean?"

There was a sudden rush of wind and Kellan turned her eyes skyward. A huge black dragon spiraled over their heads before landing gracefully on the large flat surface where they were standing. She took her humanoid form and appeared as a dark-skinned elf. Her black garments were nothing short of exquisite and finely crafted. A blazing dragon's head was embroidered on the center of her chest and she walked with purpose. She stared at Lady Kellan for a moment before offering a small nod in greeting.

She turned to Nolore. "I Serynthia come to deliver a message. You, Nolore, have been summoned to answer the questions of the High Borne."

"Yes, I figured."

Nolore approached and they walked together to the end of the balcony. He glanced back at Kellan and smiled sadly.

"You were worth it."

They jumped into the air and took their dragon forms. The wind from their wings pushed Kellan back and she shielded her eyes as the pair rose into the sky.

"I don't understand any of this. What is going on?"

She turned and looked at Rajumin who was watching her cousin fly towards the castle.

"We were forbidden to be involved with any actions not related to the three towers. Nolore disobeyed and followed your scouting party. He circled high above and watched as everything transpired. When he saw what was about to happen, he chose to save your life."

"Why?"

"The first reason is an easy one, he is infatuated with you. The second, well, that becomes a little more complex."

"What do you mean?"

Rajumin turned and looked at Kellan.

"The Stenberg lineage were the last chosen to ride the Silentclaw into battle before we went into exile. As you already know, you are the last of the Stenberg."

# Chapter 15 – The Fog of Chaos

Reitrof'nor's wise, golden eyes scanned Nolore as he lay prostrate before him.

"Raise your head, young one."

Their eyes locked and the High Borne continued.

"You know why you are here, so I will spare you the formalities. As a pack leader, I expect more from you. The allowance of our presence in the skies over Aimsire once again does not offer you the liberties to go wherever you like, not yet anyway. My instructions to you were clear, and yet you chose to transgress."

"Yes, High Borne. I admit I did and accept your judgment."

"Yet another of your infatuations with a human. You even chose to warn her. We are on the brink of another war with Nataxia; do you realize this?"

Nolore's pearl white eyes refused to hide his guilt.

"I do, and I won't deny it was the basis of my motivation. I hoped that by informing her the information would find its way back to Commander Rose so she wouldn't be sent. I knew the patrol was walking into a perilous situation."

He swallowed hard and continued. "Per your information, some have been patrolling and keeping watch over the armies advancing from the north. Based on what we knew, I could not let them linger there alone."

"You went because you wanted not to watch over them, but Kellan. Youngling, you wish to request that she become your rider. You cannot hide it, not in this place. I have looked into your eyes and the truth is revealed.

"The time of the riders is long past. That strategy was based on very specific circumstances. Though the memory of times now scribed in the annals of history provide nostalgia, God's directives are rooted in the present. This new threat affects us all and requires different tactics."

"I understand, High Borne. I don't mean to be continually insubordinate, but I must argue, the riders were a powerful force. The descendants of those that once were entrusted to the privilege are all lost to the Crevasse, except one. Lady Kellan now wields

Fallen Sky. It has passed to *her*. That means she is the sole heir to the traditions of her lineage."

"And you find her alluring."

"I do." Nolore paused and inhaled deeply. "I formally ask that I be allowed to take her as my rider."

Reitrof'nor stretched his neck up and looked out towards the domicile where Lady Kellan had been taken. Even at such a great distance his dragon sight allowed him to observe her in full detail. She was on the large portico with Rajumin, pointing and asking questions about the Vale of Ghosts. Her face was full of curiosity and when Rajumin answered it was obvious Kellan was taking in all that was said. He continued to observe her a moment before breaking the silence.

"She does have the fearlessness required, and the strength, but I cannot make promises. We will both pray on this."

He looked back at Nolore.

"Stand, youngling."

Nolore did as he was commanded but kept his head bowed in reverence.

"Sharius and Lulania guide our paths based on God's will. As they have been assigned governance we adhere to their direction. Under all circumstances we will obey the laws of God. If we are to see this through and fight these proprietors of evil who wish to take control, we must remain respectful and devoted to our tutelary for they are instructed by God on high. With that said, I will communicate your request directly to them, for you are among the favored.

"It has been decided that you are to remain a pack leader and retain authority over your flight. There is grace and an experienced champion of the Silentclaw shall not be lost due to indiscretion. I will add, Nolore, your impulses can no longer continue to be a distraction to our purpose or place on Aimsire. I expect you to understand this.

"Furthermore, you are to adhere to and remain pure in your relationship with Kellan Stenberg no matter what the outcome of this conversation. Any violation of the law of God will not be tolerated."

"Yes, High Borne. I am sorry for my lapse in judgment, and I will remain obedient to the laws ascribed to us at the Dawn Light."

"All is forgiven, youngling, and forgotten."

+++

Nidhug bowed before Nataxia as she stared at him from her throne. Her eyes traced his form angrily, as if he was personally responsible for the news he had shared. She stood and descended the ornate steps.

"Rise."

He walked with her to a massive balcony beside the throne room. She remained silent for a long while, staring at the countless frozen souls hovering in their spherical ice prisons, trapped in the Crevasse by her will.

Without turning her head, she broke the silence.

"After our fall from the Plain of Constellations and our transformation to these lesser forms, we vowed to get our revenge on those who cast us out. You, Nidhug, have been my most loyal retainer. Even as you watched your kin dwindle into hunched husks of their former selves, bound in icy chains. Finally, we found the means to free them from their amercement."

She snapped her fingers and the view of the landscape opened up before them. The flow of ardor revealed itself along with hundreds of reptilians frozen solid to the ground in prone positions. The magic was being twisted to slowly revive them.

Nidhug took it all in and then turned to Nataxia as he vowed. "It was my honor to remain by your side, my Queen, even within this depleted form. By your power on that day, you saved my brother and me from joining our kin in their frozen gallows. My loyalty to you has never been in doubt. God questioned your place and relevance amongst the tutelary fiercely, even, I dare say, unfairly. Our insurgency was more than justified."

"Was it?" She stared at him, the light in her eyes was dull. "We stood no chance against God's power, much less the collective might of those who follow so blindly. I see now that we were foolish to try. I should have known, for it was a collective I

200

existed within, a power I knew and felt, just not to the extent at which it could be wielded against us. I let my ambition blind me.

"You were by my side the entire time, Nidhug, through it all. You abetted me, in your glorious form. I still remember you black as midnight, slick scaled with wings as wide as the horizon. Your eyes, bright as the sun, and claws as long as bastard swords. You have suffered your own punishment and depletion as a result...all for my sake."

He bowed his head loyally as she continued. "We drew up our plan and inasmuch began our journey. Four creatures we created with your blood and magic, my wisdom, and a portion of my remaining power. None survived. Until..."

"The Fifth."

She nodded. "Yes, the Fifth. He was perfect in every way. Vicious enough to do what needed to be done, cunning, opportunistic, and I *thought*...loyal. And you, Nidhug, you never revealed your involvement in his making so I could remain his sole commander. I will never forget that."

Nidhug tilted his head. "Yes, my Queen, but may I ask, what is this about?"

"Without Lúth, we stand no chance. Fifth's sole purpose was to acquire this power and bring it to me, to us, as payment for the existence he was given. He chose to betray, just like the rest of creation. As you know, Lúth was always the goal. The One Power. The very life and light that God spoke into creation first, so as to be the means of sustenance for us all. There can be no victory if you do not claim Lúth from Fifth."

"I have promised I will."

"You have."

She paused and her eyes narrowed viciously.

"The return of the dragons means the tutelary are playing their final hand. They have chosen to involve themselves once again in the lives of the blasphemous mortals of Aimsire. The very creation that adored but refused to worship us, and then became so defiant to become entirely unappreciative of the gifts God offered.

"They turned away and even denied our existence. Instead of seeing, God has chosen to protect them and even offer grace. The other tutelary chose to obey, but I offer no such grace."

Her eyes flared. "If you still adore and follow me, return to me with Lúth as you have promised. If I had not been banished from Aimsire by the restraints of the others I would go with you. Crush their dragons, crush the betrayers, and I promise you rewards beyond your dreams."

"I will, my Queen." Nidhug bowed and walked away.

Nataxia turned and observed the souls of the dead again without another word. Nidhug paused just before leaving the throne room and looked at his queen. Though she tried to hide it, there was a fragility in her silhouette that he had never been there before. For the first time, she looked vulnerable. He turned and made his way to the portal that would return him to Aimsire. With her power diminishing, he knew the last time it would be activated would be to send his kin. She would not be able to do so again unless his mission was successful.

+++

Immediately upon his return, Nidhug advanced the Rage Queen's army over Pearlpoint Pass, obliterated what little was left of Pearlpoint Keep, and smashed the defenses in Riverhorn, leaving no survivors. The army then pushed down the long road into Highvale and halted after their victory.

A fast-moving storm was making its way off the Shiver Sea, and Nidhug decided to hold up where there was shelter and provisions to allow the army time to rest and regain their strength.

Sitting in the keep of the former city watch, Nidhug scanned the maps his scouts were continuously supplying from their patrols in the south. As he stared, he could not hide from his own thoughts. This excursion was becoming more a trek to see what these two had done with the new power they had acquired.

Rumors spoke of towers and lights in the sky. None of it made sense, but nothing was unbelievable, or impossible. Lúth was a power never before revealed on Aimsire, and he was determined to discover exactly what had been unleashed. Selfishly, none of this desire for discovery was being done for the service of his Queen, but he remained determined to return to her with it.

"Brother."

Nidhug looked up and bowed his head respectfully to Rezren. He walked from the table and they touched foreheads as Nidhug spoke.

"How are conditions?"

"Lorcan insists we keep moving."

"Of course he does. He's a Netherman, ignore him."

"The storm blowing in may finally convince him that we need to shelter in place. It is strange, brother, the clouds are ominous, dark, and heavy. Unnatural by Aimsire's standards."

Nidhug looked out the window.

"We must prioritize the sheltering of her majesty's army. See to it that all have appropriate protection and supplies for at least a week."

"That is a hard order to obey. There isn't much."

"I understand, but this looks to be a hard storm, and we have a lot of travel and fighting ahead of us."

Rezren walked over to the map table and spoke, "You have been driven with new life since your return and yet you have told me little about your exchange with our queen. Will you share the details with me now?"

"Her toil in exile is finally catching up with her. She sent me and has only one dose of power left to send our kin. If we are to restore her, we need to accomplish our task quickly."

"Then we shall with all haste once this storm has passed."

Rezren began to open the door and Nidhug informed him, "Brother. She is afraid, it was in her eyes."

"Fear is acceptable, quitting is not."

"She certainly has not quit, but we are her last hope."

"I understand."

Nidhug turned back to the map table. He knew they were at least two months from reaching Gryphonledge without this delay. A storm would only complicate matters.

+++

Myth'alas entered Commander Rose's council room and greeted her respectfully. She welcomed him.

"I take it you have the Netherman and his...companion situated?"

"His daughter. Yes."

"You don't find that odd?"

"That he would find a shred of compassion within him and take a young human under his care? No. Individuals are capable of making good decisions, despite the assumption's others may place on them."

"You are right, I should not judge so quickly. For the record, I am grateful they agreed to join us to fight. Others, or should I say, almost all within our ranks aren't as happy about it. That aside, if they are as powerful as you say, then their presence will certainly be of benefit."

"They are. As I told you, they wield very powerful magic and move with unexplainable quickness. When the battle comes you will see."

"Unfortunately, you're right. This situation is not a question of if, but when."

Larissa came into the room quickly and exclaimed, "Commander, come quick."

Myth'alas and Rose followed Larissa to the grand courtyard of the keep and Rose's eyes went wide. Dozens of high-ranking knights with the insignia of the Northern Guard were dismounting and being tended to. She shifted her gaze and searched until she saw who she was looking for.

"Commander Asher."

He turned as he removed his gloves.

"Commander Rose. Greetings to you."

"Greetings to me? What in the crevasse is going on? Why are you here?"

"Not the warmest of welcomes, but since you ask, The North is in shambles. We have lost many of our troops and the primary of our defensive positions. The two largest which remain are Amberwood Keep and Cliffshade Forest. I left them in capable hands to come here in order to have counsel with you."

She exhaled loudly and her heart wept for the lost.

"Apologies for my harsh greeting. I am sorry to hear this news. I have been trying to reach you for weeks and warn you of the coming invasion."

"Unfortunately, we received no word. First it was those two damned magic users, working up the coast and razing everything to the ground. They were too unpredictable and covert to track and kill. After that, the Nethermen ramped up their attacks and raids on our towns. They've been hitting everything along the border. Simultaneously, Nataxia's Army threw themselves at us like a tidal wave. Shield to sword we would have been able to hold our ground if all the coastal cities to supply us hadn't been destroyed. I don't know where the Rage Queen found those two wizards, but…"

Myth'alas spoke. "They are not working for her. They are a separate threat which we must address."

He furrowed his brow at the interruption but went wide eyed as the largest elf he had ever seen approached. Myth'alas continued his statement.

"The two you refer to are former agents of Nataxia but are now working rogue and have created an even bigger threat than her army."

"And you are?"

"First Prince Myth'alas of the Fara."

"I see. The 'redeemed' prince we have received word about."

"Yes, I was in the darkness for a time…"

"And saw to the death of many of my soldiers."

Ignoring his quip, Myth'alas continued. "We know we can fight her army. What the wizards have created however…we are still trying to find a solution."

Shaking his head in disbelief, Commander Asher Steelpike commented confidently.

"First of all, we aren't going to hang on every word or bit of advice from an elf, not even one who calls himself a prince. Secondly, everything that can be made can be destroyed. That's what soldiers do, we kill our enemies and we break their things."

Rose intervened. "Before you get so resolute, I would suggest we go take a look together so you can see for yourself."

"Very well. We have ridden hard to get here and need rest. First light tomorrow we will go see this, well, whatever it is. Before that, can you have accommodations prepared for me and my commanders? The soldiers will be fine in the barracks or tents, but my knights need solid rest."

"Of course, Commander, we will see to it. You are always welcome in Gryphonledge." Rose turned to her squire. "Larissa, please see to accommodations for Sir Asher and his knights."

"Aye, Ma'am."

Larissa left and Rose turned to Sir Trystan.

"Please see to the care of the steelguard that have arrived. Find them food, water, and shelter so they can rest. Also, please see that these horses get tended to, they look exhausted."

"Aye, Commander."

+++

Kali had been sitting for hours with her eyes closed until the day began to fade to evening. She was only a meter away from the warding, concentrating and attempting to decipher the complexities of its power. The unusually warm breeze was calming, as was the feeling of the earth beneath her.

Over the last two weeks, she had become friends with some of the soldiers. They noticed her daily pattern of study and began interacting with her. Some had even begun to stand guard to watch over her when she went to study the ward. They had never been asked to do so, a true sign of respect.

Their comfort level with a wizard in their presence was increasing. Sometimes they would even be waiting for her in the morning as she made her way up the hill. They would fall in behind her and follow, addressing her only if she spoke first.

Opening her eyes, Kali stared at the Gray Tower. The pulse of its magic, like a heartbeat, was as consistent as it had been since the first day she saw it. She watched the floating masses within the lava. They had stopped getting bigger and now just moved in a slow swirl around the middle of the magma lake.

Taking a deep breath and exhaling slowly, she pressed her fingers into the dirt. She could feel the spherical edge of the warding moving through the ground. She had mapped its location a week ago and discovered exactly which of the ardor channels it intersected. She dared not try to pass, not after what had happened to the soldiers.

As she calmed her breathing, the dragon in her heart whispered to her mind. The dragon's voice had been coming more frequently as of late. She had gotten used to it.

*"Dazzling, as always. Is it not?"*

"The beauty of it was never in question; it's the intent of those within that concerns me."

*"We could be within. You can feel it, through the ardor, the power that could be ours. You deny it, but you know it."*

"WE… are not you. You are only the shadow of my former self; you are no longer the driving force of my desires."

The dragon laughed and hissed. *"Still refusing to embrace the nature of us. A pity. Since you refuse to heed my words…"*

Instantly, the magic around the Gray Tower burst forth, and she gasped. The warding was suddenly a mixture of orange, blue, and green light, swirling like braids in concentric waves. Kali gazed in awe.

*"Child, you have become so hindered by the lack of challenges that you have become blind; therefore, I am forced to show you."*

The dragon's presence faded and Kali stood to her feet, turning to speak to her escorts.

"Do you…do you see that?"

"I'm sorry, Mistress Kali. What?"

"That! Do you see it?!"

The soldiers looked at the tower and nodded.

"Yes, the Gray Tower, the one you come and stare at every day. Yes, we see it."

"NO, the…"

She huffed, of course they couldn't see what she was seeing, but she knew who could.

"Can one of you please go and retrieve Ceridwyn and Rayann?"

"Yes, of course!"

The junior of the two soldiers departed in haste and the second soldier approached

"What is it, Mistress Kali? What did you see?"

"The answer."

+++

207

"Yes, I see it," Ceridwyn exclaimed, "What does it mean?"

"It's not just magic, it's all magic. A twisting braid, woven by the presence of Lúth. Sun, Moon, Terra, all are present. Unlike Shakyna which acts as a catalyst, Lúth is the creation force which God established at the Dawn Light. A magic unto itself. Fifth and Piramay only understand the magics of Aimsire. It's all they have to work with, as do we. There is nothing new here. There's no mystery or vast unknown. There's only the presence of a power that can weave it all together. It could never be undone by one, however, by the combined effort of those with knowledge…"

"It might be unwoven."

Kali smiled. "Exactly. If we can manage to focus our magic, all three of us, upon an isolated location, say, the weak spot I discovered, we may be able to unweave that section of the warding. That would create an entrance to allow the troops to enter unharmed. Come, let me show you."

Back in Kali's command tent, the wizards stood over the table map as Kali sketched.

"A portal frame, like the ones you can create, cousin, combined with the mixed magic of our three kinds. If we channel it against a concentrated area, we can nullify the energies and create a void."

Ceridwyn interjected. "How large can we make this breach?"

"Theoretically, as large as channeling the necessary amount of magic will allow. Obviously the larger it becomes the more power we need to expend."

Rayann spoke. "We need to open an aperture large enough to get the steelguard and knights through as quickly as possible, not to mention the siege machines. Not knowing how much energy that will require is something we need to know up front. Our presence will be needed on the battlefield; we can't be locked down simply holding open the warding."

"Any ideas on how to do that?"

"No. My moon portals are charged with magic. They can move things from one place to another, but projecting the magic continually focused on a single location, that is something I have never attempted or even thought to try."

"Well, we need to start thinking about it."

Ceridwyn spoke. "Kali, you have definitely given us a mystery to ponder."

"Isn't solving mysteries one of your favorite things?"

Ceridwyn laughed. "Yes, in fact, it is."

They said their farewells and Kali settled in for the evening. For the first time in a long time, she felt she might finally be attaining a solution.

# Chapter 16 – Winter Wonder Gryphonledge

Aeolis had arrived at first light. Ceridwyn gazed out her bedchamber window, shivering in the morning cold as she stared in awe.

"By the light Aeolis, I have never seen it snow like this."

The icy cold, stone floor stung her feet as she padded across the room, hurrying back to him, reclining on the sofa beside the hearth.

"Yesterday was so warm and now it's as if God is personally attempting to freeze the towers off the face of Aimsire."

She laid her head on his shoulder and he wrapped an arm around her to offer warmth. They stared at the fire in silence until Ceridwyn moaned.

"I just want to sit here with you all day and hibernate."

"What's stopping us?"

"Duty and responsibility. I doubt we will be traveling to see the towers in this weather, but there is still so much to prepare." She turned her head and placed a kiss on his face. "I am ready for all of this to be over so we can start watching those sunsets."

"Me too."

She whined playfully as she grabbed a blanket and pulled the covers over her face.

"Ohhh, Aeolis…make it go away!"

He laughed and pulled her in closer. Her hand came out from under the covers and she flicked a finger. The fire flared and she spoke with feigned exhaustion.

"Oh dear. I am but a fragile wizard and exhausted from casting my spell. I suppose all that is left to do is lie here and rest until lunch."

Aeolis kissed the top of her head and they settled into the warmth of one another for the rest of the morning.

+++

Most of the soldiers on watch in Still Mead had been ordered to return to Gryphonledge when the snow started coming down heavily. Kali had returned as well and was sitting in her room staring out the window in thought. There was a soft knock followed by a timid voice.

"Ms. Kali? It's me, Raspberry."

Kali opened the door.

"Good morning, Raspberry. Come in."

"Thanks. I wanted to talk to you about something, you know, if you have time."

"Of course, let's sit by the fire. Would you like some tea?"

"Do you have the honey mint kind? Like Ms. Ceridwyn makes all the time?"

Kali answered with a smile. "Of course."

Settling into her chair, Raspberry spoke, "So, I was chatting with Ms. Rayann and Ms. Ceridwyn last night. Well, they were chatting, and I was in the room listening. Actually, I was playing with Braeren, and they were over by the fire, and they were talking, and I was trying to pay attention to Braeren, but what they were saying was so very interesting, so I was kind of distracted and trying really hard to keep playing with Braeren while at the same time trying to…"

"Raspberry?"

"Yes, Ms. Kali?"

"What was said that was so interesting?"

Raspberry's cheeks flushed as she sipped her tea.

"They said you found a way through the warding that's protecting the towers."

"Theoretically, yes. I have an idea, but I am still trying to work out the practicalities."

"What's that?"

"The actions you apply to ideas to make them work."

Raspberry nodded her head. "This is really good tea."

"Thank you." Kali smiled patiently. "Is that all you came to say to me?"

"Huh? OH, no! I thought I might be able to help with the… um…practicecastleties."

"Practicalities."

"Yeah, those."

"How do you feel you can help?"

"Well, as you know, I'm a Balladeer, so I can play music and make stuff happen. I was thinking last night after I went back to my room that maybe my music could help make the opening thing happen in the warding…or something. I don't really know how, for sure, I haven't actually thought beyond the idea. But I also figured if there was anyone smart enough to chat with, it would be you. I decided to come talk and see if that might work? I really wanna help, so I was hoping you would let me try."

"Do Rayann and Ceridwyn know you came to see me?"

"No, Ms. Kali. I had to leave before the snow got too deep for me to get back to my room. I didn't have a chance to mention my idea to them. This snow is really crazy, huh? I've never seen it snow so much!"

Kali studied the halfling a moment before responding.

"You are very smart, Raspberry. You know that, right?"

She blushed. "I…ummm, well. I try to be smart."

"You are, and I think your idea has potential. Are you able to get your lute and come back safely? I would like to try some experiments mixing my magic with yours to see what's possible."

"Yeah! Sure! The guards started clearing the walkways this morning, no more trudging through the snow for this halfy! I can be back in a few minutes!"

"Great, I will refill the kettle. We have a lot to do, and we're going to need plenty of tea."

+++

Raised voices filled the hall followed by a loud clang. The door to Commander Rose's office burst open and Commander Asher Steelpike entered angrily.

"You brought a Netherman into our keep!?"

Lady Rose stood and left her squire as she approached from the table where they were working. Her voice immediately filled with authority.

"As it is *my* keep to command. Yes, I did."

"He is our enemy!"

"Do you have proof or evidence to back up this accusation, Sir Asher?"

"He's a bloody Netherman! What further proof is needed?"

"He has agreed to fight with us to assist in destroying the towers. By definition, that makes him our ally."

The guard entered, adjusting his chest plate which had a fresh dent in it. Clearly Sir Asher had shoved the man aside so he could get past. The guard reached for his sword to protect his commander. Lady Rose subtly shook her head. He released his grip but stayed, watching the northern commander like a hawk.

"For longer than history can bear witness, we have fought, bled and died in the north to keep the south safe and secure from his kind. I refuse to put *my* steelguard on a battlefield beside a Netherman."

"Then don't."

"You choose his kind over your own? You are a traitor to humanity, Commander Rose."

"Am I? I'm not the one threatening to withhold my soldiers from an inevitable battle that will determine the continuance of life for all of us."

His cheek twitched in anger. Rose inhaled a calming breath before she continued.

"Sir Asher, how would you respond if a fellow commander walked into a keep under your command, insulted you, bullied your troopers, and disavowed one of your direct orders?"

He remained silent.

"As I thought. You have no right or reasonable position to question my authority here, especially in front of subordinates. You should be ashamed of yourself."

"Not as ashamed as I would be if I willingly allowed enemies into my fortifications with open arms."

"Would these be the fortifications you build by evicting weefolk from their granted lands?"

"What are you talking about?"

"I heard what happened at Hobnob. You displaced an entire village of halflings so you could build a garrison. A garrison, I might add, that was clearly not for their protection, nor was arguably necessary except for the easy access it provided to the farmland and rivers beside it."

"So, what?"

Lady Rose paused, "Sadly, it appears the story I heard is true. I was hoping for a reasonable rebuttal, not conformation."

Sir Asher's eyes drifted to Larissa who was still standing by the table, watching him intensely. His gaze returned to Commander Rose.

"None of you central or southerners have the faintest idea what we endure in the north. The threats we face constantly would overwhelm you. Your cushy little life down here depends on us doing what needs to be done, up there, without regret."

"I'm sure creating fortifications hundreds of kilometers away from Nethermen borders is changing the course of the war effort against them."

"You have not heard the last from me on this."

"I'm sure I haven't."

Sir Asher turned and brushed past the guard. Larissa stepped forward and whispered to Lady Rose.

"What do you want to do about this, Commander?"

"Nothing. All that has happened is a disagreement and an exchange of harsh words between equals. There is no crime in that. We'll all just keep watch, for now."

+++

With the snow significantly reducing any outside threats, the city watch and steelguard were reassigned to assist the city custodians with snow removal and aiding those who needed it. The snow was falling so fast that constant attention to clearing the major thoroughfares was required.

Sergeant Erika had just finished a shift and was taking a rest in the barracks when she heard heavy footsteps approaching. She looked up as Sir Asher and his two most trusted generals, Sir Walter Eymer and Sir Donovan McFrawn approached. She hurried to her feet and saluted.

"My sirs!"

Commander Asher spoke, "At ease, Sergeant. I understand that you accompanied Lady Kellan on that foolish expedition north and have been folded into the ranks of Lady Rose's troopers."

"Yes, sir. Her squad has been reassigned as well."

"First off, I am sorry for the loss of Lady Kellan. She had great potential. Second, you and Lady Kellan's troopers are being brought back into the Northern Guard, where you belong. Her troopers will be folded in under General McFrawn's command. You on the other hand, will be reporting directly to me from now on. I am also promoting you to Command Sergeant. As soon as this snow clears, I am putting you in charge of a platoon."

"I...thank you, sir." She saluted again.

"There is another matter, one of grave importance that I came to discuss with you. Myth'alas the Elf Prince has brought a Netherman and a human companion into our keep. We hear that she is an ice witch of some sort."

"Yes, sir. I was at the meeting when they were discussing it and verbalized my opposition to the idea."

"I would have expected nothing less from you. You are part of the Northern Guard and have a much clearer head on matters of this type. Bringing that foul beast and witch into our defensive walls was foolish at best. It's even more suspicious that it was initiated by Myth'alas. He could be positioning for an attack from within. I don't buy this whole, 'redeemed prince' story I keep hearing about him.

"Though I don't have the authority to remove Lady Rose or circumvent her command, we can start gathering information and set a vote among the Council of High Commanders to have her charged with negligence of duty, or perhaps, even treason.

"I would like a report from you, as soon as possible. Make special detail about everything regarding Myth'alas, the meeting you attended and anything else you have heard or know. I am also removing you from snow removal duties so you can focus your attention. We'll let the grunts handle the manual labor. Moving forward, your mission is to keep a close eye on the vermin that sit among us."

"I will not let you down, sir."

"That will be all for now, Command Sergeant Tiliz."

+++

"Raspberry, open your eyes."

The halfling stared in amazement as she whispered, "The green light is twisting around the candle flame!"

"Yes, it is."

"So that means..."

"Yes, it does."

"WE DID IT!!" Raspberry beamed with pride. "Does this mean we can do it with moon magic too?"

"Though this is but a candle flame it is the element of fire and burns with similar attributes to sun magic. The energetic properties of moon magic are comparable, so, theoretically, yes, it should work."

"Practicalities!" Raspberry uttered with confidence.

Kali laughed before continuing.

"Do you feel tired or worn out in any way?"

"No, Ms. Kali. I'm just super excited that it worked! If anything, I'm really really happy!"

"Excellent. I will summon Ceridwyn and Rayann. Now that we know you can displace and wrap terran magic through a flame, we need to know if you can do so when two wizards are casting. After that, all three of us. Mostly, we need to know what kind of stress it might put upon your body."

"Will it be dangerous, Ms. Kali?"

"To be truthful, any venture of this kind, by its nature, is dangerous and not without risk. Think of it instead as, do you think it will be worth it?"

Raspberry didn't hesitate as she blurted out, "It definitely will be!"

"I agree. Please don't worry; we will be sure to keep a sharp eye on you."

+++

Rayann arrived after receiving Kali's summons. The emotions that flooded her when she entered the room were palpable and she smiled.

"It's obvious there is some good news to be shared. What have you two been up to?"

Just as Kali was about to answer, Ceridwyn burst into the room, closing the door quickly. Her cheeks were flushed, her robes were obviously put on in haste and everyone looked at her curiously. Rayann felt the warmth of positive, relaxed emotions and scanned her dear friend's face.

"What's going on with you?"

Ceridwyn blushed.

"Nothing. Kali sent a summons; I arrived...quickly."

Kali glanced at Rayann and playfully raised an eyebrow.

Rayann spoke directly to her friend's mind. *"Ceri, what scandalous activities have you been partaking in?"*

*"Nothing scandalous or out of decency transpired. Let's just say, in all innocence, I had a wonderful prelude to what my future with Aeolis might hold."*

Rayann winked and Ceridwyn's cheeks went as red as Raspberry's hair. Kali cleared her throat and spoke with obvious, playful chiding in her voice.

"If you two hens are done mind chatting so none else can hear, Raspberry and I have spent the better part of this snowy day doing some useful experiments."

The halfling interrupted as she blurted out, "We were able to make magic stick together!"

Ceridwyn and Rayann looked at her curiously.

Kali continued. "In a manner of speaking, Raspberry is correct. Together, we discovered that with the magic of Balaby's songs and a slow, steady casting on my part, we could weave terran magic with fire."

Ceridwyn's eyes went wide.

"You're kidding?"

"I'm not." Kali turned to Raspberry. "If you would."

Raspberry lifted her lute and started to play. She sang a song that carried through the room like the warmth of the sun on a mid-summer's day. Kali pulled the power of Shakyna through her body as she raised the energy of terra up through her feet. Green light trickled from her fingers and moved as if pushed by the music. The magic wrapped itself around the candlelight, steady and stable before finally zig-zagging in and out of the flame. Rayann turned to Ceridwyn with a look of hope on her face.

As they ended the demonstration, Kali continued, "Obviously, this was only an experiment with a candle, but it offers promise. Now we need to try putting it together. Rayann, on our next attempt I'd like you to add your moon magic to the experiment. Ceridwyn, as we do so, please keep an eye on our little magician here to make sure she doesn't begin to feel faint."

By the next morning, the snowfall had nearly stopped. The clouds were still low and heavy but most of the citizens of Gryphonledge were outside, pitching in to clear the streets.

Bold'Rock was respecting Commander Rose's request that he stay isolated as most of the knights and steelguard weren't comfortable with his being in the city. Wearing only a thin, blue, linen dress, Pela ventured out to get them some much needed food.

The architecture of the city captivated her. Never in her fifteen years had she seen buildings that reached into the sky. Some were so tall that they vanished into the low hanging clouds.

She heard children laughing and followed the sound. The streets began to widen and she found herself in the town square. Dozens of children of all ages ran and played, throwing snowballs and ducking behind the snow mounds to avoid being hit. A boy her age approached and smiled.

"Hi, my name is Alastair, what's yours?"

She looked at him skeptically before answering.

"Pela."

"Nice to meet you, Pela. Are you...*LOOK OUT!*"

He pulled her down and a snowball that would have hit her in the head exploded on the wall. Instinctually she began to channel magic to defend herself. When Alastair started laughing and packing snowballs of his own, she started to realize there was no danger. Her brow furrowed with confusion. Never in all her days had she been in a situation where someone had thrown something at her that wasn't meant to do harm.

She watched as Alastair stood, threw three snowballs of his own, and then ducked back behind the mound of snow.

"What are you waiting for, Pela? Make some snowballs! Let's get 'em back!"

She immediately understood. This was 'play', as her father had explained to her. The exact behavior she had witnessed so many times in the north while watching the children her own age run about and do such curious, fun looking activities with one another. She felt something inside her come to life. She desperately wanted to participate and followed his example, joining in the fun of it all.

Eventually, the children began to return home for lunch and warmth. Alastair and Pela were lying next to one another on top of a snow pile.

"Hey, I just realized that you're not wearing a coat. Aren't you freezing?"

"No."

"Is your family poor? Can you not afford winter clothing?"

"We can afford clothes; it's just that snow and cold don't bother me."

"Why?"

"Because I can make my own snow."

He sat up and stared at her.

"Liar."

She sat up and raised her hand. From the center of her palm an icicle formed and then twisted into the shape of a snowflake. She reached and snapped it off, handing the delicate ice crystal over in friendship. His face instantly showed fear and he stood.

"You're that girl that came with the Netherman! My father's in the steelguard. He heard everything about you. He said you're dangerous!"

"No, Alastair, I'm not. We're here to help, I promise!"

He began backing away and ran into something. He turned and looked up at Sir Asher's stern face.

"Off with you, boy. Wisht!"

He ran off as Asher turned his eyes to Pela.

"What are you doing out here? Where is the Netherman?"

"My father is in his quarters."

"HA, 'father'. Well, no matter what you call him, see that he stays there, and get yourself back there too."

Pela narrowed her eyes and stared at him defiantly.

"You don't intimidate me, witch."

She watched him cautiously as she backed away before running to the stable where she and her father were housed. It was clean but humiliating to her that they had to sleep where there had recently been horses. As she returned, Bold'Rock noted that there was no food, but more importantly, that she was crying.

"Daughter, why are you sad?"

"Some stupid knight yelled at me."

"Why did he yell at you? Were you misbehaving again?"

219

"No father! He figured out who I am and told me to come back here. He was really mean about it."

Bold'Rock sighed heavily and moved to be closer to her.

"Unfortunately, daughter, that is to be expected. The prince told me that some Northern Command showed up recently. As you know they especially hate our kind. We will find our way around them as we always have."

"I want to go home."

"I would like to go home too, my Pela, but we have no home, not after we left."

She looked up at him tearfully.

"Why did you choose me? You could have given in to the chief and let me leave alone. Then you could have stayed with your family and your clan."

"Though the chief is my brother, he was wrong to exile you once you came of age. You danced The Ceremony of Blossoms right along with the other young nethergirls."

He reached over and lifted her sleeve, exposing the jagged, rock shaped scar on her arm.

"You were marked with a knife dipped in fire as is the way of our clan when we come of age."

He gently unrolled his own sleeve and got low so their scars were close to one another.

"We are *both* members of the Rock Clan, and *you* are my family. Just because you cannot take a mate does not make you less so. Your gentle pale skin, your height, your hair, your eyes, your magic…none of that matters. You were *marked* as a clan member. It forevermore shall be by the scar on your skin. That is the bond we share.

"The humans have their prejudice against our kind; we have ours against them, because we have always been enemies. Amongst ourselves, we have no right to hate.

"To harbor any prejudice against a member of your clan unless they have broken our laws, that is wrong. You are my daughter. I declared it before the sacred fire at Stone Seat. That bond holds true, no matter what. I will never allow harm to come to you so long as I am able, my Pela'Rock."

She began to cry again as she pressed in to hug him tightly.

"Commander, he attacked your guard, that's grounds enough to have him arrested and his men removed from the city."

"I understand, but no one was hurt. We only exchanged harsh words."

"He…"

"Sir Ordin, as senior generals of the steelguard and your knights, I am informing you and Sir Gregory so you can inform your officers and we can all keep a watchful eye. Sir Trystan has already been briefed, and the city watch is on alert to report any suspicious movement or actions by members of the Northern Guard. I am not taking this lightly; however, we don't need to act unless something serious happens."

Sir Gregory cleared his throat.

"With all respect, Commander, his actions were grossly inappropriate and by the honor of our knighthood require a response."

"I don't disagree. If circumstances were different, we would likely be pursuing a different course of action. We need to remember that he is only here because the Northern Guard were pushed south due to unsurmountable losses and the decimation of their defensive positions. My decision, as your Commander, is that for now we are to observe, remain vigilant and report anything suspicious. Understand?"

Sir Gregory and Sir Ordin complied. Rose felt relief that she had two senior generals such as these that she could trust without hesitation.

"With that unpleasant information out of the way, we need to focus on the assault. As you know the Netherman, and his daughter are being housed in the stables. I understand that you both frowned upon the decision to allow him into the city, however, I have met with him and I want to offer assurance to you both that his intentions to help are genuine.

"He is loyal to Myth'alas and I am confident he won't betray us. I would ask that you give him a chance to prove himself before passing any further judgment. Agreed?"

Though there was hesitance on their faces, Ordin and Gregory nodded in agreement.

"Sincerely, gentlemen, I thank you for your trust. I realize it's an unusual decision, and though I know you will follow my orders even if you disagree, having *your* trust in this case matters greatly to me. With that said, how are we doing in terms of preparations?"

Sir Ordin pointed to the map where the siege machines were being built.

"The snow has delayed things the last few days; however, we are starting to move troopers back to Still Mead and all but one of our siege weapons are complete. The last one requires a little more work as we are attempting to construct a deployable rope bridge that can be fired from the top allowing us to cross the lava lake onto one of the towers."

"You never informed me of this idea."

"Apologies, commander, but we weren't sure it would work until recently. I planned to brief you once we knew."

"That's acceptable. So, what's the plan?"

"With two cannons mounted on the top, modified ammunition can fire grappling hooks pulling rope behind them. The Black Tower has an observation deck at the top. Our hope is to get the siege tower in range, fire the ropes and send a squad in to scout and if possible, find the slumbering wizard and slay him."

"Risky plan, but I trust you."

Sir Gregory stepped to the map.

"Once we know when and if the wizards are going to be able to get us in safely, our plan is to deploy our troops and weapons along this ridge, down through this natural trench, and up along this hillside so we can attack from three sides. We have tripled the production of canons, including some new designs the engineers have dubbed 'Tower Busters'. They have a barrel nearly three-quarters of a meter in diameter and when I witnessed a test firing, I assure you they deliver quite a wallop."

Rose approved the plan and spoke. "I do have some good news. Larissa brought word to me this morning that the wizards have discovered a way through the warding. They plan to get it in place as soon as the snow clears enough for them to do so."

Sir Gregory looked at Sir Ordin and then to Lady Rose with confidence on his face.

"We will inform the knights and steelguard to be ready on a moment's notice."

+++

The smell of manure and wet hay filled the air, accompanied by the constant scraping of a stable hand's shovel mucking a stall two spaces down. It had been going on for a long time and was starting to annoy Pela.

She sighed heavily and leaned against the stone wall. Bold'Rock was sitting nearby, weaving pure, silver wire around the bundled sticks on the end of his massive staff.

Myth'alas spoke as he and Olwa approached. "Good morning Bold'Rock, Pela'Rock. How are you feeling today?"

Bold'Rock looked up from under his bushy eyebrows and responded gruffly.

"Fine enough, Warrior Prince. To what do we owe this visit?"

"For the purpose of apologizing. I had no idea they were going to house you like this. I would have had you stay in the Glen until closer to the battle had I known. I thought your presence might break down some of their fear. Instead, they are treating you like animals."

"There is no harm, we have lived in worse conditions. At least they gave us clean hay."

He laughed and offered a seat beside himself. Myth'alas complied and sat so they could talk.

Olwa approached Pela and smiled.

"My heart sings to see you. May I sit?"

Her limited ability to trust being so recently further compromised, she paused. With a suspicious nod, she finally agreed. As he sat, she studied his face. He was beautiful and elegant, as if painstakingly carved by a sculptor without a hint of blemish or flaw. She had never seen a male that appeared so perfect in their features. A strange flutter moved in her stomach.

"I'm Olwa Pilininge, Prince Myth'alas' adherent. You're Pela'Rock, right?"

"You can just call me Pela. Pela'Rock is my clan name. It's not really necessary to say the whole thing when we're here."

"Ahh, I see. Well, it's good to meet you, Pela. Prince Myth'alas is very sorry about the conditions you are living in. He thought we should come see you. I agree with him, this isn't right."

"We've stayed in caves and run-down hovels that were far less comfortable. I admit, however, I was starting to get accustomed to that feather bed in the cottage Rayann and Myth'alas are letting us use."

"So, how long have you known Bold'Rock?"

"My whole life, he's, my father."

"Well, I mean, he's not *really* your father. He adopted you, or something, right?"

"He's my father!"

Olwa instinctually recoiled in response to the sudden aggression in her voice. Pela's eyes went down in frustration but also embarrassment. Taking a deep, calming breath, she looked up again. She decided to change the subject before continuing.

"So, what does that mean, to be an adherent?"

"It means the prince is training me, guiding me, and mentoring me."

"In what ways?"

"How to listen. How to lead. How to fight. Whatever he sees fit really. Someday I will be part of the royal court of the Fara Commonwealth. It's all just learning how to be so."

"You don't look happy about it."

He smiled at her intuition and began to lean in towards her. She watched him with wariness, wondering what he was doing, but for some strange reason she stayed still so he could bring his face closer to hers. He smelled like lavender and fine linen. She felt that strange flutter in her stomach again as his eyes locked onto hers.

Olwa whispered, "The truth is, Pela, I am loyal to the prince and I like being under his tutelage, but I'm not happy about learning to be royal."

"Then why do you do it?"

"Tradition. Duty. Obligation, maybe? Honestly, I don't really know."

"Those seem like very strange reasons to do something, especially if you don't like it."

Her response made him grin. She felt her cheeks get warm as he smiled at her words. His entrancing eyes remained locked on hers. He was about to speak again when a voice broke the silence.

"Ready, Olwa?"

Prince Myth'alas was standing behind him; clearly his conversation with Bold'Rock had concluded.

Olwa stood and looked at her in a friendly manner.

"It was nice to meet you, Pela. Until our hearts are near once again."

She smiled timidly. Pela watched him leave until she couldn't see him any longer and then turned to Bold'Rock.

"What did Myth'alas want, father?"

"The wizards have found a way through the warding. We will be battling soon and then we can return to the Glen and continue to live near he and his family with no further obligation. He reaffirmed to me that we are welcome to stay there as long as we like, even the rest of our lives, should we desire to do so."

"Father, do you know if an elf adherent lives in the same location as their elf prince?"

Bold'Rock shrugged. "I don't know the ways of the elves' daughter. Why do you ask?"

"Umm, no reason."

She blushed unrepentantly at her dishonest answer. She felt her stomach move once again knowing if she was going to be living in the glen, Olwa might be there too.

Two stalls down, Erika peeked out from under her wide brimmed hat and kept shoveling; taking note of everything she had just heard and seen.

# Chapter 17 – Lay of the Land

Ever since the snows had ceased and a solution to breaching the warding was discovered, Kali had been working tirelessly. Upon her return to Still Mead, she was treated to a wonderful surprise. The warding had kept the snows off the land within, revealing its exact location all the way around the towers.

At Kali's request, the knights ordered the steelguard to place flags ten meters apart around the entire perimeter of the warding. The entry point for the breach had been marked clearly. Salted roads were being built which would allow the soldiers to advance quickly and the siege machines to be moved efficiently.

Sir Trystan's voice came from the command tent entrance.

"Kali, are you there?"

"Yes, come in."

He entered, removing his gloves.

"The road at the entry point is completed. You may inform Rayann and Ceridwyn that they are welcome to join us when ready so construction of the breach entrance can begin."

"Thank you, Sir Trystan. I appreciate the update."

"Still with the 'Sir'." He laughed.

Kali spoke softly. "I have told you already; we cannot allow ourselves…"

She paused and took a moment to look deep into his eyes. She stepped a little closer. His glance traced her face longingly as she stared back.

"You can't allow what, exactly, Kali Fionntán, Wizard of the Terra?"

Without warning she stepped through the remaining space between them and pressed her lips hungrily against his. Surprised but unshaken, he returned the kiss, bringing his hands up her back and pulling her in close.

As he gripped her wizard robes, disturbing the pockets within the pleats, the delightful odor of hidden spell reagents permeated the air. The scents of lavender, jasmine, sage, dandelion, and salty sand swirled around them as they held their bodies close to one another. She cooed softly as he pressed in further before finally leaning back, hesitantly.

His cheeks were flush as he spoke.

"That was…much better than I imagined it would be."

"My change of heart?"

"No, how warm your lips are."

She gently brought her hands around his back before pressing her cheek against his chest as she had observed her cousin do with Myth'alas. Suddenly she could hear his heartbeat and a deep warmth raced through her. It became obvious why her cousin did this so often.

"Trystan, what I am about to say to you is so wrong, but I must say it. I keep trying to convince myself that there should be no attachments that cloud our minds. It only becomes a weapon our enemies can use against us. I've seen it dozens of times.

"I have purposely pushed you away. It was for logical, practical reasons. But in the end, Trystan, I do desire to know you more…personally. I don't want one of us to die in the upcoming battle without knowing how or where this could have gone."

"Not exactly the most romantic thing I've ever heard, but from you, I'll take it."

She laughed and buried her face in his tunic as she felt tears well up in her eyes. She also wished to maintain this embrace.

"Well, in my defense, romance is not really the sort of thing one can learn from a book. I have no experience in this."

"Neither do I."

She pushed away from him.

"Sure you don't. Every soldier has a hundred tavern wench stories to tell. It's okay, I don't…"

"No, Kali, I don't! I'm not that kind of knight, or man."

She lingered a moment and then smiled timidly. It was the first shy smile he had ever seen from her and it caused his heart to skip a beat.

"Kali, are you aware of how beautiful you actually are?"

"That's one of the few things I can say I'm *not* aware of."

"I must say, you're not a very good listener then. I've been trying to tell you this all along. To restate, you are the most amazing woman I have ever met, in every way."

Her cheeks blushed as she whispered, "Well, I better get back to work."

"Me too. Can I see you this evening after chow? Perhaps a private fire for two?"

She smiled and nodded in agreement. He turned and left. The instant the tent flap fell, the dragon locked in her heart violently rattled the cage.

+++

Rayann fussed with her robes, smoothing the front again while holding Braeren with her other arm. Myth'alas turned and smiled, leaning in to kiss her cheek.

"You look ravishing, beloved. No need to keep doing that."

"He doesn't like me; I want to at least look presentable."

"There's no cause to worry about that, Jerrin doesn't like anybody."

She giggled nervously as Myth'alas gave his wife a playful wink just before High Consummate Jerrin entered. He offered the traditional elven greeting before speaking formally.

"Good morning, First Prince, Rayann, Olwa."

Empathically, Rayann could feel Jerrin's indifference. Her stomach went to knots and she instinctively drew her son closer to her chest. Jerrin stepped aside and her mother-by-marriage, Narlea, entered with her handmaiden. The matriarchal elf smiled warmly as she approached. Rayann bowed her head respectfully before taking a step forward.

"Mother. My heart sings to introduce you to Braeren, firstborn of your son Myth'alas, and future guardian of the forests. By God's will and your matriarchal blessing, may the fae always light his path, the moon always guide his steps, the sun always warm his soul, and the song of the Fara always be sung within his heart so he may greet others with it, all his days."

Rayann gently handed her son to his grandmother and stepped back. She whispered to her husband's mind.

*"Did I get the words right?"*

*"Yes, perfect."*

*"That was harder to memorize than any spell I've ever been tasked to learn."*

He reached and gently squeezed her hand as he watched his mother hold their son.

Narlea tilted her head as she leaned in and kissed the boy between the eyes. A glowing green light spread across his face and she looked up at Rayann.

"Daughter, by God's light, may you always guide his mind, teach him empathy, provide him love, sing the songs of our forests so he may know their words, and nurture his path."

She turned to Myth'alas.

"Son, by God's light, may you show him the secrets of our forests, protect him from harm, guide the strength of his arms so he will never unjustly harm another, and plant within his heart the seeds of our traditions so he may grow, flourish and bloom."

She paused and looked at them both.

"May God give you the wisdom and knowledge to raise him in the ways ascribed to us at the Dawn Light."

Narlea turned back to Rayann.

"The song of my heart is full of joy on this day, but also sadness. It is my honor to kiss the blessing upon my grandchild, but I mourn that you are leaving him with us. I don't say this because he is not welcome, he most certainly is, I say this because as a mother myself, I know the heartache you are feeling in leaving your child behind."

Rayann fought back her tears.

"Thank-you, mother, for keeping him safe. This battle we are about to face…there will be no secure place for a child. I know that he will be out of harm's way here in Faralanthis."

"We will protect him and love him, for he is our own." She turned to Jerrin. "And we *will* accept him."

Jerrin's rigid face never changed as his mother clearly communicated her thoughts. Rayann could feel the slightest hint of regret from him, but it left as fast as it had come.

Narlea turned to her handmaiden, Rainwen, who had been staring at Olwa the entire time. As Rainwen took Braeren in her arms, Narlea spoke.

"Why don't you and Olwa take my grandson to his room? Tell the guards this is their new prince, and they are to protect him with their lives."

"Yes, Consummate Mother, I will."

She looked shyly at Olwa who bid his farewell to Myth'alas. Together they left the room as Jerrin stepped forward.

"He looks strong. We will watch over him."

"Thank you, brother."

"Come, I know you have other matters you wish to discuss before you depart."

Narlea slipped her arm under Rayann's so their elbows were locked.

"Come, daughter, let us take in the gardens."

+++

"I suppose he could be described as handsome, for a half-breed I mean. Not that I would ever condone such a thing."

Rainwen looked up from the sleeping baby in the crib. Olwa was cringing inside at her words but revealed nothing of how he was feeling in his expression. She stepped over to him gracefully, as she had been trained to do, and offered a beautifully sweet smile.

"It is good to see you, Olwa. I have deeply missed you."

Without returning her affection, he forced a silent smile.

"Did you not miss me as well?" Her voice was pouty.

"There is so much I have needed to concentrate on that I have not had time to focus on us. Our prince has assigned me many duties and responsibilities to attend to. He has been teaching me how to fight, how to listen, how to lead. The upcoming battle will be dangerous and…"

"Let's go have lunch. I'm starving."

She grabbed his hand and pulled him along. They passed the guards who nodded respectfully before moving into the room to watch and protect Prince Braeren.

Rainwen sauntered out of the castle with Olwa at her side. She was beaming and gloating with her shimmering, almond shaped eyes. Olwa Pilininge was, in every manner, the most highly desired bachelor for any elf maiden of the court in their generation. His family was prominent, wealthy and powerful…and 'attractive' only began to describe the way he looked. Their parents had arranged the betrothal decades ago. Ever since Rainwen found every opportunity she could to reinforce to all the elf maidens in the Elven Commonwealth that he was already hers.

Rainwen Bloomwhisper was the daughter of high-born elves. They were among the leadership and elite nobility, governing the province of Whisperwood in the name of the High Consummate. Her entire education had been dedicated to grooming and preparing her for life in the aristocracy. Though of noble birth herself, marrying Olwa would solidify her place among the high regency of the Elven Commonwealth forever.

She had been taught her whole life to be a perfect specimen of femininity, elven grace, and beauty. She presented herself modestly, always wearing clothing that offered just enough to give a hint but not so much as to initiate whispers. Her almond shaped eyes glistened in even the dimmest light. Her skin was smooth and delicate like lily petals and her ginger red hair was down to her waist, always braided and fashioned.

Rainwen looked at the café steward and spoke with superiority in her voice.

"Two."

The young, wild looking elf bowed his head respectfully and ushered them to a table.

"Not this one. Something over there on the balcony, where we can see the river and the gardens."

"Apologies, that table is reserved."

"I see. Well, I am Rainwen Bloomwhisper, I will just inform my father of this denial against *my* wishes and..."

"I...apologies High Elfess Bloomwhisper. I will prepare the table for you at once."

He turned sheepishly to escort them to the balcony. After removing the place card, he bowed and left in haste. Rainwen rolled her eyes and whispered to Olwa, "By the light, you would think they'd have learned by now."

Sitting down, Olwa spoke. "Who would have learned?"

"The Scruffkins. We High Fara want to see the beauty of our forests and breathe in the fresh air, not be stuffed into the middle of a room."

"You mean, The Fae. Scruffkins is an awful term to use."

"Olwa, don't be so flowery and sentimental. That is not who they are anymore. The Fae were beautiful and delicately enchanting. The dancing lights that guide our way at night, drifting from the trees and floating among us are all that's left of the memories we hold for them. Scruffkins, on the other hand, deserve their new title. They are uncivilized and uncouth, scratching a living from the forests of The Tangles or selling themselves to us, hoping to learn how to better themselves, not that any are capable."

"Fae was adopted as a means to keep the term alive in our language, but the lights that swirl are not the individuals for whom they are called. We can change the names, but we cannot change the truth of what we Fara did and continue to do to them."

"Why are you acting this way?" Her tone did not hide her annoyance.

"What way?"

"I haven't seen you for three moons and all you are being is confrontational and rude. You haven't even commented on my new dress, which I wore for you! Not to mention the fragrant sprigs in my hair, or even my recent assignment as the Consummate Mother's handmaiden. That's a position of importance, Olwa. It's one of stature."

"You're right, it is."

Angrily, she leaned back and crossed her arms over her chest. The serving attendant approached.

"For lunch today, we are offering a delightful blackberry and strawberry platter drizzled with crystalized honey jam as well as fresh bread made with cracked grains from the human region of Ravenrest. For the main course, a delightful serving of rabbit and taro root, wrapped in beet greens underdressed with pistachio nuts and basil flowers. It's then roasted over hickory wood and drizzled with a white wine reduction, sourced from the vineyards in Rubyshire. It is quite savory. Shall I bring two portions?"

"I'm not hungry."

The attendant turned his attention to Rainwen, sulking in her chair and pursing her lips, avoiding all eye contact. Nervously, he shifted his gaze to Olwa.

"Are…you hungry?"

"I am. I will take a portion. Thank you."

The serving attendant left and Rainwen leaned in.

"Living with those humans has caused you to become brutishly cold and distant. I don't like it."

232

"I am not trying to be cold and distant; I just have a lot on my mind. This upcoming battle is going to be dangerous and we still haven't fully flushed out the attack plan."

"Well, there is no battle here. You are home and I'm all you need be focused on. You should only be thinking about and paying attention to me. I am your future consort!"

"You are. I'm sorry."

Her face softened as he gave into her tantrum and she reached across the table to grasp his hand.

"Oh, I could never stay angry at you."

The food arrived and Rainwen smiled.

"My, this smells delicious."

She pulled the platter across the table, grabbed her fork and began to eat. Olwa leaned back in his chair. Rainwen chattered incessantly as she ate his lunch. He looked out across the forest and his thoughts began to drift, wondering what Pela was doing right now.

+++

Myth'alas, Olwa, and Rayann had returned to Gryphonledge late. Despite that, at the rise of the sun, Olwa was waiting in the hallway. Myth'alas opened the door and nodded with approval.

"Good to see you. I figured you would be here, but with the late hour of our return missing our normal training session would have been acceptable."

"Never, my Prince. If you are willing to give me your time, it would be rude not to accept. I still have so much to learn before the battle."

They stepped out onto the street. The cold air behind the recent snowstorm lingered. As they walked Myth'alas spoke.

"I need to make a quick stop and see Bold'Rock. My brother is not willing to commit our battalions of rangers or armies to the battle. He has offered me only twelve. Six spear bearers and six archers."

"Did showing him the towers not change his heart?"

"It's more complicated than that, Olwa. His concern is the protection of the Elven Commonwealth, which I do understand.

For now, I will take what he gives. I need to inform Bold'Rock of their arrival. They have already been briefed that he and his daughter will be fighting alongside us. I owe it to him to offer the same information about them."

They made their way to the stables. Rounding the last corner, Olwa spotted Pela instantly. She was sitting at the entrance brushing out the straw that collected in her silvery hair while she slept last night. She looked up and her eyes locked on Olwa. Her stomach fluttered before turning to the elven prince.

"My father is inside, Prince Myth'alas."

"Thank you, Pela. Olwa, I will only be a few moments."

Myth'alas entered and Pela smiled bashfully at Olwa.

"Good morning. How was your journey to Faralanthis?"

"Awful. I had to see my parents and then was forced to have lunch with Rainwen."

"I don't understand. Why wouldn't you want to see your parents? And, who's Rainwen?"

"Plainly put, my parents are awful. They are rude, snobbish, and incredibly terrible to be around. They bully our house-elf and treat everyone they consider below them with little more consideration than they would their own trash. Worst part is, they want me to follow in their footsteps. That's where Rainwen comes in."

"Rainwen is an advisor for this?" She crinkled her brow in curiosity.

"No. She is my future life-mate."

Pela's face suddenly became very sad.

"Oh...I see."

"No! I don't want to marry her! Our parents arranged it decades ago."

"They did? Why?"

"I don't know. Obligation?"

"Olwa, I admit, I know very little about elves, but obligation seems to be the reason they do a lot of things."

He huffed. "Yeah."

"It's very strange to me, especially because you really don't seem happy about it."

"I agree."

"Then why keep doing it?"

He paused before feeling sadness well up inside him. "Honestly, I don't know."

She lifted her hand, catching a tear that was coming out from the corner of his eye with her finger. She held it up and the tear formed into the shape of a snowflake. Smiling, she offered it to him. As he took it the frozen crystals melted away.

"My father has taught me that's how easy it is to let things go. Maybe even all these obligations of yours."

He was about to respond when Myth'alas approached. "Alright, Olwa, let's go get some bruises."

With a laugh, Olwa stood.

"I look forward to seeing you again, Pela. Thanks for the kind words, and the snowflake."

For the second time in three days, she watched him leave. Her gaze lingered on him until he disappeared from her sight.

+++

Myth'alas and Olwa entered the training hall. Several dozen knights were there, training as usual, but the air was unusually tense this morning. As they stepped in, Erika, Sir Asher, and eight of his knights were standing on the mat they usually practiced on.

"Checking in with your mercenary before training today?"

Myth'alas steadied his heartbeat as he scanned the group. The warrior within him remained at peace as he responded.

"I spoke with Bold'Rock this morning. Interesting how that information reached here before myself and my adherent did."

"You are in a human keep; we know everything that happens within our walls."

Myth'alas responded, containing his laughter at such a ridiculous statement.

"What can I do for you this morning, Sir Asher?"

"I am on to you. You will not undermine this battle. Those wizards you cavort with and that beast with his ice witch are not welcome."

"Has Commander Rose changed her mind? If so, she has not informed me."

"What? No! By *my* authority."

"I must admit, Sir Asher, I am not fully attuned to the command structure of the knights and the steelguard, but from what I understand, you are the Northern Commander, and this is the territory of the Central Commander, meaning, Lady Rose is the one in charge."

"It doesn't matter. Authority is authority, wherever we go."

"Is that what you told your troops as you tucked tail and retreated to the south to find shelter and protection in Gryphonledge?"

"You have no idea what happened."

"I have some idea, Sir Asher. I used to be a general in the very army that defeated you. I know exactly what they did, and how. Frankly, I'm not surprised they got the best of you."

"Are you challenging my competence and command in battle?"

"Certainly not. If you were a competent commander, we wouldn't be standing here discussing the matter. You'd be in your keep, up north, Nataxia's army under your boots."

"How dare you attack my honor!"

Sir Asher drew his sword and his knights stepped back, allowing him space. Olwa began to step forward, but with the slightest flick of his hand, Myth'alas stopped him and spoke to his adherent's mind.

*"Worry not, Olwa, this won't take long. We'll still get to train today."*

As Sir Asher spit his next words, Myth'alas narrowed his eyes and calmed his breath, settling into a balanced stance.

"You shall pay for your insult, elf, with your tongue."

Sir Asher stepped to charge and a streak of crimson passed him in a blur. The clang of steel on steel echoed through the hall.

Myth'alas slid to a halt behind him. Sir Asher stumbled forward from the impact. The flat side of Myth'alas' blade, Blue Moon, had slapped against the backside of Sir Asher's cuirass. The mythical blade was back in its sheath before Sir Asher had recovered from the blow.

The elf prince's long, bright red hair settled back in behind him and he focused. Sir Asher turned and gritted his teeth before letting out a war cry and charged again.

Myth'alas slipped the overly obvious blow and Blue Moon sang as it exited the sheath. The edge slid along the top of Sir Asher's sword and Myth'alas skillfully turned the blade flat just before it would have taken the knight's head off. Several strands of Sir Asher's dark hair drifted through the space between them.

Calm, already standing and waiting, the elf prince stared at the knight. Blue Moon was once again back in its sheath before the commander had been able to turn around.

The rage building on Sir Asher's face was echoed in his sloppy, unbalanced stance. He charged again, lifting his sword to strike. Myth'alas, the fabled 'Crimson Wind', launched himself towards the knight. Sir Asher leapt into the air and his blade came whistling down.

Myth'alas slid beneath his opponent, springing to his feet, and twisted the instant they had passed one another. Blue Moon etched a thin line of silver light through the air as Myth'alas cut the four thick, leather straps holding Sir Asher's cuirass together in one controlled swipe.

Before the commander had stopped to turn around, the metal plates protecting his chest and back crashed to the mat.

He turned in shock. His breath was heavy and his opponent was standing calmly, slightly crouched, weight centered. Blue Moon was back in its sheath. The elf had not even broken a sweat.

Sir Asher eyed him a moment before turning to one of his men, speaking through his teeth, "Pick those up."

The knight complied and Sir Asher turned, storming out of the training hall with all his soldiers in tow.

As soon as they were gone, Myth'alas glanced at Olwa with a wink.

"Well, with that out of the way, we can start our warmup."

# Chapter 18 – Breach

Sir Asher stared at the towers. After his altercation with Myth'alas, Commander Rose had ordered the relocation of his entire assembly of knights and steelguard to tents along the southeastern ridge of Still Mead. Command Sergeant Erika approached and cleared her throat.

"Pardon me, sir?"

"What is it?" He answered without turning around.

"A carrier pigeon arrived from Gryphonledge with Commander Rose's seal."

"She sent a bloody pigeon?" He turned; his face revealed his anger.

Erika handed him the sealed parchment. He read the message before crumbling it in his fist and tossed it to the ground. She bent over to pick it up but he commanded, "Leave it. We are to be among the first through the breach. We have become little more than cannon fodder to shield her own troops. This is the only level of authority she has left, so she is using it. She couldn't even send a runner to let me know."

"Sir, with all due respect, much of this seems to be because you had asked me to gather information regarding Bold'Rock. If I may, why did you shift your focus to Myth'alas and confront him directly? I'm just trying to understand."

"Understand that it is not the place of a sergeant to question the orders of a high commander. I assume no further explanation beyond that is needed?"

Her face went pale. "No, sir."

He turned back towards the towers. She lingered.

"What else do you want to say?"

"Sir, the troopers are nervous and morale is low. I am not sure what to do."

"Your reputation for doing your duty with all honor was known to me before I ever met you. When I gave you a directive to report back to me regarding the Netherman, you did so flawlessly. The Northern Armies are the best soldiers on this continent. Hands down. We will continue to protect the territories of all humankind, from all enemies, from all directions." He turned. "So, what you will do is conduct yourself as a soldier in the Northern Command."

"Yes, sir." She saluted and turned to walk away. After a few steps Sir Asher spoke again.

"Command Sergeant Tiliz."

She turned. "Sir?"

"*All* our enemies."

Erika offered a sharp salute. Her heart felt unsettled as she returned to her platoon.

+++

In the main meeting chamber of the keep, Trystan sat with Myth'alas, Rayann, and all their companions in front of a large fire. The smell of honey and mint steamed from their cups and wafted through the air as the party remained silent. All thoughts lingered on what was coming tomorrow.

"Has anyone else ever noticed if you run your tongue across the front of your teeth how much different it feels from when you run it across the back of your teeth?"

The entire group turned to Raspberry. There was dead silence for a second and then everyone burst into laughter.

Raspberry looked at them.

"What?"

"Nothing, sweet Raspberry. Only that my heart sings when you are near. I am grateful to you for lightening the mood."

Ceridwyn lifted her cup. "To Raspberry."

The entire group proclaimed in unison.

"To Raspberry!"

The little halfling felt her cheeks go warm.

"Aww, thanks chums. Not really sure what I said that was so funny but it's wonderful having friends like all of you."

With the tension broken, the next hours were far less sullen. They shared stories, memories and laughed together as friends. As the hour got late, everyone began returning to their bedchambers. Kali and Trystan lingered behind with Myth'alas and Rayann.

"Are your steelguard fully prepared?"

"Yes, Prince Myth'alas. They have been drilled and trained extensively. Everyone knows their place. It's been challenging to plan, never having faced anything like this before. Hopefully it's all for nothing and we can just move the siege machines in, knock the tower down, and everyone marches back home."

"If there's one thing I have learned, ideal situations in battle rarely come to pass. But by God's grace, I hope the best-case scenario becomes our reality tomorrow."

The two warriors clasped arms and Trystan turned to Kali.

"I will see you at sunrise in the command tent?"

"I'll be there."

He smiled, leaned in, and kissed her. Since their first kiss many weeks ago, the two of them had become nearly inseparable. Rayann felt her eyes well up as she watched them embrace. The happiness and affection she felt radiating from Kali was extraordinary. Knowing her cousin had possibly found even just the potential for love in all this mess warmed her heart.

Trystan looked up again before departing.

"Until the morrow."

He left and Kali turned to Myth'alas, speaking to him directly.

"Before I leave, might I have a word with you?"

"Yes, of course."

She turned to her cousin and spoke softly.

"You are more than welcome to stay, but my request is directly for Myth'alas. To be honest, I am not sure you will like what I am about to ask."

"I would prefer to stay." Rayann smiled nervously.

"Very well." She turned back to Myth. "We served in the Rage Queen's armies. Both of us had our own skills and tools we brought to every battle. Those skills were exactly opposite of one another. Me, a powerful wielder of magic, and you, the one capable of snuffing it out. As a wizard killer, there is something specific I need you to keep an eye out for while we are in the warding tomorrow."

"You mean if Fifth or Piramay awaken?"

"No, Myth. I mean, me."

Rayann's eyes widened as she gasped. "Kali, what are you talking about?"

"Cousin, I have been forthright with you that the Gray Tower is attempting to draw me in and bond with me. The more I attune to the warding and the magic which created it, the more that pull has increased. I have no intention of doing anything less than destroying those abominations tomorrow. Unfortunately, I don't know what's going to happen once we get inside the warding."

She turned and looked directly into Myth's eyes.

"The magic that is keeping us out could also be repressing the full power contained within. If I am to become possessed, or go mad, or fall under the towers sway…if I turn on our troops in any way, I need you to promise that you will treat me as you would any enemy– and kill me."

She reached and grabbed him by the bracer which was inset with the three gems of magic annulment.

"With your weapons and sword skills, you are the only one who will be capable of stopping me. Do you understand?"

He remained quiet for a moment before responding.

"I understand, and I agree to your request. For what it's worth, I hope it doesn't come to that."

"Neither do I."

Kali bowed her head in thanks and left the room.

Rayann stepped beside her husband and gripped him tightly.

"Myth'alas?"

"I know, beloved. I know."

+++

It was noon. The knights and steelguard were in position. The troopers of the Northern Army would enter first, followed by a second contingency of a division from the Central Command. The siege machines and Tower Busters were staged to be moved through the breach hastily. To accomplish this, an extra allotment of horses had been assigned, and it was estimated that it would take thirty minutes to get them and their ammo carts in position.

The next line would follow the siege machines and set up a perimeter to protect them from anything that might emerge. The fourth line would be the rear guard and included Lady Rose, Larissa, Myth'alas, and his entire party of allies. Three more lines would remain outside the warding as reserves, under Sir Ordin's command.

241

Sir Asher had ridden personally to inform Commander Rose that his troopers were in position. As he approached, Sir Ordin and Sir Gregory watched him closely. He ignored them.

"Commander Rose, the Northern Guard are prepared."

"Thank you, Commander Asher. As soon as the wizards open the breach, advance as we discussed and peel your soldiers to the west and cover the hill. That will clear the way for the siege machines. We will be right behind you."

He glanced at her two trusted, senior generals, then Larissa. Turning his war horse around, he returned to his armies.

Sir Trystan and Kali approached on their mounts. Trystan offered his report.

"Commander, the siege machines are ready. Sir Matthew will oversee the catapults, Lady Hillary is in charge of the trebuchets, and Sir Alex will be seeing to the canons." He turned to Sir Gregory, "Obviously you will be without the full protection of our troopers. I pray that you make it to your launch point safely. Good luck to you, sir."

"We will give it our best."

Lady Rose interrupted. "I'm still not completely sure about this plan of yours, Sir Gregory. I can't lose a man like you. I want your word that if you sense anything amiss, you will abort the mission. You are going to be highly exposed. We simply don't know what's going to happen."

"You have my word, Commander Rose."

+++

Sir Asher approached his troops. His generals Sir Walter and Sir Donovan saluted.

"All this nonsense to attack an empty field. There's enough firepower here to bring down half the kingdom."

His two subordinates agreed. "So, what did she say?"

"Nothing, she only confirmed our movement. We are to advance before hooking to the west and protect the flank."

"Protect it from what?"

Sir Asher grinned sarcastically.

"From the winter grass, and the sticks. Oh, and mind the rocks, you might twist an ankle."

The three of them shared a round of mocking laughter before moving into position.

+++

Kali, Rayann, Ceridwyn, and Raspberry approached the ornately built portal frame. Over the last week using their combined magic along with the assistance of a vine binder from Faralanthis, the branches and leaves of ironbark trees brought in from the forests of Shimmerwood had been woven together. The magic of the forests still lingered within the wood and a seat, attached to the frame, had been constructed for Raspberry to sit in while she played.

Ceridwyn went to one side of the wide archway, Rayann and Raspberry went to the other. The wizards looked at one another and then placed two lodestones each in the socket holes constructed for that purpose. The lodestones would power the portal while they were away.

Raspberry took her seat and strummed. Her voice immediately carried into the air and every person who could hear her was captivated. The lodestones began to glow softly. Rayann and Ceridwyn stepped back and chanted the ancient words of their magic. Extending their hands, light emerged from their open palms and surrounded the lodestones. Illuminated pulses shot across the open archway, mixing and merging in the center until a large swirling ball of orange and blue light fluttered and squirmed like writhing snakes.

Kali stood in the middle of the road, focusing her eyes on the Gray Tower.

*"You remain dedicated to your conviction despite my words. I respect that. Now we shall see how far you go without the true power that could be ours."*

The dragon's voice lingered in her mind as she mapped the tower with her eyes.

"Leave me."

*"We are of the same mind, child. One and together. I know what you really want."*

"There is no power worth destroying the world for."

243

*"This is only one world. The next plain is where the true power lies."*

Kali had suspected but now fully realized it. This whole situation wasn't about Aimsire, it was about the Plain of Constellations. Everything up until now was merely a set of steppingstones to a much greater prize. Her theory that Fifth might intend to challenge the tutelary became a fact. Piramay and Fifth never intended to rule these lands or its people, it would only be a sacrifice to advance their true mission. She gritted her teeth and focused on the swirling ball of light.

She whispered. "You shall not have it."

Pulling the power of terra up through her body, the intense static that filled the air created a loud buzz and her hair swirled violently around her. Effortlessly, she bent Shakyna to her will and lifted her arms, pressing her palms forward. Magic erupted from her, smashing into the mixture. The dazzling light flared outwards, illuminating the portal way, creating a shimmering, magical well of power.

Raspberry focused and concentrated her song. The wall of magical light began to pulse with the rhythm and bent towards the warding. The instant the magics touched, a glow of silver light grew from the middle and rapidly opened the breach.

Kali stared at the Gray Tower as she screamed, "For Aimsire!"

The troops advanced and she used the ardor channels to transport back to Sir Trystan and the others in the rear lines. She mounted her horse and from the higher vantage point on the ridge watched the knights and steelguard enter, fanning out into their formations. The sound of their steel armor permeated the air, and the siege machines creaked as they began to move.

Kali lifted her eyes and watched the Gray Tower. Its pulse was soft and sedated, just like it had been before the steelguard scouts had been turned to dust.

+++

Sixty minutes later, the siege machines were not in position. Sir Asher watched from across the distant field and shook his head.

"What in the crevasse is wrong with these central troopers? Those things were supposed to be hammering the walls of that tower thirty minutes ago."

"And what's with the one they keep trying to move along the cauldron lines? There's no road, just rock. No wonder it keeps getting stuck."

"Who knows? All I am witnessing is more incompetence and stupidity. How this woman became a commander is well beyond me."

"Sir, look."

Turning his attention to the ridgeline, the cannon formations raised their banners, signaling that they were ready.

"About bloody time."

They heard the bugles blaring and saw the cannoneers begin to load.

+++

"Ready! Aim! FIRE!"

The thunder of the opening salvo echoed across the Dale of Still Mead. Myth'alas and his companions watched the smoke trails produced by the massive projectiles arch over the lava lake and hammer the side of the Gray Tower. They bounced off the surface harmlessly and splashed into the lava below.

Kali turned towards the ridge. A second thunderous barrage from the Tower Busters was fired. Smoke trailed behind the cannon balls again adding to the lines in the sky until they impacted the tower. Once again, with no effect. Suddenly, she felt an incredible pulse of energy discharge from the center of the lava lake and turned towards Rayann who had clearly felt it as well.

The magma began to bubble and churn. The massive black rocks floating on the surface rolled over and quickly moved towards the shore. The troops were still a safe distance away but Kali's stomach went to knots. She pointed.

"Trystan, look."

Seeing what she brought to his attention, he dug his heels into his warhorse, Glaive. Kali was right beside him. Together they charged into the main line.

Sir Trystan screamed, "Form! Tighten your form!"

The troop commanders immediately began rallying the lines and prepared.

Myth'alas and his companions spread out and began advancing towards the edge of the magma lake. Secure on the special riding harness, Pela'Rock rode on Bold'Rock's back. Her legs pumped with each of his strides. They easily outpaced the horses and she smiled as the wind whipped her silver hair. The anticipation of casting her magic in battle excited her.

Sir Asher watched as the black rocks floated to shore. He saw Rose and her troops repositioning and raised his hand.

"Hold. We aren't moving until we know what those are."

Seconds later, the ground beneath Sir Asher's troops heaved. The winter grasses churned and split open. Countless formations of living rock, bound together with fire, surfaced amongst them. Immediately the screams of dying soldiers could be heard from all directions.

The smell of blood and burning grass filled the air and Sir Asher charged. His sword impacted one of the heads. It shattered and the creature crumbled to the ground. He watched his men rapidly being chewed up as if in a meat grinder. He spotted one of his command sergeants.

"Erika! To me!"

Her entire platoon was already dead. She began running when her commander called. Her double tipped spear swirled and cleaved each rock elemental she passed. She wove her way through the tangle of dying soldiers, making her way to him.

"Sir Asher! What do we…"

The ground between them opened and simultaneously they severed the head off the emerging creature.

"What in the bloody crevasse are these things? How did they get in the middle of us?!"

Without answering, Erika struck an approaching elemental before sprinting for a nearby horse.

"I don't know, sir, but we aren't doing any good if we stay here waiting to die."

The surviving half of the Northern Army began retreating to the rear lines. The elementals suddenly stopped along the wide hillside and did not pursue.

With his incredible speed, Bold'Rock and Pela'Rock were far out in front, charging towards the shore. A creature, much larger than the others, emerged from the lake, magma dripping off its porous, rock skin. Bold'Rock swung his tree-sized staff and an arc of frozen energy shot forth. The elemental exploded, sending razor sharp, burning shrapnel in all directions. He stopped and did his best to protect his daughter from the debris.

"Are you alright, my Pela?"

"Yes father, but we need to get back, there's dozens of these things coming to the shore."

A blast of cold erupted from her hands as a second large creature emerged. The spell hit the elemental in the center of its chest. Rearing back, the creature let out a tremendous roar and then crumbled to the ground.

"This is not a fight where we should be alone, father. We need to get back with the prince and wizards."

Agreeing, Bold'Rock turned and sprinted up the walls of the cauldron. His thundering steps announced their approach as they crested the hill. Myth'alas and Rayann were closing the gap between them, their horse's hooves pounding the ground.

Myth'alas passed Bold'Rock and swung Blue Moon. Rayann cast a sphere of protection around him and he cut down three of the smaller rock elementals that had been pursuing. He returned quickly and they began to retreat to the main line.

Myth'alas turned to Bold'Rock.

"These things just chewed up the entire western flank. We need to stick together in case they attempt that again."

Olwa looked at Pela. She was panting.

"Are you alright?"

"I don't do well in the heat. My last spell was very draining as well, but I'll be okay."

+++

Sir Gregory cursed as the machine got stuck again.

"Come on, troopers! Get those horses pulling. We need to get in position quickly!"

There was a rumble and the entire siege machine listed to the left before falling forward as the ground beneath it collapsed. A column of fire burst up and Sir Gregory yanked the reins, barely getting out of the way in time. Every horse pulling the machine was yanked violently into the gaping hole, along with all his soldiers. A massive rock elemental clawed its way up. Halfway out, it swiped at him, taking his horse's head clean off.

Getting to his feet, Sir Gregory lifted his sword and prepared to die along with his soldiers. Suddenly, golden bursts of light that looked like shooting stars smashed into the creature, blasting its head to pieces.

Aeolis and Ceridwyn were riding hard towards him. Ceridwyn drew magic into herself and projected a beam of light. It wrapped itself around Sir Gregory and she pulled. He came flying towards her. Seconds before he would have collided with her in the saddle, she leapt into the air. Casting a second spell, she slowed the knight's descent and using the elegance of her natural elven nimbleness, practically floated into the saddle behind Aeolis. Sir Gregory gently came to rest on her horse.

They rode on, intending to move out of harm's way. The ground opened again and a hand formed from razor-sharp rock gutted Aeolis' horse. Ceridwyn was catapulted over Aeolis and he went over the horse's head. They both soared through the air before landing hard. Upon impact he rolled over her, knocking the wind from her lungs. Ceridwyn coughed and clutched her ribs. He reached but she shook her head.

"I am fine. Fight."

Still emerging, only the creature's head and one arm were above the ground. Pulling his bowstring, Aeolis fired an arrow that caught the elemental in one of its glowing eyes. Ceridwyn cast, focusing on the arrow. Upon the spell's impact, the arrow exploded. The creature slid back into the earth with only half its head intact.

"Why did you come for me? That was too risky!"

"Commander Rose saw the trouble you were having getting that machine across the rocks. We volunteered to assist. Then the attack began. We weren't going to just leave you."

He nodded in thanks to them both.

The armies were attempting to regroup. The trebuchets and catapults were now firing in orderly unison. Seeing the devastation below, Sir Alex turned three of the Tower Busters and aimed them at the swarming rock elementals.

Suddenly, as the armies withdrew, the elementals stopped advancing, standing still like statues. Only their glowing eyes indicated that they were still alive.

Lady Rose moved behind the lines and found Commander Asher.

"What do you intend, Commander Rose?"

The thunder of the canons echoed through the valley again as they fired at the Gray Tower.

"We need to buy those weapons more time. I don't know why these things suddenly stopped. Maybe they will only attack when we reach a certain place."

"My troopers were put in a perfect place, right where they needed to be for a slaughter."

"Do you think I had any idea that would happen?"

He stared at her in silence.

"This is the first time any of us are seeing anything like this, Sir Asher."

"They are standing still. We need to charge."

"What if they remain frozen by our holding back? We have already lost so many. Let the machines do their work, that's why we are here."

"What if they are moving underground and about to do the same thing they did to *my* army!"

Furrowing her brow, Lady Rose turned to Larissa.

"Go. Inform the prince and our generals. We charge in two minutes."

Larissa turned her horse and disappeared over the hill. Rose stared at Sir Asher.

"Two blasts."

He confirmed her directive. "Two blasts."

Lady Rose returned to her position and sent a runner to tell Sir Ordin to advance the reserves. Kali rode up beside her.

"The tower is changing."

"How so? Are the attacks having any effect?"

"No. The vibrations of magic are getting more intense and more frequent."

"Then we need to attack while we still have time."

Myth'alas interjected. "Lady Rose?" She turned to him. "We should spread the wizards out with the armies. Bunching us all together here does not allow for the full benefit the wizards bring."

She scanned the line and agreed with a gentle nod.

Myth'alas gave orders. "Alright. Bold'Rock, you and your daughter go to the western side. Aeolis, Ceridwyn, the west middle. Kali, you and Sir Trystan take the eastern middle. Rayann, Olwa and I will take the squad of elves and advance along the eastern flank in front of the siege machines."

"My Prince, I request I be allowed to go with Bold'Rock and Pela."

Myth'alas didn't hesitate as he looked directly at his adherent.

"Be careful."

He turned his horse and the companions split to their assigned locations.

With the lines reformed, the buglers blew two blasts. The charge commenced and the instant the first boots moved forward; the entire legion of elementals responded with a rapid counter charge. They lumbered and broke apart, reforming with each step. Their heat burned the grass and lit spot fires. Their collective roar was like lava streaming from a volcano.

The two armies collided. The thin, western flank began to fold almost immediately. Olwa was doing his best to keep up as Bold'Rock thundered through the elementals. From his shoulders, Pela fired spells in front of her father and he swung his massive sword to shatter every elemental that she froze. Pela leapt into the air as he swung his staff. An arch of freezing cold magic etched a thick gap through the advancing creatures.

Pela landed nimbly and got beside Olwa. They began to fight side by side. She was concentrating and casting, freezing the advancing enemies so Olwa could finish them with his arrows. Bold'Rock was maneuvering and doing massive damage to clear the area around them. The sound of thundering hooves caught his ear and Bold'Rock turned. Sir Asher was coming in a full charge, sword up, bearing down on Pela.

Bold'Rock lunged and went shoulder to shoulder with the horse, crushing its ribs and killing it instantly. Sir Asher tumbled to the ground and his sword went flying. He got to his feet, drew his dagger, and faced Bold'Rock.

"So, this is your honor, knight? You attack those on your own side?"

"Filth like you and that ice witch were never on my side." He charged.

With lightning quick speed like a cat catching a mouse, Bold'Rock dropped his sword and grabbed Sir Asher by the head. Olwa's eyes went wide as the Netherman effortlessly lifted the Knight Commander off his feet. Bold'Rock squeezed his muscular hand and Sir Asher's head was squashed within his own helmet.

Erika was nearby and witnessed the whole thing. She stared at the body of her dead commander, dangling from Bold'Rock's massive hand and locked eyes with the Netherman, swallowing hard as she inhaled deeply.

Bold'Rock dropped Sir Asher in a heap and watched, expecting she might charge next. Instead, she gave a slight nod and turned, squaring up to the elemental that was charging from her flank. An ice spell and an arrow ripped by her, smashing the creature to pieces. She turned; Pela was already climbing into the riding harness on her father's back. They charged directly into the melee, Olwa at their side.

+++

The smell of burnt flesh filled the air as the elementals gained ground. Myth'alas was a constant streak of crimson as he repeatedly charged, lashed out with Blue Moon and made his way back to his wife's side. The elven archers were keeping many of the elementals at bay, and the spear bearers fought with ferocity.

Rayann blasted an elemental and turned to her husband.

"There are too many, it's as if with each we destroy two more emerge."

Myth'alas scanned the fields and agreed that things were getting grim.

"We must give the siege machines time. If there's any chance to weaken the tower, we must take it."

The three Tower Busters that had been aimed at the elementals continued firing, attempting to thin their numbers. Their massive projectiles soared into the crowd of creatures, decimating dozens at a time, but still had little effect. The ground beneath the ridge where the siege machines were emplaced suddenly began to give way and crumble.

Myth'alas felt his feet moving as the dirt buckled and watched in horror as a massive elemental roughly shaped like a dragon composed of fire and rock crawled out of the lava lake and began clawing its way up the ridge.

"By the light."

He grabbed Rayann and pulled her behind himself. She saw the creature as Myth'alas yelled at his elves. "Archers! Concentrate your arrows on that. You six, start withdrawing."

His elves did as he commanded. The arrows flew towards the dragon but burned to ash before they got close enough to make impact. The dragon came up over the ridgeline and exhaled fire as if the sun itself was pouring out its wrath. Every siege machine was turned to ash in seconds. The ammo carts, loaded with their powder, exploded, sending burning shards of wood, cannon balls, and rock into the sky. steelguard, knights, and soldiers screamed as they burned.

Larissa and Rose watched in horror as the hillside was engulfed in flame. Rose turned to her bugler.

"Sound the retreat. Now!"

Instead of heading for the breach, Rose and Larissa charged into the melee. They were screaming for everyone to withdraw. Through the chaos, together, they smashed every enemy that got in their way.

They found Sir Trystan and Kali. He was fighting enemies that got close, protecting Kali so she could concentrate on her spells. She was blasting anything and everything that came up over the ridgeline.

Lady Rose thundered up and yelled, "The siege machines are gone. We need to go, now!"

Sir Trystan complied and turned to Kali.

"It's over, let's retreat while we can."

Kali was exhausted. She turned and watched as a new wave of living rocks mulched soldiers into the dirt. They were being encircled quickly and at this rate she could see that none of them were going to make it out alive.

She turned towards the Gray Tower and the world around seemed to slow down. Its pulse of energy was beautiful and the dragon's words echoed through her mind.

*"Yes, the power can be ours."*

Knowing what needed to be done, Kali wiped the sweat and grit from her forehead with the sleeve of her robes. She extended her arm and rolled her hand over so her palm was facing the ground. Green light shot from her open hand and she pulled terra magic up into her body. Activating the ardor channel that passed beneath the Gray Tower, she drew in its energy. Her body oscillated wildly as the power permeated every fiber of her.

Combining the energies of the tower and the earth below, her hair began to swirl violently as if standing on the shores of the Sylph Sea. Emerald green light pulsed from within her eyes and she shifted to prepare. An explosion burst from her body. Every rock elemental within a hundred meters shattered, falling into heaps on the ground. The blast passed over the soldiers without effect, leaving nothing but a clear path for them to escape through.

Trystan looked at her in shock. She turned her glowing eyes towards him. Her body was emitting sparks of purple and green energy as she spoke with conviction.

"Run."

Trystan turned to Glaive and mounted. He grabbed her arm and helped her up into the saddle behind him. Glaive's massive hooves thundered towards the breach. As they moved, Kali spotted Bold'Rock, Pela, Olwa, Aeolis, and Ceridwyn. They had managed to rally and were keeping the enemies at bay, but she knew they could only keep it up for so long.

She screamed. "Turn, we must help them!"

Trystan complied and they moved into the swarm of living rocks that were closing in. Kali slid off the horse and ran up beside her friends. She pulled energy through the ground once again. Hissing ancient words another sphere of purple and green light even more powerful than the last exploded from her body. Every elemental surrounding her friends for over a hundred meters was

253

blown to dust and sparkling ash. They turned to see Kali's wild-eyed expression and twisting hair.

Her voice was calm. "Go. Now."

The group complied, making for the breach as fast as they could. Bold'Rock and Pela'Rock were well out in front.

A roar like a blast furnace echoed through the air to their left. Pela turned and watched as the airborne fire dragon swooped down, focusing on them.

"Father!"

As Bold'Rock turned his head and saw the beast's maw open, he reached back and grabbed Pela. He pulled her from the harness and cradled her against his chest just as the monster released its breath weapon. He sheltered her from the fire and howled as the harness turned to ash. The skin melted off his body, exposing and scorching his spine and ribs.

They all watched in horror as the scenario played out. Kali's face twisted in anger and she reached both hands towards the fire dragon that was arching upwards to turn and make another pass. The ground trembled as she drew in power and the dragon froze in mid-air.

The shattered rocks of dead elementals lifted and flew in mass at the creature followed by intense streaks of lightning from her fingertips. The beast roared as the rocks tore through it. The lightning struck and the creature exploded.

Holding up his weight with the last of his strength, Pela crawled out from under Bold'Rock. The light was leaving his eyes and he whispered, "I love you, daughter."

He plucked the magical gem out of his staff and handed it to her.

"Your...legacy...my, Pela."

His head hit the ground and Pela screamed in anguish. Kali ran over and summoned her.

"Come, we are out of time."

She gathered all her companions together quickly and got them in a tight circle. Focusing her vision on the ridge above the tents she cast her spell. The entire group vanished and reappeared safely outside the warding.

As the last remnants of the army made their way through the breach, Raspberry stopped playing. The entrance closed and she looked in horror at the wounded soldiers and gore covering the fields. Rayann grabbed her.

"Come, Raspberry. We need to get back to Gryphonledge."

+++

Fifth's eyelids flicked open. He gasped with pleasure and smiled as the surrounding magic of his tower filled him. The energy which was keeping him suspended released. His body rotated and he got his feet underneath himself. He blinked his mirrored eyes and walked out of the tower core where the magic was strongest, the same place he had been in recovery.

Naked, he stepped onto the first level and walked to the center of the room. Reaching for his robes, he removed them from their mannequin and then stepped to a large mirror and looked at his body. Satisfactorily, he noted the rejuvenated, smooth, youthful appearance of his skin. He smiled seeing he no longer had the five-pointed scar across his face from when Nataxia had created him. He was finally free from her.

Slipping the heavy velvet fabrics over his shoulders, he brushed the front pleats and his lips twisted into a wicked sneer. Kali had finally answered his call, just as he knew she would if he lured her in subtly enough. Everything was transpiring according to how he had planned it.

He transported himself to the top level. Walking out onto the observation deck he stared at the devastation on the fields around them. The armies were still doing their best to withdraw towards Gryphonledge.

"Fools." He laughed as the words slid over his lips. He turned to the Gray Tower; it's pulses of magic were still reaching for Kali but inhibited by the wardings closure. He smiled knowing she would certainly join them now that she knew what kind of power could be hers.

He turned and watched as the magma around the Tower of Flame began to swirl. He felt her presence and spoke through the bond of their magic.

*"And from the ashes, the phoenix awakens."*

# Chapter 19 – Blindsided

It had been twenty-four hours since the withdrawal. Kali sequestered herself in her room shortly after arriving back at Gryphonledge. Since then, she refused to see anyone.

Trystan approached. It was the sixth time since they had returned that he attempted to see her. He knocked on her door.

"Kali?"

He waited but as usual she didn't respond. Just as he was turning to leave the latch released. He entered and saw her seated at the window, staring out across the city. He pulled up a chair beside her and spoke sympathetically.

"Thank you for letting me in. I've been trying to check in on you. I just want to make sure you're doing alright."

"This was all my fault."

"No. It wasn't."

"I spotted those elementals floating in the magma months ago. I sat day after day, watching them grow larger. I never imagined or even fathomed. And Pela..."

He waited until he realized she wasn't going to finish her thought.

"Kali, it doesn't matter now. Even you could not have anticipated the battle would unfold as it did. Who among us could have considered such things?"

She turned to look at him. Her face fully exposed the sorrow she was feeling.

"I am the *only* one who understands and is attuned to the Gray Tower. I alone know the power within. These last months, time was of the essence, therefore I chose to focus on finding a way through the warding instead of...what is now obvious. I made a promise to Lady Rose, therefore, that was the mission. I deeply underestimated what would happen once we were inside. I desperately wanted to see what Fifth and Piramay created be toppled to the ground.

"Mistakenly, I narrowed my vision, blurring out the bigger picture. I realized right before we entered the warding that Aimsire is only a steppingstone. Those two are planning so much more. Worse, there is nothing, collectively, that we can do to stop them."

"How can you be certain?"

"There has been a voice in my head. It's the essence of the old me. The self-preserving, self-seeking, servant of Nataxia. The vicious, cruel part of me that understands how the agents of the Rage Queen think and operate. It's the part of me that only sought glory, victory…but mostly– power.

"That voice has been luring me; persuading me to tap into my darker nature once again. I believe it was my feeling the pulses of the Gray Tower which awakened it. The dragon within has been speaking to me. Thanks to its guidance, I started understanding more and more about the makeup of the protections in place, and also, the towers themselves."

"Kali, that makes no sense to me. You aren't two people. You are just…you. Wonderful you! You wouldn't pursue darkness like that."

"The citizens of Aimsire like to blame evil on darkness, but darkness itself isn't evil. God created both the night and the day. Both are full of wonderful, harmless adventures. In the dark, even you and I have discovered many wonderful moments together.

"That notwithstanding, we can't turn away from our seeking to advance. I've always desired to advance my power."

"What does that mean?"

"It means we all strive to find balance in our world. Light, dark; only fools see things so absolutely. There is a lot of gray in between; just like the tower. Some pursue blacksmithing, others soldiery. In the end we all seek something that will fulfill us and give us purpose. At the point one starts seeking, they tend to try and be the best at it. I am a wizard, and by our nature, wizards seek one thing above all; power."

"I understand what you are saying, but you would never use that power to kill and destroy."

"Trystan, for nearly my entire life, that's all I did with my power. You have only known me since I have tried to change. What I felt yesterday, that power that flowed through me so effortlessly and what I was able to do, that is what I crave."

He stared at her and felt a lump in his throat. Finally, he found the courage to speak again.

"What you did out there, the way you cleared the path so we could escape. Destroying that…well, whatever that thing was in mid-flight. I've never seen anyone do anything like that. You saved so many."

"But not before how many perished?"

"My point is, you're aware of how saving lives is more important than taking them. Yes, you once killed and sought power, but I don't believe you are that person anymore."

"Trystan, do you know how I did what I did?"

"I've never understood magic."

"After spending all that time casting spells and fighting those elementals by your side, I was exhausted and on the brink of collapse. The only way I was able to cast the spells I did was to draw upon the power within the Gray Tower. I don't know how; I only knew I could. So, I did. I made a decision at a pivotal moment when there was no time to think about it. I have always believed that's what defines a person's character."

"Exactly. You chose to protect life."

"And yet I drew upon a power I didn't fully understand and promised myself I would never use. Now the seeds have been planted in fertile soil. I created a situation where I am forced to ask myself, at what expense did I protect life? Every decision bears consequences, especially regarding magic. Anything done can potentially undo something, somewhere else."

He reached across and grabbed her hand lovingly. A tear rolled down her cheek as she looked at him. It was the first tear he had ever seen from her. She sniffled and started laughing as she continued.

"I have never allowed myself to get as close to someone as I have to you. My life has always been about hiding my vulnerabilities and shielding myself from others. It was necessary in order to not be overrun and conquered by those seeking to use me for their own purposes or gain.

"Thank you for listening. As we move forward my hope in having this conversation with you is that we can solidify our trust and faith in one another. Dare I ask, do you trust me, Trystan?"

He smiled and wiped the tear from her cheek.

"Of course I trust you, forever and always."

She leaned in and laid her head on his chest so she could listen to his heartbeat. After a moment she whispered softly, "Your faith and trust mean the world to me, especially now."

"How many?"

"It's too early to know for sure, my Lady. What I can tell you is there are far less wounded than dead. I also wanted to inform you; I sent a pigeon south, as you requested."

Commander Rose took the report from her squire and looked it over.

"In all my days, Larissa, never did I think I would see anything like that. In what possible way are we to fight an enemy such as this?"

"I don't know, my Lady. Watching the earth open and swallow our troopers, that's a memory I will never be able to remove from my head."

Larissa's face reflected her grief.

"Well, let's hope we live long enough to keep trying to forget."

Myth'alas, Olwa, Rayann, Ceridwyn and Aeolis entered. Larissa held herself together for mere seconds before rushing into her brother's grasp, embracing him in a tight hug. Myth said nothing and simply held his sister close. Her emotions released at his touch, and she began to weep uncontrollably.

Rayann stepped forward. "I can feel your anguish, Lady Rose. If you need someone to talk to, I am here."

"Thank you. We still don't know how many we lost, but already know the numbers are substantial. Has anyone spoken to Pela yet?"

Olwa responded, "No. I am going to go see her after this."

"Good, she will need someone now more than ever. What about Kali? Has she spoken to anyone yet?"

Ceridwyn answered. "Sir Trystan came to check in on us this morning after delivering his orders to the City Watch. He was asking about her as well. None of us have talked to her. She refuses to answer her door or our calls to her upon the winds.

"Rayann has been feeling her sorrow and turmoil. What we do know is she's taking this very hard. I advised Trystan to go try to be with her again. Last I saw him; he was on his way to her quarters."

"Thank you. Do any of you have any ideas or advice as to what we should try and do next?"

Ceridwyn answered. "I attempted to look into the silver waters this morning. I haven't been able to see anything for months. I wish any of us could offer you counsel but for now, I'm sorry, we are at a loss."

Commander Rose nodded softly but remained silent as she turned her head and looked in the direction of the towers contemplatively.

+++

Olwa walked into the horse stables and sat beside Pela. She was curled in a ball, wrapped in her father's travel cloak.

He could tell she knew he was there. He watched as her body would occasionally shake from the sobbing. Finally, he reached and placed his hand on her hip.

She whispered. "I can't believe he's gone."

Her skin was ice cold. He could feel it through the cloak.

"You're freezing; let me get you some blankets."

"No…I'm always like this."

He didn't respond but left his hand where it was.

Another wave of heartache washed over her and she let out a muffled wail as she buried her face deep into her father's cloak. Olwa had never seen anyone this grieved. Though he understood why, he was having a hard time knowing how to respond. Finally, he found some words he felt might bring comfort.

"Pela'Rock, I wish I could have gotten to know your father better. He was decent and honorable, that much I knew. Though I had few interactions with either of you, It was obvious he loved you and wanted to do what was right."

Her body rose and then sank as she exhaled heavily.

He continued. "I want you to know, I also want to do what's right."

She lifted her head curiously and looked at him. Her eyes were swollen and red. She sniffled and he could not help but smile sympathetically as he continued.

"I have my own room in the row beside the Keep. It is good sized. It doesn't have two beds, but it does have a very comfortable couch. I can sleep on that and I promise to mind myself."

"Olwa, what are you asking?"

"I'm asking that even though I can't bring you comfort in your loss; I can offer you the feather bed in my room. I can also offer to be near you, so that you don't have to be alone. Nobody who loses someone they truly love should be alone."

She tucked her head into her father's cloak again and inhaled deeply. His scent still lingered. She nodded, agreeing to his offer. He wanted to feel happy about it, but instead only felt her suffering.

When she was ready, Olwa helped Pela to her feet. The gem that Bold'Rock had given her was tucked tightly into her sash. They walked slowly. Olwa kept his arm around her and supported her weight all the way to his room. He got her inside and settled her onto the bed. Instinctually he reached to cover her with the blankets, but she lifted her hand and stopped him.

"I will get too warm."

He threw the blankets onto the couch. "Have you eaten anything?"

"No."

"Are you hungry?"

"No."

"Well, not to overstep and become an advisor, but some food might make you feel a little better. What I mean is, you would at least have strength. May I go get you some food?"

She swallowed hard, thinking about the times she and her father were camped outside human towns. She was always the one to go get the food. Being a Netherman, Bold'Rock was never allowed near human settlements and would have been attacked on sight. His words came to her and it made her smile.

She quoted her father as she looked up at him. "Yes, food would be nice. Be safe out there, I want you to come back to me."

+++

Evening had come and Raspberry sat in her quarters, alone. She was holding one of Lenly's old herb bags. She could never really know for sure because the question never came up, but she always had a feeling this one had been his favorite. He was constantly mending and lovingly repairing it. Though it was old and ragged and constantly in need of stitches, he continued to use it until the end.

The soft, patchworked leather felt comfortable in her hands and she could still see marks where he would hold it. She smiled, remembering how they would sit near his hearth, eating roasted lamb and potatoes. Potatoes, they were always Lenly's favorite. She looked over at her lute lying on the bed. She had tried to play since the battle but after a few chords, just felt too sad.

She let out a long breath and stood. Turning around, she gasped, dropping the bag. A kindly old fellow, wearing a puffy, bright blue shirt and a pair of the most amazing multi-colored minstrel pants she had ever seen, picked it up. Though she knew she should be scared about a stranger being in her room, she felt an odd sense of peace.

"Don't want to lose this. It's a very special item."

He handed the bag back to her before walking to the fireside and picked up the poker off the andiron. After repositioning the logs, the fire flared to life. The room was instantly filled with a strange, comforting warmth. He turned and looked at her with his kind, bright blue eyes.

"May, I?"

He gestured to the tea pot and she instinctually nodded her head. He began to whistle a delightful little tune and poured two cups of tea. Placing one on the table between the two chairs near the fireplace, he sat, leaned back and looked at her cordially.

She noted his long, wavy, white hair with streaks of black and gray. It was so thick and curly that it reminded her of rushing white water. His short beard was perfect and groomed, not a hair out of place. Most curious was his smile. The way it leapt out from under his mustache simply reached into her heart.

She stood in the middle of the room for a long time and jumped when he finally broke the silence.

"Would you care to join me before your tea gets cold?"

"I...um...yeah, sure."

Sitting down she placed the herb bag on her lap and picked up her tea.

He smiled again. "It's okay, go ahead and ask."

"I, how did you know? I mean, okay…who are you?"

"Well, I'm a little surprised you don't recognize my voice."

She tilted her head as she noticed the shimmering gold embroidery on the front of his shirt; a music note, wrapped in stars. Her face went pale as the realization struck her.

She whispered, "Balaby?"

The right side of his mouth lifted into a smile. He tapped the tip of his round nose, just like Lenly used to do when she answered him correctly. He then sipped his tea and winked over the rim of his cup.

"Oh, my." She began to get up so she could kneel. As if reading her thoughts, he lifted his hand, waving in a silly, flapping motion that made her stay in her seat.

"Wheesht. None of that formality nonsense or the kneeling that everyone seems so keen on. We are not to be knelt to, that is the way to honor God, not a tutelar. Like you, we are but part of the glorious creation. Besides, Raspberry, you and I are friends."

"We…are?"

"Of course. You talk to God every morning and every night seeking guidance…and I, as the keeper of songs, always respond with what God desires me to tell you."

"Yeah, I mean, sometimes I sorta hear a voice. Mostly I get ideas for new songs. I hear the tunes in my head."

"That is my voice."

A grin slowly spread across her face and she nodded in understanding.

"So, I am guessing you are wondering why I'm here?"

She was about to say something but he continued before she could.

"Raspberry, you have already had quite an adventurous life. My guess is when you set your first foot outside of Weefolk Wood, you never imagined where your journey would take you. You were probably even, dare I say, a little bit scared. Well my goodness, just look at you now!

"You had the bravery to step into all that unknown. You got up on those little feet and went anyway, and you've worn out many pairs of boots in the process. Now, here you are, and here I am. You, the brightest and most talented musician in all of Aimsire. And me, well, let's just say I am so very proud of you."

"Well, thank you, Mr. Balaby."

"Just, Balaby will be fine."

"Oh, okay, Balaby. Well, I do appreciate what you are saying. To be honest with you though, it's just, I really feel like I struggle more than I understand. Sometimes after I hear you, I try to play what I heard. But then, I don't know, it just doesn't sound the same."

"Raspberry, let me explain to you how journeys work. First, there's a strange desire. You won't know where it came from, or even why it showed up. It's just gonna be a funny little feeling in your tummy. It churns around, makes you even a little uncomfortable when you don't acknowledge it. That feeling is good. Whatever it is that's moving in you, that churning isn't going to settle down until you talk to it. You will never feel like you are doing the right thing until you are pursuing what's moving inside you.

"Once you take those first steps, then opportunities will arise so you can continue to grow. You did that with Lenly. You listened, you followed, you learned. You devoted yourself to something you didn't even quite understand yet, you just knew it felt right to do so. Strangely, I bet it made your tummy feel better. You weren't feeling those quirksome little churnings so strongly because you were doing the right thing.

"From there, devotion and hard work takes hold, as well as an established feeling of long standing. That one is pretty important because no journey is easy. I have watched you and I must say, nobody in all my time since God gave us time, have I seen someone pray so often and with such devotion as you do.

"Lastly is the step of complete focus. The desire to always find the next solution or in your case, listen to the next song. Together, all that leads to preparedness. The fact that you are listening and trying is what will keep preparing you before a difficult situation arises, not during, not after. There are certainly more difficult situations coming your way."

"How do you know?"

"There always are."

"Why?"

"Because, that's life, little one. The path you chose has brought you here, with me, for a reason. God established at the Dawn Light that life on Aimsire wasn't to just be one of sitting around growing mold on our feet. You were designed to walk and move and learn all about the world that was created around you and *for you*.

"As one of the Balladeers, your life will certainly be one of constant, curiously wonderful steps. A process of seeking, playing, learning and continually discovering. It is not easy and that little feeling in your tummy is never going to go away completely. What I can promise is the endeavor of pursuing music is something well worth doing.

"The difference with songs from the other arts is that you will bring the greatest joy to everyone. Every society on Aimsire has music; God intended it and designed it that way. Music is the language that ultimately binds you all together. The difference is your music also carries God's magic within it."

"Yes, I know. Mr. Lenly told me all that, well, umm, I guess you already know what he taught me. What I mean is, it doesn't always work. I want it to always work."

"It will, in time, but that doesn't necessarily mean it will work the way you think it should."

"Okay."

"You seem disappointed."

"I am, a little. Maybe I still don't understand."

He laughed and patted her on the knee.

"I think you understand better than you give yourself credit for. Please go fetch your lute. My time to stay with you is short and I have a few, personal lessons for you before I depart."

+++

Kali sat in her room the entire next day. With all the chaos since the battle, Trystan had not been able to come see her again and she had not allowed anyone admittance since his departure.

*"Your inner eye has been opened and you have felt the possibilities. You see it now, what can be yours."*

"Yes, I see it."

*"Your destiny is not here, child. It never was. You were
forged in the shadows for a much greater purpose."*

Kali watched as the face of the dragon in her heart danced
in the flames, breathing softly, watching her with burning eyes.

"What will become of Aimsire?"

*"The tower isn't stabilized; if you don't bring it into
balance, eventually the terra core will shatter and destroy Aimsire.
If you don't act, that is inevitable. In the end, however, this
creation is insignificant. Its time has passed. We can ascend and
walk amongst the tutelar, not as their servants, but as their equals.
Only you can bond with the tower. Only we can balance Lúth. It is
time to take your place and leave the insignificant behind."*

She stood and gathered her things. Staring in the mirror,
she adjusted the strap on the wizard bag her cousin had given her.
Taking a deep breath, she walked out the door.

Trystan was on duty and looked down at her from the inner
watchtower. His face brightened at seeing her out of her room and
he smiled cheerfully. She looked up at him, but didn't smile back.
Her eyes flared purple and green. He furrowed his brow as his
stomach went to knots.

He whispered. "Kali?"

She disappeared in a flash of light.

Somehow, he just knew where she went. He ran down the
stairs to the portal to take soldiers to Still Mead. It activated at his
approach and he entered, appearing on the other side.

Sprinting up the hill as quickly as he could, Trystan
watched in anguish as Kali walked towards the hollow frame of the
breech entrance.

"Kali! No!"

She stopped and turned as he ran to her.

"What are you doing?"

Kali looked at him coldly and spoke, "Surviving."

She lifted her hand and placed it on his chest. Trystan was
immediately back at the Keep, standing in the courtyard.

Larissa was near, gathering the reports when she heard him
scream. She came running to his side and watched as he pounded
the cobblestones with his fists.

"Sir Trystan? Trystan! What's happened?"

"Kali. She's betrayed us."

# Chapter 20 – Shadow, Flame, Terra

Kali didn't hesitate and stepped forward, knowing she would pass through the warding unharmed. The hollow eyes of the dead were all around her, but she remained focused on the Gray Tower. The fields smelled of rotting flesh and blood, continually stirred up by the stone elementals marching in slow, loose formations. They ignored her as she made her way to the edge of the lava lake.

Fifth and Piramay were on the shore, waiting for her. As she approached, Piramay sneered and Fifth spoke with warmth in his voice.

"Welcome home, my pupil. It has been a long time."

"It has." There was a hint of rancor in her voice.

Piramay quipped. "Did you enjoy our little surprise? How long did the steelguard last, mere seconds, perhaps?"

Kali looked at Piramay with indifference as Fifth interjected.

"Now, now, Little Phoenix. We are allies once again. The past is behind us, only the future matters now."

Piramay clicked her tongue as he turned to Kali.

"There is still contempt in your heart towards me. Good, you will need it. Your angst was always your strongest asset. I was sad to learn you abandoned it for a while. One can only imagine how much power wasn't acquired while the edge of your senses was dulled.

"It doesn't matter any longer. Once you are fully bonded with the tower, all the old magics will be insignificant."

Kali looked at him quizzically. She wasn't yet aware that during their creation, the raw elements of magic flowed through Fifth and Piramay, bonding their minds and bodies to the towers. The third tower, however, still maintained a void so that when the wizard who could control it arrived, the ritual could be completed. Fifth produced a soul well from the folds of his robes and handed it to Kali. She looked at the device curiously.

"This may look familiar to you. You were introduced to the first version when I gave you a soul pearl to complete your mission in Faralanthis. This is a soul well, the very one we used to create the Gray Tower. It is capable of storing the energy of one thousand souls. It's how we captured the life energy of those we slayed. There is only one soul left within it, for you. The power it supplies will bond you to your new home."

Instantly, he transported the three of them to the core of the Gray Tower. Kali contained her gasp as she experienced the most intense flow of magic she had ever felt. She shivered as the tower immediately began attempting to sync with her. She looked down at the stone floor. An engraving in the exact shape of the soul well was below her feet.

A triangle, etched into the floor, surrounded the spot for the soul well. Three places were marked on each of the vertices. Piramay and Fifth had already moved to their places. Instinctually, Kali placed the soul well on the floor and moved to her position. Instantly, the hairs on the back of her neck stood on end.

Piramay and Fifth began to chant. The soul well opened like a flower and the gem inside pulsed before the energy escaped in a scream. Kali watched the ghostly figure of a knight emerge. He twisted and writhed before his life energy was released in an array of sparkling colors. A tingling sensation filled the bottom of her feet and the triangle illuminated. Fire and shadow erupted from the floor and violently swirled around Kali.

She wailed in pain as the fire came at her first, licking her skin that left purple lines like bruises. It felt as if her blood was beginning to boil when Fifth's voice entered her mind.

*"You know what to do, Kali. Pull the terran energy in, push back the flames. It's the same as I taught you when you were a child to shred Shakyna. The same as you did to unweave the warding and let the armies in. Follow your instincts. Draw upon the power of Lúth in this tower like you did with the half one's music. Accept the pull and synthesize the powers around you."*

She drew in Shakyna, terra and Lúth. She focused her eyes on Piramay who's face reflected her hostility. Kali gritted her teeth through the pain and brought up her hands close to her chest, pointing her open palms at Piramay. Flashes of green light erupted from her fingers and flashed all around her like a shield, bursting the flames attacking her into harmless sparks and embers. Kali felt herself become fully present in the moment and her body went calm. There was no longer pain in her expression.

268

Not to be beaten, Piramay unsympathetically intensified her magic, trying as best she could to consume the snit. Kali inhaled deeply before calmly pressing her hands forward. The instant her fingers touched the magic swirling around her, the flames were expelled. Piramay felt the impact of Kali's pushback as her spell was banished. She took a step back letting out an involuntary gasp.

Immediately, Fifth leveled the full brunt of his spell upon Kali, forcing dark tendrils of living shadow to come out of the floor and lash at her. She shifted her eyes, looking at him with hostility. He smiled from across the triangle before unleashing a second attack that brought swirling shadow skulls in waves which burst out in a wide arc before streaking towards her to strike.

Kali showed nothing but the complete equilibrium of the energies around her and simply flicked her hands, banishing all his magic instantly. A slow-moving vortex of shadow and flame emerged from the floor and slowly coiled themselves around her. Puffs of inky darkness evaporated off her honey blond hair.

Her robes turned dark purple and the folds glowed with fire from within. A burst of shadow and sparks detonated from her body, sending light and fluidic darkness in all directions.

She murmured as the magic of the tower interlaced itself with every pore of her being. Kali's head slumped forward and she went to her knees as the sensation filled her.

Slowly her breathing calmed and Kali felt at ease. She leaned back and sat on her heels before lifting her hands to admire them. Swirling blue fire and inky shadow moved around her fingers like eddies in a river behind the rocks. Kali was no longer occupying the tower; she was part of it. She could feel the air hitting the walls outside, the warmth of Lúth glowing upon it from above, and the heat from the lava below.

"I never imagined."

Piramay rolled her eyes and laughed.

Fifth offered a hand to help her back to her feet. "It will take many weeks for the cohesion to complete, but the harmonization of our power has begun. Scales need a pillar from which the beam can hang." He turned to Piramay. "As you can see, I was right. She was exactly who we needed."

+++

Kellan gripped the spines along Nolore's neck. She adjusted her body position with each flex of his muscles as he turned tightly and looped through the sky above the Vale of Ghosts. Shortly after the request had been made, by God's permission, the High Borne communicated that if Kellan agreed, she could follow in the traditions of her lineage and become Nolore's rider. All the two had done, ever since, was practice.

Nolore shifted into a glide and Kellan leaned her cheek against the warm scales on his neck as she spoke.

"You don't have to stop on my account, I'm one of the best horse riders in the Northern Guard, you'll never shake me loose."

He laughed. "I'm sure I won't. I stopped because we have a guest arriving."

Kellan turned and saw Rajumin coming into formation beside them. She playfully nudged Kellan with her nose and then spoke to Nolore.

"The High Borne has summoned us, something urgent."

"Hang on, Lady Knight."

Kellan squeezed her muscular thighs into the riding harness to brace herself as he went into a steep dive. Her years of riding a horse had come in handy when she started learning to ride Nolore. She quickly found that flying on a dragon proved to be a lot more taxing, but also, extensively more exciting.

They landed on the large portico of the palace and Kellan effortlessly slid off, removed her gloves, and adjusted her clothing.

"I'll be here when you return."

Rajumin interjected. "Not so fast, Lady. He specifically said to retrieve *both* of you."

Lady Kellan looked at Nolore, who was as puzzled as she was. She had only had one audience with Reitrof'nor, the day after she arrived when he approved her to become Nolore's rider.

"If I had known I would have worn something more appropriate for an audience."

Rajumin smiled. "He won't be bothered by your attire, I assure you."

The three of them entered. Kellan was dwarfed by the dragons on either side of her, but she walked with strength and confidence. A whole new purpose and meaning for her life was discovered during her time in the Vale, and it showed. As they entered the grand throne room, the two dragons lowered themselves in respect and Kellan bowed her head humbly.

"Come forward."

The three made their way and he addressed Nolore first.

"They have awakened. The towers are active. The Northern Command has sustained heavy losses by the advance of Nataxia's armies. Though some significant pockets of force remain in the north, their commanders marched south for safety. Most of whom traveled were killed in a recent battle near the towers in Still Mead.

"The central armies are two-thirds strength at best. Those that live are tattered and morale is low. Our time has come, youngling. I am sending you and your flight to Gryphonledge to assist. Others are being sent to the Points of Dawn and strategic areas of importance."

Nolore complied. "We will prepare at once, High Borne."

Reitrof'nor turned to Rajumin. "I want you to accompany Nolore and his flight. They are going to need your skills."

"Yes, of course High Borne."

"Lady Kellan?" She bowed reverently once again. "For you, I also have a task. Being a rider offers more than simply going to battle side by side. It is a unique synthesis between those of us who are messengers and protectors, and those who walk Aimsire. As the only human with this privilege, you are also to be our ambassador."

"You honor me, High Borne. I am not sure I am worthy of such a position."

"God deemed you worthy enough to ride, therefore worthy enough for this. The dragons have not fought alongside the walkers longer than anyone can remember. We are mere legends to them, restricted to banners and family crests. Many doubt we even exist at all. Though they know us from time to time as "Silentclaw", humanity has forgotten the dragons and are no longer aware of our true form. They are going to need a strong voice to guide them and not be fearful when we return to dwell amongst them once again. Nolore's decision to save you, though insubordinate, opened a door to rebuild that relationship."

"I will do my best, High Borne."

"I know you will.

"Rajumin, one more matter before you depart. It is important to inform you that Kali Fionntán has become the master of the third tower."

"What?" Rajumin's voice reflected her surprise and immediate heartbreak. She turned to Nolore and then back to the High Borne. "Are you certain?"

"As certain as it is so, youngling. Nolore, prepare your flight and go with God's grace and my blessing."

+++

Sir Trystan sat in Kali's former quarters. He stared at the map she had been working from and traced his finger over her handwriting where she had been scribbling notes and strategies. He felt his eyes welling up and turned quickly when he heard a voice behind him.

"Sir Trystan?"

Ceridwyn was standing in the doorway. She had a look of sadness mixed with sympathy on her face. As soon as he saw her, he could not hold back his tears.

He looked back at the map and whispered, "How could she do this to us?"

"That is what we are all struggling with. It caught us completely off guard."

"How could she choose such a selfish path? How could she turn on us so quickly after one defeat? I never believed she would do such a thing."

"None of us thought she would do such a thing, but we *did* know she was capable."

"Because of her past?"

"Yes, Sir Trystan, because of her past."

"No. She was reformed, changed! She told me stories about her old life. She shared with me that she was now serving to bring balance and God's light to the world."

Ceridwyn approached, stood beside Kali's worktable and stared at him.

"The song in all our hearts is filled with desperate sadness over this, however, what's done is done. We can't change what she chose; we can only move forward and find a way to maintain peace and preserve life."

His face immediately showed his anger.

"This isn't a poem. How can you be so dismissive and trivialize her betrayal?"

"Trivialize?" She walked around the table and looked up into his eyes. "There is nothing trivial about losing one of the most powerful wizards who has ever lived to the darkness, Sir Trystan. I lost a dear friend. Her cousin lost the last of her family and is tattered over this. You lost a woman you have only known for a few months. I am not meaning to undermine your sorrow, Sir Trystan, but I dare say, you are not suffering alone; *all* our hearts are broken."

He looked at her and his anger melted away. He hadn't thought about it like that. Exhaling softly, he rolled up the map and looked at Ceridwyn.

"I'm sorry. You are right, I just can't…"

She reached and clutched his hand tightly.

"None of us can. What we must do now is hold on to what we have left; each other. There is still too much work that needs to be done to keep lingering on the unchangeable. Everything is at stake. Kali has become part of the greatest enemy this world has ever faced and we need to treat her as such.

Her joining the wizards who created those towers has made this situation all the more grim. Our holding together is more important now than ever before."

+++

Prince Myth'alas, Raspberry, Aeolis, Ceridwyn, and Olwa were returning from a meeting with Commander Rose, Erika, Sir Trystan, Sir Ordin, Sir Gregory, and Larissa. They had all been meeting regularly the last few days to discuss new strategies and what steps would need to be taken next. Rayann would occasionally attend, but today she opted to stay in her room.

The group dispersed and Myth'alas returned to his wife. Immediately he felt her lingering heartache. He sat on the bed where she lay and lovingly placed a hand on her shoulder. She could not escape the grief of knowing her cousin, the last member

273

of her family, had walked away from them so easily. Myth had little success comforting her. She felt a complete helplessness as her heart constricted in her chest once again.

She breathed sadly through her words. "I was never prepared for the strain of such loss. First my parents, then my brother, now my cousin. It's all such a blur of pain. How am I to be the one who fulfills the prophecy spoken over me while I am constantly needing to navigate these upheavals?"

Myth lovingly tucked some stray hair behind her ear and whispered, "Perhaps it's within the upheavals where you will find the answers you seek. You are not alone, beloved. You are surrounded by people who love you."

She reached up and squeezed his hand.

"I'm sorry, I know. I didn't mean to imply that there is nobody. I meant I have no family in my bloodline left and this *blasted* prophecy constantly lingers above my head. It doesn't add up. When Kali and I entered the Tower of Kells together, as family, I felt the first light of hope since all this started. We explored that knowledge as kin, we had so many wonderful discussions. The idea of ushering in a new era of magic finally seemed possible. Everything was starting to make sense and come together. Then this…"

"I admit, I was surprised that she walked away so hastily. It doesn't make a lot of sense to abandon us like that after watching how fervently she planned the breaching of the warding, as well as the attack. On top of that, she and Sir Trystan made a connection. It was obvious they adored one another. Everything about her actions was focused on the objective. It was so intense that even adding romance into her life didn't seem to distract her, it only intensified the outcome she desired."

Rayann looked up at him and cocked an eyebrow. "What are you thinking?"

"Just trying to put together the pieces, like everyone else."

Suddenly, Rayann's face went pale, and she sat up. Myth instantly heightened his senses and looked around.

Rayann squeezed his arm and whispered, "She's in the Tower of Kells."

+++

Over the past few days, Kali, Piramay, and Fifth could all sense the continued stabilization of Lúth as it poured through the fracture in the sky. Kali's presence and attunement to the towers was slowly harmonizing the magics and creating balance. Additionally, they were all discovering new and amazing magical powers.

Kali sat in the study at the top of her tower and traced her finger over the embossed symbol of the Fionntán on the cover of her spell book. Rayann had gifted it to her from the shelves shortly after they had entered the Tower of Kells together. She opened the book and read the inscription;

> *"My amazing, wonderful cousin. I thank God for you every day. We have seen so much already, and I know your future will be wonderful. Thanks to you I am filled with new purpose and joy. I look forward to a life of adventures together, as family.*
>
> *For the Fionntán!*
> *~ Rayann."*

She glanced around at the large empty walls and knew what must be done.

She stood, smoothed her robes which gently breathed wisps of light and smoke from the folds, and then pulled in the power of the ardor channels.

Instantly she was in the Tower of Kells. The magic wardings recognized her and released, giving her full access to the archives and artifacts within. She walked along the countless volumes on their shelves, lovingly tracing her finger over the spines of the books. They hummed with power, responding to her touch. She felt a tingling sensation which floated around her like leaves scattered in an autumn breeze.

As she reached the end of the long bookshelf she turned and removed a bag of spell reagents from her robes. Moving back along the shelves she sprinkled the magic dust, making sure to not miss a single one.

She then proceeded to the room of artifacts. Countless magic items sat on pedestals and as she passed them, she sprinkled the magic dust upon them too. The room was wondrous, full of ancient lodestones, rings, wands, odd devices, and on the far end a book titled, *"Artifacts and Relics of Antiquity"*. She began to sprinkle dust on the book when she felt a familiar presence. A second later, Rayann's voice filled the air.

"Finding everything you are looking for, cousin?"

Kali turned and Rayann could not hold in her surprise as she noted Kali's powerful new appearance. Standing in the doorway of the room, she maintained her calm and focus.

"I was hoping we would be able to see each other again, Kali, but not under these circumstances. Do you mind telling me what you are doing with our family's heirlooms?"

Kali began walking towards Rayann. The smoke escaping her robes filled the room with the scent of heather flowers. She stopped after crossing half the distance.

"They are coming to my tower with me."

"Under whose authority? I am Mistress of Kells. I am the Matron of Faemley Manor. I am the last Fionntán, and I have not given you permission to do so."

"These items are no longer the property of the Fionntán. I take them under my own authority."

"You would sink so low as to not only betray us all, but now you are going to steal all the knowledge and the legacy of the Fionntán family lineage so you can keep it only for yourself?"

"These items will do more harm than good for you. I am removing them for their own protection. Like yourself, I too have a sentimental attachment to these things. I do not wish for them to become collateral damage. Hailen Glen and Faemley Manor *will* be destroyed. As part of the old system of magic we will remove every stone and spark that holds this place together. I am not interested in these items for myself, they are insignificant to me; however, I do not wish for them to be destroyed either.

"I strongly advise you to not attempt to stop me, cousin. This is going to happen whether you want it to or not. Better to save your strength and fight for something more worthwhile, something your life is worth the sacrifice for. Even in this place, with all the power of Kells and your ancestry behind you, I promise you will lose if you resist."

Rayann could feel the immeasurable power radiating off her cousin. It was as if she was creating magic of her own rather than drawing it in. She took a few steps towards Kali. Her velvety robes rustled and she gripped the Staff of Kells tightly.

"Are you trying to convince me or yourself? Who could these books possibly cause harm to? You and those other two know that your new knowledge far outweighs anything found in these volumes and artifacts. If you aren't interested in them, why take them? Why not let them remain where they belong so they may die with this place if that's its ultimate fate?

"I agree with you on one thing, I would lose if I tried to stop you. I can feel that. The anger and power radiating off you is palpable. I pray it doesn't consume you in the end. The truth will be revealed. I hope you won't be too late in seeing it. Do what you think you must do."

Rayann vanished from the room. Kali reached through the ardor and could feel that she was now in the manor.

She whispered softly to herself. "You're right, cousin. The revelation of truth is inevitable for us all. One day you too will come to see it."

Lifting her hands, Kali spoke one word and every item she sprinkled reagents on disappeared in a flash of purple light. In the manor below, Rayann felt their departure and wept.

+++

Kali stood in her tower, staring at the items she had stolen the night before. She suddenly felt Fifth's presence and turned. As he approached, his silver eyes reflected her back on herself and he smiled hungrily.

"Very wise to remove their only remaining library of knowledge. I commend you."

"This magic is for days gone by. None of it matters any longer."

He walked past her and stared at the books and artifacts.

277

"Forty years ago, I would have killed as many as necessary to get my hands on these. I was convinced the path to Lúth was hidden in Kells. I was wrong."

Kali looked at him curiously. "When did you discover it?"

"Thirty-nine years ago."

"Why did you wait so long to acquire it?"

"Timing. I knew what to do, just not how. Keeping the secret from Nataxia was not easy, but I remained patient. When Nidhug arrived after sinking your parents ship, I could feel the power radiating from you. I knew then like I know now; you were the key. Your training to that end became my primary focus. I knew Piramay was the one who could assist me in bringing Lúth into the world, but I saw quickly that you were the only one who could balance it.

"I focused my time to hone your natural abilities, to help you understand all facets of magic. Your hunger for power was deeper than any I had ever experienced, perhaps even mine, and you didn't disappoint in your learning."

He stepped closer, looking at her intimately.

"And now that you are a woman, there is so much more."

"You clearly fancy Piramay. What are these advancements and flattery about?"

He smiled thinly. "Piramay is also a fine woman."

"Fifth, this is not why I came here and joined you."

He stared in silence for a moment. "Well, I wish I could say I was not disappointed."

"There is far too much to do. We must remain focused on the goal and not distract ourselves with such carnal desires. Especially you, Fifth. This is, after all, your plan."

"Perhaps someday when all this is completed…"

"If Piramay ever comes to trust me so we can better work towards getting it completed."

"Piramay doesn't trust anyone easily, and as you know it is foolish to do so. Trust is earned, slowly, over time. I know you because I shaped and raised you. Eventually she will come to see it as well. For what it's worth, she trusts you more now. This became especially so when she learned you took the remnants of magical knowledge from the few remaining wizards left in the world.

"As you already know, for the new magic of this world to rise, the old must be put to death. That purge includes all those who practice it. I put the notion in the Rage Queen's ear to slay the wizards of this world a hundred and fifty years ago. Nidhug and Myth'alas had already efficiently been doing the job. Of course, then Myth fell in love and left Nataxia's service before completing his mission. Piramay and I took it upon ourselves to finish the task for him. What do you think we were doing between burning cities and collecting souls?"

"That must be why Ceridwyn received no responses to her messages."

"How many did she send?"

"I don't know. I only know she started reaching out for help right after you destroyed the Hexangular."

His sinister smile spoke volumes. There was hardly any left who could or would answer the call.

"We need to visit Piramay and discuss our next steps."

He disappeared in a flash and Kali looked at the books and artifacts again before following him to the Tower of Flame. When she appeared, Piramay was staring at her with a thin smile.

"Greetings, Kali."

"Greetings to you as well, Piramay."

Piramay sauntered to the center of the room where Fifth was standing near a large circular table. Kali followed and then stared at the most incredible map that she had ever seen. It was an exact replica of the lands surrounding the towers, displaying the positions of the sun and moon as well as the weather. The map showed the area all the way from Gryphonledge to the Shovel Lands in the southwest.

Kali offered a sincere compliment.

"Piramay, this is absolutely amazing."

"It's not my greatest creation, but in the short time I have worked on it I believe it will suffice."

"It will work perfectly, Little Phoenix."

He began to talk through his plan as he pointed to the appropriate positions on the map.

"As you both know, Nataxia's army is approaching from the north. The Rage Queen wants what she considers to be hers, meaning, these towers and the power flowing through them.

Marching that army through The Bind would take longer than to march west through Mumble Branch and down into New Stone. Strategically, it makes the most sense given that the plains provide wide-open space as opposed to fighting through the hill lands between us and Gryphonledge. With the human army coming from the south, we…"

"What?"

Piramay and Kali both locked eyes with Fifth as he continued.

"The southern command is approaching with all their armies. My guess is they will be here in the next few days."

Kali nodded. "It makes sense that they were summoned. Lady Rose is getting desperate and stretched to her limit. During my time with them she barely slept and often took starshade to do so. She was also heavily despondent over the loss of her troops and knights when they attacked the towers. The reinforcements won't matter. They are going to meet the same fate as the central and northern battle groups."

"Eventually."

Kali inquired. "You don't intend for us to attack?"

He laughed. "Oh, we will fight them, Kali, but we will let them thin themselves out first. Though our magic is more powerful than anything on Aimsire, we are still subject to the natural laws of this world until we break free from God's shackles. We will be taxed and drained if we fight for too long. I will make sure that the presence of the Rage Queen's army is known to the humans and they face one another first."

"You won't need to do that. Lady Rose and Prince Myth'alas already know of Nataxia's armies."

"Interesting. Well then all we need to do is make sure they face each other before they face us."

He turned to Piramay. "Are you making progress creating your enhanced firestones?"

"The process is coming along. When they are completed, I will make sure they are appropriately deployed in the battle."

"Excellent. Kali, we will need to transport ourselves rapidly around the battlefield. As the magic of terra is your specialty, I want you to create a way for us to move around the area upon the ardor channels without taxing ourselves."

"Of course, Fifth."

Piramay glanced at Fifth and then Kali. The notion of someone not yet fully trustworthy overseeing their movements during the battle did not sit well with her. That thought aside, the little snit did bring back all the magical knowledge from the Tower of Kells. She weighed her options but remained silent for now.

+++

Later that evening, Piramay requested a conversation with Fifth. He complied and she transported herself to the Black Tower. He was in his massive work area and smiled at her.

"Little Phoenix. To what do I owe this visit?"

"Are you certain we can trust her?"

"Of course, why would you ask?"

"Consigning her to create a way for us to navigate around the battlefield is a perfect opportunity to throw us into the maw of our enemies."

"I know her and she chose to join us. She wants this power more than we do. Kali knows that doing anything deceitful will cause her to lose what she has now gained. That alone will keep her loyal. You saw her face when she attuned to her tower, it was sheer pleasure. I raised her; I imparted all my knowledge into her and forged her. I am the closest thing she has to a father, and she *is* loyal to family. If you trust me, you can trust her."

She remained quiet for a moment and then looked at his large worktable.

"What is this?"

"I have been developing a new soul well, one that does not require the enemy to die first. As of yet, this prototype is only capable of holding one soul, but if placed on the chest and the activation word spoken, it will draw the life force directly out of its victim. No more burning them to death first."

Piramay snorted. "How incredibly boring."

# Chapter 21 – Sheens of Faith

Nidhug observed the army advancing south. He had begun pushing them hard as soon as the snow cleared. Every day he felt the urgency of his mission and remained focused.

"Brother, what binds you?"

He turned to Rezren.

"Anticipation. I am anxious to get south and see these towers for myself."

"How bad can it be?"

"For several days the terra has been fluxing in a state of disarray. Energy is moving through the ardor channels in strange patterns I have never felt before."

Lorcan approached as the thunderous footsteps of the Nethermen from the Shatter Stone Clan marching by echoed through the forest.

"Our army is strong, Commander. Hardly a soldier has been lost as we've destroyed these pathetic human settlements. Our troops are hungry for victory and we have more than enough to crush any enemy."

"Don't speak too soon. We won't know what our enemy is until we arrive. For now, we need to stay focused on getting there and push hard; the energies are in flux and the moon and sun are still dim."

Lorcan huffed and Nidhug narrowed his eyes.

"I know you don't believe that magic is a change agent, Lorcan, but I assure you that whatever we encounter is far more precious to Nataxia than anything we have ever pursued. It is the purpose of our entire mission. We must capture it and bring it back to her. It's not going to be easy."

"What is it that we are bringing back?"

"Lúth. It is the magic necessary to restore her and allow her to return to Aimsire."

"Why have you waited until now to tell me?"

"Because you are a Netherman and I know the negativity you and your kind feel about magic. But I also know you are devoted. We must focus and move with all haste. The sooner we can conclude our duties and return to Nataxia, the better."

"It will be done."

Lorcan fell in behind the last of the Nethermen and Nidhug turned to Rezren.

"We are running out of time. It is a five-day journey to the Dale of Still Mead."

"We will be there in time."

The two of them turned as the reptilian troops, the last in the formation, began to pass and salute them. They were strong and bold. A mix of powerful magic users and mighty warriors, as well as the most devoted and faithful of the Rage Queen's army.

+++

"I want to thank you, Raspberry."

"For what?"

She looked at Lady Rose with innocent curiosity.

"For coming almost every night to play for me. You are a special gift to us all."

"Awww, I don't know about that. I just know it makes you happy, and it's been fun gettin' to know ya."

Rose swallowed anxiously before she spoke again.

"Do you remember a while back when I told you I...once had a calling?"

"Sure. I remember you said you couldn't bring yourself to pray anymore, and you didn't feel it mattered anyway."

Rose's cheeks went flush with embarrassment.

"Yes, that's what I said."

"Do you still feel the same way? Are you feeling like praying again?"

Rose smiled. The little halfling had a way of focusing on the obvious without pitter-pattering around.

"Let's just say, I have been seriously thinking about it. I'm still not quite sure how I feel though."

"Well, Ms. Rose, I can tell ya' how I feel. I wake up every day and the first thing I do is pray. Then I go about my day and right before I go to bed, I pray again. Now, I'll be honest, I don't always have great days, but I always have a great night's sleep. Maybe it's because it helps me remember that I am on the right path, even when I mess up...which happens *a lot.*"

"Raspberry, I would like to show you something."

The halfling's curiosity peaked as Rose led her towards a set of double doors. Raspberry had noticed them during every visit but had never seen them opened. Rose removed a key from her pocket and turned over the latch. As she pulled the doors open, a musty smell, like the place hadn't experienced new air for a long time, escaped.

Raspberry coughed and giggled. "Sorta smells like an old cave and...feet?"

"That it does."

Rose walked over and struck a set of firestones to light a large lamp on a stand. Raspberry's eyes went wide as she entered and looked against the wall. A beautiful, finely crafted set of shiny silver armor trimmed in gold hung from a wooden stand, positioned as if it was guarding the place.

"Wow! That armor is amazing! This room kinda feels like holy ground."

"It's my personal chapel. In here I used to pray every morning and every evening to God, placing my petitions before the Lord, like you do. Then I would ask Dionadair to watch over my steps and my ways."

"OH! He's the warrior tutelar of the knighthood! I've read that those most devoted can wield holy magic on the battlefield and even heal their allies."

Rose smiled sadly.

"Wait. Are you trying to tell me..."

"Yes, Raspberry. I was once a fervent Dairadonian."

"I don't understand, Ms. Rose. I mean, if you were so devoted to God that you were actually granted the ability to wield holy magic, healing people and stuff like that...why did you ever stop being devoted?"

"I have no answer for that, Raspberry. What I can tell you is that watching you, hearing you play, and observing your own devotion has roused my guilt. That guilt has led to conviction and that conviction caused me to want to pray again."

Raspberry's eyes lit with excitement. "Well, geesh! That's great! I have a...ummm, friend who told me something along those lines once. Let's just say, it's a great place for you to be in again!"

"Maybe. To be honest I'm afraid it's been so long since I have lifted my petitions that perhaps, God won't hear me. I am also

284

afraid my words won't sound sincere or true. Even worse, I could be heard and simply refused an answer."

"You know, I didn't used to always hear answers when I prayed. Recently though, I learned that God always answers, but usually when we don't hear, it's because we aren't listening so well. It's not because someone isn't talkin'.'"

Lady Rose felt her heart swell.

"You are a wise friend, Raspberry. I appreciate all you have done to help me and the citizens of Gryphonledge so unselfishly. I'm sorry that the Northern Command stole your family farm."

"You know, Ms. Rose, if they hadn't, I probably wouldn't have left Hobnob. I never would have traveled to Fogburgh or even had a chance to travel with Ms. Rayann and Mr. Rorie. I certainly wouldn't have been mentored by Mr. Lenly so I could become a Balladeer. I most definitely wouldn't have met Balaby, or any of my great new friends, including you."

Lady Rose shook her head in amazement at the halflings inspiring perspective on life.

"Well, Raspberry, tonight, I will pray. Most of all, I will heed your advice, sit in the stillness and do my best to listen."

"There ya' go!"

Lady Rose knelt and reached out. Her eyes were moist with tears and she whispered, "May I?"

Raspberry smiled warmly and then thrust herself forward. The impact rocked Rose and she laughed as Raspberry lovingly hugged her.

"You never need to ask for a hug, Ms. Rose. That's what I'm here for!"

+++

Piramay focused on the half dozen rubies floating in a slow rotation around a concentrated orb of fire. Her words drifted as she chanted her spell, laced with the new magic she had been learning. She poured her power into the flames. Though she had made firestones before, she could already feel how much more powerful these were going to be.

The jewels began to glow and tiny wisps of fire reached off the orb, wrapping themselves around the gems. The volume of her

285

voice increased and the heat spinning off the ball of fire intensified. The room began to glow brightly.

For any other, the temperature would have been unbearable, but Piramay basked in the comfort of it. Suddenly the ball of fire separated and smashed into the rubies, filling each with dazzling light.

All six rubies settled onto the table. She reached, picking one up and stared at it. A small ember glowed from within and she smiled callously.

"Concentrated fire, exactly what I need."

Kali's voice filled her head, interrupting her thoughts.

*"Piramay, may I visit?"*

With a soft sigh of exasperation, Piramay responded sweetly to the snit through mind-speak.

*"Of course, Kali. You are always welcome."*

She laughed at her own lie.

Kali appeared and walked over to the large table, staring at the rubies.

"The firestones are completed?"

"How observant."

"I could feel you were working. I waited until I didn't sense the magic being channeled any longer before reaching out to you. I didn't want to break your concentration."

Piramay hid her surprise. How Kali was so attuned already that she could feel her using magic was concerning. She bookmarked this revelation and made note to herself that precautions were going to need to be put in place so her other project could remain a secret.

"To what do I owe this visit?"

"I have completed the ferrystones. I already delivered Fifth's and wanted to bring you yours."

"I see."

Piramay looked down as Kali produced a small, very plain looking, smooth stone. As she handed it over, Piramay pushed heat and magic into her palm, pressing back against the magic that came immediately from within.

"The stone will need to bind to you in order to be used, you are probably feeling that sensation already. This is a first attempt so the range is limited and will only work when you are close to the towers. They should be sufficient for our purposes. With so little time under the influences of Lúth this was the best I could do. In the future I will work on a version that can move you anywhere you wish to go."

"Indeed, I am sure you will."

Kali instantly picked up on the disdain in Piramay's voice.

"I know you don't trust me. Please feel free to inspect and cast detection of any kind you like on that item. I won't be offended. I assure you that you won't find anything awry. The stone will only do as I was instructed to produce."

"Thank you for your permission, not that I needed it."

"Of course not. I simply wanted to…"

"Thank you for visiting, Kali. As I said, you are welcome anytime you wish an audience. We are, *equals*, after all."

Kali paused and then nodded, disappearing without another word. Piramay tossed the stone onto the table and shook the tingling sensation away from her hand caused by the object's attempt to bond itself to her. She watched as the fiery rune of protection faded from her palm.

Ignoring the stone lying on the table, Piramay turned back to her work.

+++

"It will be good to see Braeren again."

"I agree, but that will likely be the only pleasurable part of this journey."

Rayann stepped to her husband and hugged him tightly. She felt his calm, steady heartbeat, but also the trace of anxiety he was attempting to surpress. She inhaled the scent of him, lingering in her love before she responded.

"Do you not think Jerrin has come around?"

"The only thing that is certain is that I am never certain as to what he is thinking."

Rayann stepped away and her eyes welled. The full brunt of her husband's anxiety was exposed. It was rare, but when it surfaced the sensation was overwhelming. Sensing Ceridwyn's presence, she still flinched at the soft knock on their door.

"Come in."

Ceridwyn and Aeolis entered.

"Are we interrupting?"

"Of course not. What can we do for you?"

Ceridwyn turned to Myth'alas and spoke.

"My heart sings with you. Before we travel home, I wanted to make it clear that when I promised to accompany you, I also meant that I intend to be completely by your side when you speak with Jerrin and the Council of Elders."

Myth'alas smiled knowingly as he responded, "You're not one to stand aside and let matters so heavy pass without attempting to see things made right. Though I did not want to assume, the song in my heart gave me the feeling we were on this *entire* journey together."

Her brown, doe shaped eyes focused tightly on his as she stepped up and looked at him intently.

"I mean much more than that. I intend to speak my mind and do whatever I can to aid you, *my* Prince."

She bowed her head, placed her hand on her heart and then turned it over so her palm was facing his and extended it outwards in a slow gesture of loyalty.

Myth'alas hid his shock. Ceridwyn regarding and speaking to him so formally held significance. He was well aware of her enmity for aristocracy and the ruling class of the Fara, additionally, he had never heard her offer fealty in any way, to anyone. She had good cause given her experiences. Rayann instantly felt the load release from his emotions as he spoke again.

"It will be among the rare honors of my life and the few songs left which are still sung within my heart to have you stand and speak beside me, *my* friend."

Ceridwyn turned to Rayann with a warm expression.

"My Princess and dearest companion, your portal is ready to take you. Would you like to go see your son?"

Rayann's face lit up. Not just because her best friend just pledged herself to follow the lead of her prince husband, but because as a mother she knew she was only moments away from holding her little boy again.

"I am."

Together, the four made their way to the portal. Olwa, Pela, and Raspberry were waiting for them, along with the twelve elves under Myth'alas' command. The soldiers and archers of Faralanthis bowed their heads respectfully to their prince and he saluted them in return.

Ceridwyn scanned the group

"Everyone prepared?"

Their faces confirmed their readiness and she waved her hand. The portal flared to life. Myth'alas walked through and the rest followed.

Instantly they were in Faralanthis. Narlea was first to step forward and handed Braeren to his mother. The youngling instantly squealed and started playing with her hair, burying his face in her robes. She laughed and Myth'alas ruffled his son's thick, silky hair as he turned to his mother.

"Thank you for watching over him."

"Of course, my son. It was a pleasure."

Myth'alas turned to Jerrin and brought his hand to his chest and then displayed his open palm in traditional elven greeting.

"My heart sings to see you. When will I be addressing the Elders?"

"In one hour. They are already assembled, but there is other business to discuss first. I excused myself as a courtesy to come welcome you, but I must get back."

Jerrin turned to the elves that had arrived with his brother.

"The twelve of you, report for debriefing."

He glanced at his brother one last time and walked away. Myth'alas watched Jerrin depart. He didn't need to be an empath to sense the mood his brother was in.

Turning to his adherent, he spoke, "Olwa, you should go see your parents. I know you may not want to, but it is the right thing to do."

"I will obey your command, my Prince."

"It's more of a suggestion."

Myth smiled and winked at his protégé.

Suddenly, Raspberry grabbed Pela.

"Come on! I'll show ya' my house!"

"You have a house here?"

"Sure! The elves gave it to me after I helped them. It's a great story. I'll tell you on the way."

Pela looked at Olwa before practically being yanked off her feet as Raspberry tugged her along. The two walked through the streets, hand-in-hand. Raspberry was chattering away about arriving with Ceridwyn, helping her figure out what had happened to Mr. Rorie, playing music for the High Consummate, and a whole bunch of other details in between. Pela did her best to listen but was constantly distracted by all the odd looks they were receiving from the elves. She began to feel her instincts that she might need to defend herself rising.

"WOWZA!"

"What?!" Pela looked around vigilantly.

Raspberry was giggling and trying to shake warmth back into her fingers.

"Why did your hand just get so cold?"

"I...um, I'm sorry."

"Why be sorry? That was amazing!"

Pela leaned forward and whispered, "How much farther is it to your house?"

"Ummm, not far, just around the grove with the big cherry trees there."

"I am feeling very uncomfortable, and when I do, my body gets extremely cold."

"Are you gonna be okay?"

"Yes. I just need to get off the streets."

"Oh! Well, come on then!"

Raspberry started running, Pela was right behind her. Despite the anxiety she was feeling, she was simply amazed at how this 'city' was grown straight from the forest itself. All the places where elves lived or mingled were crafted out of the massive trees. She did her best to take it all in as they made their way to Raspberry's home.

+++

"First Prince Myth'alas, Princess Rayann Fionntán-Thel'Radin Wizard of the Moon, Chief Ranger Aeolis Dawnwater, and Ceridwyn Bolshoraes Archmage of the Sun and Advisor to the Fara Council of Elders."

The Caller stepped back as two blasts from the horns echoed through the council chamber and the four companions approached. They stopped in front of a large staircase which had a row of elegant, high-backed seats at the top. High Consummate Jerrin sat in the center, four elders sat on either side. All of them stared down, their eyes fixed on the group.

"Honored elders. I come before you today to report on the towers and our need to get involved. As you likely know I have had several conversations with my brother…"

"High Consummate Jerrin Thel'Radin."

Myth'alas shifted his eyes to Gintus Autumnglow, the Grand Voice of the High Consummate and first in counsel who had replaced Nimsul. He was among the oldest of the Fara Elves and stared at Myth'alas from beneath his bushy, pointed eyebrows. His deep, gray eyes held no hint of humor or respect.

"Apologies, Grand Voice Gintus. I did not intend to break protocol."

"In this place, young prince, protocol is to be adhered to. No matter your station."

Myth'alas bit his tongue at the old elf's arrogance. Had protocol actually been required, he himself would have just been referred to as 'First Prince'. He turned his eyes back to the rest of the council.

"As I had begun, I have come to report on the situation in the Valley of Still Mead within the central human territory. The towers are active and a third master has taken command of the one which was dormant. Princess Rayann and Archmage Ceridwyn have felt increasing, intense fluxes in the magic energies. The situation is becoming more dire by the day."

"Who is this third master?"

Myth'alas turned to Taralinga Vaporwind, an Archmage and the Advisor of Magic. Her unnaturally smooth skin shined and her thick red hair was pulled back so tightly that not a single strand was out of place. She was stern and pointed in her stare as she leaned forward.

"It is your wife's…cousin, is it not? The one called, Kali, who attacked our very city?"

"It is."

She leaned back smugly and turned her eyes to Jerrin.

"As I advised you, it would appear that the darkness never left her, My Consummate."

Gintus interjected, "We have already heard from the twelve our High Consummate sent with you. They have given us every detail. We have many matters to discuss today, so please continue, but get to your point without the flowery words."

Myth'alas felt his anger building. Feeling it too, Ceridwyn stepped forward to allow him a moment to calm down.

"High Elders, My heart sings to be before you today. I would like…"

"You would like to what, Archmage Ceridwyn?"

Remaining calm, she looked at Gintus as he continued.

"Perhaps you would like to bring the problems of humans into our forests? Long have you striven to do so. Long have you advocated for humanity as you turned your back on the very traditions, lineage and heritage of your own kin. We are not interested in mixing our blood with humans or spilling it by their side to aid in their conflicts. It pains me to ponder what Nimsul would think if he could see you now."

Rayann gasped as she felt the fire of emotion light inside Ceridwyn. It was a side of her that only came out when necessary.

Ceridwyn softly cleared her throat as she smoothed the front of her elegant robes. After composing herself, she began to ascend the stairs. To do so without permission when the council was in session was a direct violation of elven law. The elders murmured and looked at one another in shock.

Gintus demanded, "Halt, Archmage Ceridwyn, or I will have you arrested!"

Ceridwyn stared at him defiantly until both of her feet reached the top of the staircase. She spoke calmly, directing her words at Gintus.

"As an advisor to this council, I would advise you, Grand Voice, to remain silent, lest I abuse the power which God has gifted to me."

He immediately shrunk back after she voiced her threat.

Ceridwyn continued, "What heritage, exactly, are you referring to, Grand Voice Gintus? That of the Fara? The heritage of my lineage and family? Or maybe the weavers and workers tucked away in Rootvale whom I grew up with? I seek clarification regarding your question only because every day they struggle to scratch out a meager living and some only wish to survive while you and yours suck the fat off the land at their expense.

"Your elitist, pompous, disgusting outlook on all who don't measure into your perverted, tiny minded, limited view of this world is abhorrent. Long have you forgotten the gift of these forests that God so lovingly and generously granted us, the elves, at the Dawn Light.

"My family was insignificant to any of you until I was discovered by Nimsul and he took me under his tutelage so I could later rise to a life of wizardry. At this very moment, my mother and father, my brothers and sisters, my cousins, *your kin*, labor in the forests. They are poor, humble, pure, and perfect in God's eyes. These social status' that you so inexcusably cling to are not part of creation. They are the naïve figments of imagination by elves such as yourself. You are only better than others because you believe it and then force that belief on them against their will. It is not by some divine providence or reasonable assignment.

"I have tasted the elegance of the grand royal feasts as well as the sour bile and rumbling of an empty stomach, filled with only a dandelion leaf or two, as I feel asleep. I do not turn my back on the elves because I choose to spend time and break bread with humans. Even though I still have grievances with God over the events in my life, I obey. I do so because spreading God's light was a directive given to us, the elves! At least humans try to do the right thing.

"Of course there are exceptions, but generally, humans are humble, they are willing to learn from their mistakes, and they have some measure of compassion for one another. No, they are not perfect, but we could learn a lot from them. All these things are what this council and the Fara have conveniently forgotten."

Ceridwyn turned to Jerrin. "High Consummate, despite who controls the towers, they pose a direct threat not to humanity but to this entire world. You have seen them with your own eyes. They are real. All life on Aimsire is in jeopardy because of this new magic they channel. If we don't act soon, we will continue to fall behind. By the light, I leave it to your wisdom to make the right decision and preserve what we have left before it's too late."

She bowed her head respectfully to Jerrin before looking up once again and scanned the faces of the elders.

"Lastly, I would like to add that if the Council of Elders declines to assist, I will personally scour the city asking for volunteers. The will of my kin will then have the freedom to hear the truth and make their own choice."

Gintus blurted, "Do you see? Insolence and rebellion. The traits we have always faced when hearing Ceridwyn! From the day Nimsul brought her to this chamber she has–"

He suddenly went silent and clutched at his lips. Ceridwyn's hand slipped back beneath her sleeve and her soft eyes looked at him.

"I did warn you, Gintus." She paused for a moment as he struggled under the effects of her spell. "You stated earlier that you wonder what Nimsul would think of me if he could see me now? Well, I was his adherent and spent more hours than I could possibly count under his tutelage. Therefore, I will tell you.

"Nimsul hated the politics of this chamber. He believed that the elves, especially the Fara, had underestimated and written off humans without cause and against God's directive to us.

"He also believed in a young elf girl below his station. A brassy, cheeky weaver who lived in Rootvale. He would be proud of me. Not only for telling the truth today, but also for silencing your venom. Until our hearts are near once again, Grand Voice Gintus Autumnglow. May the light guide your path."

She raised her hand to her chest and bowed her head respectfully to him before descended the stairs. After she had moved back into rank behind Myth'alas, Jerrin spoke.

"Brother, stay. The rest of you are dismissed."

+++

"I only said what needed to be said."

"I understand, but was it the right time?"

"If not now, then when? Rayann and I have felt Shakyna waning. The sun and moon continue to shine dimly. All three towers are active and divine magic is in complete chaos. What's next? Should we wait until the very world is shaking apart?

"Aeolis, we are elves. We barely understand or contemplate urgency. Have you not yet noticed that our human counterparts see this for what it is and that it needs to be dealt with? We are losing time, something we are not accustomed to. Our light is long burning and steady, but the star of the human soul burns out so much quicker. It allows them to see that they must make the best of every moment in their lives.

"We have talked of sunsets together. I want to see those sunsets with you. The only path to that destination winds straight through those towers."

"You're right. I've always tended to be overly cautious, especially with politics."

"I know, that's why I love you. We balance each other out. You told me in Clay Water that you are a thick-headed twit, and yes, you can be. I think you also have a good heart, a level head on your shoulders and an extra measure of patience in your soul.

"If we are truly destined for sunsets together, you're going to need some patience. Though you didn't get a chance to ask me who I am that day in Clay Water before the enemy arrived, I'm a mouthy little brat from the forest. My tongue can and will run away from me… I'm working on it."

He laughed as she leaned in and kissed him. He smiled after receiving her affection and settled back into his chair, sipping his tea. Ceridwyn looked at Rayann. She had been cuddling her sleeping son and staring out the window for an hour. Her eyes were fixed on the street for any glimpse of her returning husband.

"Dear friend, your tea has gone cold."

Rayann turned; her eyes were pink.

"How long does it take to have a meeting?"

"Some of those meetings last days. Who can know?"

Rayann sighed and walked over to sit with them. Ceridwyn reached for Braeren so Rayann could settle in. She held him lovingly as Rayann spoke.

"Thank you for saying something and standing by Myth's side. I felt emotions change, but I couldn't tell from whom."

"Positive change?"

"Sort of. It was hard to tell for certain and I didn't want to pry into any minds."

There was a knock and Rayann ran to the door. Pela and Raspberry were standing on the porch. Raspberry immediately picked up on the mood and spoke.

"Is everything okay?"

"Yes, fine. Come in you two."

Rayann did her best to smile but Raspberry reached and gently took her by the hand.

"I can tell something is wrong, Ms. Rayann. It's all over your face."

Rayann confessed, "As usual, you are right, Raspberry. Let me pour us all some fresh tea and I will tell you everything."

Thirty minutes later, Rayann was smiling again. Something about the little halfling always cheered up any room she was in.

Ceridwyn turned to Pela and inquired, "What do you think of Faralanthis?"

"It's amazing. I have never imagined that trees could be sculpted into buildings. I don't understand it, but it certainly is beautiful. The lights falling from the canopy are just...I have never seen anything like it anywhere else I've ever been."

"They are the fae lights. The vine binders can control the intensity of them and even change the colors. Sadly, they are dimmed because of the presence of the towers."

"Oh, I see."

Rayann felt her husband before he reached the door. Flinging it open, she grabbed him and pulled him close.

"What happened? You have been gone so long."

He kissed the top of her head but said nothing, holding her for a moment so he could feel her near him. Finally, he closed the door and escorted her back into Ceridwyn's home. He looked at all their anticipating faces before he spoke.

"For starters, Ceridwyn caused quite a stir. The elders were completely against our armies getting involved after hearing the report from the twelve that fought with us, despite their insistence that we should."

He turned and looked directly at Ceridwyn.

"After your little speech and, how did they put it, 'show of arrogance and insolence towards the Grand Voice,' they insisted we remain in the forests and you be stripped of your title and position as well as never again being allowed to attend future meetings. Everyone but Jerrin, that is."

She smirked and sipped her tea confidently as he continued.

"As of thirty minutes ago, I have been given full authority over the armies and rangers of the Elven Commonwealth. We will begin preparation for deployment immediately. Aeolis, as my Chief Ranger, we will need to work closely to get things organized as fast as possible.

"Beloved, I need you to return with Ceridwyn to Gryphonledge. A new set of large portals will be required here and there to move our soldiers. Jerrin offered vine binders and wood from the forest to assist with their construction. I will author a formal parchment to give Commander Rose. Olwa, that will be your responsibility to deliver to her as soon as you return."

Aeolis stood and walked over to Myth'alas. He brought his hand over his heart as he proclaimed, "I am comfortable speaking for this group. We are behind you until the end, Prince General."

# Chapter 22 – Middle Ground

*"God's favor never left you, nor did the blessings that were bestowed upon you. You only forgot them for a while. I too am happy to hear your voice again, my friend."*

The voice Lady Rose heard three hours ago while she was praying still sounded as clear as a chapel bell in her ears. She stood on her balcony in the crisp, morning air, looking out over the city with confidence. Larissa cleared her throat to get Rose's attention.

"Commander, the scouting reports are here, there is some interesting news."

Lady Rose turned and took the parchments, thumbing through them.

"Movements from the south?" She looked up at Larissa.

"Last night the evening watch in the Shovel Lands caught sight of a glow on the southern horizon. They sent pigeons to Sir Trystan and then dispatched scouts to investigate. We received additional messages early this morning after contact with the group was established. It's the Southern Command. They obviously received your messages and are joining us for the battle. They will likely be here by mid-day."

Rose stared at the paper and whispered thanks to God.

"Well, it's about to get awfully crowded around here."

"Aye, Commander."

"You only know part of it. Your brother also secured reinforcements. He will be here soon so we can discuss it."

"What?!"

"See for yourself."

Rose picked up an unsealed parchment from her desk and handed it to her squire.

"Olwa brought this to me when our allies returned from Faralanthis."

Larissa's face filled with excitement as she read.

"This is unbelievable."

"Quite, but it's true."

"Shall I start preparing logistics and maps?"

"Yes, thank you. My number one priority is locating a place for this portal they wish to build. Please also inform Sir

Trystan I will need him to attend so we can discuss housing and supplies for the southern armies."

"Aye, ma'am."

Larissa turned to get to work and then stopped. "Oh, Commander Rose, there is one additional matter to discuss."

She stepped over as she reached into one of the small pouches on her belt. Rose stared at the shining symbol of Dionadair, the tutelar of the knighthood. Larissa handed it to her.

"I had a feeling you might want to start wearing this again. I polished it last night as I was preparing your kit."

Commander Rose's eyes became shiny as she responded, "Thank you, Larissa."

+++

As Myth'alas stepped through the portal, he clasped Sir Ordin's forearm. Sir Gregory approached and reached out to the Prince General as well. Larissa, standing in the background, as usual, glanced at her brother. He could see that she was bursting with questions, but protocol and priority weren't going to allow that right now. He smiled back and spoke directly to her mind.

*"Your face gives away that you have a sea of questions for me. We will talk soon, I promise. Until our hearts are near, my love to you, sister."*

She smiled and offered a loving nod of acknowledgment. As the rest of the party emerged, Sir Ordin looked them over.

"Commander Rose received the parchment from Olwa early this morning and is ready to meet when you are. She asked me to tell you that there is some urgency, but she also wants to give you time to rest after your journey.

Ceridwyn jested, "As our journey was a mere six steps, end-to-end, I believe we are okay to go see her now."

"Apologies, Archmage, I am still getting used to the notion of not dealing with those who travel over the course of months on horseback."

"Hmm, yes. Though traveling by horseback is quite delightful, we have no saddle sores or stiff limbs here today."

Sir Ordin laughed at Ceridwyn's wit. He gestured with his hand towards the large doors.

"Well then, by all means, let's go meet with the Commander Rose."

As they began to walk, Sir Gregory approached Myth'alas.

"Might I have a word with you in private?"

"Of course, Sir Gregory."

The two warriors stepped aside. Rayann turned to look at her husband and he gave her a wink, assuring her that all was well.

"As a man of honor, I need to say something to you, Prince Myth'alas. Many months ago, when we first met, I likely insulted you by rudely commenting that if you really wanted to help you could offer some of your own troops to our cause."

"In the circumstances and the moment, what you said was not an insult, Sir Gregory."

"Even still, I want to apologize. It was not right to say that. Though I believed it at the time, you have more than proven which side you're on, and I am honored to be your ally. Your friends saved my life on the battlefield. I am in their debt, and yours."

"There is no need to apologize and you owe us nothing. You and I are leaders. Sometimes that requires us to press ourselves to the breaking point and demand that others do the same. Some say that the longevity of the elves is a blessing, but the blessing can also be a curse. I have made more than my share of mistakes and it will take a long time to unwind the consequences. I thank God that he has given me grace and the time to try.

"In all honesty, I thought my brother would never allow our soldiers to join us. I was prepared to defy him and bring them anyway. In the end, he reconsidered. Now we can truly fight these threats together. Light willing; we will succeed."

Sir Gregory reached out and the two warriors clasped forearms. The Knight General then pulled his ally in tightly for a hug and spoke into his ear.

"I am honored to go to battle with you, Prince Myth'alas."

"And I with you, Sir Gregory."

The two made their way to the Commander's Quarters. Rose looked up from the table.

"Ahh, there you are."

"Apologies Commander, I needed a word with the prince."

"All is well, Sir Gregory. Larissa, the door please."

The Vine Binders assigned to assist in building the portal frames had done a splendid job. As experts attuned to the magic within the forests, they could sculpt and form living plants and trees into any shape imaginable. Ceridwyn arrived in Faralanthis shortly after the meeting in Gryphonledge and watched them put the finishing touches on the elven side of the gateway.

"Welcome home, Archmage Ceridwyn."

Ceridwyn turned and saw Jerrin approaching her. She bowed her head respectfully and placed her hand over her heart before opening her palm to him.

"High Consummate Jerrin, my heart sings to see you."

"And my heart sings to see you. I wanted to talk to you before sending the Vine Binders to Gryphonledge to complete the second portal."

Ceridwyn looked at him curiously. It was unusual for a leader to come to a conversation. Usually those they wished to speak to were summoned.

"How may I help you?"

He looked at the canopy high above the forest floor and stared at the fae lights.

"There are good things about being an elf." He looked back at her. "You know this. Yes?"

"Of course, High Consummate. I am proud to be an elf. That doesn't mean that we are above reproach, however. More importantly, God's gift to us of longevity should fill us with conviction that we remain willing to learn from our errors rather than developing haughty or prideful hearts towards the rest who were also created during The Dawn Light."

"That statement is exactly the reason I wanted to talk to you. Your bravery while addressing the Council of Elders is something this commonwealth needs. I am not formally asking you this, but I am going to ask you to please think about it."

Her forehead crinkled in curiosity as he continued. "I have removed Gintus from his position. His behavior yesterday, especially after you left, was unacceptable enough to warrant that."

"After I left?" She quirked her brows curiously.

"Let's just say, when his ability to speak returned, he had some choice words about you. Then he had a few about me. Though I am willing to listen to opinions so I can gather enough information to find solutions, there is a line that can't be crossed. This is especially true when the decision I made was correct. With that said, I would like you to consider joining the Council of Elders as my Grand Voice."

Her face barely contained her shock. She inhaled deeply before responding.

"I cannot promise that I will accept. However, per your request, I will consider it. I have never been one to sit on councils or at tables discussing what to do. I would much rather be out here, doing it."

"I understand. I am not nor will I ever demand that you accept this position. For now, your considering it will be enough. When all this is over, we can discuss things in more detail."

"By the light, you honor me. I give you my word, High Consummate, I will meditate and pray on it."

"Thank you." He turned and gestured. "I oversaw the shaping personally to ensure your specifications were adhered to."

Together they approached and inspected the work. She smiled at the Vine Binders.

"Well done, all of you."

Turning to Jerrin she offered an update.

"We met with Commander Rose this morning right after arriving in Gryphonledge. It was decided to weave the other end of this portal between The Shawl and the Freckled Forest, where the rivers meet. That location is where the trees are the densest. It is a long march to the city from there, so we will construct additional, smaller portals to move back and forth quickly.

"Prince Myth'alas and especially Aeolis liked the idea of keeping the elves in an environment where they would be most comfortable and concealed. We will of course commingle the armies as much as possible, but I fear we are running out of time for much of that.

"Additionally, the Southern Command will be arriving in Gryphonledge soon. All of humanity is uniting to fight for our world. From within the song of my heart, I thank you for fully committing The Commonwealth to the cause."

Jerrin nodded. "I have seen the towers, and I understand the threat. Let's hope, for all our sakes, that what we are doing will be enough."

"The latest reports from Commander Rose's scouts indicated that Nataxia's army will be in Goose Sky within the next two or three days."

"Well, then I suggest you get going. God's light and life to you, Archmage Ceridwyn."

"To you as well, High Consummate Jerrin."

+++

Horns blared and the clopping of hooves began to echo through the streets. Sir Trystan and the knights under his command led the procession through the main gates and into Gryphonledge.

The knights of the south were a new sight for most of the citizens who lined the streets to welcome them. The most immediate difference was they wore thick, leather armor. On their heads, instead of helmets they wore caps made of hemp cloth with wide, circular brims to protect their eyes and the back of their necks from the sun. The heat and deserts in their region of the world were not conducive to heavy steel like their central and northern counterparts.

Most wielded axes or hammers as opposed to swords. Their weapons were massive and menacing to behold. In the traditions of the ancient southern tribes, the knights of the south etched their family crests into the blades and wove multicolored leather around the handles of their weapons.

At the front of the parade was a mountain of a man. The insignia of his rank as overall commander was tooled neatly into his layered spaulders. Despite his menacing size, his smile was bright, warm and cheerful. He waved and greeted those who lined the streets, laughing and making funny faces for the giggling children. Though he was a man experienced in battle, his richly russet colored skin bore few scars and his blue eyes were kind.

On his left was a man whose shoulders visibly bulged with strength, even through his armor. His thick, black hair was pulled back into a long ponytail, and his sharp eyes never stopped scanning the crowd. He had sepia colored skin which was mostly covered with extra armor, etched with the marks of battle.

To the commander's right was a woman who radiated wisdom. A large staff was fastened to her back. On the top end a malformed, shimmering chunk of black, crystalized carbon, harvested from the throat of a desert glass wyrm was magically twisted into the end.

The staff was made of ebontine. A rare and beautiful, highly grained wood known for its ability to enhance magic. The top was twisted to look like a scorpion's tail and the stinger wrapped up and over to hold the gem firmly in place.

She sat tall in her saddle and her shimmering eyes were soft but serious. Her thick, medium length, curly hair filled with sun-bleached streaks complimented her dark skin. The locks were pinned back loosely and bounced with each impact of her horses' hooves. She gave an occasional nod to the crowd, but her eyes mostly remained focused in the direction they traveled.

Sir Trystan led them through the keep's inner wall and then moved aside. The southern army commanders dismounted, and squires came rushing in to tend their horses and the other senior soldiers that followed. Lady Rose approached.

"Commander Verik, it is a pleasure to finally meet you."

The giant of a man nodded and reached out to grasp her forearm. Even through her steel bracers she could feel the strength in his grip.

"The feeling is mutual, Commander Rose. Long have I heard the tales and victories of The Velvet Hammer. Based on the stories, we assumed you were a giant."

Rose smiled in thanks and then stepped aside as she spoke.

"This is Sir Ordin Wolfrider, my first in command, and Sir Gregory Velsandor, my second in command."

"Velsandor? Have you roots in the south?"

"I do, Commander Verik, my family came north many generations ago."

"A pity we lost a man of your size to the scrawny northerners."

He laughed and whapped Sir Gregory on the shoulder. Though he hid it well, the impact felt like being hit with the projectile from a catapult.

Sir Verik turned to his companions. "This sullen looking soldier is Sir Treyton Tilistone, my first in command, and this is Knightchanter Elce Irabel, my second."

"Welcome to all of you. The city of Gryphonledge is open to you in whatever manner you need or require. We are going to house you in the castle as it is currently the only available space for so many. You will be quite comfortable."

"We are to stay in the home of our king?! Are you sure he would approve of common soldiery sleeping on his silk pillows and purple sheets?"

Verik winked as Commander Rose was about to speak.

She paused and huffed a laugh. "He is tucked away in Pearlpoint for the winter."

He responded with obvious sarcasm in his voice, "Oh, believe me, we know. We certainly thank you for pushing him off on us for a while! He has been demanding extra protection as word began to spread regarding the battle when you attempted to destroy the towers.

"How did he put it, *'This threat to the kingdom, but more importantly, the leadership and those in nobility cannot be ignored. It is with utmost urgency that this command from your king be obeyed. Upon receiving this parchment, send a battalion of your best knights and steelguard immediately to reenforce Pearlpoint Harbor, for the protection of the kingdom'*."

"A battalion?" Sir Ordin huffed and cleared his throat as he attempted to hide his laughter.

Commander Verik turned to him and jested.

"Ahhh, another champion and supporter of the king I see."

His own laughter then boomed from his mouth.

As they all settled, Commander Rose gestured.

"It is extremely important that I introduce these individuals to you, Commander Verik. We have every thanks to give them for their contributions and insight into all that has been going on."

Myth'alas stepped forward. Verik leaned his head back and his eyebrows shot up. He and Myth were nearly eye to eye.

"Never in my days have I seen an elf your size. Tell me, what is your name?"

"First Prince Myth'alas Thel'Radin of the Fara. God's light and life to you, Commander Verik."

"Ahhh, we had heard a rumor that the elves had a presence here. I see there are a few of you."

"And more coming in the following days, Commander."

He shifted his gaze as Ceridwyn elegantly stepped forward. She placed her hand over her heart and then opened her palm in greeting as she introduced herself.

"Ceridwyn Bolshoraes, Archmage of the Sun. It is a pleasure to meet you and your companions."

Commander Verik was instantly captivated by her beauty and grace. He took her hand in his and leaned forward, kissing the back of it gently.

"It is a great pleasure to meet you as well, Archmage Ceridwyn."

"As I introduced earlier, this is Knightchanter Elce. You two, and you there…," He pointed at Rayann, "…Should all get to knowing one another. I have a feeling we're going to need your talents and abilities."

Commander Rose turned to Sir Trystan.

"We need to bring all their commanders in and brief them. Can you handle all the details out here?"

"Aye, Commander, of course."

"Thank you, Sir Trystan."

She looked at him and felt a pain in her chest. She realized she hadn't spent much time with him since Kali's treason and regretted that. Though he had been doing his duties to the utmost of her expectations, the pain still lingered in his eyes. Now that she was feeling the flow of God's holy power moving in her again, she felt much more empathy.

"Sir Trystan, please come to my office at sunset, and bring your appetite. I would like to have supper with you and debrief you on the meeting I am about to have."

"Of course, Commander. I will be there."

He saluted sharply and she returned the gesture.

The group began to move and Elce caught sight of Erika near the back of the assembled steelguard. She furrowed her brow as she focused on her and then elbowed Sir Treyton. He turned and Elce pointed.

He caught sight of her and whispered, "Erika?"

Pela sat, staring out the window. The day had been a whirlwind of activity and now that night had fallen, she began reflecting on all that was happening around her.

"Here ya' go! Two fresh cuppers."

Pela turned and looked at Raspberry as she took the cup. She focused her magic and the stoneware mug frosted as she cooled the tea.

"Thanks. I had never had tea until I came here. Everyone drinks it all the time."

"Sure! I love when you do that to your cup. We should start calling your version 'ice tea'! I admit, I wasn't much for it either, until I met Ms. Ceridwyn. I always thought it tasted like dirty water, but she made it in such a way that you just always wanted more. I don't know, maybe it's all the great talkin' she does while we drink it that helps."

Pela smiled sadly.

"You, okay?"

"No, not really. Knowing we are about to go to battle again... I just... I really miss my father. I've never gone anywhere without him. I keep reflecting on the whole mess that brought us here. First, accepting Nataxia's gold to go fight Myth'alas and his family. Then making our way north and seeing all the armies that were coming to shore. Then agreeing to come here and fight these enemies with you.

I just keep wondering: if none of that had happened, would he still be alive? And if he was, what we would be doing, together, right now."

Raspberry looked at her a moment before responding.

"Hmm, well, you were way up north, right?"

"Yes."

"Nataxia's army is marchin' straight down here and it sounds like they're doing some really bad stuff. You might have had to fight them alone. I know you two were really tough together but, from what I've heard at the meetings where Prince Myth'alas is talkin' about them...I don't know if you would'a survived."

"I guess." Pela shrugged indifferently.

"Hey, I don't know. Maybe you would have. One thing I've figured out for sure though…Mr. Bold'Rock really loved you, didn't he?"

"He did. Anytime people figured out that we were together they would always say the same thing, 'How could a Netherman be compassionate and keep a human child?' But he did. And he really cared for me."

"Tell me your story."

Pela looked at her. Nobody had ever asked her to talk about herself. Though she was trying to not be suspicious all the time, she couldn't help her lifelong instincts from surfacing. Sitting here with Raspberry, though, she knew it was a pretty safe bet that things would be alright.

"What part of my story do you want to know?"

"All of it! I love stories. I love telling them. I love hearing them. Our stories are who we are. We really can't get to know one another unless we share what journeys and adventures we've been on. I'll make a deal with you. Tell me your story and next, I'll tell you mine!"

Pela smiled. "Okay. Well, my father was the brother of the Chief of the Ice Rock Clan. Nethermen are gathered into seven major clans. There's the Shatter Stone, the Bog Mud, the Ice Rock, the Crush Skull, the Hawk Screech, the Grim Howl, and the Iron Bark. There's also a lot of smaller clans that hold or claim allegiance to the big ones. We call them the 'Broken Clans'.

"Clan leaders aren't organized by family or anything like the humans do. You must fight to become chief, so the chief is always the strongest in the clan. Where I'm from, Stone Seat is the biggest settlement. In human terms, it's our capital city, where the chief and his greatest warriors live.

"One day, Bold'Rock and some of the other warriors were patrolling along the southern border. They were on the human side, moving along the cliffs close to Amberwood Keep. As they made their way through some very dense trees, they heard a baby crying. Bold'Rock approached and picked up the broken basket I was in. My mother was near me, torn to shreds. He looked inside the basket and found this beside me."

She reached into her bag and removed the crystal that used to be in Bold'Rock's staff.

"It was all I had with me besides the clothes I was wearing. The other Nethermen that were with him wanted to eat me. Netherman will do that, but Bold'Rock sensed something was different, especially because of the crystal, so he protected me.

"He was looked down upon when he brought me back to Stone Seat, but since he was one of his brother's finest warriors and his brother was chief, I was allowed to stay. He raised me, among the other netherchildren. Of course, they were all much bigger than me, so I had to fight for everything I needed. Nothing is given to you in Nethermen society. You must be strong enough to survive or die. As a human, I was at a major disadvantage."

Raspberry swallowed hard and leaned in, listening intently.

"I was seven when another nethergirl snatched my roasted rabbit from me. We had been in exercises and I hadn't eaten all day. I was so hungry. She knew it and of course, they all wanted me gone anyway. I reached to get it back and all she needed to do was hold it above my head, out of reach. Several of the other children approached and started chanting 'Ech'chta' which means, 'little pinky'. I was furious. I felt something in me that day, a desire to make the teasing and the pain go away. I reached out my hand and a shard of ice exploded from my palm, blasting a hole in her chest."

"What?"

"In Nethermen society, that is not a crime. Killing for no reason is a crime, but killing as a means of rising in the ranks is considered natural. There are laws and rules, but in cases like this, especially with children– killing when your food was stolen is not against the rules, it's done to advance your place in the clan order.

"After that, the other netherchildren left me alone. Many even let me go before them at lessons and mealtimes. Only a few continued to bully and put pressure on me, but it was done in a much different manner. The girls finally started accepting me as part of them, and at eleven, those in my age group began our journey of passage."

"What's that?"

"It's the lessons of adulthood. All netherboys and nethergirls are separated and instructed by the elders, the warriors, the laborers, the wardens, and the greenreapers. We are taught and tested, ultimately put into our potential positions through which we will serve the clan."

"What position were you put in?"

"Warriors." Pela's smile was shy, but proud.

"As I grew, my abilities in magic continued to intensify. By the time I turned twelve, most of the clan feared me."

"Wow. How old are you now?"

"Fifteen. I mean, as close as father could guess."

"What happened next?"

"In my thirteenth year, I danced The Ceremony of Blossoms with the other girls."

"The Ceremony of Blossoms? What an amazing name!"

"I know. It's a time of great feasting and celebration, but it has incredible significance as well. It's very cold in the Ice Rock Mountains, so we only get flower blossoms in high summer and for a very short time. That's when the ceremony occurs. We go out into the hills and pick the blossoms, as many as we can find. Then, we braid them into our hair, weave them into adornments like necklaces, headpieces or bracelets. We even tuck them into all the seams in our clothing, wherever they will stay put.

"After that, on the last night of the waxing moon, right before the sun goes down, the elders light a huge fire and we start to dance. The tradition is, because it's the brightest light available, the fire lures the boys who have been learning to hunt, to come and 'hunt' us girls.

"The boys have their own ceremony too. It's called The Ceremony of Bones. They go out on their first hunt one new moon before The Ceremony of Blossoms. They come back wearing their trophies on their armor. They emerge from the trees and dance with us. Slowly but surely, the next generation of adults pair off to begin our journey as life mates.

"Of course, the girls wait for the biggest, strongest males to court them, especially the ones wearing furs or the skulls of bigger animals. The males look for the prettiest females and the ones adorned with the most blossoms. You know a couple has agreed to become life mates when she is wearing the tanned hide of his first kill and he is wearing some of her blossoms on his armor. It doesn't always work out evenly though. That year, I was the only girl without a hide on her shoulders."

"I'm sorry."

Pela looked at her and smiled sadly. "Don't be. It was never realistic that I could be a Netherman's mate. I admit, I was sad, but deep down I knew the reason. I'm human."

Pela sipped her tea and Raspberry waited with anticipation for her to continue.

"After the night of dancing, the next morning all the youth assemble at Big Fire, in the center of the village. The Foremost Greenreaper places a blade in the hot coals until it glows red and then etches the clan mark on your arm. It's the same blade that has been used for as long as anyone can remember. The blood of every single one of your clan members is baked into the metal. Once you are marked, you are part of the clan forever, even after death."

"Did you get marked?"

Pela lifted her sleeve and showed Raspberry the symbol of the Ice Rock Clan etched on her arm. The little halfling reached and looked at Pela for permission to touch it. She nodded in agreement, so Raspberry traced her fingers along the scar.

"Did it hurt?"

"Yes and no. I mean, it hurt a lot…but it was strange. There was this sense of belonging and accomplishment that came with the pain. My father was staring at me, proud as can be. I will never forget his face as he smiled at me."

"I don't think I would want to be burned and cut. I admit though, it does sound nifty to be part of something like that. What I still don't understand is, after all that, why'd ya leave?"

"We had to. Well, *I* had to. Once I was of age and could not realistically be a Netherman's mate, the chief banished me."

"What?"

"Father argued with him, but once the chief gives a command, it's final. I had no choice; I had to leave or be executed. He refused to let me go alone, so we left together."

"He did love you."

Pela's fingers caressed the mug holding her iced tea.

"Yes. Yes, he did."

# Chapter 23 – Kinetic Objectives

Ceridwyn and Rayann stared at the elegantly woven foliage with satisfaction. The human commanders had gathered near the portal gateway and were in assembly to welcome the elves.

Rayann spoke to Myth'alas. "All is in place. On your command, Ceridwyn will transport herself to Faralanthis so we can activate the portal from both sides simultaneously."

Myth'alas' eyes shifted to the archway. It was massive, large enough for twelve individuals to walk through shoulder to shoulder.

"They are ready for her. I told them noon sharp."

Rayann gave Ceridwyn a nod. The Archmage reciprocated and transported herself to Faralanthis. Within seconds, she could feel the magic start buzzing through the portal. Taking a deep breath, Rayann began to chant. Shakyna swirled around her and many of the central commanders shifted uneasily as they felt the static begin to build in the air. The southerners were far more comfortable with magic and stood in place without flinching.

As Rayann drew the power of the moon into her body, she mixed the two flows of energy and blue light erupted from her palms. The magic hit the center of the open space in the portal frame, orange light erupted behind it. The flow shimmered and spread like water until it reached the edges. Faralanthis could be seen as if in an underwater distance.

Aeolis turned to his companions.

"I will be right back."

He stepped through as Rayann turned to her husband.

"Are you ready, beloved?"

"As ready as one can be."

He lovingly brushed her cheek with his fingertip and turned as Jerrin stepped through the portal in his magnificent armor. Red Sun held firmly in his grasp.

Myth quirked a brow and stepped up to his brother. He spoke with whimsy in his voice.

"Well, what are you doing here?"

"Following our commonwealth's Prince General on some foolish quest. I have it on good report that the world needs the elves in order to save it."

Rayann felt her husband's emotions burst like a wellspring. She watched as Jerrin reached out an arm and Myth'alas gently batted it away, hugging his brother tightly instead. Jerrin gave pause but finally brought one arm around and patted his brother on the back.

The High Consummate smirked as the embrace ended.

"I certainly couldn't let you do this alone, little brother."

Jerrin approached the humans and brought his hand to his heart before turning his hand over and showing his open palm.

"Commander Rose I presume? From my brother's descriptions I figured you would be much larger a lady."

"HA! That's what I said!"

Jerrin turned to Verik curiously at the interruption before returning his gaze to Commander Rose.

"Light and life to you. I am High Consummate Jerrin Thel'Radin of the Fara. The Elven Commonwealth stands with you. May God be with us as we fight these threats in unity."

"It is our honor to finally meet you, High Consummate Jerrin. Your brother speaks very highly of you."

"Does he?" Jerrin turned to look at Myth'alas.

"He does. We were not expecting you to come with your troops. It will be an honor to have you on the battlefield with us."

As Jerrin continued with the introductions, Myth'alas turned to Rayann. She was crying with joy.

"I had no idea, husband. This certainly does bring more light to chase the darkness."

"Indeed, it does."

Aeolis and Ceridwyn emerged, followed by line after line of Faralanthis' elven rangers. They were dressed for battle, their faces stoic with dedication to the task. Olwa reached and brushed his fingers on Pela's hand. She responded immediately, bringing her hand around so they were palm to palm and their fingers interlaced. She looked at him and he smiled. Turning back, they watched the formations arrive. Olwa had never been so proud to be an elf.

+++

313

The human commanders were amazed as they observed how effortlessly the elves blended into the forest. One would have expected them to gather and bunch up around the portal as they came through, but the elves slid into the shadows as fast as they arrived, shadowskipping hundreds of meters at a time towards their assigned encampments.

Over a thousand elven rangers and twice as many more soldiers of the commonwealth were now in human territory with many more to arrive over the coming days. They were already setting their lines along the southern edge of Still Mead. Once the ceremony ended, the human commanders were given leave to get back to their duties and preparations.

After the arrival of the elves, Sir Treyton made his way through the barracks until he came to the armory. He stood in the doorway and stared at Erika. She was meticulously retethering one of the blades on her double ended staff with a weave of hemp rope and leather.

"We assumed you were dead."

"Well, I'm not." She pulled the braid tight so the leather made a snapping sound and continued to work without flinching or turning to face him.

"Clearly."

He approached and watched her work without saying anything else.

"What do you want, Treyton?"

"I want peace between us."

She slammed her hand on the table. "Do you?" She stood, turning to face him. "Do all of you want peace? Did the family have a meeting and agree to this?"

"I am sure those who are still alive would agree to peace."

"What?"

"Mother and father are dead."

"What? When?"

"Last summer."

"How?" Erika tried to maintain the stone look on her face, but her eyes welled up.

"A raid by the Saber Wolves. They attacked in force, several hundred strong. Both of our parent's companies were wiped out."

Erika sat and her eyes welled up. Treyton placed his hand on her shoulder.

"They never forgot you after you left."

"I had to leave."

"Your defiance insists you did. In reality, you didn't."

"How would you know?"

"Because I sat with our parents at the evening hearth every night for months and observed them grieve the loss of you as they discussed ways they could have handled it better."

Erika looked at him and her lip twitched. She desperately wanted to counter his statement but instead turned her eyes back to her weapon on the table. After a long pause she finally spoke.

"Is that all you came to tell me?"

"No, I have already said, I want peace between us. I am the third of seven. You are the seventh, the last of our line. Tradition says the last shall remain disburdened. You were to carry on the lineage without the need to go to battle or defend our lands. That falls on the elders, not the youngest. It bores deep in me that you shortened your name. But you are still a Tilistone."

"I wanted to wield the same steel as my brothers, sisters, and parents. I was denied that. I was told I must remain in the background, marry, tend our lands, have children; that is not the life for me."

"Obviously. You were denied squireship, so you enlisted. Look at you now. A command sergeant of the Northern Guard and among the survivors of the remaining northern armies. I dare say you have proven your point."

Erika swallowed hard.

"Listen, sister. I would fold you back into my ranks in an instant. I will leave that to you to decide. But for this battle, there are few choices for you. With all their commanders dead, the remaining northerners are to be absorbed into the ranks of the central knighthood and steelguard for this battle. Would you rather charge with me or with a stranger?"

"With you."

"Good. I have already requested to Commander Rose that you be transferred into my units immediately, depending on the outcome of this conversation. I am going to put you in command of some conscripts. Yes, I know, they aren't steelguard, but the soldiers of the south are not going to blindly follow a sergeant they don't know."

She stood and saluted. "I understand. Thank you."

"There is nothing to thank me for. One last thing; if we survive this, consider coming home."

"No promises."

"I never expected any."

+++

Piramay tapped her fingernails on the table, staring at the ferrystone. She had cast every detection spell she knew, but the object proved itself true to form. Snatching it up, she transported herself to Fifth's tower unannounced and waited patiently until he looked up from his worktable.

"Little Phoenix? To what do I owe this unexpected visit? Not that it bothers me to see your sensual form."

"When will we go to battle? Only through the slaying of our enemies will we know that the snit is truly on our side."

"Still so slow to trust."

"She is still not trustworthy."

"Would it reassure you if you had a backup plan?"

She lingered a moment in the question before responding. "I'm listening."

"As you know, I have been working on a new design for capturing souls. The prototype has been completed."

He removed the device from within his robes. It looked different than the others, more like a dagger handle.

"This is a soul dagger. When activated a blade will appear and take the soul of its victim. If I gave it to you, with the understanding that you were to only use it if necessary. Could I trust you to show restraint?"

"My dear Fifth, whom else could you trust further, or deeper?" Her voice was suddenly flirtatious.

"None."

"That's right. None."

She leaned forward so the top of her dress fell open ever so slightly and kissed him softly on the cheek.

As she pulled away, he slipped the device into her hand and whispered the activation word into her ear. She winked and the device disappeared into her tight-fitting clothing.

"So, I take it you don't trust her either?"

"I trust her implicitly."

"Then why give me the soul dagger?"

"Because I need your focus right now. The next few days will determine our future and alter this world forever. Until you stop obsessing about Kali's loyalty, you will not be able to focus on our mission."

"We still don't know the plan. How are we to focus until you tell us?" She narrowed her eyes on him.

He began pacing around the table and spun with a sneer. "So glad you asked."

*"Kali, please join us in my work chamber."*

Kali appeared within seconds and bowed her head respectfully.

"Good evening."

Piramay's expression instantly became one of welcoming.

"Good evening to you as well, Kali."

"Thank you for joining us. As you both know the southern army has arrived. Nataxia's army has advanced through Black Bee Valley and will be here soon. These two forces…"

Kali interrupted, "Three forces. The elves are here too."

Piramay and Fifth looked up in surprise. "The elves?"

"Yes, they began arriving at noon via portal."

"Where?"

"I have not been able to pinpoint the exact location, but it is somewhere in The Shawl."

Piramay inquired. "Why did you withhold this information until now?"

"Why have we still not heard Fifth's plan? Why do you labor secretly, deep in the belly of your tower? I didn't realize that joining the two of you meant I must divulge everything I learn while you two keep your discoveries to yourselves." She turned to Fifth. "Is this how it is to be?"

"Of course not. Piramay?" She turned and looked at him. "That's enough."

317

Inside she smoldered but outwardly she nodded and turned to Kali. Her voice was dripping with sarcasm. "My apologies. Obviously, we have all been very busy. I am sure that you planned to let us know the numbers of our enemies were increasing by the minute as soon as you had a few spare moments of your own."

"Where, approximately, is this portal?" Fifth brought their attention back to the map.

Kali pointed to the center of The Shawl. "As best I can discern, here. I could feel Ceridwyn and Rayann's signatures. There was also a third source of magic, one I am not attuned enough to trace."

Piramay chimed in. "That's a good location. I am sure you are feeling the location correctly. The elves would prefer the forest over the open plains. The center of The Shawl gives them quick access to the entire southern line of trees that border Still Mead. With their ranger's ability to shadowskip, they can cover that entire tree line with ease."

"Agreed." Fifth pointed towards New Stone. "As the Rage Queen's army finishes advancing, my guess is they will spread out along this opening between the forests. The humans and elves will have no choice but to stack up between the old roads, putting their backs to us."

"And that's when we strike."

"No, Piramay, that's when we enjoy the show."

Kali looked up. "You still plan for us not to attack?"

Fifth laughed. "Dear Kali, we are going to attack, but only when the time is right. There are tens of thousands of soldiers, archers, and machines that will be facing one another. As I've already told you, even with the might of the towers to fuel us we could not fight so many, not yet anyway. Our casting will be effective and longstanding, but eventually even we will succumb to the energies and exhaust ourselves. We will linger, let them chew themselves to pieces, and then strike."

"Where's the fun in that?" Piramay exhaled her frustration and traced her finger on the map. "If Nataxia's armies are here, and the humans are here, my best guess is the elves will line up in the trees. Some may already be positioning in this northern point of trees as well. That would create an opportunity to attack both flanks simultaneously. Their arrows could cover a great deal of ground from those locations."

Fifth approved. "I agree. When we strike, Kali, I want you in the middle. You can move the fastest and mobility will be key in that position. Piramay, I want you on the southern side, where the trees are the densest. I will move along the northern edge. If the elves have a presence there, I will handle it. Once we advance far enough, we will all collapse to the center and show them that our power is not to be challenged.

"Once we strike and end this, we will be the last power on Aimsire. From there, we will focus on fully stabilizing the rift and open our own portal to the Plain of Constellations."

Piramay giggled. "I'll begin preparing my pets for the battle." She turned to Kali. "As always, it was a pleasure seeing you." She vanished in a twirl of fire.

Kali turned to Fifth. "Are you sure about this?"

"Yes. I believe it's a solid plan."

"No. About her."

Fifth turned and stared at Kali with his mirrored eyes. "I grow weary of this war between you two."

"I have no war, Fifth. I have ambition and aspirations. You assured me that we would work together, the three of us, as a unit."

"And we are. After we have shed blood and burned our enemies together, she will see you in a different light."

"What of those creatures she is breeding?"

"What of them?"

"There is a strange magic in them."

"All these new magics flowing through the rift are strange, Kali. None of us have felt them before. Trust me, Piramay wants this victory more than you or I."

She looked at the map. "She's right about the elves. They will spread out and try to stay in the trees. Their forest magic is their greatest advantage against us."

"I'm sure they will."

"Have you tested your ferrystone?"

He reached into his robes and removed the object she had given him. "Not yet. I did feel it attune, however. Quite an interesting sensation, almost…erotic."

"It must take a small measure of your magic to work. That is the way of artifacts."

He laughed. "I know how artifacts work, Kali."

"I know you do." She reached and brought her hand over his. The ferrystone cinched between their palms. "I trust your plan. Our victory is inevitable."

"Indeed, it is." He dared to lean in. She didn't withdraw and he gently kissed her neck.

With a smile, Kali vanished and reappeared in her tower. The instant she arrived she bitterly rubbed the moisture from her neck where his lips had made contact. She then lifted her hand and looked at her open palm. A soft, purple glow on her skin where the ferrystone had touched slowly faded away.

+++

Commander Rose, Commander Verik, and their subordinates sat on horseback, staring at the towers. Jerrin, Myth'alas, Aeolis, Ceridwyn, Rayann, Larissa, and Olwa accompanied them.

The group was positioned on Still Mead Ridge and looked out over the valley. From this high point they could see the towers in the cauldron, the forests on either side of the valley, and the edge of the Shovel Lands to the east.

"We have tactical problems no matter where we set lines."

"Agreed, Verik, but we must set them somewhere."

"So, what do you propose?" Commander Verik turned to Sir Ordin.

"To your point, the options are limited. Our defensive strategy has always been to draw approaching armies through the pinch of trees created by Narrow Wood and The Shawl, it's only a kilometer or so in width before the valley opens up. With the towers in the center of Still Mead we certainly can't do that now.

"Setting formations with the towers to our back is not an option as we don't need to find ourselves between two enemies. Even though our information says those three wizards aren't working with the Rage Queen, who knows what they will do when an army of such size and strength arrives. They might decide to

320

align. Every defensive option the valley once provided is compromised. These towers saw to that."

"Is protecting Gryphonledge the number one priority?"

The Commanders turned to Myth'alas. "Yes of course."

"Then it doesn't make sense to set the armies anywhere other than between the city and the enemy. Both enemies."

"How, Prince General? We can't bring the southern armies in without marching them past the towers. What if the wizards attack while we do so?"

"Knowing what I do about magic users, I don't think the wizards will attack. They have been biding their time. If I was up there, I would let the two armies have at one another from a safe distance. What need is there to get involved if someone else can bleed for you?"

Verik turned to Rose and shrugged. "The elf prince has a point. I still don't like the idea of marching my entire army right past those things in the open." He looked back at Myth. "We need to get my armies safely through the valley and into positions. How do we do that?"

Jerrin interjected. "We have a hundred Vine Binders with us. They could part the trees and cast swift hooves along the newly opened passages through The Shawl. The pathway could be made wide enough to move your armies quickly and under concealment.

"As for us, the trees on the south side of the valley will provide adequate cover for the rangers. The elf warriors can move easily through the thickets near the wetlands. I can also have the Vine Binders build a series of bridges over the rivers in case we need to retreat."

Myth'alas continued the strategy. "This plan would force Nataxia's armies to circumvent the towers and funnel themselves into us. We have withdrawal routes, the trees, and three rivers as natural positioning points."

Commander Rose asked. "To Verik's point, what if the wizards see the Rage Queen's army and chose to align with them? What then?"

"At least they'll be in front of us and we can respond accordingly."

Rose continued. "All of this requires us to move fast. Sir Gregory, what is the latest report on Nataxia's army?"

"They are split on either side of the river but occupy Old Stone and New Stone."

Rose turned to Jerrin and Myth'alas. "Then they are in the process of crossing the Black Bee River by ferry boats and still need to march across the Shovel Lands. That's going to buy us a little time. Can all of this be done quickly enough?"

Myth'alas responded. "Yes, Commander Rose."

Verik boomed. "Well then, let's get moving."

+++

Two days later, with the elves' assistance, the southern armies had advanced through The Shawl and were now encamped along the rivers. The rangers had fortified their positions in the trees and the elven warriors were set in their positions amongst the human armies.

Olwa sat twenty meters inside the tree line, observing the landscape to the west. He was doing his best to remain in the moment, but his thoughts lingered on Pela and his wish that all this chaos would end quickly. He wasn't afraid, it was just becoming more and more obvious that his heart wasn't to be a part of the rangers or serve the commonwealth. His keen eyes scanned the landscape as he snapped himself back to the moment. He was supposed to be keeping watch, but the subtle movement of the grass and the light constantly captivated and distracted him.

He heard a soft rustling and turned around. There was nothing behind him. Suddenly, he felt a movement of air to his left. He turned. Again, there was nothing. After a moment he returned his gaze to the landscape he was supposed to be scouting. Myth'alas was there, sitting cross legged with his back to Olwa.

Without looking he knew his adherent was scrambling to compose himself. "Save your salutes for another time, Olwa. Come, sit with me."

Olwa did as he was instructed. Myth'alas never turned to him, instead, he gestured to the landscape.

"When you look out there, what do you see?"

"My Prince, I see the advantage of the shadow line coming off those outcroppings. The tree line comes halfway through the rock shadow and would create a path of opportunity to circumvent enemy movement and attack from behind..."

"Perhaps my question was not clear. I asked what *you* see, not the ranger in training." Myth'alas looked at him.

Olwa took a breath and whispered, "I see ten thousand colors commingling to create a splendid, harmonious balance. I hear the robins as they flutter and land, tapping for worms. I feel the vibration of every doe and stag as their hooves press gently into the soil. I hear the soft breathing of the mountain cats as they hunt. There is not a single line but a blend of shadow and light, wrapped in the elegance of purity but surrounded by a frame that won't hold the painting within its edge.

"I hear every whisper of the breeze through the needles and the branches. The difference in their tones and the harmony that is created by their song. Not a single spec of the landscape is out of order but set in unison against the neighbors that exist within God's creation. In all, I see a natural perfection that not even the elves could dare attempt to improve upon."

He looked at Myth who was smiling with satisfaction. The elf prince spoke.

"You constantly excel in your duties and training. You are an obedient and loyal adherent. Though you thrive and I am very proud of you, you also hide, Olwa. Not from me, but from yourself. You are not a ranger; you are an artist."

"My Prince, you know I want that path. I am not afraid of battle; I just don't wish to pursue it. Please understand, I do know there is much worth fighting for, more now than I ever imagined there could be."

"Yes, and above all you must remember that. Everything you described and see before you are at risk. If we don't defeat this enemy, there will be no more landscapes to paint. This will be my last lesson before the war, so listen well. Keep your focus, keep your wits on the field, and most of all, protect Pela. You will be fighting beside her. You shall be her shield. Wizards and sorcerers are most vulnerable while they cast their magic. Do you understand?"

"I do, my Prince."

"I know you love her. Some would say that may cause you to take unnecessary risks. I disagree. I feel it will cause you to do whatever you can to protect her and keep her safe."

"I will."

Myth'alas squeezed Olwa's shoulder like a father who was proud of his son.

Olwa smiled sadly and turned his eyes back to the landscape. He caught a glimpse of movement and whispered, "Prince Myth'alas."

He pointed and they both stood, staring across the long span of winter grasses at the tree line on the far edge of the fields. Three figures moved with purpose from shadow to shadow.

"Reptilian and two humans. By the manner of their armor, they appear to be scouts."

Myth'alas nodded. "It begins. May God's light be with us."

# Chapter 24 – The Battle of Still Mead

Nidhug stared at the towers. They were mesmerizing. His body quivered, reacting to the energy pouring from them. His tongue flicked and his pupils dilated as he focused on the one made of fire.

"Commander?"

Nidhug turned to the small reptilian. Her scales were crystal blue and slick like water.

He spoke. "Report?"

"We have scouted the tree lines around the entire perimeter. The stench of humans and elves is everywhere, but we saw nothing until we got past the towers. The human and elven armies are entrenched along the eastern side of the valley."

"Clever. They intend to draw us in and force us to advance past the towers."

"What other choice do we have?"

"None." He turned and yelled. "Lorcan!"

The massive Netherman stepped up and bowed his head respectfully.

Nidhug gave his orders. "It is time. We advance to the east. First, we crush the human and elf rebellion, and then we deal with the towers."

"How are we going to march past them?" Lorcan looked at the towers with suspicion and fear.

Nidhug spoke angrily. "The same way we traveled here."

Lorcan's face showed apprehension, but he saluted and left to prepare the armies. Nidhug whispered under his breath as he turned to Rezren.

"Imbecile."

Rezren narrowed his eyes. "You are trembling, brother. Are you alright?"

"I am fine. We must engage the enemies of our queen and return Lúth to her as quickly as possible. If we attack the towers first, the humans will take advantage. We must crush them, then we can deal with the towers."

Rezren felt a deep concern for his brother but obediently complied.

"I will inform our kin."

Prince Myth'alas stood with his companions. They stared at the black lines advancing around both sides of the lava lake that surrounded the towers. His sharp eyes identified the troops approaching. Netherman, orcs, giants from the northern islands, humans, but he saw no reptilians.

Aeolis leaned his head into Ceridwyn's neck and whispered, "May God's light protect us, and may it shine upon you until the end of our days."

"May those days last another thousand years and more. My heart will not sing until I see you again."

She brought her arms around him and pressed her lips to his before he slipped away into the shadows to be with his rangers.

Ceridwyn inhaled deeply and Rayann sensed the rage building within her friend. Suddenly, she felt Myth's hand on her back and turned to him.

"I will shield you, wife. Give it everything you have, or all will be lost."

"I love you, my prince husband."

Olwa felt Pela tingling with power. It radiated from her and was building with each beat of the enemy's drums. Her hands continually flexed open and closed and her eyes were fixed on the Nethermen formations.

"Pela?"

"Yes!? What!?" Her head snapped to look at him.

He reached and took her hand. It was ice cold.

"I love you."

"You...you do?"

"More than anything in this world. I will protect you today, at all costs. This is my vow."

Her cheeks flushed as she smiled, "I love you too." She stepped in and hugged him tightly.

He pulled her in as close as he could and whispered, "May God's light shine upon us and protect us this day."

Raspberry stood with confidence beside her friends. Her lute held firmly in her grasp. She hadn't bothered to bring her daggers. She knew she wouldn't need them today. She stared at the advancing army and felt Balaby's guidance fill her as she prayed silently to God. She was ready to fight alongside her friends to protect their world.

+++

Lady Rose Fairwind watched the armies advancing against them. She was calm and centered. Her armor blazed in the sun and she felt the warmth of Dionadair's guidance within her.

"Commander?"

Rose turned to her most trusted friend. "Yes, Larissa?"

"We are ready when you are."

Rose gave one last look at the approaching horde. She pulled on her gloves and reached, feeling the sturdy handle of the warhammer sheathed on her back. She ascended the steps and mounted her horse. Quickly, Larissa mounted hers and took formation with her commander.

Rose turned to Larissa. "No matter what happens today, know that you are my dearest friend and most loyal companion. I never could have asked for a squire sounder of mind and heart. We need to see about getting you a knighthood when this is over."

Larissa blushed. "Thank you, Commander, but I am not interested in knighthood. I am happy enough for this life I have. May God's light protect us."

They approached Sir Ordin, Sir Gregory, and Sir Trystan. The commanders of the south were on Rose's left, and she saluted Sir Verik, Sir Treyton, and Knightchanter Elce.

"May Dionadair guide us so we may strike true and defeat this threat upon life. May God strengthen our arms, watch over us and shield us from the darkness that invades our world."

"AYE!" All the commanders shouted in unison and broke off to their positions.

+++

The war drums echoed through the valley for hours as Nataxia's massive army advanced around the perimeter of the three towers like a blight spreading over the land. Fifth, Piramay, and Kali stood on the observation deck of the Black Tower.

327

Piramay lazily traced her fingernails along the railing. Kali watched her closely, wishing she could read her thoughts.

Fifth observed the formations. "Since the knights have decided to draw them in as opposed to using the perimeter forests, this changes our plan."

"How? They are all still going to burn." Piramay turned, there was a feral look in her eyes.

"Naturally, but we must adjust our tactics and positions. Kali?" She looked at him. "I will take the middle. The formations are close enough to the towers that the ferrystone will provide adequate movement for me. I want you to protect our northern flank and make sure none of them escape into the forests."

Kali could not hide her anger but remained silent.

"Say what you want to say, Kali."

"This is your plan; you alone have been calling the strategy from the beginning without our input. You told me I would be in the center. Why change at the last minute?"

"Because it is necessary to achieve our victory."

"You said our victory was inevitable."

Piramay laughed and stepped between them. "I will go so you two can have your little spat. See you on the field." She vanished in a flash of fire.

Kali narrowed her eyes angrily. "I have been preparing since you told me my position. Everything I have strategized was based on being in the center of the field."

"You are quite capable of making the necessary adjustments. I saw to that when I raised you. I filled you with the ability to think on your feet and alter the plan to be victorious. Then I gave you these towers; the most power available to any wizard on Aimsire. I do not doubt you or your abilities."

"She is up to something. I can feel it as I can feel terra. I request to be put back in the middle so I am closer to her and can respond if she betrays us."

"These towers work on a system of balance. She will not compromise that. If Piramay destroys one of us she loses all the power she has gained."

His lip quivered and Kali saw it. He was confident that he had them both hooked.

"Your request is denied."

"Very well."

Fifth placed his hand on her shoulder. She could feel his callousness through her robes and wanted to vomit.

"Soon, Kali, this world will be ours. We will use it as a steppingstone to achieve godhood of our own. We are the most powerful beings to ever exist. Not the wizards, not the Silentclaw, not the tutelary, not even God can challenge us. Stick with the plan and in the end, we walk away with all that we desire."

His hand trailed down her arm and slipped around until it came to rest on the small of her back. He could feel the gentle curvature of her spine. She looked up at him and forced her eyes to whisper compliance, but her guts were churning.

"By your lead, Fifth. We attack at your command."

He released her and stepped back.

"Today is our day."

Kali disappeared and arrived in her tower. Immediately she went to her knees and pounded the floor with her fists. Having absorbed his magic through the ferrystone and hearing him speak his words just now solidified her suspicion– Fifth was the dragon that had been speaking to her. It wasn't her former self or any form of sinister, evil nature she was still harboring. He had infiltrated her mind as he slept and lured her in. Isolated in her tower, she clutched at her stomach and began to cry.

After several minutes she took a deep breath and composed herself. She stood and walked to the mirror in her dressing chamber. After washing her face she combed her hair until it was shiny again. She flipped the latch on a small wooden box which had remained closed since her arrival and removed an ivory hairpin in the shape of a warhorse. Trystan had given it to her on a moonlight walk two nights before they attacked the towers.

She tied it into her hair, tucking it back so it couldn't be seen before smoothing her robes. She stared into the mirror and focused on her own face. Her thoughts raced with what these two creatures had done and the damage they intended to keep doing. She knew the fate of the world depended on successfully executing the plan she had crafted while she sat in her room after the first battle within the warding. The time had finally arrived.

"Aviyana, provide me with your guidance. God, give me your strength today."

From an impossible range, elven arrows filled the air and struck the front lines. The first blood hit the winter grasses and Lorcan shouted the charge. The sound of battle quickly filled the air as the steelguard charged, meeting the enemy in a rush.

Lady Rose thundered through the lines with her calvary. Her hammer broke the armor and bodies of her foes. Larissa was right beside her, protecting her commander's back and cutting down the enemy.

From their flank, two Nethermen rushed in. Larissa stood on her horse's saddle and launched herself into the air, twisting her body before landing on the shoulders of the one in front. She thrust her sword down where the armor ended near the neck and the Netherman went to his knees.

Distracted, the second grabbed for her. He never saw the strike from Rose coming. His face caved in and his body fell to the ground, lifeless. Rose began to round back towards Larissa when a spear narrowly missed her leg and pierced her horse's heart.

She was thrown and hit the ground hard. Larissa helped her up and the two of them charged the approaching enemy on foot.

Pela cast a spell on Olwa's arrow just as it left his bowstring. The arrow streaked through the air with a trail of frost behind it, striking a giant in the neck. He howled and grasped at the hole in his throat, the cold spreading across his skin like flowing water. He wasn't dead yet, but Olwa could see the wound was fatal and saved his follow up shot.

Lifting her hand, Pela let loose a blast of frost at four approaching humans. Three collapsed but the fourth was only stunned. Olwa finished him with a precisely placed arrow. Immediately, they ran forward.

Sorcerers of the Rage Queen's army fired a volley of ambient magic at Prince Myth'alas and High Consummate Jerrin. Myth'alas rubbed his finger down the gems in his bracer and the spells dissipated when they hit the sphere of magic annulment.

"Glad you still have those."

"One of the greatest gifts you ever gave me." Myth spun and Blue Moon bisected an incoming soldier. Jerrin flipped over his brother, landing on his feet and Red Sun ran through a large woman who was closing in on them. Her crescent moon shaped battleax landed at his feet in the grass.

Rayann stepped outside of Myth's annulment field and brought up her hands. Concentrating on a five-meter-tall giant, she discharged a gravity spell. The giant teetered and fell but began to get to his feet quickly. She drew magic again and surrounded the beast's head with a sphere of containment. She flicked her hand. The sphere collapsed and crushed the giant's skull.

Several balls of fire streaked through the air and smashed into an advancing group of humans. They screamed as the fire cooked them in their own armor. Ceridwyn stepped up beside Rayann and blasted a female warrior in the chest with a burst of concentrated sunlight as Jerrin came up beside her and issued a command.

"Ceridwyn, we need to get to the top of that rise."

She followed the High Consummate up the hill, blasting enemies as they went.

Arrows streamed from the trees in steady barrages. The elven rangers were picking off the enemy with pinpoint accuracy. Aeolis would occasionally spot a blast of fire, or a burst of flames. He would then see Ceridwyn's pale yellow robes among the steel and black armor of the enemy and breathe a sigh of relief.

He wished he could be at her side but knew that she was well protected by their High Consummate. He watched as Jerrin and Ceridwyn advanced up the hill. Two Nethermen were cresting from the other side. From his position he could see his ally's wouldn't see them approaching and they would meet at the top.

"Protect our High Consummate!"

Several rangers turned and released their arrows. The distance was great and the arrows seemed to linger in the breeze for eternity. One of the Netherman was peppered and fell to her knees, the other managed to receive only harmless impacts against his thick armor. He ignored the arrows and crested the hill, bearing down on Ceridwyn.

Jerrin swiped fiercely and the beast parried the blow. He swung his fist, narrowly missing Jerrin's head. Nimbly, Jerrin used the energy of his miss and flipped through the air. The female Netherman was on her feet again and approaching. Jerrin ran her

331

through and twisted the shaft as he withdrew the spearhead, spilling the life from her body.

Fire erupted behind him, and he spun, fatally striking the remaining Netherman who was now in flames thanks to Ceridwyn's spell.

Ceridwyn pointed as she proclaimed, "They are still coming around the towers. By the light, how are there so many!?"

Olwa and Pela had taken position behind a line of steelguard and knights so Pela could catch her breath. She was panting heavily and trying to regain her strength. Olwa picked off soldiers that came into range but kept looking at her.

"Are you alright?"

"Yes, I just need a minute. Keep firing."

Sir Trystan and Sir Ordin charged into the northern lines. Their steelguard smashed into the enemy and broke through the shield bearers so their troopers could pour in. Quickly, they were beaten back. Sir Gregory arrived with his units, but the enemy was using the trees to fire their arrows and hide their numbers. War cries erupted and the trees came alive with a massive influx of fresh troops.

"RALLY! RALLY TO LINES!"

Sir Ordin tried to gather his men, but they were getting overwhelmed quickly. Sir Trystan managed to rout a small bulge of enemy troops but was rapidly getting surrounded and pinned into a pincer. Sir Gregory and his soldiers broke through one side, opening an escape route, and the steelguard were able to create a new shield wall of their own. The Rage Queen's army bashed into them, slowly thinning out their numbers.

Sir Trystan turned to Sir Ordin. "We need to retreat; we can't hold them. They are obviously trying to break in and get behind us from here."

Raspberry had been healing the wounded. Anytime she saw one of the knights or steelguard fall, she played her music and focused on them. The enemy noticed and shouted to advance on her. She turned from healing another ally and saw a massive orc coming straight at her with his ax held high.

Calmly, she took a deep breath and focused, strumming the next chord of her song. The lute let out a blazing light, blinding the warrior. He stumbled forward, landing on his hands and knees. His ax slide along the ground and Raspberry easily sidestepped the weapon as it passed her. He attempted to stand but an arrow struck him in the chest, killing him instantly. She turned to see Olwa and Pela running straight at her. She could see that Pela was exhausted.

"Are you okay, Raspberry?"

"Yup, I'm fine. Nice shootin' by the way, Olwa!"

He looked at her curiously, not understanding the cheerfulness of her voice.

Raspberry focused her attention on Pela and began to play again. The song wrapped around her like cool water and her breathing calmed. She felt the heat and exhaustion leave her body immediately. Within seconds she turned and released shards of ice from each palm, striking three different enemies.

"Thanks, Raspberry!"

"Come on, those soldiers in the middle need our help!" The halfling charged towards the vanguard, Pela and Olwa were right behind her.

Erika was doing her best to rally her conscripts. They were farmers and tradespeople, not warriors. Her side of the advancement buckled quickly. She managed to fight in reverse until she found her brother. He split his troops, and several came to Erika's aid. They were holding, but the enemy's crushing push through the middle of the field made it necessary for them to keep fighting on their heels.

The overwhelming numbers and strength of the Rage Queen's armies were simply too much, even for the savage southern knights and steelguard. Commander Verik's voice could be heard over the battle. He was shouting a retreat, back towards the river.

Raspberry looked at Pela and Olwa. "Come on, we gotta get back."

She played again, the grass swirled around their feet and Raspberry yelled, "Run!"

As if carried by the winds, the three of them fled towards the rivers behind the lines.

Elce swung her staff and bursts of fire erupted from the shimmering gem at the top. Multiple warriors of the Rage Queen's army fell. Two of her knightchanters came in beside her and cast holy light to shield them from the advancing enemy. As Verik shouted his retreat, Elce looked at her companions.

"This is madness, it's as if they rise up from the ground."

She swung her staff again; fire engulfed an onrushing orc. A Netherman came from the side and punched a knightchanter in the face, caving in her skull. With a spin he swung his massive double-bladed ax and narrowly missed Elce, breaking her staff in two. A crossbow bolt hit her in the shoulder. She screamed and fell to her knees. The other knightchanter brought up his hands and was about to cast when a second Netherman cleaved him in half.

The pair laughed and one reached down, lifting Elce off the ground with ease.

"I have always wondered what a knight wizard tastes like."

He opened his mouth and began bringing her towards his sharp teeth. Sir Verik's hammer came up over the top, crushing his skull and he collapsed in a heap. The second Netherman lunged but met the axes of two southern knights. Verik dismounted and grabbed Elce by the back of her leather armor, effortlessly lifting her across the saddle of his own horse.

"Come on, trooper, we're not done yet."

She pointed to the side of her staff with the malformed gem twisted into the end. A soldier tossed it up to Verik. He handed it to Elce and they retreated back towards the rivers.

Myth'alas and Jerrin were a whirlwind of death. The brothers moved with such grace and fluidity it was obvious that their training together spanned hundreds of years. Where one would parry, the other would spin and strike. Myth would shadowskip away in a blink and the confused enemy would suddenly find themselves impaled by Red Sun.

With their elven brother protectors beside them, Ceridwyn and Rayann were laying waste to any enemy that dared approach. Theirs was the only part of the front line that was holding. When they heard the retreat being sounded, Myth'alas looked up.

"The vanguard is collapsing."

"I see it."

Jerrin focused on the retreating knights.

+++

"They are ready."

"Excellent."

Fifth smiled at Piramay before turning to Kali.

"Are you prepared?"

"Yes, Fifth…I am ready."

Her face was resolute. The three watched the battle unfolding. From their high vantage point, they could see the northern line beginning to fold and the central vanguard buckling. Almost half the human and elven army was dead or injured.

"We strike, now."

Piramay disappeared in a flash and Fifth turned to Kali.

"I will see you when this is over. We will celebrate."

The look on his face exposed his underlying intent. He disappeared and Kali felt the muscles in her jaw tighten. She had one chance to make this work. In a flash, she appeared in the northern line of trees. Four of the dark army's soldiers jumped in surprise and then rushed her. With one wave of her hand, they were vaporized to dust.

She looked along the northern lines. Nataxia's troops were rallying and reorganizing for a second push. She spotted Sir Trystan and Sir Ordin on their horses. They had managed to get their troops gathered but were nearly surrounded and fighting for their lives.

Kali pressed her palms into the ground. Several rock elementals exploded from the dirt in the middle of the Rage Queen's army and started smashing the soldiers to pulp. They paid no attention to Trystan, Ordin, or their troops.

"What in the blazes!?"

Sir Ordin watched in shock as the rock elementals emerged. With the distraction he started rallying the remaining soldiers to retreat towards the rivers.

"Sir Trystan! Get them back!"

Trystan wove through the fray, screaming at his steelguard. He heard a war cry behind him and spun his horse. A giant, four meters tall, was closing in quickly, baring his double row of teeth and a massive warhammer. Sir Trystan knew he would never be able to counter the blow or get out of the way in time. He brought up his sword to block but braced for certain death.

The giant exploded as if a keg of gunpowder had detonated within his chest. Sir Trystan's ears rang like church bells as he wiped the blood from his face and looked around in a daze. He quickly returned his attention to the battle and withdrew his remaining troops through the new gaps that were opening as the enemy fought the elementals.

Kali lowered her hands after casting her spell and watched the lifeless body of the giant slump to the ground. She turned her attention back to the battle after seeing that Trystan was now free and clear to ride to safety.

Fifth appeared in the center of the battlefield and immediately began casting. Some victims he hit with dark energy which melted the skin from their bones. Others exploded spontaneously. He showed no favoritism. Anyone that was within range was fair game and the soul well dangling from his sash pulsed every time someone died by his spells.

The central and southern soldiers began withdrawing as the dark army formed a circle around Fifth. He merely smiled and watched as Nidhug approached.

"You have something of our Queen's. We have come to retrieve it."

"Anything you wish to leave with, you will need to take from me. Nothing is free, Nidhug." Fifth laughed.

"Kill him!"

Reptilian wizards began appearing out of nowhere, firing spells at Fifth. He vanished and the crossfire smashed into the circle of soldiers that were surrounding him. Nidhug felt the ardor channels buzzing and followed the energy. Fifth appeared on a nearby ridge and continued blasting the Rage Queen's army. Nidhug roared and the reptilians he was holding in reserve for this very moment emerged and started charging towards Fifth. He then turned and searched for Kali. He could feel that she was nearby.

An ear-splitting shriek erupted from near the towers. The fighting slowed as the ground rumbled and a gap opened in the side of the cauldron near the Tower of Flame. Piramay emerged riding atop a massive flaming dragon elemental. Three more followed and they took to the air. Myth'alas and Jerrin watched as the elemental dragons split into pairs. Piramay looped around and attacked, setting the southern tree line ablaze where the elven rangers were positioned.

The screams of the dying rangers echoed over the battle. In a systematic pattern, the other two dragons began crisscrossing areas of the valley, burning the soldiers beneath them. They were concentrating on Nataxia's army, but the elven brothers knew it was only a matter of time before the attention was turned on them.

Ceridwyn screamed as she watched the tree line become engulfed in flame. She began to run but Rayann grabbed her.

"No! Don't!"

Ceridwyn shook free of Rayann's grasp and vanished. She appeared in the middle of the inferno and began searching for Aeolis. The heat and ash were intense. She shielded her face as she called out to him. She felt for his presence, reaching to sense his heartbeat. There was nothing but burning bodies and splintered, smoldering wood.

Rose and Larissa were near the rivers and looked up in horror as the elemental dragons took to flight. Larissa gasped as the elves were burned alive in the trees. She began to run towards the forest.

Rose grabbed her. "Larissa, no."

Larissa turned in compliance, realizing there was nothing she could do.

Commander Rose closed her eyes. She inhaled deeply and reached out with her prayer.

"Holy God, this cannot be how it ends. Not after what you told me when you answered my prayer…"

## Chapter 25 – Of Towers and Dragons

The light dimmed and Rose looked up.

A dark, obscure cluster appeared, fluttering as it eclipsed the sun. Bellowing roars echoed just before the flight of dragons spread out, transitioning from vague silhouettes to identifiable forms. Swiftly they spiraled downwards, moving in perfect synchronization. Streaks of fire, lightning and frost blazed through the valley as Nolore's flight attacked the forces of the Rage Queen.

A small silver dragon landed behind the lines. Unsure of what was happening, the soldiers lifted their weapons and prepared. There was a flash of light and a beautiful, raven-haired woman stood before them.

"Fear not good citizens of Aimsire. The Silentclaw have been sent by God and are here to aid you this day."

"Rajumin!"

Raspberry sprinted and smashed into her friend. She hugged the halfling tightly and spoke with warmth in her voice.

"Greetings, little one. My goodness your face is a mess."

"Yeah! We've been fightin' pretty hard all morning! I knew you were comin', Balaby told me last night! I'm sure glad you came when you did, we could use the help!"

She wiped some of the grim from Raspberry's forehead and smiled as she continued, "We will have time for greetings later. Come, we need to tend the wounded and aid the armies."

Looking at the exhausted soldiers in the rear of the lines, she continued, "Play the song you just started hearing in your heart, little one."

Raspberry smiled and began to play. Rajumin mixed her magic effortlessly with the song, amplifying its volume across the mass of soldiers and knights. All that heard felt their strength and courage renewed as their wounds instantly healed.

Rose ran to Rajumin and bowed.

"Thank you for coming."

"Do not bow to me, Lady Rose. We are but messengers and servants, here to assist you." She reached and touched the Knight Commander's arm. "May God, strengthen this arm and may the weapon in your hand strike true!"

Rose flexed her fingers as her exhausted muscles tingled with new life. She looked at Rajumin in silence and awe.

"Go now, Lady Knight. Fight for your world."

Rose felt an incredible warmth fill her. Emboldened, she turned to her renewed troops.

"Rally to lines! It's time to push this filth from our lands!"

The revitalized armies cheered in a war cry and immediately assembled into formation, preparing to charge.

Piramay snarled as she watched the dragons arrive. She climbed high and called her other two elemental dragons to her. The four began to circle and came down on a pair in Nolore's flight, a large red and a black. The two elemental dragons on her left tore into the black, shredding him with their claws. She issued the command for breath weapons to the one she was riding and the one to her right. The charred body of the red dragon crashed into the fields below.

Nolore and Lady Kellan circled high above and gasped as Piramay effortlessly took out two of their flight. Nolore roared and went into a dive. Kellan reached for Falling Sky and Nolore spoke to her mind.

*"We will be going too fast for you to strike. Just hold on."*

Two of his dragons came in beside him and they streaked downwards, breaking through the center of the four elemental dragons. Piramay was nearly knocked off her mount as the turbulence caught them but managed to break off and swung wide of the attack to readjust herself. The dragon to her right caught a blast of lightning from Nolore's largest dragon, Niamh. Its fiery, ashen scales opened and molten innards sprayed over the battlefield below. The dragon exploded on impact, covering dozens of Nataxia's troops in burning blood.

Jerrin watched the aerial dance of the dragons fighting above the fields. He turned as Myth'alas approached.

"Has Ceridwyn returned?"

"No."

"We need to find her."

Rayann spoke. "You two are needed on the battlefield. I will go."

Myth reached for her, "Ray…"

339

"Beloved, she is my best friend. I am highly attuned to her magic signature and emotions. I have a better chance of finding her than anyone."

He looked at the inferno of burning trees.

"God's light protects you, my wife. Come back to me."

"I will, husband."

Rayann mounted a nearby horse that had returned without its knight. She skillfully kicked into the haunches and raced towards the forest.

"Come, brother, she will be fine."

Myth'alas looked at Jerrin and growled, "Let's finish this."

The lines on the northern side where the bulk of the dark army was massed were reinforced. The knights began their charge. Kali appeared as the groups clashed. She fired spells at both sides. Her magic tore the ground up and churned it over. The dark troops were smashed under the weight of rock and dirt while the armies of steelguard and elves appeared to be crushed but were instead transported back to the rear lines within the thickets where their reappearance would go unnoticed.

Kali felt Trystan's presence and looked over at him on his horse. He had just finished off a Netherman and was staring at her. His face twisted in hatred as their eyes locked. Her heart sank as she saw the rancor he was projecting towards her. He screamed to his troops, and she watched as he spun his horse away to continue engaging the lines of the enemy.

She turned as she felt magic building and watched two sorcerers approaching. One cast a shield while the other began to chant. As her heart continued breaking, Kali walked towards them.

The sorceress' spell fired and Kali brought one hand up, twisting her palm inwards. The energy passed harmlessly over her robes. She magnified the magic with her own before thrusting her other hand forward. The sorcerers were caught in a violent vortex before their bodies gruesomely twisted apart.

Using the sleeve of her robes she wiped a single tear from her left eye before hearing a malicious hiss. Rezren stood just off the tree line and narrowed his eyes on her.

*"Brother, she is here."*

Nidhug appeared. "It is time to die, traitor."

"You…"

"After I killed your parents, I had a feeling I shouldn't kill you as well. I was right. Now you are the gateway to enter those towers so I may take back what is rightfully our Queen's."

Simultaneously, Rezren charged and Nidhug cast two spells. The earth beneath her churned and a blast of fire exploded from his palm. Kali vanished and reappeared behind them. She reached out and the magic Nidhug cast was drawn back towards her. Nidhug shielded and the ball of fire exploded harmlessly around him.

Rezren slid to a stop as the churning earth approached. He jumped and kicked off the rising soil, charging back at her again with inconceivable speed.

Kali felt the power Nidhug was drawing from the terra. She had a small window as he gathered energy. She focused on Rezren. His tail swung wildly, and his two swords flashed in the sunlight. She waited until he was right on top of her. Lightning surged from the ground at her feet, discharging from her fingertips. The ignition triangulated on Rezren's steel armor. The electricity tore through him and his smoldering, lifeless body slid to a stop at her feet.

Nidhug lost concentration and his spell vaporized harmlessly. He roared as he stared at his brother's lifeless body.

"You will pay for that."

"How? I can see the fear in your eyes. You can't beat me and you know it."

Nidhug raised his hands and Kali countered quickly pulling power directly from her tower. The spells collided right in front of him, blowing him backwards. He smashed into the trees in a cloud of soot and smoke.

Sir Trystan rode hard, breaking the enemy with his mounted knights, opening gaps for the steelguard. A tremendous roar thundered through the air on their flank. He turned and watched as one of Piramay's elemental dragons swooped in, preparing to release its breath weapon.

A flash of silver appeared on the elemental dragon's blind side. Trystan saw that this dragon had a rider. The gleaming armor flashed as a sword with distinctive patterns of banding and reminiscent of drifting clouds trailed behind it. The warrior swiped and gashed open the neck of the elemental dragon. The beast fell through the air and landed off the edge of the battle, exploding as it hit the trees. The silver dragon tipped its wing and rapidly gained altitude.

Kali transported herself back into the fray. She felt a powerful, familiar magical signature and searched. She found Pela and saw that Olwa was with her.

Seeing an opportunity to adjust and advance her plan, she moved towards them. From her right, two reptilians rushed in, but were blown to pieces with a simple swipe of her hand.

Pela felt the powerful magic and turned. Immediately Olwa fired an arrow. Without lifting a finger, a glow of energy detonated from Kali's body, disintegrating his projectile.

Myth'alas saw Kali appear and begin to advance on the younglings. He watched as she effortlessly defended herself and activated his bracers. She was a hundred meters away and he would need to cut a path to her. He was determined to keep his vow and strike her down as she had asked him to do.

Kali transported herself so that she and Olwa were face to face. He reached for his dagger. Kali lifted her hand. He froze, stuck as if made of stone. She brought up her other hand, his eyes filled with fear, silently begging for his life.

"The battle is over for you, Olwa."

She spread her hands apart. An illusion made it appear as if Olwa burst into flames. His body collapsed to the ground and burned to ash.

Pela screamed, "No!"

Kali turned as the young sorceress' spell exploded towards her. She pushed her hands forward and the ice shards melted away. She cast an illusion and made it appear as if Pela was turned to dust, in reality she was transported to the rivers behind the lines, out of harm's way.

Myth'alas watched in horror as he witnessed what looked like both his adherent and Pela had just been killed mercilessly by Kali. He had cut his way through the enemy and charged. Kali caught him out of the corner of her eye. Using her magic she spun away as Blue Moon barely missed her neck. She twisted and followed his movement, lifting her hand to hurl a transport spell that would send him off the battlefield as well.

She lost concentration as she felt terra vibrate under her feet in warning. Jerrin's incoming thrust was aimed for her chest.

342

Unaffected by Myth's bracers, she released the magic she was holding, knocking the spear off its trajectory, but the spearhead cut her robe and sliced through the outside of her shoulder. She gritted her teeth through the pain. To stay and fight the brothers was futile and would not advance her plan. Instantly, she vanished into the ardor channels.

Piramay descended. The pair of elemental dragons ignited the trees along the northern edge of the valley. The dark army troops screamed as they were burned alive. She repositioned the two elemental dragons and moved to circle around for another pass but were intercepted by four of Nolore's flight cresting the ridge.

Blindsided and with no alternative, Piramay engaged the ferrystone, vanishing just as both of her remaining elemental dragons were torn to shreds by breath weapons. She appeared in the burning trees and closed her eyes as the blazing warmth of the inferno surrounded and renewed her.

Kali felt the ferrystone activate and gasped as Piramay's magical signature was drawn into her own body. The last reagent she needed was now in her possession.

Ceridwyn shielded her face. The intense fire licked at her robes and dried her eyes. Suddenly, she felt a faint heartbeat. She ran as fast as she could and found Aeolis. He was trapped beneath a burning log. His legs were broken and his chest, along with both arms were burned black.

"Aeolis! By the light!"

His breath was shallow and weak. She knelt and opened his waterskin, pouring some of the contents onto his face. He coughed weakly and opened his eyes.

"Ceri."

The fire blazed as Ceridwyn reached into her robes and removed spell components. She was getting dizzy. Her lungs burned as she inhaled hot soot. She attempted to spread the reagents, but her hands were shaking fearfully, and she couldn't release her grip on them. Consciousness began slipping away when suddenly a blue light erupted around her.

Rayann focused with all she had. She could barely see them through the swirling flames and thick smoke but managed to get her sphere of protection in place. She could feel her friends' fear and spoke to her mind.

*"I feel you. Don't you dare give up, Ceridwyn."*

She heard her friends voice and scattered the reagents before taking a drink to flush the ash out of her mouth so she could speak her spell. Drawing on Shakyna and the power of the sun, she and Aeolis were instantly transported to the rally point behind the three rivers.

Rayann exhaled in relief as she saw them leave. She turned to mount up and realized that her horse had panicked and fled. While she was concentrating on her spell to keep her friends safe, the flames had enveloped her. Desperately she searched for an escape route.

Over the roar of the inferno that was rapidly hemming in around her she suddenly heard a song. Raspberry walked through the fire, unburnt, playing her lute. She smiled as she continued to strum the chords.

"Hi, Ms. Rayann. Come on, I can help get you outta here."

Pela ran to Ceridwyn and Aeolis as they appeared. She knelt and shook Ceridwyn.

"Wake up…please, wake up!"

She then noticed Aeolis' broken, morbidly burned body and stared in shock and horror.

"Steady young one. They will be alright."

Pela looked up as Rajumin knelt and placed a hand on each of the injured elves. Emerald green light filled the area around them and Ceridwyn coughed as the heat and ash escaped her lungs. Simultaneously, Aeolis felt the pain leave him and his body become cool. His legs were healed and his skin renewed. He flexed his stiff fingers and looked around curiously, blinking to bring his eyes into focus.

"Where? Where are we?"

"You are beyond the rivers. The battle still rages in the vale. You have been restored and made whole by God's grace."

Ceridwyn hugged Aeolis tightly. Her chin was on his shoulder and she saw Pela looking at them, crying.

"Pela, what is it?"

"Kali…she, she killed Olwa."

"What?"

Aeolis' jaw clenched as he stood, staring across the battlefield at the Gray Tower.

Piramay glanced down at a former soldier who was now a pile of ash. Drawing on the flow of magic from the towers, she picked up a handful of what remained and threw it into the air.

The ash collected like a marble and she ignited a spark, drawing the forest fire towards her. A devilish grin crossed her face. It was exhilarating to feel so much power without having to worry about seals or boiling her own blood.

She stepped through the burning trees and onto the battlefield. The flames followed her like the wake off a ship and she stopped on the edge of the fighting.

Bringing her hands up, the fire rolled out in front of her and formed into a massive cone. She systematically directed the flames, roasting every unfortunate being in front of her.

Kali reappeared near Fifth. Every direction his hands moved, something died. He was smiling with furious satisfaction as his power grew in the melee. She blasted an enemy that was approaching. He turned to look as he felt her magic.

"Do you feel it, Kali? The time of the towers has begun!"

"We have problem."

She pointed. The flames exploding off Piramay bellowed into the air.

"She's spending herself too quickly. We need to stop her."

"Piramay knows her limits. She will retreat to her tower when she needs to."

He noticed the tear in her robes and the blood.

"Who injured you?"

"The brother elves caught me in a surprise attack."

Fifth snarled. "Are you well enough to fight?"

"I will be fine."

"Come, we will find them and turn their bones to dust."

They moved to higher ground, scanning the battle.

Fifth pointed. "There."

The elven brothers were a ferocious dance of elegance that was dealing death to everything that came near them. Fifth and Kali transported close enough to attack.

He sneered. "Let's make an example of them. Once we have killed them, I will resurrect them as undead pet rats for you."

Fifth began to draw magic so powerful it pulled the sound out of the air. Standing twenty meters to his right, Kali joined him, secretly drawing in the energy from all three towers, terra, and Shakyna simultaneously. She felt Fifth focusing on Myth'alas.

Fifth sensed his magic mixing with Kali's and shouted the final words of his incantation. His shadow orb left his hands and burned a blackened trench across the ground, heading straight for the Prince General.

Myth'alas was unaware of the wizards near him and looked up. His eyes went wide, the orb was too close to counter. Kali released her spell. The energy of her magic spread out behind the elven brothers.

She pulled the energy back towards herself. It passed over the elves harmlessly and caused the orb to reverse course. The speed of her countermove was so fast Fifth had no time to respond. He lifted his hands instinctively, but the spell exploded against his body with its full force.

Fifth went flying like a ragdoll into the burnt forest behind them. Myth'alas turned and saw Kali, realizing what she had done. Just as they made eye contact, she vanished from sight.

+++

Olwa felt the cold stone floor under his cheek. He sat up. The air smelled clean and fresh like springtime rain.

It was pitch black and his natural night sight was ineffective through the darkness that surrounded him.

"By the moon I wish I had some light."

The perimeter of the massive, round room illuminated. With surprise, he glanced around. There were no seams in the stone walls or the floor. It was as if they were masoned from a single piece of rock. He stood and thought about his thirst. A table appeared with a water skin on it.

"And I would like some bread?"

A loaf of warm bread appeared beside the water. Curious as to what was happening, he whispered to himself, "Am I on the Plain of Constellations?"

"No, Olwa, you are not dead."

Kali hissed words of magic. The stored energy of Fifth and Piramay's signatures, harvested by her ferrystones shot from her palm into the floor. The energy spread through the ardor channels and nullified Piramay's ability to transport back to the towers.

Olwa clenched his fists and scowled.

Without turning towards him she spoke, "Stop it. If you were supposed to die you would be dead already."

She knelt and traced her finger along the stone. A line of shadow formed, opening a hole in the floor. She reached in and removed a large velvet bag of specially prepared spell reagents. Instantly the air filled with a sweet, delightful smell. Next, she withdrew her leather wizard bag containing the spell book her cousin had given her and slung it over her shoulder.

"Come here."

"Why?"

"Olwa, we don't have time for explanations. I have done what I can to keep Piramay from transporting back, but she is clever. Should she find a way around my efforts she will burn you until there aren't even bones left. I will not have the energy to fight her and protect you. I already told you that if I wanted you dead, you would be. Now, come here."

He approached. She reached into the hole one last time and removed a finely crafted elven sword. The blade hummed with ancient power, and frost dripped from its edge. He was mesmerized by the beauty of it. She smacked him on the arm with the flat side of the blade.

"Wake up. I need you to pay attention."

Olwa snapped back to reality as she handed him the sword.

"Stand right here and keep watch. Do you understand?"

He nodded in compliance.

"I am going to leave so I can spread these reagents. When I return, we need to stand with our backs touching and I am going to cast. Do not disturb or interrupt me otherwise we will both die. If this spell misfires there won't be any way for me to save either of us. It is far too powerful."

"I understand."

She vanished. Olwa looked around the room. His throat was dry and he wished that he had taken a sip of the water when he had a chance. He dared not move now. His stomach was in knots as he waited.

He jumped when Kali suddenly reappeared. She pursed her lips in disappointment before transporting to the perimeter of the room to spread more of the magic powder. Olwa watched as she worked quickly. Finally, she stepped around behind him. He felt her press against his back before she spoke.

"Not even a peep, Olwa. Only move if Piramay shows up, and if she does, give her the crevasse. That sword will help. You are my only defense while I am casting."

The torchless light flickered as magic filled the room. The hairs on the back of Olwa's neck stood on end. Static built and a vortex of wind picked up the reagents, swirling them around the perimeter. A dazzling display of colors expanded from Kali and the room became so bright that Olwa had to shield his eyes. Kali's voice grew louder.

The immense power created by the mixed sources of magical energy filled her. Kali lovingly called upon Shakyna to weave the energy into place. Her covert mission to end this threat was one final action from coming to an end.

She paused and thought about, Rayann. She reflected on how her cousin had trusted her, brought her into their family estate, treated her with kindness and respect despite the vile actions she had attempted against her. More than that, how she forgave without any further judgement.

Her thoughts moved on to how Rayann had found love and started a family of her own through all this mess. Finally, her eyes welled up as she thought about Braeren and her charismatic, crooked smile appeared as his little face came into her mind's eye.

Kali felt peace enter her heart and mind. She did not know if she would survive the release of this magic and get the chance to see Rayann again to tell her the truth. She closed her eyes and sent a message like a whisper along the winds quoting the valediction that Rayann had inscribed in the spell book she gifted to Kali in Hailen Glen, hoping it would be heard.

*"For the Fionntán."*

She released her spell. The dazzling light was sucked into the tower walls and the room went pitch black.

Through the rift in the sky, lightning flashed, blowing holes into the ground. Rapidly, the lightning walked itself towards Kali's tower and swarmed the walls with writhing blue lines. The winds swirled violently from the base and the armies stopped fighting, looking for anything solid enough to hold onto so they wouldn't be swept off their feet.

The rift gave one final flare of intense light and began closing. The winds stopped and the energy around Kali's tower was drawn into the ground. There was dead silence across the entire glen for a mere second.

Without warning, the base of the Black Tower flashed from within. The slick exterior exploded outwards. The tower teetered and then began to buckle under its own weight. A second explosion rocked the base of the Tower of Fire. The two towers fell towards one another and collided, crumbling as they came down. As if time had been slowed, both towers fell into the molten lake of magma with a rolling, thunderous crash.

+++

Piramay felt the undeniable signature of Kali's magic and watched Fifth fly up and over the hill behind her, tumbling through the air into the burning forest. She removed the ferrystone from her pocket and attempted to transport to her tower. Neither her tower or the stone responded.

She ran up the hill so she could see the magma lake and furrowed her brow as the base of the Black Tower exploded. Then her own. She watched the two towers collapse before shifting her gaze to the Gray Tower which remained standing.

Knowing the battle was over for her, she turned with a scowl before the towers had settled into their resting place and moved in the direction she had seen Fifth go flying. She felt the new power she had managed to attain begin to leave her body.

After a short walk, Piramay came upon a trench etched into the blackened soil. Fifth lay at the far end against an outcropping of rocks. His leg was broken, and he clearly had a shoulder out of joint. A long, burned tree impaled him through the small of his back and exited his abdomen, keeping him pinned to the ground.

She sauntered up slowly. He had an expression of relief as he watched her approach.

"Little...Phoenix. Kali be...betrayed...us."

Piramay spoke compassionately.

"Of course she did."

She knelt and lovingly rubbed the tip of her finger down Fifth's cheek.

"We... I, m...mean, you, need to ki...kill her."

She studied the wound where the tree had impaled him. With time and proper care, it would likely heal.

"The...rift. We only have...a moment, before it closes. Use what...power you have left. Destroy her."

"Indeed, I will. Time is of the essence, my sweet, Fifth." She gently took his hand. "I warned you the girl would be trouble and you blindly ignored my wise and thorough counsel on the matter. Even after all these years in planning and service to this great goal, you prove yourself to be nothing more than a narrow-minded fool, but I forgive you."

She smiled warmly. "And, as I have forgiven you, I hope that in the afterlife you will forgive me."

His eyes went wide as he heard her speak the activation word for the soul dagger he had given her. He looked down as the device flared to life. She slowly pressed the ethereal blade that formed from the bottom into his chest.

He twitched with a snarl, released her hand, and reached for her throat. His arm was fully extended but the tree piercing his body held him down. His fingers were centimeters from her neck.

Her smile became vicious as she leaned into his weak grip, allowing him to attempt to choke her.

"Yes, Fifth. Go ahead, fight for your life. It is so much sweeter that we depart each other's company like this. Your brand of magic is powerful, not like the towers, but the energy of *your* soul should provide enough to serve my next purpose. Thank you for sharing it with me."

He gasped and his grip loosened. She watched his reflective eyes go dull as his life faded. His skin shriveled and a soft gurgle escaped his lips as his body collapsed into his robes. He was too weak to scream, but the look on his face showed he died in agony.

Piramay deactivated the soul dagger. As she knelt over her former partner, she watched the gem pulse softly and hoped he could still see her from within. Just before she stood, she noticed the soul well on his sash. With a sneer she removed the device and tucked it away into her tight-fitting dress.

Turning her head towards the battlefield she stared with conviction. There was one more matter to deal with before she would depart.

+++

Rayann and Raspberry were making their way back to the rivers when Rayann faintly heard her cousin's voice on the winds…, *"For the Fionntán"*. She gasped and stopped walking. Raspberry looked up at her.

"What is it, Mrs. Rayann?"

Rayann looked towards the towers and Raspberry followed her friend's gaze. They watched as the two towers exploded and came tumbling down. Rayann began to cry. Raspberry cheered and looked at Rayann.

"How do you think that happened?"

Rayann whispered as she looked up and watched the fracture in the sky begin to close.

"It was Kali."

The two of them could see the Rage's Queen's army begin to retreat in a chaotic fashion. Lorcan was on the main ridge, bloody and exhausted, ordering the unorganized withdrawal. They hastily began to traverse the long distance between themselves and what remained of the scar upon their world.

In the distance, on the edge of the magma lake, two figures unexpectedly appeared.

+++

Piramay was making her way back to the battlefield and turned quickly as she heard a noise to her left. Nidhug limped towards her with his hands up. She huffed as his injuries gave her a quick assessment as to the threat of him.

"What do you want, Nidhug?"

351

"I have watched all this unfold. I have crossed the distance between the plains on behalf of our Queen and marched down half a continent only to see there is no hope left for her. Though the towers have collapsed, I still know where power remains. Piramay, Mistress of Fire, I would ask that we align and work side by side."

He bowed his head respectfully. Piramay knew the way of the reptilians. They were the fallen dragons. The twisted remnant of the rebellious allies Nataxia had recruited to attack the Plain of Constellations. Nothing they did came without a price.

"You humble yourself before me with an offer of alliance, therefore I must ask, what's in it for you…and me?"

"I have only had one goal in mind. I desire to shed this decrepit form. Without the power of Lúth, there is no hope for Nataxia, or me. I dare not return without it. Though she is humbled of her power, she is still a tutelar."

"I am not hearing a bargain, only what you desire."

"I will aid you in claiming the tower that remains. It is of the terra, and I can help you find a way. Once obtained you will use that power to restore me and my kin. In return, we will be the spearhead of your new army."

She inhaled deeply and a thin smile crept across her face.

"I shall hold you to your vow. I accept; however, I'm in charge, Nidhug. We do things within my timeline."

"Agreed. I will be loyal and obey."

"Then we have an accord. I am on my way to kill Kali. My first order to you is to transport us out of here when I am finished. There is a place in the north that I have prepared, this fire gem will show you the way. Wait at the edge of the burned trees and take us there when the time is right."

+++

Olwa spoke as he and Kali walked from the shore of the magma lake.

"Never in my days have I experienced magic that powerful."

"Aren't you a little young to be saying things like that?"

Suddenly Kali looked towards the burnt trees and whispered, "We aren't done yet, Olwa." She grabbed him by the arm. "This way."

Together, they ran up the hill and from cover watched as Piramay emerged from the burned tree line.

"Listen carefully. Piramay is vindictive and motivated by a lust for power. There isn't a bone of kindness in her body. She is not going to allow the loss of this magic without a fight. The rift is closing, but it will be most advantageous to confront me now while she still has some measure of this power. She doesn't know you are with me, which gives us an advantage. Do you understand?"

He nodded.

"She practices magic differently. Her natural abilities use containment seals. Though there are remnants of the tower magic my guess is she will resort to releasing her seals and fighting me with the magic she truly knows."

Olwa nodded and looked around. He set down the sword and grabbed a bow and quiver lying beside a dead archer.

"I am much better with this."

Kali pulled an arrow from the quiver and wrapped her hand around the broadhead. She whispered and the arrow shined briefly before going dull.

"Nock that arrow and stay hidden, use it only when you see an opportunity."

"How will I know?"

She tapped the symbol of the Fara Rangers on his armor.

"Follow your training."

Piramay magically increased the volume of her voice and chortled. "Come out come out wherever you are, Kali…let's get this over with."

Kali stepped out from behind the rocks. Her face was calm as she approached Piramay. The fire sorceress sneered and when Kali was in range she spoke mockingly.

"Well played, little snit. You had him fooled until the very end. Unfortunately, what you stole from him you also stole from me. I have come to collect your life in payment."

She lifted her hands and the seals which limited her magic appeared. She touched the center and moved her fingers outward before turning the fiery symbols like clock hands. They all faded away and she narrowed her eyes.

"I do not intend to fool around with you, Kali."

Instantly a massive draw of power filled Piramay. Flames materialized and she stepped forward, sending an enormous ball of fire towards Kali.

Without hesitation, Kali brought up her hands and the winds whipped around her. The fireball was caught in the vortex, circled behind her, and flew back towards Piramay.

Kali knew that Piramay could not be burned, so she directed the spell into the ground a few meters in front of her, hoping the impact would blow her off her feet.

The ball exploded and sent shards of rock and dirt right into the fire sorceress. The precious seconds gained by blinding Piramay allowed Kali to transport behind her. Piramay was shielded and unhurt. Feeling the directional shift of Kali's magic signature, she turned and drew the dirt and debris into a fiery vortex of her own, thrusting her hands towards Kali.

Kali was reaching for a bag of reagents when the attack came. She cast a field of protection, but not in time. Rocks and fire tore through her robes and painfully impacted her skin. She gritted her teeth and clutched the bag of reagents tightly so she wouldn't drop them.

Reaching into the bag, Kali threw the sparkling sand into the air across a wide arc and cast a sleep spell. Piramay tilted backwards and felt the simple, basic magic hit her. She considered it an insult that Kali would resort to low-level pub room tricks.

"A sleep spell? Really? You are a filthy little witch."

The spell effects began to take hold. She went to her knees and pressed her palms into the ground. Flames appeared under her hands as she breathed, attempting to resist.

Seeing the fire sorceress on her knees and struggling, Olwa stepped out from behind the rocks and fired the arrow. It streaked through the air, heading straight for Piramay's midsection.

Kali disappeared and fell back, appearing across a large gap, slightly higher than Olwa's position and watched as the arrow moved towards its mark.

Just as the arrow began its descent, Piramay's hand came up. The symbol of her magic was burned into the soil where her palm had been. Her spell plucked the arrow from its course.

Twisting her hand over her head, the fire sorceress stood and thrust her arms towards Olwa. A burst of energy propelled the arrow at blinding speed.

Immediately, Kali realized the deception and cursed under her breath for falling into the trap. She assessed the distance and Olwa's vulnerability as the arrow streaked towards him. He was too far away for her to transport them both. She had to make an immediate decision. There was only time to save one.

She mistimed the distance and cast her spell too soon. Olwa disappeared just before the arrow's impact. Piramay compensated and flicked her wrist. The arrow changed course and detonated on the rocks below Kali's feet with the force of a full powder keg.

Kali was blown back violently. The explosion sent fire and razor-sharp projectiles directly into her.

Olwa reappeared on the grass below, dazed by the sound of the explosion. He ducked into a small cavern and watched from safety as shards of rock landed all around him. Kali's limp, bloody, burning body tumbled down the rocks, finally stopping at the base of the ridge, thirty meters from him.

Piramay watched with satisfaction as she felt Nidhug appear beside her. She turned and took his hand. A flare of light sent the two of them into the ardor channels.

# Chapter 26 – Recompense

Olwa crawled out from where he had taken shelter. The dust was beginning to bellow down the rocks and obscure his vision. Though he was losing visual contact, he began moving towards Kali's lifeless body. Suddenly he felt Pela grab him and pull him into herself. He could barely hear her weeping over the ringing in his ears but put his arms around her and embraced her tightly. As she sobbed into his neck, he heard the murmur as a crowd began to gather around Kali.

Trystan came sprinting in, throwing his helmet aside but stopped outside the group. Myth'alas, Rayann, Ceridwyn, and Raspberry were huddled around Kali. Ceridwyn turned to comfort Rayann who was sobbing after seeing the extent of the injuries her cousin had sustained. Raspberry had already begun playing, but to no effect.

Rajumin approached and everyone watched in silence as she knelt beside Kali. She exhaled softly and assessed the injuries as a single tear moved down her cheek. Most of the skin had been seared off the left side of Kali's face. Her robes were tattered to ribbons and she was blistered and burned.

A large shard of rock was embedded in her hip and both her left wrist and leg were clearly broken. Despite the blood on her skin, she was barely bleeding. Most of the wounds had cauterized in the blast.

Leaning forward, Rajumin whispered into Kali's ear. Her face twitched ever so slightly, the first sign of life any had seen since she was blown off the rocks. Placing her hands over Kali's chest, Rajumin began to pray.

A soft green light glowed and pulsed around her fingers. The light shone for a few precious seconds and then disappeared into Kali's body. Her breathing was labored but steady. Rayann let out a grieved cry of gratitude.

The charred skin slowly disappeared, but the scars remained. Rajumin inhaled deeply and turned to look at Rayann.

"God has granted your cousin enough healing to survive, but she is destined to walk her remaining mortal days carrying the scars of her decisions, under Aviyanas guidance. What she did was forbidden. She defiled God's creation in the wielding of Lúth."

Rayann shook her head instinctively. It was obvious in her face that she was not happy with this conclusion.

Rajumin reached and touched her.

"For now, know that she has been forgiven and will live."

"It's not fair. She sacrificed and fought this evil from within. We all thought she betrayed us. We were wrong! She had a plan and destroyed the desecration that was brought here. She saved countless lives! How can God not show appreciation or recognize her sacrifice to save us all?"

"The fact that your cousin lives is proof her sacrifice *has* been recognized, despite her choices. This world was given to you along with the promise of free will, therefore, when choices are made there are consequences, good, or bad. It doesn't mean there isn't grace. These scars she now bears will serve to remind her that she lives by grace alone, not by any actions she took."

"I don't mean to question God; but I am angry, and disappointed in this decision."

"God's grace to us all is long-suffering. So much so that you too will be given plenty of time to heal as well. Maybe in that time you will also come to understand."

Rayann turned and cradled her cousin's head. She leaned down and whispered, "Kali?"

Kali opened her eyes and Rayann gasped. The unburned side of her face looked completely normal. Her crystal blue eye stared at her cousin. The scared side was marbled and purple, twisted like the flames that had burned her. Her left eye was no longer blue, but a blazing orange and yellow, glowing like the sun as the intense power within her radiated outward.

Immediately Rayann heard a gentle, faint voice in her head. *"...through their combined actions the 'one of different eyes' will usher in and establish a new era of magic and enlightenment on Aimsire. An age filled with balance and rediscovery of the old ways which God established during The Dawn Light."*

Rayann began to cry. Immediately she knew she was not the one of The Prophecy. So much of what had happened immediately came into focus.

She turned to Ceridwyn, the urgency in her voice was louder than her words.

"Can you please take us to Hailan Glen?"

"Of course."

Rayann turned to Myth'alas.

"I need to take her where she belongs so she can heal and recover. I will see you soon, beloved."

Rayann, Ceridwyn, and Kali disappeared as the spell activated. Myth'alas approached Sir Trystan who was still standing off to the side.

"She will live, but she will never be the same."

Myth'alas handed Trystan the burned, warhorse hair clip.

"This was dangling in her hair; looks like something you would have given her."

Trystan started weeping guiltily. It hit him like a punch to the guts. She had never betrayed them, nor forgotten him. All the anger and hatred he felt towards her after he watched her depart stabbed him from within. How on Aimsire could he have been so wrong about her after all they shared in those weeks together?

+++

Nolore landed and his rider dismounted. The commanders approached as Nolore took to the air again. He circled and called to gather his remaining flight and assess their losses.

Lady Rose approached, bowing her head respectfully.

"We cannot thank you enough for your aid, rider. Surely, we would have been slaughtered had you not arrived."

The silver armored knight removed her helmet and her long, blond hair cascaded out from underneath.

"Lady..."

Rose immediately stepped forward and embraced Lady Kellan affectionately. She squeezed with all she had and for the first time ever, Larissa saw her cry.

"We thought you were dead."

"I did die, but the Silentclaw rescued me. It's a long story, I promise to share it with you sometime, Commander Rose."

"MY LADY!"

Kellan turned as Erika sprinted over and stopped hastily, kicking up the soot around her feet. She composed herself and saluted sharply with tears in her eyes. Kellan saluted in return and then stepped forward, grabbing her sergeant in a tight hug.

"I can't believe it. I saw you die in the snow."

"You did, but God had other plans."

Sir Treyton approached and Lady Kellan saluted the knight commander. Her armor bore no symbols of the knighthood or her ranking. He saluted in response but inquired, "Erika, you obviously know the savior of the day."

"This is Lady Kellan Stenberg; I was her sergeant for six months before the invasion began."

"I see." He turned to Kellan, "The Stenberg name carries with it a great deal of stature in the north, and the south." He looked up as the dragons made a pass overhead and turned back to her. "Looks like the minstrels weren't exaggerating…for once."

Lady Kellan bowed her head respectfully. Erika was beaming as she took in Lady Kellan's presence and the fact that she was alive.

"Sister?" Erika turned to her brother. "Come, there will be time for reminiscing later. We have injured and assessments to tend to."

Lady Kellan spoke softly. "Go, Erika, attend to your duties. We will talk again soon."

+++

Jerrin spoke with jest in his voice.

"I suppose all this means you won't be returning to do your duties in Faralanthis?"

Myth'alas turned. Jerrin was smiling as he continued, "I didn't think so."

The two embraced and Jerrin patted Myth'alas sharply on the back.

"I guess I will just have to keep finding ways to get your duties done for you, little brother."

As they separated, Myth spoke, "My wife will likely have a lot to do while nursing Kali back to health. I may be able to find a little time to help with the Commonwealth while she's busy."

With a nod and a slight chuckle, his brother responded.

"Your assistance but more importantly, your opinion will always be welcome."

Jerrin left to assess the elves he had brought to the battle.

359

Myth'alas noticed Raspberry sitting on a rock all alone. He approached and sat beside her.

Without turning to him, she said, "I couldn't heal her."

"Kali?"

Raspberry turned her head.

"Yeah. I healed and helped everyone else that I sang and played for today. I even knew that if I played just right, I could walk into the fire and get Mrs. Rayann out. It's just...Kali's the one that maybe endured the most pain of any of us today. I played so hard...I tried, I really tried! I still don't understand, why?"

"Raspberry, you know that Kali and I once served the Rage Queen together, right?"

Raspberry's hair bounced as she nodded her head.

"Any chance you've got time for a story?"

Raspberry's beautiful smile crept across her soot covered, tear-streaked face.

"Sure! I always have time for stories!"

*To be continued...*

Made in the USA
Monee, IL
18 March 2025

14195457R00203